UNSEELIE

IVELISSE HOUSMAN

UNSEELIE

inkyard PRESS

ISBN-13: 978-1-335-42859-2

Unseelie

For questions and comments about the quality of this book, please contact us at CustomerService@Harlequin.com.

Inkyard Press
22 Adelaide St. West, 41st Floor
Toronto, Ontario M5H 4E3, Canada
www.InkyardPress.com

Printed in U.S.A.

For kids like me,
and for those who help us find our place in an unwelcoming world—

Yes, especially you, Sam.

Stories tell of children stolen away by faeries,
replaced by inhuman look-alikes.

These look-alikes, they say, could be identified by their strange speech or silence. They cried without reason or never showed any emotion at all, and struggled to relate to a world that seemed foreign to them. Folklorists theorize that these stories were early descriptions of autistic children—proof that autistic people have always been here.

But once, they called us changelings.

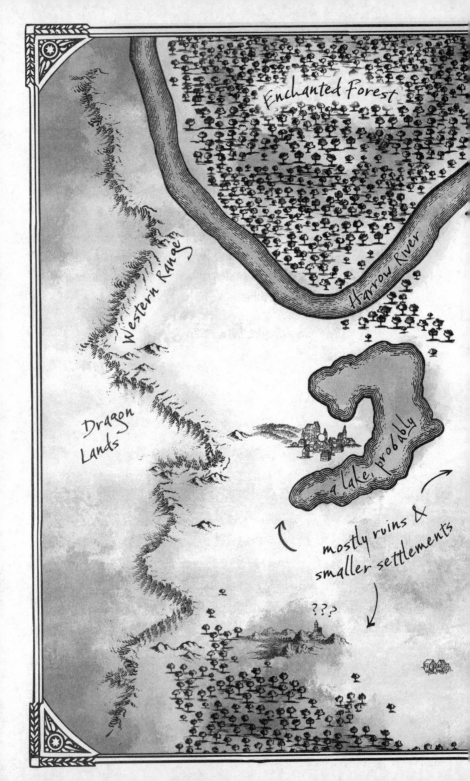

PART ONE

chapter one

On the night the faerie world collides with ours, anything can happen and wishes come true—and right now, I'm wishing I had stayed home.

I struggle to keep up with my twin sister as we push our way through the crowd. Revelnox is summer's closing act, when day and night balance perfectly on the edge of the world. In the smaller villages, where people lead calm, productive lives in predictable patterns—*back home*, I think, with an ache in my ribs—this means that children stay up late, bonfires are built in the middle of town, and offerings are left on the edges of the fields to prevent unwanted faerie mischief. There are special cakes, and the liquor flows freely, but all the merriment is a thin muzzle over the sharp teeth of the truth. You don't go anywhere alone, and you *don't* go into the forest.

Not if you want to come back, at least.

But here in the city—Auremore, the shining jewel between the forks of the Harrow River—here, it's something else entirely.

I have to fight not to lose my sister in the crowd of faces and languages blending into a waterfall of color and sound. Children call to each other in the streets, even though it can't possibly be safe for them to be out alone on *this* of all nights. But they're not really alone: it seems like everyone in the city is out, despite the late hour. The ever-present sound of voices crashing over each other is even louder tonight, volume rising with people's spirits (and the amount of spirits they've consumed). Music threads through it all, sparkling and twanging in the air.

The bonfires are the same here at least, adding their roar to the commotion. Each city district has its own, and here in the center of Market Square, everything is golden and cheerful, surrounded by dancers and the sweet smell of candies for sale. Here, they welcome the Seelie, the faerie realm of good intentions, of order and politeness—or, at the very least, neutrality. Pouches of herbed salt meant to ward off evil swing from the torches that keep the darkness at bay and paint the whole block in brilliant amber.

I seriously doubt that the faeries of the Unseelie Court will be scared off by what is essentially steak seasoning, but it's a nice thought.

We squeeze past a man wearing an elaborate mask with goat horns curling around the back of his head. That's the other thing about the Revelnox celebrations here: everyone is masked, and no one dares to utter their own name. For just this one night, faeries walk among us—and the less power they can claim over you, the safer you are.

It's all fun and games for the faeries, whose visits to the Mortal Realm are usually limited to one human at a time, in remote forest glens or moonlit crossroads. For changelings, the not-quite-human-but-definitely-not-faerie in-betweens, *walking among mortals* is less of a novelty. We grow up with humans, hated for being almost like them but not enough. Most of us find our way back to the faerie realms by adulthood. I've never felt that pull, though. My magic and I have what you could generously call a troubled history, and if Revelnox is the closest I ever get to the faerie realms, it'll be more than close enough.

Also—and on a potentially unrelated note—it's my twin's seventeenth birthday.

I can't exactly say that my twin and I have the same birthday, since I'm not sure if changelings even *have* birthdays. I don't think anyone actually knows where we come from. For all I know, my essence might have been floating around in a cloud of faerie dust for centuries.

Or maybe I formed out of thin air the moment a faerie lifted Isolde from her cradle, stiletto fingernails digging into her soft, honey-colored skin, to exchange her for me.

I don't know.

What I do know is that ever since our parents adopted me, Isolde and I share a birthday every year. Back before it was just the two of us on the run, we always had a homemade cake and presents, and we would all sit outside in the grass and watch the stars come out. It was usually uncomfortable, near the end of summer when everything turns sickly sweet and starts to crumble, but that didn't matter.

It was still my favorite day of the year. And often, that day happens to fall on Revelnox.

The man in the goat mask meets my eye, flashing white teeth at me before turning sharply and disappearing into the crowd of disguised faces.

I shiver, clinging tighter to my sister's hand.

"Too loud?" Isolde murmurs, pressing close to my side. She wears all-black, as usual, from the tips of her scuffed boots to the roots of her glossy black hair.

I shake my head. It *is* loud, but in a weird way the overwhelming sensations are soothing. My boots feel more solid on the cobblestones, my body more real and alive than ever. Even the heat—of all the bodies, the radiant glow of the fire, the last warm breezes of summer—makes me feel strangely at ease, instead of just sticky and miserable.

No. If I seem on edge, it's thanks to the buzz of magic in the air, a living hum that I don't hear so much as feel, like a mosquito hovering at the back of my neck. I don't think Isolde can sense it.

Magic is technically a part of me, fizzing in my faerie blood, and this is the one night when it isn't considered dangerous and wrong. One night when it's safe to be the thing I have to be every day. But maybe that's exactly why I'm so terrified of it—because I've seen firsthand what magic does.

I stop short, jerking Isolde's arm back, as a woman with a small reddish dragon draped over her shoulders cuts in front of me, obliviously strumming a stringed instrument and belting out a song that would make the most seasoned escort blush.

My sister smashes into me, and we both pause to make sure our masks are still in place. They're the cheapest we could find, a simple painted covering of the eyes and cheekbones held in place by a fraying ribbon. I'm pretty sure they're made of rowan wood to protect against faeries, because mine is starting to itch abominably. It's a familiar itch, and for a second, I'm ten years old again, being held down by a clump of other ten-year-olds while they take turns pressing charms of rowan bark and iron to my skin to watch it blister.

The moment passes, and I somehow maintain the willpower not to rip the mask off my face.

As I slide it back into place, my fingers twitching nervously over the surface, I pull Isolde closer. I lower my voice, even though it's so loud in the streets that no one could possibly hear me anyway. "Are you sure this is a good idea?"

"It's Revelnox," Isolde reassures, her easy grin slipping back onto her face. "The manor is empty, and everyone will be too drunk to even notice us. We'll be long gone by the time they even realize we were there. Trust me, Seelie."

This is the part where I pause to say I *know* it's an unfortunate nickname considering…what I am. I wish that my parents had thought of that before Isolde's toddler tongue bumbled *Iselia* so many times that it stuck.

I hesitate, but I've never been good at saying no to my sister. The fight goes out of me with a rush of air before I straighten my shoulders and squeeze the soft, worn fabric of my favorite dress in my fist. "Let's make it quick, then."

"Quicker than lightning," Isolde promises.

I glance up nervously at the clear, dark sky as glittering orange sparks drift up from the bonfire, dancing on the breeze.

As we wind our way upriver, the world flashes by in vignettes of chaos.

People push through the crowds in chains with their friends, arms linked, songs in the air colliding with the louder instrumental music. Some wave flags or toss flowers into the air. Yapping excitedly, a small dog chases at the heels of a group of kids who can't be older than thirteen. The normally drab buildings are draped in garlands of rainbow-hued flowers and tiny pennant flags.

And then there are the faeries.

Even though faeries are an expected part of tonight's festivities, they slip through the mortals almost unnoticed. But I'm not quite human, either, and I keep finding my eyes wandering to balls of light floating over the crowds, or catching the smell of a meadow in the breeze of someone running past. I accidentally make eye contact with a woman wearing a feathered mask that covers from her cheekbones up to the crown of her head, then realize with a start that it isn't a mask.

She winks, her blood-red mouth curving into a smile. Then she turns and blows a kiss towards a pair of revelers sitting at a wobbly wooden table in a brewer's booth. They're deep in the conversation of close friends, hands wrapped around their cups and separated by exactly the right amount of distance so their knuckles don't brush. When the faerie's breath washes over them, the speaker doesn't seem to notice at first.

The listener, on the other hand, stiffens noticeably, something strange and hungry coming over their expression.

My heart stops. Faerie magic is dangerous, and I don't know what—

Then the listener, without a heartbeat's space to think, surges forward, crashing their lips into their friend's.

I wince. Not deadly magic, at least.

Still dangerous.

The speaker freezes for a second, mouth still open in the shape of whatever word was cut off by their friend's lips. Then they melt into the kiss, eyes closing blissfully.

I turn away, blushing hot enough that I worry my mask might burst into flames. The pair will probably regret this tomorrow. They don't need my invasion of their privacy on top of it.

The feather-faced woman is still staring at me with wide, owlish eyes. Then she turns, and her eyes flash red like a cat's in the night. If I hadn't been sure that she was a faerie before, I am now. That gleam in the darkness is the one thing faeries can't change about their glamours.

The one thing that reveals a changeling's true nature.

A cold breeze rushes over my skin, trailing chills as we let the scene fade behind us.

Isolde releases my hand, adopting an exaggerated drunken swagger. She crashes into someone with gold leaf painted over their cheekbones and lips and stops, slurring apologies and patting the person's shoulders.

I roll my eyes as she falls back into step with me. "Can't you at least save it until we get there?" I mutter, barely moving my lips.

Isolde's hand slips out of her pocket, withdrawing a silver-plated compact mirror that she definitely didn't have a few seconds ago. "Where's the fun in that?"

"You're not here to have *fun*. You're here to get into the house, grab as much as you can, and get out, ideally without getting us arrested." I know my voice is coming out too harsh, but I don't know how to fix it, so I settle for nudging her in the ribs with my elbow.

Isolde looks at me sideways for a moment, as if she's just now remembering the seriousness of our situation, before stuffing her loot back into its hiding spot with a chastened sigh.

I am not a pickpocket.

I don't mean that in any kind of morally superior way—the truth is that even if I *wanted* to be a pickpocket, I don't have the talent for it. Not like Isolde.

Isolde steals, grifts, pickpockets, and pawns. I keep us fed. We don't need to be wealthy. We just need to survive until we can scrape together enough to reunite, to start over in a place where no one knows my face.

The noise of the festival fades as my fingers drift to the vial on a leather cord around my neck.

Our parents—Mami, a midwife, fierce and tough, with her homemade remedies for everything from a cold to stubborn zits; Papa, gentle and strong and always coming home from his studio with clay under his nails. They wouldn't want this life for us. They're good people. Honest people.

And they aren't safe as long as I'm around.

So we left three years ago to run from city to city, to steal and cheat and lie and scratch out a living, telling ourselves it would be justified. It would all be worth it when we had enough to make our family a new home. When I could walk down the street without flinching every time someone looked at me a little too long, worrying they'd seen my face on a wanted poster somewhere.

We're coming up to the bridge now, boots pounding an uneven rhythm on the cobblestones as the crowd around us thins. The streets are too choked tonight for horses or wagons to force their way through, leaving extra space on the wide bridge. The sour smells of warm human bodies pressed together and beer subtly ebb away with every step.

This side of the bridge is plain, a smooth transition into the arch of stone over the sluggish water. Weeds poke up through the mortar and along the muddy banks. On the other side, garlands of golden paper flowers curl around the gleaming brass streetlamps, and an enchanted ball of light changes color every few seconds.

"Last chance to back out," I mutter, as a woman dressed in sky-blue silk passing from the opposite direction stares at us for just a second too long.

"You worry too much." Isolde catches the woman staring and meets her gaze with a brilliant smile.

I move a half step faster, trying to look casual as the dazzling sights of Gilt Row come into view.

Gilt Row is less of a row and more of a blob-shaped tangle of streets draped in more opulence and wealth than anyone knows what to do with. The houses, like the rest of the city, are pressed tight together, tall and narrow, but here they're all white stone and pastel-painted brick, with gardens out front and just the right amount of emerald ivy crawling up their fronts.

Entire eight-story houses, each for just one family. It's hard to imagine what the buildings might look like inside—and I pride myself on my colorful imagination. And presiding over it all, flanked by iron gates and a perfectly manicured lawn, Wildline Manor looms three times the size of any of the others. It's huge, imposing, and—since Leira Wildfall is sponsoring Gilt Row's Revelnox celebrations—totally empty. They might as well have painted a glowing target on it.

I haven't spent much time in this part of the city. Among the perfectly maintained streets populated by well-dressed, respectable families, Isolde's and my rags stick out like thistles in a bouquet of exotic flowers. Someone who looks like we do can't just walk around, without someone rich assuming they're up to no good and signaling the city guard.

To be fair, most of the time we *are* up to no good…but *they* have no way of knowing that.

But tonight is different. I can feel it in the air, smell it in the spaces between smoke and sugar and expensive perfume. Tonight, anyone could be a faerie in disguise, and everyone receives equal respect.

Well, besides a few wrinkle-nosed looks from people who think I can't see them.

Despite that, the crowd we melt into on the other side of the bridge is still almost entirely made up of people dressed in dazzling garments of violet chiffon, tangerine velvet, indigo silk, pure white linen—every color you could imagine and some you couldn't. Gold gleams on throats and wrists and fingers, in embroidery along skirts and cuffs. Each mask is more impressive than the last, each custom-made and totally unique. Servants, dressed a bit more simply but still wrapped in the decadent midnight-blue velvet of Wildline Manor, mill around serving snacks and drinks.

I couldn't possibly feel more out of place, with my plain mask, my simple slate-blue dress, my dusty brown boots. For someone like me, there's no point in throwing away money on a gown that would only be worn for one night—no matter how enchanting it is.

My sister looks even more at odds with our surroundings than I do, but her aura of confidence doesn't waver, even as tiny beads of sweat trickle under her mask. Isolde is the sweatier twin, but that's more because she wears layers of all-black every day, no matter the weather, than because of any innate dampness.

Even though we're identical, I can't remember a time that we could be mistaken for each other. It seems laughable that the fair folk thought leaving me in her place would be an equal trade. Our olive skin and dark brown eyes are exactly the same, but her wavy hair never falls any longer than her shoulders before she chops it off, and I keep mine in a thick braid tied off neatly at the small of my back. Our identical heavy eyebrows look bold and dashing on her face but almost always seem troubled on mine.

I can feel them bunching into that concerned twist now. "Do you know where you're going?" My fingers twist in my apron, fidgeting as always. We've been planning this for weeks, but we're not exactly criminal masterminds. Once Isolde sneaks in the servants' entrance, I don't think there's much of a plan beyond grabbing anything that looks shiny.

"Relax," she replies, taking a flower from a girl dressed in petal-pink handing out bunches to everyone who passes. "Just stay on the lookout, and try to enjoy yourself. This isn't the kind of party you get to see every day, you know." The flower twirls between her fingers before she drops it, leaving it to get crushed underfoot.

We follow the trickle of people towards the center of the district and their bonfire. It's getting late now, and most of the children have been sent to bed.

Which means the party is really getting started.

"Who here'sss try'n'a get…a *wisssh granted*?" shrieks a faerie, so drunk on Leira Wildfall's liquor that they don't even bother hiding the shimmering wings sprouting from their shoulder blades. A shout ripples through the crowd around them. Then there's a flash of pearly light, and when it fades, the faerie is gone. A stack of gold coins remains where the faerie had been standing, and I don't know if they intentionally vanished or were banished back home by some Seelie rule about not getting drunk off your ass and offering wishes to mortals.

As people frantically dive for the coins, I lean to speak into my sister's ear. "Those coins are super cursed, right?"

"Oh, *incredibly* cursed. For sure." She squeezes my hand and chuckles. "You know what you're supposed to do, right?"

I groan. My job, of watching the servants' entrance and drawing the attention of any guards who might get suspicious, was supposed to be easy. "How can I possibly top that distraction? What goes on around here? There's something wrong with rich people, Sol. That would have ended the night across town."

Well, across the bridge. All the way across town, in the Twilight District, I've heard rumors that they celebrate the holiday with much more unsavory magic, and a few cursed coins would probably be the *least* of their problems.

"You'll figure something out." Isolde grins, slipping away from me. "See you in an hour."

Then she turns her drunken saunter back on with all the ease of the highest-quality actor and stumbles into the crowd, ready to dip her hands into their gilded pockets.

chapter two

Try to enjoy yourself, I repeat mockingly in my head. Isolde darted through the crowd like a shadow, but to me it looks like a solid wall of rioting color.

Try to enjoy yourself.

I straighten my mask and take off in the opposite direction— towards the bonfire. We should end up at the same door, but splitting up makes us less conspicuous. If our timing is right, she'll just be slipping inside by the time I arrive to stand guard.

But maybe our timing won't be right: we've never done anything like this before. We're pickpockets, not burglars. Breaking into someone's house, grabbing more than loose coins and jewelry… It seems more *personal*. And I might feel bad about it, if it wasn't for the absurd excess of Wildline wealth.

Everyone's heard of the Wild line.

Once, far enough back for even a faerie's memories to grow fuzzy, the Mortal Realm was united under one monarch. But that kingdom was destroyed, and now all that's left is the cities, their territories, and the leaders who rule them. In Auremore, for as long as anyone can remember, that's the women of the Wild line—the last of the shapeshifters, mortal enchanters who can transform themselves into any (nonmagical) creature. An ability passed down from mother to child along with the maternal prefix of their surname. *Wildstorm*, *Wildrun*, *Wildcall*: all spring from the Wild lineage, but right now the manor is ruled by Leira Wildfall, and she doesn't seem to want to let anyone forget it. This is *her* party, in *her* neighborhood, in *her* city.

The closer I get to the fire, the thicker the feeling of magic in the air wraps around my skin, calling to the magic within me. Despite the warmth, chills rise on my arms and over the back of my neck.

My fingers go to the vial under my neckline again, like I need reassurance that it's still there, or a reminder of why I don't use my magic. My fingers wrap around its familiar shape, smooth and solid skin-warmed glass.

Going out tonight was a bad idea.

"Care for a drink, miss?"

I trip over myself to avoid bumping into the servant who materialized in front of me while I was distracted. He's tall and broad and suddenly filling my whole field of vision, bearing a tray covered in tiny cylindrical glasses of a bubbling pinkish liquid.

"Oh, um—" I'm flustered, fumbling for a lie.

The servant doesn't budge. "It's free tonight. Courtesy of Leira Wildfall." I can hear the curve of a smile in his voice.

Try to enjoy yourself.

I'm not much for drinking, not like Isolde—and I've made my disapproval abundantly clear to her on numerous occasions.

Then again, it *is* our birthday. And it's free.

I snatch up a glass and drain it, savoring the slightly sweet taste of the stinging, fizzy liquid. Wiping my mouth gracelessly on my sleeve, I place the glass back on the tray, maybe a little rougher than necessary.

The bubbles are already rising straight to my head as my eyes turn up, actually taking in the servant, who still hasn't moved, for the first time. Blinking, I realize the man isn't a man at all, only my age, maybe a little older.

Realizing I've just used the phrase *my age, maybe a little older*, I feel the need to clarify.

This boy doesn't have dazzling green eyes or a crooked smile that makes me feel weak in the knees. This isn't like *that*.

He's just...*here*, towering over me, half-hidden eyes glimmering in the firelight. The only remarkable thing about him is his bright red hair, which curls over his collar in messy, shaggy waves.

I can't see much of his face from behind his simple mask, but his cheeks and middle were round with what I would call *baby fat* if it didn't seem so unlikely that he'd ever grow out of it. His boots are shiny and look too expensive, but his trousers are worn and dirty. The buttons of his ill-fitting servant's uniform strain like the coat is struggling to hold on, but that doesn't seem to affect his good mood. He grins down at me over the tray, like he knows something I don't.

I hate him, and his expensive boots, and his absurd smile, instantly.

The sweet berry taste of the drink I gulped is still rolling over my tongue. It's the best I've ever had, sweeter and sharper than the cheap cider and mead I can afford. Without invitation, I take another drink from his tray.

I expect my rudeness to chase him away before I can finish off the whole tray, but instead, he nods his head approvingly. When he speaks again, his tone has lost the measured politeness of a servant. "Nervous?"

My mouth twists into a frown as the liquid burns its way down my throat, savage and sparkling. "No."

"Just thirsty, hmm?" He doesn't even flinch as I slam the second glass down on the tray, and he lowers his voice conspiratorially. "Might I recommend water, then? This stuff's pretty strong—"

"Who exactly are you?" I interrupt. I don't dare to raise my voice and draw unwanted attention. I need to stay calm, to avoid doing anything likely to get Isolde and me tossed over the bridge. Or, worse, noticed by the city guard.

"Someone like you," he says, quiet and smooth. Like he's telling me a secret and doesn't really fear the consequences. "Though, I was wondering what it is *you're* doing here."

My breath catches in my throat, making my heart stutter and ache. His eyes don't shine back at me, the light isn't right for that, but how else could he know? Pain pricks my palms as my hands curl into fists. "A changeling?" I whisper.

The boy recoils at that, making all the drinks on his tray clink precariously. "Oh, Fate, no. I meant…someone who doesn't belong here. Didn't you—" He cuts himself off.

I'm regretting the second drink now, even though I'm fairly sure its effects can't kick in *this* quickly. My head feels like it's buzzing as I try to understand. Of course. The ill-fitting coat, the ragged trousers, the air of general mischief. He's in disguise. He doesn't belong here any more than I do.

His surprise melts into a bemused curiosity as he leans back in. "Are you really a changeling?" It's strange, but his tone isn't accusing, just fascinated. By me.

I swallow hard, summoning anger to chase away my nerves. "No, I'm a cave troll in a very clever disguise. What's it to you?"

"Nothing!" I get the feeling that he would put his hands up to deflect the venom in my voice if they weren't occupied with the tray. "Just wondering. What *are* you doing here?"

I cross my arms. "What are *you* doing here, pretending to be a servant?"

The grin returns to the boy's face, pulling at his round, rosy cheeks and making me think that maybe I judged his appearance a little too quickly. "Causing a little trouble."

There's a pause, in which I consider just walking away and pretending this conversation never happened, and he stares at me like he's waiting for me to answer a question he didn't ask.

Finally, he gives up.

"Your turn."

I look around quickly, but no one has noticed us. I probably should have walked away, but I'm feeling a little reckless now. "Same as you," I whisper, feeling the smile steal onto my lips as a little thrill of excitement runs up my spine.

"We should…probably get back to work, then," he says, but he doesn't look like someone who wants to get back to work. He looks like someone who wants to memorize me, to reach out and pull my long braid loose around my face.

"What are you staring at?" I check to make sure my mask is still in place—something about my appearance must have alerted him that I don't belong here, and I should fix it before anyone else notices.

He's still staring down with those thoroughly human, dark blue eyes. "I've just never met a changeling before," he says, with a breath softer than the summer wind.

And just like that, I'm angry again.

"You almost certainly have," I reply, snapped out of my delirium. "Most people don't know—"

His tray trembles again with a delicate tinkling and the shifting of glass, and he leans precariously forward, ignoring the drips that slosh over the rims. "I didn't mean it like that," he says gently, which doesn't really make it better.

I stare at my fluttering hands. Anything to avoid meeting his eyes again. My voice is barely more than a breath, too quiet to carry over the sounds of the crowd still swirling around us unless you were really listening. "Then, what did you mean?"

"I've never met a changeling so *pretty* before," he says, and I should brush it off as empty flattery, but when I look back into his face, he seems so *earnest*.

"Raze!"

A voice leaps over the sounds of merrymaking before I can figure out how to respond, and the boy's head turns suddenly to its source.

A girl even taller than he is, wearing an equally badly fitting servant's coat, strides towards us. The bonfire's light dances over her dark brown skin in a way that almost makes her look as though she's lit from within, and her twisted locks of hair are pushed back from her face by a hair wrap under a simple leather mask.

"Raze!" she repeats, fully taking over his attention. "What are you doing? We don't have time for you to flirt. Our *appointment* is—" She glances at me and cuts herself off quickly. "We need to get going. *Now.*"

He sighs deeply, shoving the tray into my hands before I can protest. As he does, he leans in close.

"We'll have to continue this some other time, I'm afraid, changeling," he murmurs, with that same grin that I've officially decided, after several turns of changing my mind, is *definitely* irritating and *not* charming.

"Don't count on it," I hear myself say, not looking up at him.

"Raze," the tall girl snaps again.

Then they disappear. They melt into the crowd as if they'd never been there at all, and I'm left standing on my own, holding a tray of half-spilled drinks, mouth still hanging a little open.

chapter three

I stand there stunned for several moments, while the world keeps turning around me, until I remember I need to get to the servants' door. The tray is getting heavier by the second. People dance past, twirling carelessly and slinging flowers as they snatch glasses from the tray. Glass crunches underfoot, mingling with crushed petals, shards left from those who couldn't be bothered to return their glasses.

I hear a cry of alarm, and for a second, my heart leaps into my throat, and I'm completely sure Isolde's been caught.

I'm already planning our escape from prison by the time I realize it's a totally different kind of cry. It's spreading now, waves of awe and fear rippling through the crowd. The music stops abruptly as musicians' fingers freeze on their instruments, and a hush falls over the wildest party of the year.

I, with everyone else, push toward the source of the disturbance. I elbow and shove, and when I see a bewildered-looking servant, I hand off the tray with its mostly empty glasses.

I'm shorter than nearly everyone in the crowd, and all I can see is shimmering silk tunics, dusky-purple sleeves, deep crimson coats, the backs of flower-adorned heads. People are pressing in now, too tight, and I can hardly breathe.

Then I'm at the front of the newly formed mass of people, and I can finally see what's going on.

A wolf walks through the middle of the street.

Nearly as tall as my shoulder, all lean muscle under thick golden fur, it pads forward calmly. The crowd parts as its eyes sweep back and forth. For a second, the wolf meets my eyes, and there is something far too intelligent about its steady yellow gaze. My breath catches in my chest.

Then the wolf turns its head. Its form flickers, blurring into one golden smear. When the colors resolve, it's in the shape of a chestnut mare.

The crowd goes wild, cheering and gasping. I stumble back.
Shapeshifter.
Leira Wildfall.

I never thought I'd actually see her. But there's no one else it could be, unless she has a secret heir she's hiding from the public. I watch as the mare tosses her mane and picks up her pace to a cheerful canter. The crowd parts wider, and then she's galloping circles around wide-eyed mortals and disinterested faeries.

She shimmers again, this time taking the shape of a glowing white swan.

Now everyone is talking over each other, and the bonfire smoke diffuses in the air with the faint, indescribable scent of magic. I force myself to turn and head to the manor, but the crowd around me keeps moving forward, drawn toward the shapeshifter as if she's magnetic. They've almost formed a circle around the swan now, with a few stragglers still holding murmured conversations or chasing down servants to grab another drink.

Still, as I elbow my way against the current, I catch glimpses between the fine dresses and cloaks. The swan raises her ash-white wings and throws her head back dramatically before transforming one last time. This time, she's human. I guess I had some sort of image of what members of the Wild line would look like in my head—brooding and mysterious, maybe, with hair and eyes dark as a raven's feathers and features sharp as its beak.

Instead, the woman at the center of the crowd is in her midthirties, relatively plain, with freckles and a pinched expression that suggests she's used to giving orders. Her strawberry blond hair is piled on her head in an elaborate updo, and she wears a gown the same intense white as the swan, embroidered from throat to toe with a frosty covering of shimmering silver thread.

Most noticeably, she isn't wearing a mask.

"Good evening, everyone," she says in a voice that must be magically magnified, because despite its soft tone, I can hear it from across the square.

The crowd applauds riotously—at least, the mortals do. It's easy to spot the faeries now. They're the ones with crossed arms, rolling their eyes. Faeries love spectacle, but to them,

Leira's whole production must be like watching a child screaming for attention as she executes a crooked handstand.

Leira motions for quiet, and the crowd calms. "Thank you so much for joining me this evening. I hope my hospitality is to your liking." Another cheer, which Leira allows with a gracious smile.

After that, I tune her out. She keeps the crowd's breathless attention with occasional sparks at her fingertips as she gestures, and they cling to her every word.

I reach the side door, which is wide open so that the servants can come and go with their trays. Golden light spills from the house, along with the clattering of pots and the sound of people yelling at each other. I lean against the ivy-covered wall casually, and no one gives me a second glance, thanks to the same plain clothes that made me stick out so badly in the crowd.

A servant wanders outside, trying very hard to look like she's working while she cranes her neck to see what's going on in the packed circle of people. As she pauses, I snatch several miniature almond cakes off her tray and stuff them into the pocket of my apron. Then, since she's still distracted, I take another handful, popping one into my mouth.

The cake is delicious, delicately sweet with a dusting of sugar clinging to the top that puffs up as I bite down. The sugar is going to make my pockets a mess, but there will be plenty of time to clean my apron later. Each bite dissolves in my mouth, leaving a faint, nutty aftertaste coating my tongue. I start mentally deconstructing the ingredients, wondering how they got it so fluffy without the richness of eggs in the batter. I've been baking with my father since I was old enough to hold a spoon, so I know a good cake when I taste it, and this is definitely—

"We need to go," Isolde huffs into my ear. "Now."

I startle, bashing my elbows into the stone behind me. My twin has materialized, as if out of nowhere. There's still at least half an hour until we were supposed to meet back up. But before I can even think of questions to ask or respond to the breathless urgency of her tone, Isolde is already hauling me away.

"Sol—" I start, panic leaping up my throat. Was she caught? What went wrong? Then I realize she's pulling me inside the house, instead of sprinting for the bridge. "Where are we going?"

She looks over her shoulder, grinning. "I found something."

Wasn't that kind of the point? I think, but I let myself get dragged along, ducking to avoid the chaos of the busy kitchen. The sounds and smells all clash in the air, making it impossible to pick out any details other than *loud* and *delicious*. At least all the servants are so focused on whatever they're doing that they're too busy to notice two nonuniformed girls slipping inside.

Isolde moves quickly, with the confidence of someone who's taken this route a hundred times. The kitchens lead into more service areas, through twisting knots of hallways, until they eventually spill into the main house.

We slow as I trip, and Isolde hauls me back to my feet. It's not my fault, though: my imagination failed me. My mind can't even understand what I'm looking at as someone's house. It's impractical, with ceilings almost three times my height and not an inch of wall that isn't covered in some kind of gilt adornment or tapestry or painting of golden-haired Wildline forebears. The hallway seems to go on for miles, intricately laid wooden floor covered in a plush rug with the design of a hedge of roses, lit by the even yellow glow of a ball of light like the one out in the street. It's totally breathtaking.

It's totally ridiculous.

Golden hallways and staircases streak by, all one unmemorable blur. I have no idea how Isolde can remember which way to go, but in just a few moments we're standing before a door grander than any of the others.

But before I can memorize the look of the gleaming gold inlay or the exact height of the soaring arch it's set into, Isolde is dragging me into place. "Watch the hall."

The door boasts an enormous lock, the likes of which I've never seen. Isolde has some practice with lock picking, along with a natural light touch, but I can't imagine she's ever laid a hand on something as complex as this.

The tightness in my chest loosens just enough that I can whisper, "Sol, *why* are we here?"

She looks up at me from her crouch and scratches the frame with a fingernail.

"Don't—" I start, but she's already scraping gold shavings from under her nails.

"This is *gold*, Seelie. Real gold."

I sigh. "Okay, why am *I* here?"

Ignoring me, she twists her lock picks in the shiny brass opening. "Because it's the only lock I've ever seen that takes four hands to open. Or a special key, but four hands should do it. Which means…?" she prompts, still focused on the lock.

"There's something very special back there that no one

wants us to see," I mutter, leaning to look around the corner. It's too far to see what's on the other side from here, which means if anyone's coming, we won't have much time to get out. I try to breathe slowly. To count the seconds. To stay as calm and steady as my sister.

My hands flutter anxiously. We're totally exposed, with nowhere to run. "What if they have guard dragons?" I blurt, giving my wildest anxiety a voice.

"No such thing," Isolde says, a pick held between her gritted teeth. "Dragons are fluffy little pets with dulled teeth and clipped wings. *Guard* dragons are a myth rich people invented to keep poor people from doing—"

Click.

"This," she finishes triumphantly. The lock springs into place, and I feel my knees go weak with relief...but the door doesn't open.

"Hold," Isolde says urgently, her elbows angled awkwardly so I can take hold of the picks. "Exactly like that. Yes, perfect. Don't move!"

Now I'm staring at the lock, at her hands fitting another smaller set of lock picks between whatever it is I'm holding open, at my shoes, at the shiny floor. My eyes blur a little. I can hear my heart beating in my ears, louder than the Revelnox drums. It feels like someone could spring on me at any moment.

But I stay perfectly still.

A queasy churning in my stomach is making me start to regret those two drinks earlier, but my head is completely clear from the terror of being in here. My palms are sweaty, but I can't let the lock picks slip.

Then I hear something else: a soft click, click, click—like footsteps, but not quite. Whatever it is, it's going to be around the corner any second now.

"What's that, Seelie?" Isolde whispers, still focused on the lock.

Was I still supposed to be keeping watch? I'd been given a new task, but—

Then the sound echoes around the corner, revealing a dragon slightly smaller than the wolf. Its scales are a mottled green, like weathered copper, and its undersized wings are held tight to its thickly muscled neck. Its mouth hangs slightly open as it paces, showing hundreds of spectacularly maintained white teeth. I know that firedrakes—the giant, wild, fire-breathing dragons—are long extinct, but I always imagined they'd look about as scary as this.

"Seelie?" Isolde repeats, as a chill runs all the way down my arms, and I squeeze the lock picks tighter in an attempt not to drop them in frozen terror.

"A myth," I whisper, hoping its hearing isn't great. It hasn't spotted us yet, but that's only because its snout is stuck to the floor, and it's clearly puzzling over our unfamiliar scent.

Isolde glances up for less than a second and returns to the lock, swearing quietly as she tries to pick it faster. I manage not to let go and run screaming, but my hands are trembling so hard I can't imagine it's much help.

Less than a second before I'm about to make a run for it anyway, the lock gives, and the door glides open on silent, oiled hinges. We throw ourselves inside, not caring what might be lurking in the total darkness of the room beyond.

I ease the door back as far as possible without letting it actually click shut: I don't want to risk being locked in here. Wherever *here* is. We wait several seconds, trying to listen to the dragon's approach over the sound of our own shallow breathing. It pauses in front of the door, snuffling loudly, and Isolde squeezes my hand as we both try to stay completely still.

Then it moves on, and its claws click, click, click down the hall before disappearing. Finally, after another long pause, we slump in relief.

"What is this place?" Isolde asks, voice still cautiously quiet.

I'm imagining piles of gold, or some kind of treasury hiding magical artifacts, something that would warrant a lock like that on a door like that, when soft yellow light floods the room's corners. Isolde and I both jump instinctively, backs bumping against each other, as we wait to be caught—but it's only another ball of enchanted light, just like the ones in the hall.

The enchantment must activate whenever someone speaks. There isn't actually anyone here.

Finally, I take in our surroundings. Nothing inside the room suggests the same kind of grandeur as the intricately decorated door. We must have passed a dozen studies that look exactly like this on our way up: a small, tidy space with a desk and soft carpeting and bookshelves lining the walls. The only things that seem out of place are a glass display case next to the desk and a tacked-up map covered in scribbles.

The Harrow River cuts a sharp curve across the map like the slash of a dagger. One side is taken up by the Western Mountains, a range of rocky cliffs on the opposite side of the continent from the foothills of the Eastern Range, where I've spent my entire life.

The Eastern Range butts up against the sea, dropping down in a sheer sheet of rock. I've never been as far as the Western Mountains, but I know they're the border between us and the Dragon Lands, a plateau of active volcanoes, covered in sleek obsidian and riddled with unmarked gateways to the Unseelie Realm. So, basically, uninhabitable for pretty much any other species besides the one that gave the land its name, back before fire-breathing dragons were hunted to extinction.

Throughout the ages, more than one power-hungry half-wit has had the brilliant idea that a mountain castle overlooking the Dragon Lands would be badass, inevitably ending in disaster and littering the cliffs of the Western Mountains with grander, stranger ruins than the normal ones scattered from sea to sea. It's this border that's been marked up the most on Leira's map, concentric circles closing in on a spot she can't seem to find. Some of the circles are crossed out with violent slashes.

I freeze uncertainly, but Isolde takes a step closer to the case and peers inside. "It's just a compass," she says.

The door bursts open, and the red-headed boy from earlier tumbles inside, landing in a heap at my feet. I step back, stifling a scream with my hands over my mouth, as he glares up at me from the floor. "You!"

"*You!*" I echo.

Isolde's knife is already drawn. "Who's this?"

"By all means, Raze, bust the door down." The girl he was with follows him inside, pulling the door half-closed behind her. The boy stands up with as much dignity as he has left, which isn't much, hand resting on the hilt of his own dagger.

The four of us stare at each other.

Finally, the tall girl breaks the silence. "Who are you? What are you doing here?"

Isolde's blade twists lazily in her fingers. "I could ask you the same thing."

"Okay, clearly we're all breaking in." Raze says it good-naturedly, but there's an edge to his smile I don't like. "But you see, changeling, it was our idea first."

At the word *changeling*, Isolde shoots me a wide-eyed look. Then she smooths her face out again, addressing him. "Well, we got here first."

I feel like I should say something, like maybe if I was cleverer there would be a perfect string of words that would make everyone put their knives down, but I'm too tongue-tied. At least it doesn't look like they're going to turn us in.

Raze looks past us, taking in the room. His smile flickers, and he lets his hand drop. "I have to admit, it's a disappointment."

"Hoping for treasure?" Isolde's tone drips honey, as if mocking him for the exact same thing we were doing. Before he can respond, she flicks the case open and snatches the compass.

"Olani, now!" Raze and the girl both lunge forward. I'm pretty sure they don't know what they're grabbing for; they just don't want *us* to have it. I shove myself forward, too. I may not have a weapon, but at least I can stand between them and my sister. Unless she meant for me to run, in which case I'm in trouble.

Raze trips over me, dropping to the floor for the second time, and this time taking me with him. We land in a heap, cushioned by the soft carpet, and Olani leaps over us to make another grab at Isolde, who dodges nimbly out of the way.

"Well, this is new." I can't see the speaker, but it definitely isn't any of the four of us. The voice sounds lazy, almost amused, and as cold as ice cracking over a frozen river.

Caught, I think through total panic. *Caught, caught, caught.* I kick Raze viciously away, not caring where I hit him as long as it untangles our limbs.

He doesn't resist. He's perfectly still.

I look up in the direction of his gaze and see a figure standing in the display case...or perhaps the display case is standing in him. He's tall and ghostly pale, slightly translucent, and I can make out the glass through his torso. He looks down at himself, a little annoyed, and steps forward to remove the offending furniture from his lower half.

"What an interesting bunch," he says. "I don't think I've seen any of you before. Oh, is this a heist?"

Isolde and I exchange a look. I don't know what he is, but he isn't human. And I don't think he's any kind of sentinel guarding this space, because he doesn't seem particularly upset that we're in here. Her eyes dart from me to the compass in her palm. "It's broken," she murmurs. "The needle doesn't move." She looks up at the figure. "Is this yours?"

His lips twist. "I suppose you could say that."

Olani snatches the compass from Isolde's hand. In the brief second that it passes from palm to palm, the figure flickers and disappears, before crackling back into existence. "I'd prefer if one of you would hold onto that," he snaps. "It's very disorienting going back and forth like this."

"What are you?" Raze's voice is soft as he stands up, peering more closely at the ghostly figure until they're practically nose-to-nose.

"If this *is* a heist," the figure says, ignoring Raze's question and looking at each of us in turn instead, "you'd better get on with it. I've been in Leira's keeping too long, I think, and I can't imagine her letting you just stroll out of here if you keep wasting time."

I finally find my voice and blurt, "So you're…in the compass?"

"Something like that." He smirks again. "But think of it less as a compass and more as a guide."

"A guide to what?" Raze asks, reaching to the tall girl to take the compass. She hands it over easily. The figure flickers but quickly schools his irritated expression, meeting Raze's eyes with a slow smile.

"The great Wildline legacy, of course."

In the silence that follows, the sound of footsteps echoes from far down the hall—humanlike, this time, several pairs of boots. If the dragon's with them, its claws are lost in the noise.

"And that'll be Leira's people," the figure says lightly. "Better hurry."

chapter four

Olani jumps up and peeks out the door. "Clear for now," she says. "Raze, what do you want to do?"

"Not so fast," Isolde says, swiping for the compass. He tries to hold it up out of her reach, but she's too quick. "We had it first. What legacy?" We all stare at the figure.

"Anyone and anything Leira's ancestors deemed too dangerous to be out in the world. Some might call it a prison. Some might call it treasure—all hidden away here in one convenient location."

"Here?" I repeat.

He shrugs. "I was unlucky enough to be on their list. I believe they once called it the Mortal's Keep. Let me out, and the rest of it's yours."

Raze is making a strange face that I can't read, so focused

on the translucent figure he seems to have forgotten that Isolde is still holding the compass. "Why hasn't Leira freed you yet, then?"

"You don't think she's tried? It wouldn't be a very good prison if I could just *tell* anyone how to find and unlock it, would it?"

"Sol," I mutter. A very bad feeling crackles at the edges of my awareness: *danger.* "Put it back."

"Someone's coming," Olani says from the door.

"Take it now," the figure says, urgently. "Leira couldn't figure out how to make the compass work, but you seem like a bright bunch. It could all be yours. Please." Desperation seeps into his voice.

Isolde looks between me and him, back and forth. "Seelie," she says. "Treasure."

I feel the same temptation I see in her eyes, but the awareness that something is wrong here, that this figure isn't someone to trust, is stronger. I shake my head.

"Please," he repeats. "Help me."

"I'll take it," Raze offers, reaching for the compass. She pulls it back quickly, swinging her arm in a wide arc away from him.

He grabs for it again, pushing her. His arms are longer, but she's quicker, and then they're scuffling. Neither of them draws their daggers, so it's just a blur of his hands swiping, her arms reaching, elbows knocking into ribs. The ghostly figure flickers in and out of existence as the compass changes hands back and forth.

Something shiny flies across the room as Isolde's frantic grappling knocks a simple ring from his hand. Raze's attention switches immediately, a hand closing tight over the compass as his eyes scan the plush carpet for the missing ring.

"Someone's coming *now*," Olani repeats. "We need to go."

"Olani!" Raze chokes, doubled over with one of Isolde's arms tight around his throat, but she doesn't seem to hear. She's too focused on keeping watch. He holds the compass just out of Isolde's reach, bending closer to the floor to continue his search, and her fingers tremble with the effort of stretching toward it.

"Both of you, stop it!" Impulsively, I snatch the compass out of his hands.

As soon as my fingers close over the metal, the figure winks out of existence and doesn't reappear, but for a heartbeat I could swear he looks right at me—right through me. A shock of cold runs up my arm, chilling my veins, and the compass simply…vanishes.

Not quite. The weight of it is gone, but the biting cold isn't. Metallic liquid puddles in my palm, clinging to my skin. Panicked, I try to wipe it on my apron, but it doesn't even smear. Holding my hand close to my face, I can see it slowly seeping into my skin, like a stain on cotton cloth.

"Where'd he go?" Raze demands, but his question seems faint, at the edges of my awareness. Far less pressing than whatever's happening to my hand.

Tendrils of silver run ice-cold under the surface of my skin, like they have somewhere to be but they're not in a huge rush to get there. The primal urge to stop it, to tear it out if I have to, is only held back by the observation that it's running *through* my skin, not below.

"Sol?" My voice comes out a choked whine. I don't know what to do. I don't know what's happening to me.

When I look up, Isolde and Raze are both staring at me, just as uncertain about what to do now as I am.

At the door, Olani swears quietly. "It's Aris," she says. A flash of light brightens the hall outside like an explosion, which makes the decision for all of us.

"Run!" Raze says, unnecessarily.

Isolde takes my other hand, and we sprint out into the hallway, bolting like rabbits from a hole. I can make out a handful of uniformed guards in the hall we came from, accompanied by three snarling dragons, so retracing our steps is out. We'll just have to find a different exit.

Another flash of light, and something like a sunbeam streaks past us, leaving a smoldering hole in the wallpaper. I dare to turn around, expecting Leira or a somber enchanter in the manor's uniform. Instead, I see a teenager with tawny skin and dark brown curls barely long enough to be tied back from her face. All her features are pointed, precise, as if they'd been painted on by a fine-tipped brush. But it's her eyes that stand out—shockingly green as they narrow, cat-like, on the four of us.

"Olani, you *traitor!*" the girl shrieks. "Get back here!"

Isolde's grip tightens on mine, squeezing all the blood from my hand. Raze and Olani are still ahead of us, cloaks billowing behind them. They may know a way out, but that girl seems to know who they are. Which means if we split up, she'll be more likely to follow them...and we'll be more likely to escape.

We go faster and faster, the thunder of boots behind us,

blasts of light shooting at us like arrows. At least the girl seems
to be the only enchanter among them. Finally, the hallway
branches off. I watch Raze and Olani, still a few yards ahead
of us, turn right, and I drag Isolde to the left.

"Don't let them get away!" the girl shouts behind us, but
her voice is already fading as she turns the opposite direction.
A few of the guards follow her, but most—and the dragons—
are still on our trail. Unlucky, but all we have to do is get out
of this house, out onto the street, out into the crowd, where
we can disappear. Easy.

I have no idea where we are. Every hallway in this giant
house looks the same to me, and I'm just choosing turns at
random. The dragons are practically snapping at our heels
now, and even though I know they don't breathe fire, their
breath has a strange chemical smell. It's amazing it doesn't
throw off their ability to scent us.

But something else might.

We come to a long, grand staircase that descends at least
two stories. I slip a little on the slick marble but manage to
keep myself upright. Too desperate to be embarrassed, I dig
a handful of smashed cake out of my apron pocket and sling
it behind us, hitting one of the dragons in the nose. It stops
abruptly to process the smell, and the other two crash into it,
sending all three of them careening in a pile across the pol-
ished floor.

Isolde's laugh at the ridiculous sight rings through the grand
entrance, echoing off the stone and up the stairs. I miss one of
the steps and she catches me, and I can't help but laugh along.
There are two doors ahead: one that could be the main en-

trance, which I definitely don't want to go through, and a smaller, plainer one off on the side wall.

Praying for good luck, I stumble off the last step and lead Isolde across the slippery stone floor to the smaller door.

It's unlocked. Better yet, it isn't a broom closet. Fresh summer air sweeps into the house with the smell of bonfire smoke, and Isolde and I escape into the crowd.

We slow a little as people press in close around us, catching our breath. We don't have to blend in perfectly, just to squish into the spaces the guards can't fit. Where they can't see.

"Why do you have cake in your pockets?" Isolde laughs, pulling me through a tight space between two people. I open my mouth to respond—

"There they are! Stop those girls!"

At the guard's call, the crowd splits around us, leaving us vulnerable and exposed. We break into a run again, my boots catching on every uneven cobblestone, and Isolde's pace growing ragged. Our fingers press into each other's palms, digging in.

They're behind us: the guard who called after us, her two companions, and a few other vigilantes who apparently have nothing better to do with their holiday.

We're almost back to the bridge now. Maybe if we can make it to the other side...

I waste a precious second glancing behind us. They're still back there, and I can't tell if they're gaining ground or losing it.

The bridge is coming up now. I grab hold of any decorations I can reach as we streak past, flinging them in the path of our pursuers. A lantern smashes, spreading fire up a strand of banners, and a faerie appears on the eaves of one of the houses, giddily playing a small flute that makes the flames dance and leap. That isn't exactly my fault, but it helps, too. One of the guards has to stop to deal with the fire, waving the others on to follow us.

I catch a sideways grin on Isolde's face as she looks back at the chaos. Confused and outraged shouts trail us with every step. Each heavy breath stabs my ribs with pain, and my limbs are starting to ache. But I can't stop. I can't allow myself to feel it.

"Stop those girls!" one of the remaining guards shouts.

My heart takes a break from pounding painfully to twist, but I don't have time to worry. We're crossing back into Market Square now, and everyone is too busy with their own merrymaking to worry about a few petty thieves. We squeeze right into the thickest part of the press of bodies and slow, but I still can't catch my breath as we shove and elbow people out of our way.

A wall of people cuts in front of us. The music on this side of the bridge is still going strong, pounding in my head. I turn in place, trying to fight my way through.

"Got you!"

Suddenly, I'm hauled back by the collar. My hand slips, and before I know what's happening, Isolde is lost in the crowd. I choke as the hand squeezes the back of my dress, pulling me into the arms of the city guard. My hands flail uselessly, and my feet kick as I try to free myself, but he doesn't let go. He's taller than me and at least twice my weight; there's no question about which of us is stronger.

The guard's head tilts in confusion, taking in for the first time that my face is identical to Isolde's. "Wait…"

"LET—ME—GO!" I choke out, trying desperately to kick his knees. My head thrashes as I try to find Isolde in the crowd. She'll come back. She'll find me. We're still going to get out of this.

The guard lets out a heavy sigh. "Look, it's Revelnox. Don't you think I have enough to do without—"

And then he really does look confused and surprised. I half expect blood to start leaking through his shirt, to see the tip of Isolde's knife and her sharp, focused eyes. But she's not here, and he hasn't been stabbed. Instead…

It all happens so fast.

A pained cry escapes his lips as his teeth grow, gums stretching aside with a wet, disgusting noise. The cartilage of his nose cracks and bends as his skull reshapes itself, stretching horrifically out of proportion around wide eyes being swallowed by the dark brown of his irises. Short, gray hairs poke from every pore like eager seedlings, covering his face within the space of a heartbeat.

The face of a donkey.

I stumble back, and this time he releases me. The guard holds up his still-human hands in front of his long, gray nose. His dark, glossy eyes widen in horror, and he lets out a distressed bray. He's clearly terrified, but at least the pain seems to only have lasted in the moment of his transformation.

"Don't worry."

Suddenly, there's another face behind the donkey's, a feathery female face with crimson eyes that flash in the darkness as they meet mine. "He'll be back to normal in the morning. No cost from you, changeling. You've already paid enough."

The faerie winks at me just as she did when I caught her eye across the crowd earlier, an extremely self-satisfied smirk occupying what I can see of her face.

Faeries don't offer gifts. The rules that dictate their behavior won't let them give anything freely, without an equal bargain. If I accept this, will it come with a hidden price tag of a thousand years of service, or the ability to see the color orange? Should I respond?

It doesn't matter, because I am unable to speak. I have to concentrate to even make my heavy heart keep beating. My jaw drops, and every word I've ever learned stalls on the tip of my tongue.

"That…was a close one," Isolde says, gasping. Finally, I see her, a heap of black in the middle of the street like a discarded rag doll. Someone must have knocked her down, and she's run herself too ragged to get back up. Still, even that can't kill her irreverent grin. I offer her my hand and pull her unsteadily to her feet.

When I look back, the faerie is gone. The donkey-man is still braying in distress, probably wondering if he still has to finish his shift.

chapter five

I solde and I huddle close together as we shuffle into the crowd, but the rest of the guards seem to be gone. For a while, we walk silently in a combination of exhaustion, residual fear, and spiraling thoughts. Buildings and people and fires and faeries blur past. Heading home should feel comforting, but there's a chill settling into my spine. If Market Square was dull compared to Gilt Row, then this neighborhood is a dump. It's still technically in Market Square, but on the outskirts, backed into a corner, bordered on one side by the peacefully sluggish Harrow River, and by the Twilight District on the other.

The streets are full here, too, but not with pulsing waves of revelers like the ones back in the middle of the square. They're furtive, holding whispered conversations, tugging each other by the hand back to the safety of the bonfire, kissing in darkened corners where no one can see them, glancing over shoulders and clenching hands into tight, nervous fists. Finally, when there's no one within earshot, Isolde speaks.

"Seelie, you didn't...you didn't ask that faerie...for a favor, somehow?"

My heart stutters. "Fate, no. I have no idea why she helped us." I don't know what kind of fool Isolde takes me for. Everyone knows better than to make deals with the fair folk. It always turns sour, no matter what they offer you, no matter how airtight you try to make the contract. It's the first lesson parents teach their children, the cardinal rule, more a fact than a law. No matter how desperate the situation, faerie bargains will only make it worse.

But I don't have time to be offended because Isolde has already moved on. "The compass?"

During the chase, I'd managed to forget why my hand was going numb. But the silver metal is still in there, and when I hold my hand up, my stomach drops. Intertwined loops are marked into my skin, like the petals of a blooming flower, surrounded by a thread-fine circle. Four points. The impression of an arrow piercing the design, intricately spanning from the dip of my wrist to the space between my middle and ring fingers. I can feel the magic simmering in the silvery ink, like an infection, if I concentrate.

Isolde grabs for me, but I pull away. Urgency tightens her voice. "Does it hurt? Are you okay?"

"Okay," I echo. Another deep breath as I try to make my heart beat normally, to make the words obey. "I'm not... I can't do this right now. We can look at it when we get home. Are *you* okay?"

"I'm always okay."

"Isolde." I fold my arms and look her over. She collapsed in the street. I saw how exhausted and battered she was, but she seems fine now—unless she feels worse than she's letting on.

"Seelie." She parrots my name back to me in the same serious tone. Finally, she allows herself a grin. "I'm fine. What about that guide or whatever he was? Is he still...?"

The question trails off into empty air. I stare down at my palm, remembering the voice, the cold, disinterested stare. The half second that his eyes met mine before he disappeared and a flicker of genuine surprise shone in their flat white depths.

This time, I let her take my hand and brush her fingers over the design, as if she was holding the compass. It was her touch that awakened him the first time, after all. But nothing happens. "He's gone," I say. Which is a relief, because if I started projecting sarcastic apparitions whenever someone touched me, I might actually disappear into the forest never to be seen again.

"Okay," Isolde says, releasing me. "Since it looks like neither of us was mortally wounded...that was pretty cool."

"Yeah, well." I huff, crossing my arms. One hand fidgets with the hem of the opposite sleeve. "Don't start getting sloppy and expect a faerie to show up to fix everything with magic. This has been, hands down, the worst birthday ever."

My twin laughs softly, and I let myself relax a little. Tonight has gone about as wrong as it possibly could, but we're walking away together, in one piece. I can still hear the Revelnox celebration behind us, but it all fades as we move quickly down the dark, empty streets no one bothered to decorate.

Isolde considers a small flask she must have taken from someone's pocket earlier. She unscrews the top, sniffs at the contents, shrugs, and—before I can stop her—raises it to her lips, drinking deeply.

My senses are coming back to me, and even the horrible smell of the city is strangely calming. I'm okay. Everything is okay.

Isolde extends the now much-lighter flask to me with a questioning look.

I glare. Then again, I'm not exactly in the position to take the moral high ground tonight.

If the drinks at the party were fizzy, pink, and delicate, this is molten silver, hot, and bright all the way down my throat. Coughing too loudly to try to play it off as something else, I hand back the empty flask.

"What are we supposed to do *now*?" I think I might sound accusing. It's hard to tell. I don't think changelings are supposed to have as many human emotions as I do. I've never met another who's lived with humans as long as I have (at least, that I'm aware of), though I know they exist. "Isolde." I grab at her arm. "What happened back there? Why didn't you just stick to the plan?"

Isolde wipes a hand across her sweaty hairline, right above her mask. She isn't looking my way, but I can sense her mouth puckering into a sullen frown. "What about you, huh? Who were those people? How did they know about—?"

"Shh!"

I hush her as a trio in cheaply painted skull masks stumbles past us, screeching with laughter. I stare at my boots as they pass, trying to keep my eyes in the shadows so they don't flash with light. So no one else finds out I'm a changeling.

I'm tired.

When it seems safe enough, I tug on Isolde to bring her closer. "I ran into him at the party. It...it just slipped out."

Curses. I should have lied. I should have told her that he'd noticed my eyes, anything to not make myself look *this* foolish. But her face is already twisting in surprise and something else, something almost angry but not quite. Her mouth opens—

"He didn't seem suspicious or anything," I lie, covering her half-started word. "And then the girl showed up and dragged him away, and—well, *then* they seemed kind of suspicious."

Isolde's mask is slipping off her face. She shoves it up roughly, and I'm met with a dark, quiet stare. "You know we have to get out of town," she says finally. Her voice is rough and quiet. "First thing in the morning. At the latest."

She's right. Between Leira Wildfall, that girl with the beams of light, and the city guard, we'll need to be careful for a while. Even once we get out of the city, we have no way of knowing if they'd follow us to the next place we happen to settle in.

"I know," I say. "You're not going to make a habit of making me help you pick locks, are you? I don't think our parents—" I cut myself off suddenly, seeing the faintest twitch as Isolde flinches.

They didn't raise us for this life, but we found it anyway. Easily. As if it's what was always meant for us.

Isolde looks offended. "Of course not. I was just...so sure there was something great in there."

There's a chance that my sister's brush with the faeries that stole her left her with a touch of magic. Not like my enchanting magic—more like uncanny luck, a skill with illusion. Her fingers are lighter than an autumn breeze. People tend to avoid her, and I don't know if it's because she's always hanging out with her weird changeling counterpart or because she has her own kind of otherworldliness.

But we don't talk about that.

I tell myself to take another deep breath. I don't want to fight with my sister. Not really.

We finally pass out of the edges of Market Square, trailing the walkway alongside the river choked with darkened barges that will carry things in and out of the city in the morning, when the world creaks back to daily life. We're almost home.

I squeeze my hands into fists, trying to ignore the slight tingle still lingering at the back of my mind, itching over my palms.

The wide path hugging the river along the outskirts of the city is all but abandoned. The moon is the only source of light now, washing silver over the river and the jagged silhouette of the crumbling ruins at the city's edge. Auremore is a city built on the bones of an older civilization, with very little respect for whatever calamity wiped the original out all those centuries ago. It's easy to forget all the history that lingers beneath when you're in the city, but here at the border, the old and new butt against each other awkwardly.

I force a little smile and try for a joke. "Next year, all I want for our birthday is to not endanger our lives."

Our birthday. I force myself to say it aloud, to claim it. I belong in this life as much as she does, and the circumstances of my birth don't make us any less sisters. Doubts lurk in the dark corners of my mind, telling me I'm only lying to myself. I turn from them, pushing their whispers away. Just like Mami taught me to do.

Isolde's hair catches the moonlight, silhouetting its sweep over her shoulders, and she gives me a gleaming, innocent smile. "No promises."

Our home is parked in a solitary spot on the other side of the river, across the bridge that separates Auremore from the countryside. Other enchanted wagons and regular, horse-drawn caravans are spotted along the banks, but the Destiny is (in my admittedly biased opinion) the most beautiful of the bunch.

The solid wood box has been our home for the past three years, and I still feel lighter every time I see her cheerful paint job—emerald, accented with mint green—even tinted indigo in the night. She's maybe six feet by fourteen, propped up on beautifully carved wooden wheels, with a domed roof, a little tin chimney poking out of the top, and round windows in each side. One large rectangular window in the front, currently closed off by curtains inside, lets the driver see without being exposed to the elements in even the worst weather. Two fold-away steps lead up to the door and a small platform in the front, used by the previous owner as a stage.

Golden light sparkles off the Destiny's varnish from another caravan's bonfire, which is still surrounded by masked people of every age and background talking and laughing, their voices ringing to the distant mountains.

"Think we have time for cake before we make a run for it?" I lean against the sleek, smooth wood and watch Isolde pick the lock. After three years, you'd think we would have found time to buy a new lock, or at the very least have a key made. We keep telling ourselves we'll get around to it someday.

Someday is starting to look more like *never*.

Finally, her thoughtful look loosens up into a smile. "There's always time for cake." One thing we do have in common: a monstrous sweet tooth.

The lock clicks, and the door swings open, as if the wagon is welcoming us home.

I reach for the closest lantern, twisting the dial that sparks a small flame onto its wick. I probably would have lost my mind in a claustrophobic fit long ago if not for the abundant light let in by the windows during the day. We don't have an inch to spare. Two stacked bunks, partly hidden by a bookshelf, butt up against the back wall. A tiny wood stove and what I can only call the suggestion of a kitchen line one side. On the other, a heavy wooden chest secures our possessions and doubles as a bench.

Home.

I let out a sigh as my fingers scramble with my mask's ties. Isolde stretches, shrugging off her carefully curated streetwise persona like an itchy coat. She kicks off her boots and tears her mask off her face, plopping down cross-legged on the floor next to the bench. I catch the look she gives my hand and bury it surreptitiously in my skirt, out of sight. But she doesn't bring it up again. She knows there's no point trying to talk to me about something before I'm ready. And I'm not... I can't—

Focus. One thing at a time.

It's a relief to take my mask off. I'd almost gotten used to its itch, but the sudden breath of fresh air on the upper half of my face is a relief. I hope it won't leave a lasting rash. I toss the cheap, ugly thing next to Isolde's in the corner.

A distressed meow splits the dim atmosphere, followed by the scuffling of footsteps.

Of course, we don't have a cat.

One cold night, just a few months after we claimed the wagon, I found a tiny, injured kitten, the color of fuzzy midnight. We took it in to nurse it back to health and only discovered later that it wasn't actually a cat. It never had been.

"Don't be like that, Birch," I scold. "We'll pick them up later."

I go to work quickly, swaying on my toes as I reach for our battered tin plates. The shelves are stacked to the ceiling to take advantage of every possible inch of space, and I get the sneaking feeling that Birch put the plates up where I'd struggle to reach them for his own amusement.

Our resident brownie came to us in the disguise of a kitten, but he spends at least half his time invisible. After we'd let him in, it had been impossible to convince the house spirit to leave—despite our protests that the Destiny isn't really a house.

We could have chased him off with charms or salt, but our parents raised us better than that. Even though brownies and other faerie creatures are less powerful than the fae themselves, they're still not to be trifled with—and besides, many of them have lived in the Mortal Realm long enough to consider it home. So we leave little pieces of leftover food in front of the stove, and in return, he helps out with the dishes and scolds us for leaving things out of order. He's fond of my baking, especially anything with lemon.

I'm going to have to dig the rest of the mashed-up cake

crumbs out of my pockets sooner or later, but I manage to find two pieces that weren't completely obliterated in our escape, along with one smaller, brownie-size portion, which I place on a napkin by the stove. It's not the same as the elaborate homemade birthday cakes that Papa and I used to make, but there's still comfort in the familiar motions. I've always loved the process of baking as much as the end result, clearing a moment for a tiny slice of joy, sharing that joy with someone else, even if it only lasts a short time. Each plate gets a drizzle of honey and a sprinkle of cinnamon, which does very little to hide the beating they took in my pocket.

Isolde sits deep in concentration, splitting up the night's profits into messy piles grouped by function or material or some other factor I can't quite grip. A wave of emotion washes over me when I look at her. She's been taking care of me, fighting all my battles, since we were kids. I just want to be able to return the favor.

"Come on," I say softly. "Let's go sit outside. Just like old times."

chapter six

When I said the Destiny's stage is small, I wasn't kidding. We can dangle our feet off the edge and lean our backs against the caravan, heads tilted to the inky-blue sky.

The air is cool out here without the fire and the tight press of bodies, alleviating the stuffy humidity of the last days of summer. A breeze sweeps in from the countryside, blowing the city smells away from us. The distant diamond stars wink at us as we bite into the cake. It's almost better than before it was smashed: soft and sweet, with a warm hint of spice.

But it's not the same as home—our real home.

"Hey... Seels." I don't like the look in Isolde's eyes, the nearly black color of rain-soaked earth. It looks too much like pity. She puts her fork down. "Everything okay?"

I hadn't realized she was watching me. I must have let my

disguise slip, let all the places I was falling apart leak through the cracks as I thought about home and everything we've lost. My fingers curl around the vial on its leather cord, pulling it out from under my neckline.

I take a deep breath, doing everything I can to keep my voice from wavering. I even manage a mockingly stern look. "You *cannot* shorten my nickname to a shorter nickname. It's unconscionable."

A mischievous grin slips naturally over her face. "You like it." The cheerful look is gone as quickly as it came, but she doesn't look away. "Seriously. What's wrong? And I can tell it's not just what a disaster tonight was, so don't even try lying."

I miss home. The words don't come. Tongue-tied, I just stare into her eyes, softer for me than for anyone else in the world. But I don't have to say it. My twin can look at me and know what I'm thinking.

I do miss home. I miss it like I would miss a chunk of my heart removed from my living body. We're leaving this city that sheltered us for the better part of the spring and summer, but we still can't go back. I miss the embrace of the familiar, the rhythm of daily life with our parents. And I know that they don't—*can't*—miss me back.

My fingers squeeze the vial, knuckles going white. I know it's my fault we're on our own. My uncontrolled, reckless, *dangerous* magic that made me a criminal before Isolde had ever so much as set her eyes on a lock pick.

I miss home excruciatingly every day. But it's worst on days like this.

Moving instinctively, my head settles onto Isolde's shoulder.

The ends of her dark hair tickle my nose as her head leans on mine, sheltering me.

"Want me to tell the story of how Mami and Papa adopted you?" Another birthday tradition. They told that story every year. I can hear the smile in her voice. Is it forced or real?

"You weren't there." Another forkful of cake turns to glue in my mouth. "I mean, there's no way you remember. You were less than a month old."

"You don't know that."

"How old you were?"

"That I don't remember."

I snort. "Go ahead, then."

There's a pause as she chews. "Well," she says with her mouth full, "I don't remember, honestly. But from what I've been told, it was easy to tell, even as a newborn, that you were a changeling. Mami had been around enough other babies, after all. And don't tell me that newborns don't have a personality, because if they didn't, one of us wouldn't be here."

I'd helped our mother, the town midwife, with dozens of births before everyone found out I was a changeling and suddenly wouldn't allow their children within spitting distance. Up until that point, I'd considered myself something of an expert on the subject. "I wasn't going to correct you," I interrupt.

Isolde hums. "Sure you weren't." She gives up on her fork, lifting the cake to her mouth with her bare hands. "Worried over what would become of her other daughter, she decided to come find me herself. She left in the night, because she knew Papa would try to stop her. You were in a sling tied close to her chest as she traveled through the forest for three days."

The faerie realms lay along our own, each world like a layer of cloth, each life like a line of stitching in a tapestry. In some places, threads weave between the worlds. Other places are riddled with holes, where it's all too easy to slip into a different world. The forest Mami ventured into bordered our village to the south. It was safe enough, as long as you stuck to the path. In its depths, it was said you could slip between the human world and the faerie ones without even noticing until it was too late.

Every year, our mother spun this story for us.

And every year, she refused to talk about what she'd seen in the forest.

"And three nights," I add.

"I was getting there. Would you like to tell it?"

I kick my feet idly in the open air. The scent of smoke and the sound of laughter carry over to me on the breeze from the bonfire at the center of camp. A temporary peace settles in my stomach. "No, go ahead."

"She must have been a sight—you know that face she does." Isolde's features stretch into an almost *too* good imitation of Mami's you-already-know-what-you-did expression.

I laugh. "Only from when *you* got me in trouble."

Isolde ignores me. "Turns out, it works equally well on the five-year-olds *and* the faerie court."

The smile freezes on my face, draining away slowly.

Technically, there are two faerie courts: the one governed by the Seelie, a world of order and chivalry and pleasure, of endless summer and endless green forest. And the one ruled by the Unseelie, who revel in chaos and power. They aren't good and evil, exactly—no matter which court, faeries are self-interested above all else. But at least the mortals who end up in the Seelie Realm sometimes live to write stories and songs about it.

Like our mother. She never told us much about the court she'd visited, but it must have been the Seelie. After all, she hadn't just returned, she'd returned with exactly what she was looking for.

"She was so stubborn that something in her amused the faeries, and they gave her a chance not many get—" Isolde is getting to the good part now "—'One of these children you bore. The other is of faerie make. You may leave with whichever you choose. Pick carefully.'"

I close my eyes, envisioning the scene. Mami, standing before a court of faeries, their glowing eyes lit up with mischief as they await her decision.

And our mother, without a second of hesitation, lifted us both from our ivy-woven faerie cradles and gently tucked her newborn daughters into her arms.

"Calmly and quietly, she said, 'I came for the daughter in your possession. I never agreed to return my adopted child.' This cake is great, Seelie." Isolde pauses to take another bite.

I headbutt her gently. "It's okay. Keep going!"

"Bossy," she mutters, but she continues. "She didn't meet their glowing eyes or wait for permission. She turned on her heel and left, wise enough to know not to look back. She brought us home."

I smile. "And Papa was beside himself with worry. He was so overjoyed to see her return that he almost crushed us in his embrace."

Isolde's voice warms. "He picked you up and cradled you.

They looked us both over, and they thought that we were both perfect."

I imagine us as babies. I imagine myself perfect. Two wrinkly, chubby-cheeked infants with a lick of Papa's dark hair, held up next to each other, right where we belonged.

"Papa didn't know it before just then—he'd been too sleep-deprived—but as he held you, he realized that our family had been missing something. And you were the piece that made it whole."

A lump forms in my throat, choking me as I try to swallow it down. Dewy tears prick at the corners of my eyes. I sit up and twist to meet my sister's gaze. "Happy birthday, Isolde."

She beams back at me. "Happy birthday, Seelie."

A tear tracks down my face. I wipe it away, embarrassed. "Sorry. I just—"

I just miss them so much.

The words stick yet again.

"I know," Isolde whispers, wrapping her hand around mine. "Me, too."

My nose is running, and the tears are flowing freely now. I sniffle.

"Oh!" A goofy grin lights her face, promising something that will dry my tears—literally or figuratively, I'm not sure. "Here, wipe your eyes." She digs out a silk handkerchief I've never seen before in my life from one of her pockets. "I'm pretty sure it was clean when I stole it."

Laughing and crying at the same time, I accept the handkerchief and blot at my tears. "Isolde?"

She's just crammed the last bite of cake into her mouth

and set her plate to the side, licking honey off her fingers. "Hmmf?"

"Do you really think we can do it? Just…start over somewhere new, as a family?"

Everything about her transforms in an instant. She's resolute now, as perfect and severe as a statue, staring off over my shoulder.

"Yes," she says quietly, and this time she's the one who won't meet my eyes. She reaches for my hand. "Now, let me see."

I reluctantly hold my palm up to her. The compass's needle twitches as my hand wavers.

Isolde's fingers trace over the design as her brows come together in the middle of her forehead. "We all touched it," Isolde murmurs. "Why you?"

I tap my feet on the stair and don't respond. I know it'll only take her a moment to think of the one thing different between me and everyone else in that room.

"Oh." Pause. "You're sure you're okay?"

"Yes," I lie. It's not pain, it's just an uncomfortable awareness of something that's not supposed to be there. I shake my head, not trusting the right words to come to the tip of my tongue. "No. No, it doesn't hurt, I mean. Yes, I'm okay. It's okay. It doesn't hurt. I–it's an enchanted *compass*, Isolde," I stammer. "And maybe my magic took it—but I didn't mean to. You know I wouldn't."

"Seelie," she half laughs. "We were there to take stuff."

I know I sound like a pouting child, but I can't help it. She isn't the one with magic crawling under her skin. I didn't want this. "I was trying to put it back."

"You heard what that man—whatever—what they said. The Mortal's Keep. *Treasure*. This could be *it*, Seelie. The chance we've been waiting for. You expect me to believe you really wanted to put it back?"

"Yes, but only because I knew you'd get *like this* about it."

"Like this?" she repeats, and she could be angry, but she's not, because she's Isolde and picking my arguments apart like snarled threads is a hundred times more interesting than getting offended. She lets my hand go, and I lean back against the wagon. A smile pricks at the corner of her mouth below rising eyebrows.

Oh, no.

I know that look in her eyes. I've seen it hundreds of times, right before she got an amazing idea that always ended up with both of us in trouble—for instance, right before we crossed the bridge into Gilt Row. Or the night we ran away from home, and instead of just vanishing, we *borrowed* our wagon and went charging off across the countryside.

I roll my eyes. "You know exactly what I'm talking about. You get all worked up—"

One hand rumples her short hair, tugging like it's impatient for a task to do. "Does it point north?"

My nails dig sharply into my palm. "West." I let out a breath. "The Western Range was circled on the map in the vault. Leira must have figured that part out." The part of my imagination I've been trying to hold back surges forward like the needle is pulling me west, filling in the gaps with visions of treasure and wealth, more than we could ever find slinking around and stealing trinkets.

Meeting Isolde's eyes again, I can tell she's thinking the

exact same thing. I want her to tell me that it might just be a curse, and that it's safer for us to not find out which of the two options is at the end of this path.

But since it seems like she won't, I have to.

"N-no," I say. I'm stammering, backpedaling, fighting what it is I actually want to do. "No way. You heard them, Sol. Everything in that place was locked away for a reason. We have no idea what else—"

"Seelie." A second's flicker of concern crosses her face. She reaches for my hand, catching it palm-up. Gentle. Soothing. "Don't you get it? This Mortal's Keep thing could be your ticket home. You'd be rich enough to buy Mami and Papa a big fancy house like that somewhere no one knows our face. You'd be rich enough that even if you did get in trouble, you could buy your way out of it. This would all be over."

The dream shimmers for a moment. It's tempting. It's everything I want: paying my way out of this life, being together as a family again without fear that consequences for my actions would fall on the people I love, picking up exactly where we left off.

I give one last weak try. "We don't know—" I whisper.

"Isn't it worth a shot?" Isolde squeezes my hand. "Seelie, we have to follow this thing or find a way to get rid of it. I might not be an enchanter, but I wouldn't even know where to start looking to get rid of *magical tattoos* trapped under your skin. And whoever those people were, they wanted it, too. They're probably already looking for us now."

"Oh." I knew that already, but it still feels like a blow to hear it put so plainly.

"We have to try."

I frown. We don't *have* to do anything, besides survive. Our current situation isn't *home*. Not by a long shot. But it's the closest thing I have right now. I've always lived on routine and familiarity, clung to it like a life raft in a storm. Maybe because some part of me (a part I prefer to keep locked away) still feels like I belong in the faerie realm of constant, unchanging summer.

Isolde's hand pulls mine away from the vial. The tiny forget-me-not flowers inside, now uncovered, glow with soft blue light. My sister lifts the bottle away from my skin, frowning thoughtfully. She's clearly remembering the last—and first—time that I dug deep into my reserves of magic.

The last time we saw our parents.

I'd had no choice but to leave, and of course Isolde was going with me. It was the only way I could spare our parents from the pain they'd brought down on our family just by loving me. But we also knew that if we just disappeared, they would stop at nothing to bring us back home. That our mother would insist that sheltering us, and paying the price, was what they were meant to do.

So I'd waited until the latest hour of the night and called on my magic to steal the memory of their daughters—all the emotional ties that held us together—from their peaceful, sleeping minds. The memories floated like a blue mist in front of me before I reached for one of my mother's dozens of scattered jars and vials and trapped them inside.

After that, I'd been struck with a headache so bad that I briefly lost my sight. As I faded in and out of consciousness, Isolde had dragged me away to our getaway vehicle. I couldn't remember anything after that until I awoke the next afternoon, so weak I could barely stand. My parents' memories were stolen but safe, as long as I kept them trapped in the bottle. If they escaped, I didn't know if they'd return to Mami and Papa or disappear forever. The mist inside the vial, which was still clutched in my fist, had resolved itself into the shape of forget-me-not blooms.

Magic has a cruel sense of humor.

Ice shivers down my spine.

Isolde reaches to tuck her pinky finger into mine—a promise. I let her, despite the weird, numb feeling frosting over my fingertips.

"Fine," I bite out, before I can stop myself. "We head west first thing in the morning."

Maybe I'm imagining it, but I think I feel the magic simmer with satisfaction in my palm. I squeeze my fingers hard enough to leave ragged nail imprints in the silvery mark, as if that will stop it from spreading to my veins.

chapter seven

I'm left staring at the distant gold smudge of faraway flames long after Isolde jumps up excitedly to start getting every-thing ready. I know I should move, but I can't shake off my heavy thoughts. My fingers move over the compass in my palm in absentminded, endless circles.

Looking out over the rest of the riverside encampments, I see people dousing the bonfire and picking up their scattered mess and staggering home to catch a few hours of sleep before the world begins anew. As the parties wind down, faeries that are too weak or lazy or drunk to summon up a physical form drift out of the city in faint, bouncing balls of light. Half in this world, half in theirs.

They say the border between worlds used to be blurred,

and not just at Revelnox. The faeries lived among mortals, bargained with them, fell in love with them. They allowed humans into their realms as equals, artists, and friends. But that was a long time ago, and now the divide between mortals and faeries is deep and filled with distrust. The faeries spend as little time in our world as possible, and mortals can only enter the Seelie and Unseelie Realms through faerie-made portals.

It's better this way.

Except for those of us with a foot in each world, yet belonging in neither.

Finally, I force myself to get to work. We need to leave as soon as we've caught a few hours of sleep, and I have to make sure the Destiny is ready for the trip.

The tight space between the wagon's underside and the grass presses in on me like a hug as I crawl between its wheels in the stillness of late night. I can hardly see, now that the fire's down to embers and the moon is the only source of light.

Luckily, I've done this chore so many times that I don't need to see. My hands move automatically, unlatching the box attached to the Destiny's rear axle. The lid falls open on smooth, oiled hinges, and I dodge to the left. That box has given me more than its fair share of black eyes and bloody lips, but refueling is one job Isolde can't do for me.

I take a deep breath, crushing my ribs against the ground, and let a trickle of magic flow to my fingertips.

I'm not sure how the device actually works, what mechanism it uses to store the magic it collects, and I don't really care. As long as I remember to channel magic into the box every week or so, depending on how far and fast we've been traveling, the enchanted wagon runs. There's a limit to how much magic each mortal enchanter can call on at once, but I've only reached mine once, on the night we ran away from home. At least, I think I did. I might have been able to draw even more if I hadn't passed out from the pain.

It doesn't take much magic to replenish the Destiny, since we haven't budged from our spot on the bank in so long. I'm pretty sure the only time the wagon has moved in the past six months is when it got bored and decided to roll itself into a sunnier patch or drift sideways at an angle that would better display its paint job. The only downside of having an enchanted wagon is that the magic gives it a bit of personality, which makes it charmingly unpredictable.

After everything else tonight, I feel like I should be spent from the effort of pouring magic into the wagon, but if anything… I almost feel refreshed when I pull my fingers away from the cool brass and latch the top back on the box.

No. No, I can't enjoy this. Even when I was a little kid, I did everything I could to push magic away. I'd had to hide my ability to blend in. I couldn't get sucked into it now. All I want is a normal life, to pick back up exactly where I left off the last time we dropped everything and ran.

Not that enchanters are *that* rare, but my faerie side is a deep cave that I have no plans of exploring as long as I can help it.

I hop past the little stash of gold Isolde left out for the wandering faeries, spring up the steps, miss the landing, and grip the side of the wagon to swing myself back on balance.

Something cold prickles on the back of my neck. I turn, looking over my shoulder.

A cool breeze kicks up around me, scented with warm summer grass, campfires, and a promise of rain. The stink of people and alcohol and magically overperfumed flowers is far away now, with the lights of the parties still going on across the river. I know Raze and Olani will be after us, but since they have no idea about the Destiny, the riverbank is the last place they'll look. For just a few hours, we're still safe here.

I fill my lungs, go inside, and latch the door.

Isolde looks younger in her sleep, tucked on the top bunk into a messy nest of blankets that twist around her arms and legs when she tosses and turns. The lantern is still burning, casting the whole inside of the caravan in soft amber light, but it's so late I can't blame her.

Besides, Isolde can fall asleep anytime and anywhere. It's like…well, magic.

Following the same thoughtless rhythm I do every night, I slip my hair out of its braid and pull my dress over my head, draping it with my apron at the foot of my bed. I settle into my own neatly made bunk, sitting with my back pressed against the wall.

Across the wagon, Birch sleeps in outstretched feline form on the hearth, next to an empty plate. He looks so small and sweet that it's hard to remember that he isn't actually a cat. Especially with the adorable silvery-pink pads of his paws turned out to me, just begging to be squished.

I let myself flop down on my pillow, pulling the blankets tight around me. I didn't realize until just now how *cold* I am—freezing. The air around me is warm and still, but the cold is in my bones.

I know I'm exhausted, but I've never felt more awake. Too much happened today, and too much will happen tomorrow, and I can't believe I've agreed to this reckless, near-impossible quest.

But if it means I might get to go home…

My hands fold together again, tracing circles over the design without looking. The repetitive movement is comforting, absorbing my attention and calming the frantic beat of my heart. I slowly sink into sleep so smoothly I don't even notice the moment everything goes black. Everything is dark and quiet and close, with the blankets pulled tight around me.

It would *need to be a changeling, wouldn't it?*

The voice is familiar, sending a bolt of panic down my spine. My heart stutters, and my eyes try to fly open, but it feels like something is pressing down on my chest, holding me in sleep.

Shh, shh. Just relax. Don't mind me. I'm just along for the ride.

I know that voice. I heard it earlier today, in that room in the manor, bored and aloof one moment, desperate the next. But just like the compass went from metal to magic, the presence has changed, too, from something I could physically see to a voice I don't *hear* as much as *feel* vibrating in the back of my mind. Too close to touch, cold as winter wind.

Where's your magic? Don't tell me you're the world's only changeling without magic.

It feels like my throat is closing. I want to wake up, to scream, but I can't move. I can't even breathe. *I have magic*, I think back at the voice. Maybe if I can appease it, it'll leave me alone. *I just don't use it.*

Chilly condescension washes over me. *You must have used it at some point. Come now, let me see.*

I want to protest, but I'm already slipping away from myself, reaching for words that aren't there. I scrabble uselessly at the edges of my own consciousness...

My own memories fold me in like heavy blankets, pulled up over my head by unfamiliar hands and a soft, freezing voice.

chapter eight

The first time I saw the Destiny, it was painted sky-blue with marigold accents.

I've relived this day time and time again in my nightmares, watching the Destiny rumble on spoked wheels down the dusty road, as if for the very first time. I had seen enchanted caravans before, but this one caught in my mind and wouldn't let go, for two reasons.

The first was the craftsmanship. Even before I had ever seen the inside of the caravan, I could tell how beautifully made it was.

The second was the giant gold lettering on the side advertising REDBROOK'S FIRST-CLASS HEALTH POTIONS AND FAE PREVENTION MEASURES, which was and is a mouthful.

As the caravan rolled into our sleepy little town, a crowd started to gather. Nestled between a faerie forest and the Harrow River, Rurava wasn't exactly a destination for out-of-towners. There was the occasional traveling merchant or adventurer on their way to something better, but even the most mundane visitor was cause for excitement and speculation—and this wagon was anything but mundane.

It passed the orchards, the apiary, the blacksmith's forge, and stopped under the ancient oak in the middle of the main square without any regard for the regular daily activities going on there. Tall, golden grass shivered under its wheels, and sunlight dappled its shiny sides.

"Let's go see," Isolde begged, tugging me by the hand. We were fourteen and thought we knew everything.

As my twin and I stood near the outer fringe of the group, where I wouldn't feel too pressed in, a man stepped out onto the little stage with so much force that I wondered if he'd kicked the door down. He looked maybe my parents' age, with neatly parted mousy-brown hair down to his shoulders and a gleam in his eye I couldn't read at all.

"Good afternoon, folks! I am Cassius Redbrook, and I am here with solutions to all your problems! Unless it's problems with love, in which case you're on your own."

He was warming up the crowd before they even had a chance to question him. A few people chuckled faintly. Isolde rolled her eyes like only a fourteen-year-old can.

And then he quickly launched into his sales pitch for various kinds of garbage—for hair loss, hair removal, coughs, headaches—

"You name it!"

He dazzled the crowd with a too-white smile and tossed out samples and big, brash promises, and then he reeled them in with what made him unique: the fae prevention and repellant measures.

What a joke. Faerie mischief is just a part of life. Anyone with common sense accepts this and does their best to coexist, with bribes of milk and shiny things. Keep your head down and *don't bargain with them*, and you'll mostly be left alone.

People with common sense are rare.

Everyone knows someone who knows someone—someone who was unlucky enough to cross the faeries and woke up the next day dead…if they were lucky.

Some woke with flowers sprouting under their skin, vines curling around muscles that made every movement more and more painful until they eventually choked to death on the leaves filling their lungs. Others lost their sense of taste, their memories, their most-beloved skill. There were stories of people who cried pure, crystalline salt, whose raw faces and unseeing eyes bore the scars of thousands of tiny scratches. I'd even heard of some who could never feel warm, no matter how many layers they wrapped themselves in, who burned themselves alive just to relieve the cold.

Most of these stories were probably not true—but why take the risk?

Redbrook's so-called fae prevention was even worse than the rest of his stuff: special herbed salts to ward off brownies, potions to drink to safely cross the forest at night, dust to throw at a faerie if it approached you. And then it got worse.

I should have walked away.

Isolde squeezed my hand and gave me a look. *Are you okay?*

I stared forward, crossing my arms. I didn't want to know what she was thinking at the moment.

Redbrook produced a tiny iron bracelet stamped with charms, meant to go on a baby's wrist to protect them from the thieving hands of a faerie. A powder to mix with water to determine whether a child had been swapped with a changeling. And worst of all...

"Ladies and gentlemen, I present to you my totally unique Changeling Exchange Tonic!" This exclamation was accompanied by a swish of cloak and the brandishing of a green bottle appearing seemingly out of thin air. As he held it over his head, a hush fell over the crowd. "*This*, I am certain, is unlike anything you've ever seen before. For those parents already afflicted with a changeling—" my insides boiled "—your solution is here! Just a small sip of this tonic, every day, *will* restore your human child to you."

"What's in it?"

I looked around with everyone else for the source of the shout before realizing it was *me*.

"Uhh—*what* was that, miss?"

Was I stepping forward? Apparently, because people were whispering and clearing a path for me. "I asked what was in it," I said, looking up at the man and, for the first time, hoping the light would catch on my faerie eyes.

"Well, miss, *obviously*, I have to keep my formulas a secret—"

"Is it safe?"

The man's face turned red, then white. "It's perfectly safe for a changeling," he said cautiously.

"Why don't you try a sip, then?" What was I *saying*? What was I *doing*? It was so unlike me, and yet more like *me* than ever.

He pressed his lips together, whether to keep from saying something careless or in subconscious fear of the tonic he was selling, I wasn't sure.

"It's poison, isn't it?" I said. "Changelings are *children*, in case you weren't aware. We—"

Everyone had known my secret for almost four years now, and I'd seen the results. My father was barely keeping his pottery shop open, and Mami hadn't delivered anyone's baby in months. They were starving us out, eliminating the unlucky family foolish enough to love a changeling child with slow, quiet persistence. I started again.

"We didn't ask to be this way."

I almost tripped, and only then did I realize I was shaking. I didn't know if I was scared or angry. Both?

Isolde was still standing where I had been, as shocked as everyone else at my sudden outburst. I was standing just in front of the platform, squaring off with the salesman with my fists clenched. My hands stung, like their restlessness had found its way to my skin.

"You're selling people poison and calling it hope!" I shouted. My voice carried farther than I had known it could. "Don't you know that's *wrong*?"

Redbrook was too surprised to answer. His mouth opened and closed as I turned to address his audience.

"If you can only love a child that exists within the boundaries of your expectations—if you would harm them to make them what you want—then you have no business being a parent at all." I'd heard my mother say this a hundred times.

"There's no *cure* for changelings, and you shouldn't let this quack convince you otherwise. We deserve to live the way we are!"

Something gripped tight around my arm. I turned to see Redbrook had hopped down from the stage and was now standing over me, holding my arm so I couldn't move. "That's enough of that," he snarled quietly. Then, to the crowd, "I would say that the misguided creature has proven my point. Changelings have no place in our world, and this tonic is a guaranteed solution!" I twisted viciously, trying to pull away, but I was small and weak, and he was a grown man, crushing me with his full strength.

And the crowd—people I'd known my entire life, people who might have once thought of me as sweet or harmless—let him.

Isolde let out a cry of protest, pushing her way to the front. But she wasn't a hardened criminal with years of practice taking down people much bigger than her. She wasn't armed with a blade. She'd never even fought anyone except the kids who used to bully me. She had no idea what to do next.

"Now," the man said pleasantly. He wasn't speaking to *me*, really, just addressing me like one of his props. "How about a free sample?"

It was a valiant attempt, but there is *literally* no menacing way to say *free sample*. I almost might have laughed, if not for the vial that was waved in my face, the heady, eye-watering smell of something sharp enough to make me light-headed.

"No!" I struggled harder as he tried to force the bottle to my lips. All I managed to do was drag him sideways to the oak, away from his wagon, as he fought to keep a hold on me.

"Settle down, now—"

All my fear and anger boiled under my skin, building into a strange, tingling sensation. It pulled me along like a riptide, clearing everything except purpose, leaving my mind totally blank. With one furious burst of strength, I managed to elbow him in the gut and pull free. My burning hands flung out in a wide gesture.

A jet of flame arced in their path.

The heat seared my skin, startling me, but didn't burn. The flames slammed into the oak tree hard enough to shake its roots and splinter the wood. It caught instantly, crackling loud in brilliant gold, angry and hungry.

Someone screamed, but the sharp, cracking sound of splitting wood was even louder.

I pulled my hands tight to my chest, fingers curled. I hadn't meant to do that. I'd never shot fire out of my hands before. I didn't want to hurt anyone. My mouth was dry, and violent trembling started overtaking my brief rush of bravery.

For a second, I was weightless, as Isolde grabbed me and threw me to the ground, shoving me out of the way with her full weight. I landed in the dust *hard*, catching myself on my hands and knees. Something cracked, and I howled with pain. A fair price for the magic.

The tree groaned and snapped, and then a flaming branch bigger around than I was came crashing down, exactly onto the spot where Cassius Redbrook had been standing. I was the only one close enough to hear his short, whimpering sound of pain turn to a guttural moan before he went silent.

Everyone started moving and making noise then, totally ignoring me and Isolde—running for water to put out the fire, trying to clear the area around the tree, trying to free Cassius from the branch.

But it was too late. He was already dead.

I didn't want to get up after that. I wanted to curl up as small as possible and lie on the ground until my bones turned to dust. The one thing that had kept me safe all these years, even after people found out my secret, was the fact that I was relatively harmless.

Now no one would ever look at me, or my family, the same.

But for some reason, Isolde wouldn't let me wither away. She dragged me onto my feet and through the crowd, past the still-blazing tree down the dusty road to our home at the edge of town. Our father's adjoining shop was open but empty as usual.

After that, as my mother splinted my sprained wrist, we had to explain what had happened. I had to watch their expressions tighten with fear. When Isolde and I went to bed that night and pretended to sleep, we had to listen to our parents' hushed voices discussing packing up and leaving the only home we had ever known.

It was all my fault.

That was too much guilt for one fourteen-year-old to bear.

I had never been well-liked, even before everyone found out that I was a changeling. Honestly, I'm surprised it took them ten years to piece it together. My eyes were always too focused, too intense for a baby's. I learned new words frighteningly quickly, outpacing my sister. My hands never stayed still, either fidgeting with my skirt or catching in my sister's hair or windmilling through the air for something to feel. I cried and no one could understand why. I wandered off into fields of wildflowers higher than my toddler head.

But even with all the words I understood, I hadn't been able to talk to anyone outside of my family until I was ten. No matter how hard I tried, the words stuck like someone had poured glue down my throat. It was like there was a code that everyone knew but me, and they all hated me for not being able to puzzle it out.

Or maybe they just hated me because somehow, deep down, they could always sense my faerie nature.

The next morning, a group of people with serious faces rapped on the door while I was still huddled in bed. Their voices were indistinct, but the meaning was clear: *Bring us the changeling. She needs to face consequences.*

I heard both my parents arguing, my father forcing his insubstantial frame in front of the door so they couldn't come in. I was a child. It was an accident. They had no right.

The men left, but we all knew they'd be back.

After several hours of weeping on Isolde's shoulder hidden in the leaves of our favorite climbing tree, she told me to pull myself together.

"How can we fix this?" she whispered, her voice blending with the wind in the leaves.

"We can't," I blubbered. "I ruined everything. That man, I—" I couldn't make myself say it.

I killed him.

"No," she said fiercely, holding my hair back so I was forced to look at her. "It was an accident, like Papa said. You were only defending yourself."

I wiped my nose on the shoulder of my dress. "I should just go away. Everything would be better if I never existed."

Isolde looked wounded. "Seelie, you know that's not true. I'd probably have gotten myself killed doing something stupid long before now if you weren't around."

I managed a sliver of a smile at that.

My sister smiled back, then turned serious. "I need you."

All I could do was shake my head and look away. "It's not fair," I whispered. "It's not fair for me to ruin Mami's and Papa's lives. They deserve to have a home and be safe. I'm the only who should have to run."

A strange sense of calm came over me, and suddenly I knew.

"I'm leaving, Sol. Tonight. I'll run away so no one can find me, and Mami and Papa and you can live your lives without a changeling messing everything up. Don't say anything, because I've already made up my mind."

She was silent for a long time. She must have been able to tell that there was no way to convince me to stay and let our parents destroy their lives around me.

Finally, she said, "Okay. But I'm going with you. You can't get rid of me that easy, Seels."

"Don't call me that."

I stole our parents' memories that night. The connection that bound our family snapped as I bottled them up. Maybe the townsfolk would remember a changeling girl who once lived among them, but not as the midwife's daughter, not as one of them. Eventually they, along with my parents, would probably figure out they were under a spell…but that was a problem for another day. Fighting through my magic-induced haze of pain, we commandeered the Destiny, struggling to use the remaining trickles of magic I had left at my fingertips to hijack the mechanism and storm into the darkness.

The next day, after I came to, we scrubbed off the scorch marks, repainted her green with Isolde's first stolen haul, and dumped all of Cassius Redbrook's belongings into a river. We renamed the wagon, giggling, so that we could say that, wherever we ended up, we'd been carried there by Destiny.

My splinted wrist still hurt, but the bone-deep stabbing was turning into fire tearing up the surface of my skin. Except it wasn't just my wrist.

My palm is now frozen stiff, aching from the skin down to the delicate ice-cold bones.

This doesn't feel right. This isn't how the memory is supposed to go. The cold spreads up and down and burrows in deeper, sinking thousands of tiny teeth into my muscles.

There, now I'm all caught up. Was that so bad?

I think I'm opening my mouth to scream, but then the last bit of my mind is overtaken, and I sink into merciful oblivion.

For real this time.

chapter nine

I wake to a flash of light.

I'm sitting up before I'm even awake, cursing myself for falling asleep, buzzing with energy. I narrowly miss bumping my head on Isolde's bunk.

Then the low roar of thunder rolls across the night sky, and I come to my senses. My left hand curls close to my chest, but the icy tingle of magic is gone. The roar of rain patters on the Destiny's tin roof. The promise of a vicious late-summer storm is finally being fulfilled.

I only slept a couple of hours, but I'm fully awake now. The moments before I passed out are a blurred haze.

The cold.

The voice.

The breathless feeling of something on my chest.

I stretch my neck and shoulders, trying to ease the permanent knots of tension. It's flat black outside the caravan's windows, and inside, at least an hour until dawn. Not that there's much to see. I know every inch by touch.

A scurrying sound flutters from the corner by the stove, like a trapped bird: Birch, suddenly shy, scurrying out of sight.

I lift the lid off our makeshift basin of washing water and splash my face to wake myself up a little. My fingers follow the water droplets down the planes and curves.

Isolde's face. Stolen to fit me.

It's too early to start thinking like that, I scold myself, creeping in bare feet to the front of the wagon. *Or too late. Whatever.*

At least I don't have to worry about waking Isolde when I light the lantern. My sister could sleep through a wildfire.

The glow licks over my still-outstretched hand. It trembles in time with the flickering shadows as I slowly turn it over.

Silvery ink, spinning within my skin. Searching. Wobbling vaguely westward.

I land in the navigator's seat, folding as the chair spins in place. The compass in my palm wavers but returns to the same point.

The Destiny's navigation system looks more like it belongs in a boat than an ordinary wagon: a spinning leather chair bolted to the floor in front of a spoked wheel; several levers and switches along the front panel control speed and direction; and there's a small built-in table to one side of the chair. We haven't figured out what the table is supposed to be used for yet, but we use it for snacks.

The Destiny is, to put it mildly, not easy to drive, and we had what I could generously call a *learning curve* when we first stole it. Luckily, the wagon was built sturdily enough to with-stand ramming into a tree every other day or so.

It's second nature to me now, though. I plant my feet on the floor. The gold velvet curtains covering the front win-dow are one of the few aesthetic choices we never replaced. I like the rich, heavy feel of the fabric when I pull them back almost as much as I resent the man who put them there.

Lightning. Another crack of thunder.

It takes some maneuvering, but I manage to get us out of our riverside spot and on the main road, steering around the ugly stone remnants of the keep that once sat where the bridge is now. Once you've seen one set of ruins, you've kind of seen them all, even though the dozens of simultaneous disasters that tore the world down all those years ago were all slightly different. Here, I think it was flash flooding, water moving so fast it carved through stone and wiped out the city.

Hopefully we're not in for more of that with this torrential autumn rain, which is already churning the road into slick mud. It's still dark, the only spots of light sparkling on rain-drops as they splat loudly on the front window.

We're on our way. There's no going back now.

I remember that ice-cold voice in the back of my mind: *It would need to be a changeling, wouldn't it?*

I've been *needed* before. People say lots of things about changelings—that we're less than human, that we all have magical power beyond measure, that we don't feel joy or sor-row or pain. They try to bend us to the shape of the child they'd wanted or despair completely at our very existence. But they also say that we can grant wishes, or return a changeling baby to the faeries, or solve any alchemical equation, or every other absurd request I've had to turn down over the years.

It's an inconvenience to be unwanted. It's a curse to be needed.

By the time my sister wakes, the sun has been up for hours. The inside of the wagon is lit in pale pink and gray light, and rain still taps gently on the roof. The smell of freshly brewed coffee drifts from the pot still sitting on the stove as I sit cross-legged in the driver's seat, sipping my cup.

Isolde wakes with a jolt and a scream. I glance over my shoulder. She's flailing, almost falling out of bed.

"Good morning!" I say cheerfully.

Her hair sticks up in every direction, a mess as confused as her sleepy face. "Seelie! Wha— Where—?" She looks around, dazed. "We're moving."

"We needed to leave as early as possible." I look down at my palm, which I've been studying over the more boring stretches of road, and I realize I may be coming off as a little frantic.

Isolde blinks at me. "You should have woken me. How long have you been up? Where are we?"

"You need your rest." If people think *I'm* a monster, it's only because they've never seen my sister when she's tired. "We've been on the road since I got up—that puts us right between the edge of nowhere and the middle."

Isolde groans, rubbing her face in her hands. "Do you *ever* sleep?"

I respond with a noncommittal noise.

"You should have woken me up," she repeats and stretches as her toes meet the smooth wood of the floor.

"Everything's gone fine so far." I flick a long strand of hair away from my face. I braided it as the sun came up, and it's already slipping free into my eyes. "Not like it's my first time disappearing into the night. I've had practice."

Isolde snorts half-heartedly, pours coffee into our other chipped enamel mug, and breathes in the sweet-smelling steam. "That's the spirit." She stands beside me, leaning on my seat as she peers out the window.

The road is mostly empty at this hour, in this weather. Perfect. We can go as fast as we want without fear of crashing into some poor farmer's mule-drawn cart and destroying his crop of cabbages.

Not that that has ever happened before.

The road cuts through a patchwork of grassy meadows scattered with trees, which at this point all look exactly the same as they pass in a gray streak. This isn't the Destiny's first time carrying us down this road, but this time, we don't turn at the crossroads that would eventually take us to the unfriendly seaside city of Faeport, or the walled Crowhold. We're banned from both those places anyway, after two separate incidents involving pickpocketing and dozens of socks.

I'm not sure how much time has passed when a sudden chill makes me shudder. I'd managed to let my mind go blank for a while, not thinking about anything except the pattern of raindrops and the feel of the wheel under my hands. The wheel jerks with me, but I recover quickly, swerving back onto the road.

Maybe Isolde didn't notice.

"Are you sure you're okay? Do you want me to drive?"

Of course she noticed.

I flinch, turning to look at her. Isolde sits on her spot on the floor, flicking one of her knives casually in her free hand as she pretends to study a map.

My shoulders hunch defensively. "Would you put that thing

away? We don't have enough space in here for you to start practicing a knife-throwing act."

"That's what you think." She tosses it lightly in the air. The blade turns end-over-end before she snatches it by the hilt, flips it, and slips it back into its sheath.

"Stop showing off!"

"Seelie…" She grabs the driver's seat and twirls it around. I shrink into the leather, looking up at her. "I'm driving!"

"The road is straight for miles. We need to talk."

My stuttered protests die in my throat. "I didn't sleep well." My hands curl into fists, nails pricking me again. "I'm fine now."

Isolde frowns. A little crease forms between her eyebrows. "Is it…you know?"

I hold up my hands helplessly. "I don't know. Ever since I…ever since…ever since I…" I know what I'm trying to say, but I can't get it out. My breath catches in my throat.

"Since you picked up the enchantment?" she asks gently.

I nod. Finally, I find my voice again. "It's like I can *feel* its magic. *And* mine. It's all so…*loud*." Isolde knows how I feel. She knows I'd do anything to be mundane, for things to be simple.

Which is why I'm so shocked when she says, "Maybe that's not a bad thing."

Hurt floods through me. "How can you *say* that?"

Isolde folds her arms across her chest, looking down at me impatiently. "Seelie, I know you don't like it, but…magic is a part of who you are. Maybe this means it's time to stop pretending it isn't."

A strangled noise escapes my lips before I can stop it. "It's not part of who I *am*!" I hear the way my voice is rising in volume and pitch, but I can't stop it.

"You're a changeling, Seelie. All changelings are enchanters." Isolde sounds frustrated, but she follows quickly with, "And there's nothing wrong with that!"

It doesn't make me feel better.

"I don't *want* to be a changeling," I shout. "I just want to be your sister!"

I'm not going to cry. I am *not* going to cry.

"You *are* my sister." Her dark eyes crinkle with concern. "But you're also—"

"No!"

Suddenly, I smell ozone.

A tight, hot ball of anger churns in my chest. I can feel the lightning within me, searching for a release. I press it down. "You don't understand, Sol. You *can't*."

"Please—" Isolde stops short. She's staring over my shoulder. Her jaw drops, and my heart sinks with it.

What now? I turn my chair back around, just in time to see two dark-cloaked figures on horseback, perfectly still in the middle of the road. At this rate, we're going to collide with them head-on and smash us all into kindling. I can already imagine the crunch of my bones breaking.

I'm dimly aware of screaming, but I don't know if it's my voice or Isolde's or both. Birch joins in with a yowl, never one to be left out of chaos. My hand flies to the chain dangling over my head, and I pull the brake down as hard as I can.

Everything in the wagon that isn't bolted down—me, Isolde, and most of our belongings—flies forward.

"Seelie!" Isolde screeches, and Birch follows with an inhuman noise just as unhappy with my driving.

I realize I should have just steered around the riders, but it's too late now. Our wheels flounder in the slippery mud, sending us spinning in circles. Clattering fills the air as everything skitters back and forth over the floor.

In all the sound and movement, my focus sharpens. The world shrinks to the most insignificant details: the rain pattering on our roof, the feeling of the wheel clenched in my white-knuckled hands, the brush of loose hair on my face. The knowledge that there's absolutely nothing I can do now but see what happens.

Luckily, we don't die.

The Destiny slows to an awkward crawl, and when she finally runs out of momentum, she comes to a rough stop just inches away from the motionless riders.

Before I can even process what just happened, Isolde is storming out the door. I follow, poking my head out into the rain self-consciously.

"What is wrong with you?" my sister shouts at them. Something feels very wrong here.

Cautiously, I hop down the stairs. "Isolde…" I warn.

"Hey!" Isolde's boots splash mud as she stomps forward, ignoring me. "I'm talking to you. You could have gotten us all killed!"

The two figures dismount with a long, flat stretch of road still between us, silhouettes stark against the far-off trees and rolling mountains. Their horses immediately trot down the hill and out of sight, but that doesn't seem to bother the riders: they're fully focused on us.

My mind runs through a quick list of all the people we've pissed off in the past twenty-four hours: Wildline Manor's enchanters, the Auremore city guard, Leira Wildfall herself.

But it isn't any of those people.

"Hello there, changeling. Imagine running into you here." I know Raze's voice instantly.

Isolde's back goes stiff. I know she's thinking the same thing I am. *How did they find us? How did they beat us here on horseback?*

"Hand over the compass." The taller figure takes a step forward, towering over Isolde with the easy, muscular grace of a lioness. The outline of a quarterstaff balances perfectly in Olani's hands.

Isolde pauses. I imagine the trace of a cocky smile on her face, even though I can't see it with her back to me.

"What compass?"

Self-consciously, I bury my hand in my skirts, nails digging into my palm.

"We don't have time for this," Olani snaps, talking more to her companion than to us.

He acknowledges her with a slight nod, still studying us from the shadows of his hood. "Whatever you think it's worth, I can pay more. Just give it back."

Isolde looks at me. I shake my head, trying to still my trembling hands with the familiar fabric in my grip. It's a good offer, but it's one we literally can't accept. I can't get rid of this enchantment, no matter how much I want to.

But they don't seem to know that. They must not have seen the metal dissolve into silvery ink, sink into my skin, and shimmer under its surface. They think we still have it in our pouches or the folds of my dress.

I don't know what they'll do when they find out that's not the case.

chapter ten

"I'm afraid that giving up the compass is no longer an option," Isolde says. "Now let us pass."

I try to act like it's already settled, taking half a step back to the wagon. I'd drag her with me if I could, but Isolde is already on high alert, preparing for a fight.

"We can't do that," Raze says, almost apologetically—and I know he means it. They're planted solidly in place, and even if we could get back to the Destiny without being attacked, they would just catch up to us again.

Which makes what comes next inevitable.

There's a pause, a moment when no one breathes and tension pulls tight in the air.

Then, without warning, Isolde bounds forward.

She doesn't get far before the quarterstaff is solidly in her path, swinging to strike. Isolde dodges, but it's a near miss.

How did they find us?

Olani slides easily into another pose, swiping her quarterstaff sideways into Isolde's ribs—

Even if we wanted to, how can I give them something that's embedded in my skin?

—and narrowly missing, as Isolde ducks under the blow and presses closer to her. If she can get in close enough, the staff will be useless.

Olani seems to realize that. She backpedals, feet steady in their stance. Her face scrunches slightly as she and Isolde size each other up.

My sister and I are both the same size, built like dollhouse miniatures, so no one ever expects her to be able to hold her own. She might not have size or strength to her advantage, but she has something better: an uncanny and almost psychic ability to simply *not* be wherever her opponent expects her to be.

At least, usually. The girl she's facing now is clearly a gifted and experienced fighter.

I watch Isolde dodge swings, sending the girl reeling off-balance, and kick with the grace of a dancer. She pounces like a cat, blades flashing. The quarterstaff meets her mid-air with a blow that doesn't manage to hit her square in the chest but does knock her wrist hard enough to make her release one of her knives.

"Ow!" The yelp is bitten off swiftly. Isolde lands crouched, waiting for her next chance to spring.

I want to yell for them to stop, but I can barely breathe, and it's pointless for me to make myself a target without some kind of plan. I need to do *something*, ideally before Raze realizes that *he* should be doing something instead of standing by with his mouth gaping.

At the same moment I think that, I see Raze reaching for a knife at his belt, even though he doesn't seem sure what to do with it. Isolde and Olani are moving too quickly to get between them without endangering both.

I sprint forward, but Raze is already moving, surprisingly swift for someone his size. It happens so suddenly that I don't even see the blade move, and I don't have time to make a new plan before he's bearing down on me with its wicked, silvery point.

"Listen, changeling, I don't want to hurt you!" he says, which seems strange for someone pointing a knife at one of my more vital arteries.

For a moment, though, I almost believe him. There's a flicker in his eyes of something that might be earnestness, and I *want* to believe that he wouldn't hurt me. Hope flutters briefly over his face, like he thinks I'd actually give up without a fight.

Isolde's wide eyes meet mine, and I watch her considering running over to defend me. Behind her, Olani pulls a small dagger from her boot and swings.

"Isolde, look out!"

But one moment of distraction was more than long enough. Isolde just barely manages to twist away so the knife slams into her bicep instead of her chest. She screams, falling back as her hand goes to the injury.

I could have expected the rush of *feelings* at the raw pain in my sister's voice.

What I don't expect is the rush of magic.

Power flows through me, coursing with my anger and fear to the rhythm of my speeding heart. That *pull* under the surface of my mind fills my blood with a bubbling feeling, rolling over me and within me.

And this time, I let it. The rain pours down harder, drenching all four of us down to the skin, and the wind picks up. I bring my hands down in a sharp gesture, tapping into everything I've been too busy to really feel. I haven't used magic in so long that I almost don't know what to do. Panic builds up quickly with all that undirected power.

And then something sparks. I don't have to think about it at all, once I let my instincts take over. I'm a storm cloud, and what I do next is as natural to me as breathing. My hands rise on their own. I don't know what I'm about to do, and I don't care.

With a long exhale, I release a burst of lightning. It tickles my skin as it rolls over me, but there's no pain, no burning, nothing that I should have felt. Olani throws a hand up, but it's too late for whatever she was going to do. She and Raze are both thrown back, landing hard in the mud several yards away.

I don't pause to watch what happens or wait to let the price of the enchantment catch up with me as I sprint to my sister's side.

There's no way to tell how much she's bleeding. Cursed black clothing.

"Are you okay?" Shaking, I reach for her, gripping her back and her uninjured arm.

She groans, pulling the blade out of her own arm. I'm relieved to see it isn't buried deep enough to damage the muscle. Just enough to hurt like hexes.

An ugly hiss escapes her lips. "I've been lightly stabbed," she says through her teeth.

"Lightly," I repeat, brushing wet hair away from her face. But she doesn't seem to be weak or in shock. I'll have to patch her up later. I try to pull her, but she resists. This is still a fight we can run away from. We just need to get to the Destiny before Raze and Olani can form another attack.

A clatter from behind me. The sound of a door slamming.

The Destiny's mechanism roars to life. It picks up speed quickly, splattering mud everywhere as it swerves from where we skidded to a stop and takes off down the road.

Without us.

Isolde and I both cry out together. She breaks into a jagged run, uselessly trailing it until it's so far in the distance she gives up and slows to a stop. I just watch our home disappear into the gray smudge of horizon.

This isn't the first time the Destiny has bolted. It's powered by my magic, which has a mind of its own, and if it feels too endangered or penned-in, it decides to take off. Cue me and my sister, out of breath and sweaty and swearing, spending an entire day chasing our home from the crest of one hill to the next until it finally decides to let us capture it again.

It's never been at quite such an inconvenient time before, though.

That's when I discover that I've made a huge mistake. This lesson takes the form of a strong arm slamming across my shoulder, fingers digging roughly into my arm. The smell of sage and leather and sweat crowds all my senses as Raze squeezes me hard enough to make me wonder if my ribs are going to pop.

I fight with all my strength, pull his cloak and his hair, scratch, lash out. I'd bite him, if I wasn't facing the opposite direction. I reach for my magic, but the second I actually want it, it dips out of my grasp, leaving me leaning unsteadily over a deep chasm.

"That really hurt," Raze growls in my ear. Then he sighs, and his voice takes on a tone that's totally different, but just as grating. "Just listen to what we have to say, and no one has to get hurt. We need—"

I spit, and it mostly misses him, but it's the thought that counts. In the corner of my eye, I can see Isolde limping forward to rescue me, but Olani is faster. She swings for Isolde's neck, and my sister throws herself out of the way. Olani is already attacking again, stabbing forward before Isolde can land back on her feet.

No, no, no—this can't be happening. Isolde actually stumbles, splashing backward into the mud. She groans as her injured arm absorbs her weight, curling in on herself.

Olani looms over her, biceps flexing as she stands perfectly balanced, quarterstaff posed to strike. "Just hear us out," she says, sounding more exasperated than anything in between gasps for breath. "We have…an offer…for the changeling."

Isolde freezes there, catching her breath, eyes locked on the other girl's.

When she moves, it's a flicker, as fast and inevitable as the crashing of a wave, straight up off the ground. I think it takes even her by surprise, but she's back on her feet in less time than it takes to blink, getting a slash to Olani's arm before staggering backward.

Olani swings her staff, a second too late. In the brief opening, Isolde tackles her, gracefully using Olani's momentum to force the girl to her knees and twist her arm behind her back.

Olani is bigger and stronger, but she isn't quick enough to twist away before Isolde's blade meets her throat. She's pinned.

Raze and Isolde face each other, each with a blade to their captive's throat.

From an outside perspective, it might almost be funny.

Raze lets out a deep, dramatic sigh. "Please let her go," he says lightly. Then, for the first time, I feel him waver. The metal burns on my skin, trailing a cold itch behind it. Iron. His voice trembles almost imperceptibly on his next words. "Just calm down. All we want is to make a deal. I don't especially *want* to slit your…sister's throat today, but I will if you don't give me another option." He emphasizes the word *sister*, so it simmers in the air like a question mark.

He wouldn't.

Would he?

My throat is closing, each breath shallower and more useless than the last.

Isolde's face flashes with panic. Most people, looking at her large doe eyes and softly round cheeks, would have said she looked completely calm. I know her better than that, but she doesn't let her voice give anything away, either. "Oh, calm down. I wasn't going to hurt either of you."

She looks down at Olani, who's trying to reach for her staff again, and stomps down hard on her fingers. Olani takes in a sharp gasp of pain and says nothing.

"Not badly, at least," Isolde amends.

"How kind of you," Raze snorts. "But I'd be more inclined to believe you if you put down the knife." His own blade digs harder into the exposed skin of my neck.

Isolde wears a sunny grin. "After you."

I reach again for my magic. I can see that my twin is fading fast, that behind the wet curtain of her hair, her eyes are blurred with pain. She's pretending to be strong, but she can't keep it up much longer. And I can't think straight with iron poking against my skin. The magic that's always lingered just under the surface keeps slipping out of my grasp.

"Now," Isolde continues, "I'll make *you* a deal. You release my sister right now, and I'll let you walk away with all your fingers."

I shiver at the ice in my sister's words. Raze doesn't relax his hold on me for even a second. The cool glass of the vial I wear under my dress digs into my chest under the pressure of his arm. "How about this deal?" His voice lowers, but he never loses that faint note of affability. "You let Olani go, or I take your sister with me, claim whatever's in the Mortal's Keep for myself, and *then* kill her."

Isolde hesitates, dark eyes flicking back and forth between his face and mine. She doesn't know if he's bluffing.

I think I feel resolve in his grip, but I'm not sure, either. Then the sting of cold iron on my sensitive skin reminds me: our brief flirtation at Leira Wildfall's party means nothing to him. My life means nothing. I'm just a *changeling*. He'll kill me, and whether he hesitates to do it or not won't matter when I'm facedown in a pool of my own blood.

Isolde holds my gaze steadily, like she's trying to tell me

to do something. Her words are addressed to Raze, but she doesn't look away for a second. I don't know what she's trying to tell me. My chest tightens. "She's holding back now, but just wait—"

Her words are cut short by a sharp crack and a groan. Her eyes roll back in her head, and she crumples like a poorly pitched tent in a storm, falling hard to the ground.

Olani *knew* which of Isolde's arms was injured and couldn't maintain its grip. She was only waiting for the right moment to strike, and now she's kneeling in the mud with her staff in her hands, looking down at Isolde's unconscious body. I curse myself for not realizing what she was doing sooner. "Isolde!" I lunge against Raze, not caring if he'll do it or not. I need to get away. I need to get to my sister.

Raze struggles to hold me back. "Will you just…calm… down!"

My elbow snaps up between us, catching him hard in the nose, and I manage to pull myself free without getting stabbed. So he *was* bluffing.

"Listen, changeling—"

And with that one word, I know what he thinks of me. He doesn't see me as something with the capacity to actually *care* whether Isolde lives or dies. I'm just a *changeling*, a shell that only looks human—and I have the compass. He keeps talking, but the words might as well be the sound of the wind passing through the rain, because they don't mean a thing to me in the moment. I don't care what he's saying. I don't care how destructive magic is. I don't care that I hate it, that it's just as likely to tear me apart from the inside out as to do what I want. Maybe both.

The feeling is cold and foreign, and it slithers dangerously into the back of my mind.

Destroy him.

I don't just want to protect Isolde, to get away, to survive on the run, I want him to see what I can do. I want to *hurt him*.

I reach for the clouds, embracing the rain that drips down my sleeves and into my open mouth. The lightning is like an excited dog, all too eager to come when I call again. I fling my hands apart, and it answers.

Lightning snaps through the sky, brilliant and white and as refreshing as screaming at the top of your lungs as you run into a cold winter sea.

"Raze!" Olani dives forward, tackling Raze—but the lightning just consumes both of them.

The first strike was a test, weaker than what a real storm would produce. Enough to knock them backward but not to do permanent damage. I was holding back then. This time, what I call down *is* the storm, all of its energy in one concentrated blast.

But when the air clears, they're still planted in the same spot. Olani's hands are up, trembling, as if she's holding an invisible shield, and sparks of lightning linger there long after they should have dispersed.

My breath catches in my chest, and I freeze in place.

She's an enchanter.

Her face is twisted with the effort of deflecting my attack, but we both know it has to go somewhere. Magic always has a price. "Sorry," she mouths, right before everything explodes in brilliant white light.

All of the raw power I'd directed at them rips my world in

half, striking the middle of my chest. It's not how I expected it to happen, but there it is—the price of magic.

My muscles all betray me at once, trembling and stiff. My skin burns. My insides burn. I'm completely lost in time and space, and all I know is the blinding, white-hot pain.

And then it stops.

I've fallen to my knees, but they can't hold me any longer. I drop to the ground beside my sister, a horrible ache radiating out from my chest. I need to get up. I need to fight.

I can't move.

My vision is going blurry, fading out.

I see Isolde and thank Fate that she's still breathing, though a trickle of blood runs from her temple down her cheek. Everything else is fuzzy. The pain is so bad that I'm ready to be swallowed by the blackness in the edges of my vision.

Flashes of gray sky, of rain falling down on me, of the tall grass surrounding my limp body.

A big, blurred shape a little farther off separating into smaller shapes—one dark, one pale.

A smudge of copper red against the clouds, a boot digging into my aching shoulder, a voice pulled taut by anger and exhaustion.

"I believe you have something that belongs to me, changeling."

PART TWO

chapter eleven

There's a long blur in my memory after that. Consciousness slips in and out of my grip, until finally I grit my teeth, seize onto it, and force myself to take in my surroundings.

I'm still alive, which seems like a good sign.

Then the aching kicks in, and I'm not so sure. The lightning strike made every single muscle in my body convulse uncontrollably, and they're all complaining about it now. My head feels light and fuzzy, buzzing like it's full of bees.

"I told you…we're not…any way…" Isolde's voice sounds like it's coming from very far away, her words slipping just out of my understanding. The pain behind my eyes intensifies, and I groan. "Seelie?" The voice sounds a little closer, and suddenly she's right here, shaking my shoulder and repeating my name.

"Ow," I croak, barely moving my lips.

"Seelie!" She crushes me in a hug, which makes everything hurt worse, but I can't really be mad.

It's still pouring rain, and the cool water clears my head a little. I crack one eye open.

I have no idea how much time has passed since I blacked out. Over Isolde's shoulder, two tall, hazy shapes loom over us.

Curses. I'd hoped I had dreamed that part.

"All right, that's enough," Olani says. She kneels, examining my arms with a surprisingly light touch. "The burns aren't too bad. Do you feel dizzy? Nauseous?"

"Get...get...get off me." I manage to prop myself into a sitting position, speaking through a sore, scorched throat. Why is she touching me? Why is Isolde letting her? Why isn't everyone fighting? Even though it doesn't make sense, it's a relief to not be trying to kill each other. I have nothing left to fight with, nothing left in me to fight. "I'm f-fine."

"Of course you are," Raze says sarcastically. Everything is slowly coming into focus. He stands a few feet away, arms crossed and shiny boots splattered with mud. Blinking, I look down at myself.

Oh.

My sleeves and dress are shredded and burned, like they'd been attacked by a beast with fiery claws. I can see glimpses of my undershirt, which is luckily still intact where it really counts but also looks the worse for wear. And then it gets really bad: all down my arms, the skin left exposed by the missing fabric is etched in raised red marks. They almost look like ferns, branched and delicate and extending tentatively over my skin.

Suddenly, I think of something else. My hand flies to the

base of my throat, but the leather cord is still intact, and the glass vial hasn't broken. I exhale deeply, hand pressing around it like it'll make anything better as my eyes go back to my dress.

I'm coated in mud. My favorite (ruined, destroyed) dress will probably never be robin's-egg blue again, but that's the least of my concerns.

"Isolde…" My voice is still a little slurred. "You okay?" The rain has washed most of the blood from her, and someone bandaged her head and arm while I was out. Why would they do that?

"It's just a bump on the head. Are *you* okay?"

I give her a doubtful look but surrender. "I… I've been better."

Olani cuts in, her gaze on me so intense it almost stings. "The burns will heal. You'll dry out eventually. I won't even steal the compass and leave you to the mercy of Leira Wildfall's guards, which is more than you did for us."

"Olani." Raze sounds tired when he says her name, like a little brother asking for a reprieve from teasing. But he isn't looking at her. He's looking at me. His gaze tingles uncomfortably as I realize that Olani pulled my left arm palm-up to check it, and he's openly staring at the enchanted symbol in my skin. His eyes lock on it, rather than me, as he says, "Look, we don't want any trouble."

"Could have…fooled me," I mumble, struggling to stand.

Isolde's wiry arm slips around me, helping prop me up but also holding me solidly to the ground. "You followed us," she accuses the other two. "I don't care what you want. *We* walked away with the compass, fair and square. It's ours."

There's an awkward pause. Raze ruffles his wet hair, and Olani takes a sudden, intense interest in her fingernails. They both look like they're really hoping the other will speak. Finally, Olani says, "It's working now. Whatever she did to it, the needle is pointing to *something*."

Raze interrupts, ignoring the pointed glare she shoots in his direction. "So. How'd you manage *that*, changeling?"

I scowl.

He sighs, and his broad shoulders slump. Rivers of rain run off him, making him look like a dejected umbrella. "Listen, I don't really care how you did it. We just need it back."

I doubt the vague response of *I have no idea what I did to it* will be enough to satisfy them. Besides, working with them is out of the question, and I suddenly remember that I have other problems. We have to get out of here. Every movement hurts, but I'm increasingly frantic as I look around, hoping I'm misremembering things, hoping I'm wrong.

There's nothing in any direction but empty, muddy road, the two horses, and crushed grass.

"Seelie, calm down. Breathe. What's wrong?" Isolde tries to put a hand on my shoulder, but I'm already pushing her away, breathing hard.

The Destiny—*my* wagon, the only home I've had for the past three years—is gone. Birch must be so frightened, lost and alone in the countryside, all because of my unpredictable magic.

"It's…" Words fail me.

I think that's when I start crying. With the rain pouring down my face, it's hard to tell.

Isolde figures out what I mean quickly. "It's gone."

I cover my face with my hands and bite down on one finger, trying not to start wailing, and shake with the effort. Olani and Raze try not to look too stricken.

"What's gone?" Olani says tentatively.

Raze's face is pale, his hair stringy and darkened by the water, falling in front of his eyes every time he tries to brush it away.

"Our wagon. Could be anywhere now."

Olani is stony, unrelenting. "We don't need your wagon." Then she turns to talk straight over our heads, like we aren't even here. "We need that *compass*. You heard what—"

"I can't," I interrupt. Shaking, I hold my hand up palm-out, so they can see the mark more clearly. I know they saw it, but I want them to *see*. To understand. Magic, woven into my skin.

Even if I wanted to, I couldn't give your precious compass back.

"You will," Olani replies. "If it means I have to take your hand and leave the rest of you bleeding out in the mud, you *will* give us that compass."

Isolde draws her blade, but she's still not fully steady. Even so, she says, "I'd like to see you *try*."

And then Raze has a knife out, too, and this is all spiraling out of control again too quickly to follow, but I know that we can't take another fight right now.

Another long silence follows as they all glare down blades at each other and the sound of rain gets louder and louder in my head. The headache that doesn't seem like it's going away anytime soon—holy hexes, lightning *hurts*—pounds behind my eyes, smashing to pieces the thought that's trying to form.

"Listen," I mumble. Everyone looks at me. My voice is weak and shaky, but I try again. "Listen."

Their faces are expectant, but I can't get anything else out.

"Listen," I repeat. I tug on the end of my braid, which has mostly fallen apart at this point. It's soaked with rain, everything's soaked with rain, possibly down to my bones. "I…

I…" The words build up at the back of my throat, choking me. Why can't I speak?

Isolde sheathes her blade again with a sigh and crouches, squeezing my hand in hers and gazing at me steadily. "It's okay," she says soothingly. "Take your time. You can do it."

"I… I can't," I say. Good. That's new words. "Get rid of it. The compass." I squeeze my hand to demonstrate that it's truly trapped in my skin, not sure if I'm making any sense.

Isolde is silent. Raze's lips press together in a tight line. He and Olani exchange a glance, and she nods.

"Listen," he says. "Why don't we make an arrangement? We don't even care about the treasure that much."

"Well—" Olani interrupts, before cutting herself off quickly with a glare in his direction.

"What does that mean?" Isolde asks, voice hard.

Raze takes us both in. "Thirty percent," he says finally. "I'm just looking for whatever he meant by the Wildline legacy. Nothing else matters. Get us there, and you can have thirty percent of the treasure—or whatever it's worth in gold. Whichever you prefer."

I close my eyes for a long time, trying to make the pain recede so I can put my thoughts in order. They need us. We don't need them. But they seem a lot more prepared for this journey and whatever might be at the end of it than we are. And they've already chased us this far, which means that even if we try to run now, they're just going to track us again.

Which means there isn't really another choice.

"Fifty," I say.

Raze responds too quickly. "Done." I should have asked for more.

Isolde's voice lowers, so only I can hear. "Seels, are you sure about this?"

I nod. She's the better strategist, but if there's a way out of this, it's out of both of our reach.

"So you're in?" Olani asks.

She looks to Isolde, who nods. "If she's in, I'm in. We find our wagon. *Then* we'll take you…wherever it is this thing leads." Isolde really doesn't look well, but her voice is as firm as ever.

Raze shakes his head, and my heart sinks so quickly I start to feel sick. "We don't have time to waste on a wild-goose chase," he says, an edge in his voice.

"You don't get to…to decide that!" I complain.

He frowns, crossing sturdy arms over his chest. "Oh? *You're* the one who stole the compass and ruined everything. You have no idea how important this is to me. I don't care that you lost your wagon, I don't care that you're sitting here in the dirt bleeding—" he gestures to Isolde, then to me "—and burned alive. But I'm pretty sure you'll be worse off trying to wander the Western Range without us. *You* should be paying *us*. It's downright generous of us to offer you even a *thought* of payment, instead of—how did Olani put it?—taking your hand and leaving the rest of you here in the mud."

His words sting, and I don't know why. My hands cup my face and rake through the roots of my hair.

"I-I can't do this right now," I say, still stuttering on every couple of words. Once I get going, though, I can't stop. "You want to complain? Okay. You got us caught at the manor, and somehow I ended up with an enchanted tattoo—which, by the way, I didn't even mean to take, and now I can't get rid of it even if I wanted to. We lost our wagon today—our home—

while you two were busy trying to kill us. I got hit by my own bolt of lightning, and my sister got bashed in the head, and I still don't know how serious it is. We were knocked unconscious in the mud at the side of the road, beaten worse than we've ever been, and drenched to the bone with rain, only for you two to start making demands before I was even fully conscious. But no, I feel *so bad* for you."

"You know, *you* two were the ones who attacked us—"

"I wouldn't have had to steal it in the first place if you hadn't been trying to take it from my sister!"

"—was trying to explain before you knocked me out—"

"—actually *held a knife to my throat!*"

Isolde and Olani wear strangely similar stunned expressions, watching us spit back and forth like two alley cats hissing at each other.

Raze also looks stunned, but before he can prepare another retort, Isolde blows a sharp breath out of her nostrils and cuts in. "Listen. The way I see it, we have something you want. You can go after the wagon with us, or my sister and I disappear forever with the compass and no way to get rid of it. You don't scare me, and you're not in a position for negotiation. So, everyone. Do we have a deal or not?"

I close my eyes and wipe mud from my face, defeated. I know what I'm about to say, and I don't like it. Maybe if I say it quickly, I can put all this behind me. "I'm in."

"Us, too," Olani says gruffly.

Raze starts to protest, but then she gives him a look, and he sighs. "Fine."

I take some comfort in the fact that everyone seems equally unhappy with our arrangement.

chapter twelve

"**Y**our name isn't really *Seelie*, is it?" Raze asks, even though no one was talking to him.

I'm stretching my arms and rolling my shoulders, but that doesn't do much to relieve the stiff aching. It's hard to stomach the thought of walking several hours in the chilly rain when my body already feels like it's been trampled by a vengeful herd of unicorns.

Seeing the look on my face, Isolde reaches down to help me up.

"It's short for *Iselia*," I snap, trying not to groan in pain as I ease to my feet.

Isolde frowns as her hand slips from mine, looking at me funny. "No one calls you that."

I grit my teeth. The nickname has always been a problem,

but I still like it. I just don't want to hear the scorn in the way Raze says it. "Well, maybe I'm trying to rebrand."

"You'd bother going through all that trouble just for me? I'm flattered, Iselia."

He says it with a smirk and a tone that makes me immediately regret switching to my full name. Either his good spirits bounce back remarkably fast, or he's provoking me on purpose.

Before I can snap something back, Olani steps between us. "Raze, behave. We can all fit on the horses, but we'll have to share. It's a few hours' ride to the nearest town. We'll stop for the night, get some supplies…" She looks Isolde and me over. Isolde's all-black wardrobe won't stain, but my clothes are ripped and muddied and burned beyond the point of no return. "And maybe some new clothes for the changeling."

We have to double up on the horses, and of course Raze and Olani are both too large to share one, so—

Well.

Isolde jumps on Olani's horse faster than I can think to claim it. That leaves me wedged uncomfortably between Raze and his roan horse, squished back against his broad chest with his arms squeezing me from either side.

Raze and the horse don't seem too excited about it, either.

"I usually like to get to know a girl a little better before getting this cozy with her," Raze says as we start down the road. I can't see him, but I picture the anger in his glare as he reluctantly struck our deal with Isolde. This new tone of voice is such a quick turnaround that it must be an act. But why would he pretend to stop being angry? How can he *joke* at a time like this?

"We don't have to talk," I snap, because if he thinks he

can trick me into sparing him the acidity I feel with smooth words, he needs to think again.

"We don't *have* to," he agrees. "But it would help pass the time."

I say nothing.

Before long, the pressure of being squeezed in Raze's arms makes me feel like I'm going to scream. I don't like being touched in the best of circumstances, and with the burning marks down my arms stinging more and more with every one of the horse's steps, it's unbearable.

Besides the physical discomfort, the all-consuming, skin-crawling nearness of a boy whose relationship to me is best described as *not killing each other—for now!* is excruciating. I need to think about something else. Anything else.

"Why *were* you there last night, anyway?" I blurt. He didn't seem to know what he was after any more than we did, but what are the odds that in a manor with hundreds of rooms, we'd end up behind the same locked door, vying for the same treasure? Maybe he knows more about it than he's telling.

There's no reply, and for a moment I think that Raze didn't hear me. Or maybe he's decided to ignore me now. Then he says, "To talk to pretty girls, mostly."

Glaring at him isn't worth the effort of twisting my aching neck around, so I settle for staring intensely at the space between the horse's ears. "I was being serious."

"So was I."

Fate, he's irritating. If he's trying to prove that he can shut down any question or attempt at conversation, or to make some kind of point about the irony of me trying to talk after cutting his efforts off so coldly just moments ago, it's working.

"Never mind," I mutter.

For some reason, that seems to offend him. "Well, what were *you* doing there, changeling?"

"Don't call me that," I say, ignoring the question.

After a lingering pause, he lets out a little snort. "Well, if I can't call you that, and I can't call you Seelie, then what *am* I allowed to call you?"

"How about you just don't talk to me at all?" I suggest.

"Ah, but you're the one who started this conversation, Iselia."

Isolde was right. I've only ever been called by my full name by our mother, and only when I was in trouble. Even though it doesn't hold the danger on Raze's lips that it might on a faerie's, I've still made a huge mistake in handing it over. "That's worse," I inform him.

We both give up after that. We're headed up a gradual incline, and the horse's stride gets more and more uneven as the road gets rockier. I'm not an experienced rider, and I know I'm doing this wrong, but I don't know what to do differently. I'm tense all over, trying to keep as much space between Raze and me as possible, and it's using muscles I didn't even know I had.

I wobble in the saddle and try to counterbalance it by throwing my weight the other way. All that does is make me wobble *more*, and then I'm so off-balance that I have to throw my hands to the sides to try to recover, and then my stomach flips because I'm *falling*—

I hear myself scream.

Instead of landing under the horse's hooves, I'm stuck, tilted at an awkward angle until my wrung-out muscles inevitably give up. The horse flicks its ears in irritation at my incompetence as I reach desperately, trying to cling onto its neck for dear life, but every time I move I just make everything worse.

Just when I think I'm about to splash down into the mud, Raze is lifting me back into place, squeezing his arms tighter around me. Pain flares in every burn etched over my skin, but mostly I'm relieved. I let myself lean in to him, too tired and scared of falling again to resist.

"Please try a little harder not to die." Raze's mouth is way too close to my ear now, and I can't tell if that's softness in his tone or restrained irritation.

I'm tired, I can't think clearly, and words are becoming more of a burden alongside the pain I can't be distracted from any longer. "Just leave me alone, Raze."

"I never told you my name." Ugh, he's close enough that I can feel his breath when he speaks. I can't tell if it's a realization or an accusation.

"I'm tricky like that," I mutter.

"It's Raze." Yes, *obviously*. "Raze Wildborn."

For a moment, I'm almost thankful for the crushing force of him holding me on the horse, because if he wasn't, I'd probably fall off from surprise. He's related to the Wild line, on his mother's side. He's connected to Leira Wildfall, to the same enormous mansion he was breaking into, to generations of untold political and magical power—probably as a distant cousin who's spent about as much time with her as I have, but still.

For every question Raze's family name answers, it raises ten more. Like, what was he doing pretending to be a servant in Gilt Row, wearing those ragged clothes? It's no wonder he's so desperate to get this treasure, but if it's really his family legacy, why did he have to break into Leira's house to take the compass? With a lineage like that he must be an enchanter, if not a shapeshifter himself…so why hadn't he used magic when we fought earlier? Why is he *here*, with me, on a horse, in the middle of a rainstorm?

"That's personal," Raze says tightly, a little bit of the teasing tone drained from his voice.

"What?" I jump, suddenly afraid that he's a mind reader, too.

Behind me, he tenses. "I mean…all of it. How would you feel if *I* asked you what a changeling's doing out on the road with her human counterpart?"

Defensiveness washes over me before understanding, and then I'm relieved and embarrassed all at once. "Oh, Fate," I mumble. "How much of that did I say out loud?"

Raze snorts. "Sorry, did I interrupt your conversation with yourself? I was waiting to see how long you'd go. It's like I wasn't even here."

I *wish* he wasn't even here, but I shut up after that, concentrating on keeping my thoughts from bubbling up into a mindless monologue. It's hard to focus on any of my questions about him, given that my mind feels like a half-frozen river, numb and sluggish and pierced with ice. Drawn out by my racing heartbeat, magic prickles at my fingertips.

Even though Raze is too close to me for comfort, and Isolde is practically within arm's reach, I feel like my only real company is the pain in my head and my muscles and my skin.

And, of course, the rain.

Tears build pressure in my throat. None of this is how today was supposed to go. I'm hurt and *so* overwhelmed and lost and confused and maybe a little bit broken.

Not now. Not yet.

It'll all have to come out eventually. I can't shove it down forever—but I can for right now, and I am *not* about to let this cursed boy see me cry.

I've never ridden a horse for longer than half an hour before, and let me tell you, moments after being struck by lightning is *not* an ideal time to start learning horsemanship. It's hours of trial, precarious balance, and awkward squeezing as Raze struggles to keep both of us on the horse. He tries to rekindle conversation a few times, but I pretend I don't hear. Even if I *wanted* to talk to him, my mind isn't putting thoughts together into words anymore.

By the time we reach the outskirts of the nearest town, sore, tired, soaked through, burned, and bloodied, I'm starting to rethink my stance on not crying.

The town—Farpoint, a chipped sign proudly proclaims—isn't one we've visited before. It's larger than the village where Isolde and I grew up but much smaller than the cities I've gotten used to, clinging dangerously close to the edge of a cliff to peer curiously down at the sea. It feels new, without any centuries-old shadows clinging to its heels. Goats and chickens wander freely among a respectable collection of shops and tidy homes, a few open-air market stalls, and far more people looking at me than I'm comfortable with.

Not that any part of me is *comfortable* by now.

Besides, I can't really blame them. We must be quite a sight.

I'm pretty sure I only imagine the horse breathing a sigh of relief when we finally dismount at the only stable in town, next door to the only inn. The rain has finally let up, and the clouds part tentatively to reveal a faint orange smudge of sunset. The air is rinsed sharp and clean, tinged with a hint of salt. I can hear the distant crashing of waves as the strong sea breeze cuts through me.

"We can't stop so soon," Isolde says, dismounting with unfair ease. When she meets my eyes, I can tell what she's thinking: *the Destiny.* It could still be going full speed right now, farther from our reach every wasted hour.

I want to keep going, but I'm completely drained. I'm going to stop soon either way, whether it's taking a break or passing out and falling facedown into a ditch on the side of the road. Isolde seems to soften as soon as she takes in my appearance. I'm so stiff that Raze has to help me off, awkwardly working one arm around my waist and lifting me off the horse as if I weigh nothing. My boots splash into the mud that I assume must have once been the street, before the rain.

Isolde props me up with her shoulder. "You don't look so good."

I thought I'd been doing an okay job hiding how much I feel like crawling out of my skin and leaving it behind as I sprint away at top speed, but apparently not.

Olani, who's quickly shaping up to be the most functional of the four of us, delegates before we can start bickering again. Raze is sent (whining) to find me some new clothes, and she accompanies Isolde and me to arrange accommodations for the horses and ourselves.

I hesitate when I see the iron horseshoe nailed above the inn's door—a ward against faeries. It won't keep everything out, but it's effective as a warning to banshees and wandering faeries: *Stay away. Harassing the mortals here is not worth your trouble.* I have no intention of harassing anyone, and I still shiver as I pass beneath it.

Isolde and I are silent as Olani makes the transaction with

an economy of words that is impressive even to me. We have so much to talk about, but I don't know what's safe to say in front of strangers.

Isolde, however, can only hold her tongue for so long. "Just one room?" she asks sharply, as we climb the stairs to the third floor. Every step sets my muscles on fire.

"Unless you can pay for another," Olani replies bluntly.

That shuts her right up, but she slumps. We don't have a coin to our names. Everything we had—*everything*—had been in that wagon.

But I can't start thinking about that again.

Our room is a tight little space with two narrow beds, which is another problem I can worry about later. It's relatively clean, as far as these places go, with a thick, bubbled pane of glass that looks down at least a hundred feet of rocky cliff face to the churning ocean, a lantern that barely lights the corners of the room, and—thank Fate—a basin of water.

"Okay," Olani says, as soon as the heavy door clicks shut. "Let me see that head wound."

Isolde's hands go to her hair. "It's nothing. Really. You already bandaged it."

Olani rolls her eyes. "I grew up in an apothecary. Let me see it." Ignoring the moment of silence under our matching confused stares, she adds, "You're no use to us so concussed that you can't think straight. Or dead."

My sister blinks, but she doesn't have a sharp comeback to that. Maybe that head wound is worse than I thought. "Fine," she sighs. "Just let me wash up."

Without warning, I realize I'm so devastatingly exhausted that I can hardly stand, but I don't want to draw attention to myself by crossing to the beds at the center of the room. Instead, I press my back against the wall and slide to the floor. My knees fold to my chest, and I start unlacing my boots.

Isolde looks strangely vulnerable without her black clothes, discarded like an old shell in a pile on the floor. Her soft sand-colored undershirt and leggings are exactly the same as mine, a mirror image I'm not used to.

After unwinding the bandage that wraps around Isolde's head, Olani prods my sister's thick skull. Her movements are surprisingly gentle. She tilts Isolde's face to examine her eyes. "What did you say your name was?"

"Isolde Graygrove," she says. It's been so long since I heard my real surname that the sound of it rings in my ears. For a second, I wonder if we should have given false names, but then I realize we couldn't keep that up for the unknown days (or weeks) ahead. Besides, our family name isn't instantly recognizable, unlike *some people*, so it doesn't really matter. "And my sister, Seelie."

Olani nods. "Olani Fullbrace."

I don't bother mentioning that we already knew her first name. I don't say anything at all. I just stare at the flat plane of my open palm, decorated by enchantment. I roll my hand back and forth and watch the arrow adjust itself to point one constant direction—*to what?*

Olani digs through a small bag previously hidden by her cloak. She pulls out a jar and dabs an oily substance on the gleaming wound at Isolde's temple before winding it with a fresh, white bandage. "Now your arm."

Isolde obeys, holding out her bare arm. "Ow! Careful."

Olani applies more of the stuff from the jar to her arm. "Don't be a baby. No one learns how to fight like you can without their share of pain. This is nothing."

Isolde offers a crooked smile. "Yeah, well. I've never been stabbed before." The smile slips briefly before hoisting itself back up.

"Sorry about that." Olani doesn't meet her eyes, focused instead on her fingers as she nimbly ties off the bandage.

Isolde shrugs with her uninjured shoulder. "Don't be. No one's gotten the better of me like that in a long time."

"Guess you'll have to practice more for next time," Olani says lightly. They exchange a wavering look of amusement.

Fantastic, I think. *At least* they're *getting along*.

"Okay, ch— Uh, Seelie. Your turn." Her attention on me is clinical, but it still makes my skin crawl.

"But there's nothing wrong with me!" I protest.

Isolde gives me the look she gives when I'm being especially difficult and childish. "Seelie, don't make a scene. Look at yourself."

She has a point.

When I give in noncommittally, she and Olani face away to give me a moment of privacy as I retreat to the corner.

I peel off my damp, stained dress with a sigh. My skin itches from being trapped in the wet fabric for so long, and it's like taking a breath of fresh air. Scrubbing away the mud the rain didn't get out of my scalp and off my face and legs is another relief. I check that my necklace is still intact and that the knot in the leather cord hasn't loosened, pull the few strands of hair still clinging to some appearance of a braid loose, and tie it back at the nape of my neck.

Then there's no more delaying it. I examine my arms.

It's worse than I thought.

The skeletal flowers etched in my skin are raised and pink and tender, edged with angry red. They reach all the way up from the backs of my hands and wrap around my shoulders, and I don't know how much of my back they might cover. Brushing a finger lightly over the fronds along my collarbones, I trace the burns back to their origin point: right over my heart.

It could have killed me.

Maybe the lightning should have killed me, but it didn't. Whether I'm glad for that or not is still being decided.

Once I've taken a second to compose myself, I cross the room and perch on the corner of the bed with so little of my weight that I feel like a bird, ready to take flight at any moment. Olani crouches in front of me, studying me with warm brown eyes the color of sunlit afternoon tea. Slowly, like I really am some wild creature that might vanish if startled, she places one graceful hand on my shoulder.

I stiffen, fighting the urge to scramble back as my eyes quickly flicker away from hers. No one but my parents and my sister has ever looked at me like that before—trying to understand what's wrong and piece together how to fix it.

"You're in pain," she says gruffly, surprising me.

My muscles have nearly locked in place, and they still ache with tension. "Yes."

Her hand doesn't move from my shoulder. A weird feeling flows through me, like drinking something warm and sweet on a cold morning. Then hotter, brighter pain sparks when her other hand brushes over the lacy burn marks. "That's strong magic. I can still feel it."

I hesitate, not ready to take ownership of it. My own magic, turned on me.

By her, something spiteful in the back of my mind reminds me. *She should pay.* I shove the thought down.

Olani frowns a little in concentration, shifting so her long fingers stretch over my shoulder blade. I don't know what she's doing, but I don't move.

That soothing sensation intensifies until I'm sure I'm not imagining it: she's doing *something* to me. There's tingling just under the skin, the feeling of a foreign magic butting up against mine, and that soft, warm feeling, and then— unexpectedly—relief from the bone-deep pain.

I gasp. "You... You're—"

"A healer," Isolde finishes, just as surprised.

Olani leans back, studying both of us again. Her sleeveless shirt looks bleached at the hem, little tendrils of white streaking up her torso against the previously ocher-colored fabric. She looks at the spreading stains—the price of a magic that cleanses and purifies—and lets out a little sigh of annoyance. "Something wrong with that?"

I shake my head, still stunned, stretching my arms and rolling my shoulders. The ache still lingers just below the surface, but it's quieted for now.

Isolde leans forward with her elbows resting on her sprawled knees, eyes bright. "Why didn't you say something?"

A brief trace of a smile crosses Olani's face. "Enchantment...not really my strongest suit. This, and one shielding spell every month or so. That's about all I can do with it."

"Thank you," I say quietly. "I'm sorry for, you know—"

Olani waves me off with one hand. "I don't care what you did. I don't care if you like me or not. I'm not Raze." Our eyes meet again. "You shouldn't let him get to you," she adds. "He's a spoiled brat, but he's trying his best." I turn my gaze to the floor, refusing to even consider discussing this. "I think," she adds.

"Does he pay you to say that?"

Olani surprises me again by actually chuckling at that. "You're funny, changeling. Sorry—*Seelie*. I'll work on it."

I feel a different warmth that has nothing to do with healing magic. It fades quickly, drained away by the question that bubbles up inside me, refusing to be ignored.

"Do…do you think it'll scar?"

My voice is barely audible. Olani is packing her bag, hanging it up on one of the hooks on the wall beside her drying cloak. She pauses, staring at me strangely. "You've…never done that before, have you?"

I don't answer, but I think the stiffness of my posture as I stare down at the floor tells her everything she needs to know.

"I don't know," she replies honestly. "If it was just lightning…well, the burns themselves don't look too serious. It'd probably fade. But magic is…less predictable."

You're telling me, I think, balling my fingers into a fist, pushing my nails into the tender center of the compass in my palm.

"It's greedy," she continues. "Magic always takes, from someone or something. Even if you don't see how at the time. It won't…it won't want you to forget the price." Olani must see the looks on our faces then, because she quickly adds, "But I can make you a salve for it. No promises one way or the other."

At least my head isn't splitting open like last time. At least I'm still conscious. I look down at my arms, streaked with the echo of lightning that still stings and blisters with its own malevolence.

I hate myself, and the magic simmering within me, more than ever.

chapter thirteen

Unsurprisingly, the clothes that Raze brings back for me are too big. The neck of the rust-orange gown scoops a little lower than I'd prefer, sliding crooked over my collarbones every time I move. But the sleeves are wide and mercifully loose on my tender skin, abruptly narrowing a few inches above the wrist into a tighter swatch of embroidered material that almost covers my hands, so I can't complain too much.

I still feel self-conscious as we descend the stairs again, tugging at the fabric and trying to get it to sit right, tucking my necklace under the collar. A few inches of blistered pink skin peek out from the edges of the sleeves and the neckline. My singed apron has been replaced with a hemp belt, wrapped twice around my waist to make it fit, and I feel the absence of my familiar scraps of ribbon and leather like I'd miss one of my own fingers. I pluck at the embroidery on one of my sleeves instead.

"I think I did well," Raze says, valiantly attempting to stab a pick in the frozen surface of discomfort between the four of us. No one responds.

The ground floor of the inn is a swarm of people, lit in buttery pools of flickering light by lanterns scattered throughout. And they're *all* talking over each other, the overlapping sounds of speech and laughter crescendoing by the second.

"I want to go back upstairs," I murmur, low enough that only Isolde can hear me. Waves of damp hair tumble, still loose, down my back. I twist one strand nervously between my fingers as I resist the urge to hide behind it.

"Too bad," she whispers back. "The least we can do is eat dinner together. We're a team."

"For now."

My sister gives me her classic, top-shelf Warning Look, but it doesn't work on me this time. Looking at her face, her brow wrapped up in that bandage, all I feel is sorry. I've only been thinking about myself this whole time. I can't *stop* thinking about myself, and what a nightmare this whole thing has become, and how my head won't stop buzzing and I feel like a tracked rabbit, predators closing in, and my magic is still simmering—put away for now but near enough that I have an unfamiliar awareness of it.

But this day has been hard on her, too. All she's doing is her best, holding herself together by clinging to the hope that we can make this arrangement with Raze and Olani work out.

The nice thing about being saddled with the two of them is that, unlike Isolde and me who disappear in a crowd, they force their way through easily. People clear out of their paths, and in a room that had seemed overrun down to the last inch, we find a table in a corner that's almost quiet. It's right under one of the lanterns, next to a couple playing cards and flirting drunkenly. I try not to stare at the blue-gray, hound-sized dragon curled sleepily around their feet. Even though they're extinct in the wild, I'm used to seeing dragons of every size and color as pets, but still—surely that isn't allowed in here?

The table is slightly, unnervingly sticky. No one else seems to care.

"I feel like we may have gotten off on the wrong foot," Raze says, once we're all settled.

I frown. "Do you mean the time you tried to slit my throat, or the time you cornered us while we were passed out and forced us to work with you?"

Olani takes offense at that one first. "We weren't trying to kill you," she protests. Everything she says is so low, so mild, that it's hard to tell if she's upset or just insistent. I'm pretty sure I don't ever want to see her truly angry. "We were just trying to talk."

"Sure," Isolde says. She leans back in her seat, but I can tell she's still far from relaxed. "Why do you need the compass so badly, anyway?"

They both grimace, exchanging an uncomfortable look.

"We didn't know what we'd find in that room," Raze says eventually, as if that explains everything. I realize that what I thought was mindless fidgeting is actually him rubbing the spot where his ring must have fit onto his finger, before Isolde knocked it off and it got forgotten in our escape from the manor. Since Isolde is still glaring at him, he adds, "We just knew it was important. The Wildline legacy, that's... It's more than I ever dreamed of. Plus, Leira spent years trying to figure out how to activate it, and the changeling here did it in less than a minute. Any chance to make Leira look bad is worth whatever it takes."

I stare down at the design rippling over my palm. I never meant to *activate* it, but it's alive with magic now. Just my luck.

"Hmm. Okay." Isolde frowns, like she's filing that information away. "You two don't exactly strike me as each other's type. How the hexes did you end up working together?"

"None of your business," Olani says, at the same time Raze says,

"It was kind of an accident."

Isolde presses her lips together, dark eyes flicking back and forth between them. "Mmm-hmm."

Tension crackles in the air. No one wants to be the first to speak, to give up any more information.

Raze's fingers drum dully on the sticky table, his eyes focused on a point somewhere over my shoulder. Slowly, a smile flickers at the corners of his mouth. He stands. "How about I go grab us some food?"

Olani crosses her arms. "Grab us some food, or flirt with that lovely girl at the counter?" Her eyes move pointedly towards the spot he'd been staring at, and mine follow, my whole body twisting to see behind me.

Across the crowded room, I easily pick out the girl in question, standing by the bar and trying diligently to pretend she's hard at work. She's pretty in a way, with long dark hair framing her bright blue eyes and rosy cheeks carved out by a warm smile. She doesn't look down at what she's doing as the rag in her hand scrubs repeating circles, over and over, on what has to be by now the cleanest spot in the entire inn.

"Don't stare at her!" Raze hisses, his already-pink face growing a little pinker. At Olani's raised eyebrows, he composes himself again, slipping back into easy charm as effortlessly as a swan into water. "And who says I can't do both?" With an even brighter flash of a grin, he wades into the crowd.

After leaning over the counter to put in an order for our dinner, he strikes up conversation with the girl easily, casually. As naturally as breathing.

Isolde mercifully breaks the awkward silence at the table. "What's in that stuff you put on my head?" she asks Olani, touching a hand to the bandage. "I think it's really helping."

Olani shrugs. "You know, stuff. Apothecary stuff. It's boring." She studies her fingernails.

There's another pause. I look down at the compass. The road here took us north, so now it's pointing slightly more southwest. It's strange how not-strange it feels.

Isolde tries again. "You said your parents were apothecaries. Where'd a healer like you learn to fight like that?"

Bright, high-pitched laughter rings out behind me. With a twinge of irritation, I glance back to see the dark-haired girl pressing a hand to her mouth to stifle the outburst, while Raze watches on, pleased with himself.

Olani doesn't pay him any attention. Her mouth quirks up slightly in the shadow of a smile. "I have three older brothers. And one younger."

"They taught you?" Isolde leans in, interested.

Olani scoffs. "No. They're all gentle healers. Easy targets. I got sick of watching them get teased and beat up by the other kids. And…well, things kind of got out of hand from there." Her free hand brushes the smooth wood of her quarterstaff propped against the wall behind her, almost subconsciously.

I glance at Isolde, begging her silently not to say, *Yeah, I also started fighting to defend my useless sibling!* She meets my eyes, and I think she understands. Maybe she's just surprised she and Olani have something like that in common.

I need to turn this conversation, fast. "Is Raze's family *really*… Wild line?" I blurt, before embarrassing secrets about our past can come tumbling out.

Olani gives me a funny look. "Yes."

I guess some part of me had still thought—or hoped?—he was lying. "So he's an enchanter, right? Why didn't he… Why hasn't he… Does he, you know—?"

"Is he a shapeshifter?" Isolde says, cutting to the heart of the question with the cold efficiency of an iron blade.

Olani doesn't look at us. "Yes."

Okay, then.

I look over my shoulder again, and I'm struck again by how much he doesn't look like a shapeshifter—like anyone special, really. Currently, he's standing by the blue-eyed girl, who giggles as she leans over the counter to ruffle her fingers through his messy red hair. It gleams gold as it catches the light. A tray loaded with what I can only assume is our dinner rests dangerously close to his elbow.

"Raze!" Olani calls harshly, just loud enough to snap him out of it without everyone else in the room turning to stare at us.

I watch Raze smoothly excuse himself, apologizing through

soft laughter, and pick up the tray. Despite holding enough to feed four people, it looks so small and light in his hands. The girl stands on her toes, says something almost earnest with a teasing laugh quivering at the corner of her mouth, and turns back to the counter.

I want to scream. How dare he pretend to be *charming* and *friendly* now, after I had to deal with *difficult* and *antagonistic* the entire ride here?

It's been too long since I last ate.

"What took you so long?" Olani complains, before he's even set the tray down. "We have *things to do*, Raze. We can't all come to a grinding halt for every pretty face that turns your head."

"That doesn't seem fair," he replies lightly, snagging a cup from the tray. I take one, too, and sniff. Apple cider, slightly warm and spiced. I sip tentatively and am relieved to find that it doesn't have the bitter sting of something harder.

All the food is served in large bowls and vessels to be shared between all of us—fragrant, buttery flatbread, fried sausage, apples from the outskirts of town, and some kind of vegetable medley that's been mashed beyond recognition.

Obviously, I start on the bread first.

We eat in silence. It feels like I've been to the edge of the world and back since the bite of lunch I had at midday, so I could probably eat sand and be satisfied.

At least, that's what I think until I put a spoonful of the vegetable mash in my mouth.

My entire body revolts. It's like cold glue sticking to my throat. I panic. It takes all my willpower, and a huge gulp of cider, to keep from spitting it out. Even as I manage to swallow, a shudder crawls over my skin.

The dragon at the next table is the only one who seems to notice, looking up at me with curious, liquid-mercury eyes. It lifts its head and sniffs.

"So," Raze says eventually, glaring down into his cup like he's trying to gather the courage to drink it. "We know the wagon went this way...but it could have turned or changed directions. Do you have any way of tracking it?"

I take my time, chewing and swallowing very intentionally. "No." Tracking spells are a precise, formulated magic, not something you can just do off the cuff. I've never seen the need to study them, a fact that I'm only now starting to regret.

"Oh."

I reach for one of the apples. "If *you* know any tracking spells..."

"I trust you." He says it loftily, then attempts a smile at me like we're just enjoying a bit of friendly banter. What is he *doing*, trying to get along now? I look away.

"Hey!" Raze's sudden protest makes me jump. "That's mine!"

Isolde pauses, flask halfway to her lips. It's the one from last night, the one I thought nothing of at the time but which she must have snatched from Raze while they were wrestling for the compass, for no reason other than she's absolutely incorrigible. She makes a big show of examining it. "Oh, is it? I don't see your name..."

He scowls, and I wonder if *this* is what it'll take to make him finally show off his magic. "You *stole* it from me!"

She stares him down, not even breaking eye contact as she

raises the flask to her mouth and drinks deeply. "You held my sister hostage. Let's call it even."

He sighs, his hands flying up defensively. "I wasn't actually going to *do* anything to her. Besides, she tried to fry me alive with *lightning*." His attention turns to me. "Where did you even learn how to do that?"

I remember the sting of iron on my skin. I bite the corner of my mouth, pinching it between my teeth until it hurts. "None of your business."

"Look at yourself. You clearly don't know how to control it. How do I know you won't do it again?"

Isolde's eyes narrow, and she breaks in angrily before I can respond. "You don't know us. You don't know anything about Seelie or her magic, and you don't *need* to know anything."

"Believe me," I snap, "it won't happen again." He has no right to complain when it's *my* skin emblazoned with the memory of lightning, not his.

Raze snorts. "Oh, sure," he says sarcastically. "Why *wouldn't* I believe you? I trust you both implicitly with my life!"

"Everybody stop!" Olani growls, slamming down her cup. Sweet apple cider sloshes over the rim and puddles on the table.

Well, that would explain the stickiness.

"Raze," she says calmly, "would you like to find the Mortal's Keep?"

He turns his glare to her. When it becomes clear she isn't going to let him off the hook until he responds, he says, "Yes," in the quiet, sullen mumble of a scolded child.

"And you two," she says, alternating her hard stare between Isolde and me, "would you like to get paid to guide us there?"

Isolde's fingers twitch, clutching the flask harder. "Don't—"

"Would you?"

She sighs. "Yes."

Olani lets the pause drag out just long enough to become an uncomfortable weight on our shoulders. "Then, we're all going to have to put up with each other. So can we try and cut down on the squabbling so I don't have to play at being anyone's mother?"

Isolde rolls her eyes. "I'd be willing to share," she mutters, holding the flask out to Raze.

His eyes flick to her for a short moment, and some kind of stiffness leaves his shoulders. He accepts. "Okay. Let's just get down to business. We need to be on the road by dawn."

I'm about done speaking for the night, but I bark a sharp, humorless laugh at that. I'm too exhausted after everything to even think about waking before the sun. "Absolutely not."

Raze lowers the flask from his lips, swallowing hard. He lets out a long-suffering breath. "And why not?"

"Do you want to hear again about the day we've had?"

He shakes his head in disbelief. "Every minute we're asleep is a minute we're falling behind. Do you want your wagon back or not?"

He's right, but I'm too tired to deal with this.

"Seelie, maybe we should—" Isolde starts, but this time, I'm the one who interrupts.

"What are you so scared of, Raze?"

He turns away, biting his tongue.

"That's what I thought. I think I can safely argue that if whatever's rushing you isn't a big-enough threat for you to tell us about it, then we don't need to worry about it. And

I *will* argue." I'm looking beyond him at the stone wall, my eyes blurring out of focus.

"I heard that changelings don't need sleep."

My glare shifts to him, skimming his blue eyes and landing at the tip of his nose. "You heard wrong." I stand abruptly, not sure what I'm going to do.

Every lantern in the room flickers, flames responding to a command I didn't mean to give.

I can't lose control of my magic now, not with all these people here. I stuff it down, panicked, already backing away. I need to get out of here, *now*, before I catch the whole building on fire. I stand, ready to bolt for the stairs.

Before I turn, I let out one last attempt at intimidation, despite the fact that I'm tiny and trembling like an lapdog and probably the least imposing creature in the world. "And if you wake me before sunup, you can forget all about your precious treasure, your compass, your *legacy*."

It's an empty threat, and he knows it.

"Then, you can forget about the treasure, too!" he snaps. "And good luck getting rid of that tattoo!"

"That's fine!" I lie.

"Fine!"

My chair slams into the table loudly enough to pause the chatter in the room and make the dragon lift its head again. I turn on my heel and stomp up the stairs.

chapter fourteen

Somewhere between the second flight of stairs and the door to our room, the bubble of anger beneath the surface bursts, leaving behind a storm of *feeling* I can't define. Everything I endured today, everything I pushed through, everything I shoved down and ignored, all slams into me as hard as the bolt of lightning. I feel it overtake me.

The door slams behind me, my back pressed against it like I'm bracing against attack. Something heavy and invisible pushes down on me. My limbs tremble. I can't breathe.

This isn't how today was supposed to go. This isn't how any of this was supposed to go. And now I'm streaked with burns, the Destiny is lost, and I'm facing an unknown journey with unknown people who might betray us at the first chance. It all crowds in around me. It's too much. It's all too much.

Sobs seep out from between my lips, shaking my chest. Hot tears streak down my face, and I hear myself wailing like a child.

There's a draft in the room, wind whipping at my loose hair and drying the tears as they fall. I stumble to the little window looking over the inky darkness of the sea, but it's already closed.

The wind is coming from *me*. A cyclone, building around me, twisting circles around the room, lifting and whirling around everything it can: the blankets on the beds, Olani's cloak and bag, the curtains, the skirt of my dress.

This is what power feels like. Don't try to check it.

The thought is unwelcome, and it's exactly why I don't mess around with magic—because I can't say it isn't tempting. And I don't know how to control it. I can't think straight. I'm powerless as the rising wind fills the room, cold and harsh.

My nails scrape up and down my arms, bringing the pain Olani had soothed back to life. I don't *want* to hurt myself. I don't know why I'm doing it. But I can't stop.

Before I can bring down the entire inn around me, Isolde forces the door open. She has to struggle against the winds to pull it open with a slam. It closes behind her just as loudly.

The wind whips her short hair around her face. From far away, I can hear her voice, but I can't understand her words.

You can't do this now, some part of me tries to argue. *You don't get to fall apart. Stop it.*

But these thoughts are useless. I'm completely out of control.

"Seelie!" My name breaks through the haze. Isolde pushes toward me, fighting the wind trying to push her away. Her scrawny arms wrap around me, squeezing mine to my sides, like a shield. Like a promise that she won't let go.

"Seelie, please. Please stop. You're okay. It's going to be okay." Her words are barely a whisper.

The wind stops abruptly, leaving the room uncomfortably quiet and still. My legs won't hold me up any longer. I collapse onto the floor, and Isolde slowly lowers, too, crouching next to me.

I curl in on myself, squeezing my arms tight around my knees.

Stop it, stop it, stop it.

I taste salt and feel wetness on my lips.

Stop it, stop it, stop it.

I can see everything around me like I'm looking straight through it, like I'm not really here. There's a gentle hand on my hair and soothing words.

It doesn't fill that terrifying emptiness inside my chest. A deep, dark emptiness that feels like it's dragging the rest of me in. I put my head in her lap, burying my face in her dirty shirt.

"I'm sorry," I hear myself grind out. My voice is raw. "I'm sorry." And then I can't stop repeating the words, over and over, as my tears soak her shirt.

"Shh, shh…" Isolde comforts me. Her pickpocket's hands are incredibly gentle as she strokes my hair. Just like our mother's hands, soothing away our childhood fevers. She's so much like our mother.

I will never see our mother again.

Never.

A second wave of sobs rips from my chest.

Isolde sits with me for what might be a long time, rocking

me softly and whispering soothing words. Swallowed by the tide of emotions, I lose all concept of time.

My thoughts cycle through the same doubts and fears and self-loathing over and over and over again, and it feels like maybe I'll be curled up here on the floor, aching and weak and confused, for the rest of my life.

But I'm too tired. Without permission from the part of me still raging like a hurricane, my energy runs out. My tears slow, and I'm left shaking and hollow.

I finally regain enough control over myself to sit up. Isolde rubs my back lightly, just like our mother used to as my fits blew themselves out. Just like she has ever since we left home, and we had no one to take care of us except each other.

"I'm scared, Sol." My voice is trembling, weak, high. I hate it. I hate how I sound like a helpless child. I hate the way the magic ripped recklessly through me.

She takes her time before responding. "Me, too."

I can't bring myself to ask what scares her. I can't bear the possibility that the answer might be me.

I sleep even worse than usual that night.

It's disappointing, because I need the rest more than ever. All night, I linger in that strange, slow place halfway between sleeping and awake, tossing and turning in the bed I share with Isolde—who, of course, passes out the second her head hits the pillow.

Olani claims the other bed, and when Raze finally wanders in long after the rest of us have gone to bed, he pulls a bedroll out of his bag. He unrolls it in the narrow space between the two beds and settles into the slow, steady breathing of sleep almost immediately.

My eyes open against my will before dawn, and I stare wide-eyed into the perfect darkness of the far wall. I'd hoped I could sleep it off, but my head is still buzzing. The persistent ache all over hasn't gone away, either.

I wait, alone with my thoughts. They churn restlessly in my head, turning back again and again to Raze and Olani. There's so much we don't know about those two.

As the black shadows start to gray in the faint light of sunrise, Olani stirs. She stretches slowly, taking her time before sitting up. When she stands and walks to the basin silently, I turn over and pretend to be asleep. I listen to the faint rustle of her dressing, preparing herself for the day. The door eases open, then clicks shut.

I'm alone again.

For several heartbeats, it's like that. The syrupy, sleepy predawn closes in around me as I listen to my sister's and Raze's steady breathing.

Just as I've started to relax and doze again, the door bangs open. Olani bounds in, considerably less calm than she had been just moments ago.

I give up my act instantly, sitting up. "What's wrong?"

She's already reaching for her staff and her bag. "Um—" She looks afraid but not sure what to say. "Nothing. We just need to leave." She pokes Raze roughly with the butt of her staff. "Now!"

Though I'd prefer to know what exactly the threat is, I believe her. I shake Isolde, gently at first. She groans, smashing her face deeper into the pillow.

"Come on, Sol. Weren't you the one telling me we didn't have enough time to sleep last night?"

"That was before I fell asleep," she mumbles. "I'm on Team Sleep now."

In a truly cruel and heartless gesture that might prove that not all the horrible things they say about changelings are false, I snatch the blankets off her. "Too bad. Something's wrong. We have to get going."

That gets her attention. Her head pops up, hair sticking out around her confused, half-closed eyes. "What's—?"

"I don't know." I stand, already reaching for my rust-colored dress. "Olani won't say."

This is directed pointedly at the girl behind me, but she doesn't hear. She's too busy whispering something frantically to Raze, who looks like he's only getting about every third word. Then his eyes widen.

"She sent *her*?"

Olani scowls but nods.

"You're sure? I thought she was too *precious* to leave the city."

She looks back at us, uncomfortable. "I saw her with my own two eyes. If they tracked us this far, we don't have much time. *Get up!*"

Raze is already scrambling to his feet, his face even paler than normal.

Isolde gets up too, still grumbling about it thoroughly. "You saw *who*?"

They pretend not to hear her.

"I feel like you at least owe us the courtesy of letting us know who's hunting us down," I say. My fingers braid automatically, moving swiftly down my shoulder.

Raze turns to me, arms flapping wildly as he tries to stuff

them into his coat sleeves, irritation clear. "I believe you've already met Aris. In passing, at least."

I take in the hunch of his shoulders, the way Olani's knuckles tighten around her staff. The way neither of them will look directly at me.

Slowly, pieces come together. A threat Isolde and I dodged by leaving them to face it. "The enchanter who chased us on Revelnox?"

Silence, interrupted only by the sound of clothes being pulled on rapidly and bootlaces being tightened.

Then, with the simple bluntness Olani makes into an art form, "Yes."

Isolde seems almost awake as she ties her boots, yanking the laces like they'd insulted her. "So if she's downstairs, how are we going to get past her without getting caught?"

Raze and Olani exchange a look.

"No," he says. "It's way too early for that. I *just* woke up."

She raises her eyebrows and crosses her toned arms.

He sighs deeply, running both hands through his shaggy hair. "I hate you. Open the window." As Olani obeys, he turns back to Isolde and me. "I'll cause a distraction."

I'm only partly listening as I pace back and forth. I can't believe this is really happening. I should still be asleep.

"Everybody ready?" Raze shoulders his bag, backing toward the window. Olani's is slung on her shoulder, her cloak draped over her back. It feels like we should have something to hold, too, but Isolde and I lost everything when we lost our wagon, so I guess we're lucky to even be standing here fully clothed.

And then...

I don't know how to describe what happens next. The best I can do is this.

Every color, from the russet of his hair to rosy skin to the long sweep of dark cloak and brown of his shiny boots, blurs. The streaks of color fold in on themselves, then fold back out, resolving themselves into a different shape.

The shape of a hawk.

The hawk circles overhead once, then dives out the window with a scream.

Olani lets out an exasperated sigh, shaking her head. As she passes, I think I hear her mutter, "Dramatic little jinx."

I'd seen Leira Wildfall shapeshift before, but that was different. She never seemed like a real person. Raze...

But I don't have time to be wonderstruck. Olani doesn't hesitate before opening the door and running down the hall. Isolde squeezes my hand, and then we follow.

Headfirst into danger.

The perfect start to any morning. Who needs coffee when you have the icy shock of mortal terror?

chapter fifteen

At the bottom of the stairs, Olani stops so suddenly that I almost crash into her. Isolde grabs my arm and yanks me back on balance before I can send all three of us sprawling on the floor.

"Shh!" the healer hisses, peeking around the corner.

I follow her gaze, trying to make myself as small as possible. From here, we can see the front door and the counter where Olani paid for our room. It's surprisingly crowded for this early in the morning—

And they're all decked out in Wildline Manor blue.

I strain to hear the conversation. Aris is the only one speaking, her back turned to us. Her hands, wrapped in thin strips of cloth, drum impatiently on the desk. Given how nervous the innkeeper looks, she must be threatening him. At least it doesn't look like they brought the dragons with them.

"Saw them—with two other...but they didn't...could be wrong."

She mutters something that makes his face turn red. Then she waves her hands in a circular motion, and a ball of light forms between them—not fiery or flickering, but shining white, like a tiny sun.

My breath catches in my chest. It's one thing to know what she can do, but it's another to actually *see* the magic spring from her fingertips. I've never seen someone manipulate light like that. She must be the one who enchanted the lights at the Revelnox party and in Wildline Manor.

"Olani, how—?"

Before I can finish my question, the front door bursts open. Raze, back in his human form, slides in as if he'd sprinted with his full weight into the door. "Aris!"

Her green eyes wide, she turns sharply, and so does everyone else in the room.

He stands there panting for a second, possibly for dramatic effect. Then an irreverent grin breaks like the dawn across his face, and he says, "What's a girl like you doing in a place like this?"

That breaks the spell. "Get him!" Aris commands. She shoots the ball of light across the room at Raze.

It's headed straight for his chest, but he's already transforming back into the hawk. Instead, it explodes against the doorframe, leaving a singed black crater.

Raze swoops out the door, and half the room chases after.

The other half holds back, clearly confused and trying to look like they aren't.

We wait a moment for the chaos to peak, to make sure that Aris, who I'm pretty sure is their leader despite her age, is following Raze.

"Now!"

With our heads down, we quickly cross the room. I realize in a flash of panic that I have no idea where we're going, but it's too late to ask.

I glance back over my shoulder as we pass the smoking hole where one of the hinges used to be. It seems impossible that Olani, tall and striking as she is, has slipped by without notice, but no one seems to be looking at us.

Before that can change, we sprint to the stable.

"You two take Raze's horse. You know how to ride, right?"

We hesitate. "Yes?" Isolde says.

Olani groans. "Doesn't matter. We don't have another ch—"

A ray of white brilliance blasts over her shoulder. Behind us, Aris and a pack of her accomplices are advancing quickly. I knew a simple getaway had been too good to be true.

"Too late," Olani says, bolting uphill. "Run!"

"To the *cliff*?" I shout. "What about—?"

But I don't have enough air in my lungs to argue. We fly past the stables and any hope of escape, behind the inn, until we're out of space to run. The sea crashes against the rocks below.

"Don't tell me you're about to jump." I back away from the edge nervously.

Olani quickly realizes it's too far to fall without smashing into the rocks below. "Well, I'm not *now*!"

Then a flash of light blinds us all.

In the whiteness that follows, I hear my sister cry out like she's been hit. My footsteps crunch in the dirt as I turn, trying to pinpoint where she is. Then a heavy, anonymous thump, and the upsettingly familiar sound of the breath being knocked from someone's lungs.

My vision clears slowly, and I realize I'm facing the cliff, dangerously close to its edge in my temporary blindness.

"Show me the compass, and none of you have to get hurt!" Aris snarls.

I whirl, blinking away the zigzagging lights crawling in front of my eyes.

Isolde is several paces back, entangled in an extremely undignified schoolyard tussle with Aris, who is currently trying to pin her down. Aris is already sweaty and breathing hard, spent by the magic she's used. Good. It'll be at least a few minutes before she can fire off another spell. Dark hair blurs in the air as they punch and claw, trying to restrain each other.

"I have…no idea…what you're talking about!" my sister grunts. The bandage on her head is starting to slip, gray dust staining the crisp white material.

Before my muddled mind can begin to make sense of it, before I can even launch into an attack, the rest of Aris's crew catches up. One runs for me, drawing his sword. I have less than a second to act before I'm going to be sliced in half, and I have no idea what to do.

But I don't need to know what to do. I let go, let my instincts take over, since so far they seem to have a better idea of how to keep me alive than I do.

Immediately, I feel more aware of everything around me. Magic rushes through me like a river, eroding away doubt and rational thought. It tingles beneath my skin, blazing through the raised fingers of the burns that cover my arms.

My hands cross in an *x* in front of my chest, then swoop apart.

A strong gust of wind weaves between my attacker's feet as his sword pulls free from its sheath. He tumbles to the ground. I press my advantage, kicking the sword out of his hand and over the edge of the cliff.

Behind me, I hear the crack of Olani's staff.

My attacker rises again and charges for me with his bare hands.

I don't want to kill him. I can't even bring myself to crush the lost spiders that find their way inside the Destiny.

Then again, I don't want to get pummeled off the edge of the cliff, either.

I'm not as quick as Isolde. He gets a good hit in, square on my cheek, and I can't stop myself from crying out as the bruising sensation bites all the way through my face. Somehow, I *taste* pain.

No, wait—that's blood.

But the man isn't expecting me to crumple instantly, which is what I do.

It only takes him a moment to recover from the surprise and raise his boot to stomp on me, but I've already rolled out of the way.

My jaw throbs with uncomfortable warmth.

Olani looks as calm as if she was enjoying a lively game of cards as she fights off two of our attackers at the same time. They've been forced to go strictly on the defensive, and it doesn't look like they'll last much longer.

"Seelie!"

Aris twists Isolde's injured arm, and a feral shriek of pain rings out in the clear morning air. I've never heard that specific note of panic in my sister's voice before.

Let's see what this magic can really do.

It burns through me—literally, dancing through the mark on my outstretched left hand and bursting from my fingertips. Excitement leaps through my veins, a kind of sick thrill that I've never experienced before and don't expect.

I don't see it spark or catch. One moment, the man is pulling back to attack me, and the next, he's on fire.

Fire, it turns out, makes an excellent distraction. I have to assume the man isn't being paid anywhere near enough to burn to death, and as soon as the flames start spreading up his sleeve, he completely forgets me in his frantic scramble to put himself out.

I push past him, closer to the fighting. Just in time to see a streak of light miss my sister by less than an inch.

But she can't dodge the spell and the enchanter at the same time. She cries out in pain as Aris kicks her in the stomach.

"Don't worry," Isolde gasps. "Go—" She chokes on her words.

A screech rings out over the cliffside. I look up. A hawk circles above us, swooping over the ocean as he descends. The sun glints copper off his feathers.

Raze!

I expect him to transform back, to conjure up some kind of magical attack.

Instead, he dives for the nearest person in blue, vicious claws extended.

Isolde is still struggling on the ground. I can't let Aris get to her again, not like this. My fists clench, power flowing through me again.

Before my magic can provide me with an attack, Aris sweeps a hand out toward me. Her teeth grit with the effort it takes as massive roots emerge from the earth in a shower of dirt and pebbles and wrap around my middle, pinning my arms in place. Trapping me.

A scream of frustration tears from my throat. The branches squeeze my tender skin, pressing the fabric of my dress into the burns until I can feel every individual fiber against my skin, alight with pain.

I kick and thrash, but it's about as effective as the beating of a moth's wings against glass. Each movement scrapes my skin, more painful than the last. There's nothing I can do but *watch*.

Aris laughs hoarsely, pushing sweaty curls back from her face with a sniffle. "Come on, Olani. You really thought no one would find out you were sneaking around? Or did you think no one would care?" She's cocky, but I notice that she's still gasping to catch her breath. "Throwing in your lot with *Raze*? I didn't think you were that stupid."

Olani's staff smacks into her opponent, and for a moment, it's just her calmly facing Aris. She lets her staff fall a little, leaning on it casually. "Right," she says, as if daring an attack. "Much more embarrassing than working thanklessly for Leira Wildfall indefinitely, waiting for a promotion that's never going to come."

Is she talking about Aris or herself? Maybe both.

"It's not like that!" Aris replies, hands balling at her sides. Her magic is exhausted, but she's still trying to prepare for another attack.

Olani doesn't flinch. "She was only ever going to see me as a fighter. I'm tired of being used like that. Aren't you?"

Before Aris can respond, the person Olani just smacked aside rallies back to their feet, drawing a dagger. Olani's stance changes instantly to the defensive, and she's back to the battle.

She's good at this—but she wants more. Whatever it is, it's something she thinks she'll find by helping us get to the Mortal's Keep.

Isolde struggles back to her feet, panting and sweating and possibly angrier than I've ever seen her. Instantly, she's sprinting back into the fight, knives already in her hands, despite the looseness of her grip on her injured side.

"Isolde—"

"Wait there!"

It doesn't seem like I have much choice in that. I kick my legs uselessly, straining against my bonds. It does absolutely nothing against the might of the huge, gnarled roots. "Isolde!"

A dagger flies through the air and lands at my feet—not an attempted attack, I realize quickly. The woman whose face Raze's talons tore into abandoned it to throw her arms over her head, screaming at a pitch even higher than the bird's. Blood drips from the scored claw marks down her face, and she curls into a shivering ball.

Raze's form blurs and shifts back into his human shape, landing heavily on his feet.

The woman doesn't get up.

"If you have something to say about me," he pants, advancing on Aris, "you should say it to my face."

She smirks, looking not even a little surprised by his sudden transformation. Her fingertips start to glow, white light beading into a ball hovering over her wrapped palm.

Raze takes another step forward, flexing his fingers at his side. Preparing for her attack? Or an attack of his own?

Then Raze's eyes widen, his knees give out, and he stumbles.

The morning air is shattered by a loud retching as he heaves the contents of his stomach over the edge of the cliff.

My own stomach clenches—because it's gross, *not* out of any concern over him.

"Raze, *why*?" Olani growls, even though it seems obvious: he's red-faced and nauseous from over-exerting his magic. Isolde is at her side, a furious storm of blows and flashing blades.

It takes everything in me not to turn my head and squeeze my eyes shut. I need to watch, no matter how horrible it is. I need to be here for her.

The woman Isolde is fighting holds her own surprisingly well, but she can't land an attack. I watch her dodge and parry and shift her eyes away just long enough for Olani to knock her in the back of the head with a hollow thud. She collapses like a rag doll. Is she dead or unconscious?

It doesn't seem to matter to anyone else.

"Thanks for the distraction," Olani says breathlessly, but Isolde's attention is already focused over her shoulder.

Isolde flicks her wrist back, then sends her knife in a gleaming streak that narrowly misses grazing Olani's cheek. It buries itself in the shoulder of the man sneaking up behind her, narrowly missing his heart. There's blood, instantly, so dark it's almost black on the blue of his clothes. I can hear the wetness and smell the iron in the sea-salt air.

I hear myself let out something like a strangled whimper.

The man stiffens, swaying on his feet. It seems like he might drop to his knees, but then Olani swings her quarterstaff, knocking him neatly off the cliff. The churning waves are too far down to hear the splash.

I look back to Raze. Aris crouches by his side, one hand raised and full of light, sweeping her lovely green eyes over him disdainfully. She twists his red hair in her delicate fingers, wrenching his head up. "Tell me how you got it to work," she says, dangerously quiet.

He coughs, looking the least dignified anyone has ever looked with a string of drool trailing down his chin. "Got... what to work?" he says, unconvincingly.

Someone has to do something, before she gets bored of playing with him like a cat with a wounded bird.

I look down at the roots trapping my limbs and crushing my ribs. My arms burn with pain where the roots wrap around the lightning marks. I can feel a bruise blooming painfully on my face.

Tree! I think at my magic. *Make the tree do the thing. Undo the thing. You know what I mean.*

It does not know what I mean.

My magic doesn't care about my thoughts and reasons. It only responds to—

Instinct, I realize. *Emotion.*

I need to get out. I need to be free. To save everyone.

A flash of light and heat. Isolde screams. I scream.

By the time I realize my body is encased in blue flames, they're already gone. The roots burn off of me like rum-soaked rags, but I'm unscathed. I stretch my arms and flex my fingers. The healing blisters protest, but they're the only marks on me.

I've definitely got Aris's attention now. Her bright eyes lock on the palm of my outstretched left hand, realization dawning. For the first time, she looks at me like I might be a real threat. Her eyes flicker with confusion as she tries to figure out what I am.

I'm going to pay for that later, but I'm not worried. I feel light-headed and airy. Even after using so much magic, more of it swells through me in a wave of warmth. I'm shaking with the effort it takes to hold it back, trembling from my fingertips down into my boots, from my boots into the earth.

Then I realize that the ground beneath my feet is trembling, too. Magic flows down, spreading in ripples around my feet, making the loose pebbles of the cliff's sandy peak shiver and bounce.

"Don't come any closer!" Aris warns, still gripping Raze's hair. There's the tiniest flash of fear in her eyes, and I don't mind it.

"Release him and let us go," I say, taking one shaky step forward. "We're not telling you anything."

As soon as I move, I know I've made a mistake. The fear on Aris's face hardens into something dangerous, and her hand snaps out, firing concentrated light in my direction.

I don't know if she misses my heart accidentally or on purpose, but the beam still burns a clean tear through my sleeve. Pain follows immediately, a searing red line over the already-tender burn scars from yesterday. I knew to avoid her light, but I had no idea it would hurt this much. It feels like the breath is being torn from my chest, ripping all the way down into the earth. My cry of pain echoes off the cliff as I squeeze my fists tight and pull them back in a quick snap.

The wind responds, surging around me. I'm wary of lightning now, but the air is just as eager to obey my call, to bend to the tiny voice inside me that wants to see her dead.

End it now. You're more powerful than her.

My hair and dress wave wildly in the storm-force winds that gather around me like a shield, so much building force I don't know what to do with it. Aris's eyes are wide, and I watch her release Raze with satisfaction, fingers grasping at her throat.

The wind had to come from somewhere. I've pulled it straight from her lungs.

Her green eyes get round and shiny, and I see all the pain and fear I felt reflected in them. I *want* her to feel it. I want her to know what it's like to be helpless. I call more and more wind, enough to make her hollow ribs ache.

"Seelie," Isolde's shaky voice breaks through the storm around me, the storm in my head, and all of a sudden, I realize what I'm doing.

What am I *doing*?

Panic mixes with the dregs of my rage, and I push the winds with all my might. All the air rushing around me knocks Aris square in the chest, and it feels like a release of all the built-up pressure. Her breathing relaxes, even as she goes tumbling off the edge, voice too ragged to scream.

Raze, looking like he might throw up again, meets my eyes, and this time, the fear is much less satisfying. "Run!" he shouts, forcing himself to his feet and sprinting back the way we'd just come.

We don't think. We don't pause. We don't double-check that she's really gone. We just run, as fast as our legs will take us.

chapter sixteen

The inn is starting to wake (possibly due to the sounds of battle outside), and the stunned faces of a few early risers blur as we stampede past. Raze is already stumbling and looks like he might be sick again, and Olani has to support his weight, dragging him along beside her.

"Horses?" Isolde pants. A slow drip of blood trails down the side of her face from her reopened wound.

"No time!" Olani says, slumping Raze forward. Raze. The shapeshifter.

Isolde looks at him, considering. On Revelnox, Leira Wildfall morphed into a huge, beautiful mare. If Raze could do the same, even for a short time, he might be able to get us a head start. "Can't he—?"

"Not really," Olani interrupts. "Hurry!"

That settles it. Our only hope is to dodge and hide and hope they lose our trail on foot.

We skid into the sleepy town. The smells of breakfast, farm animals, woodsmoke, fresh hay, and coffee pool around us. Chickens flee, squawking indignantly as they narrowly avoid getting stepped on.

I twist abruptly to avoid knocking over a mother carrying a wailing toddler to the center of town and instead crash into a man with a cart selling coffee.

Luckily, he only has one tin cup in hand that sloshes over his canvas apron as steaming droplets splash my chest and sleeves. "Hey!"

"Sorry!" I don't stop running.

Not so far behind us, I can make out flashes of deep blue pushing forward through the gathering crowd.

"They're catching up," I gasp, catching Isolde's hand in mine. I try willing my legs to go faster. Olani would have left us in the dust by now if not for the burden of Raze stumbling along slung half over her shoulder.

"This way!" Without hesitation, Isolde leaps over someone's fence and slips into the narrow space between two houses, pulling me along behind her. Olani curses behind us, slowing down to step over the fence.

We come out on the other side of the houses on another street and take off in a random direction, trying to get lost in the maze of small, humble buildings. Maybe, if we lead them far enough away, we can circle back around to the horses.

It isn't a plan, exactly, but it's all we can do. Especially at an hour when we should still be snuggled up in bed.

The town is coming alive quickly, though. The sun is almost fully overhead, the sky barely streaked with pink. People bustle all around attending to their own business, either making far too much effort not to stare at us or far too little.

Eventually, we turn a corner and find ourselves in the town square. It's full of people chattering and calling out to each other in the early light. At first, I don't see what all the fuss is about.

And *then*—

I stop short, almost tripping over my own feet.

"Look!" I shout, not thinking. I'm too excited to think, too overwhelmed with delight and disbelief.

Isolde grabs for my hand to keep towing me along, but then she sees, and she freezes, too.

Past the gathering throng of townspeople, a familiar emerald-green paint job shimmers in the pink early-morning sun.

The Destiny is *here*. Finally, our luck is turning around. I could laugh out loud.

Raze stops, bending in half with his hands braced on his knees as he struggles to catch his breath. "Need...to keep going." He looks a little green now, and it isn't just because of the light bouncing off the wagon's shiny paint.

Before I can reply, or foolishly run forward, the Destiny's door bangs open. I suddenly notice two men, separate from the crowd, who had been leaning against her side and trying to scratch gilt from the adornments, as they startle with a laugh.

Isolde grips my wrist in one frigid hand and wrenches me to the side. She catches Olani with her other hand, and we all do our best to make ourselves invisible in the crowd, hoping everyone will ignore that we're out of breath and sweating.

"Cursed cat!"

A man's voice is muffled as he emerges from the wagon, disheveled. He tugs his tunic back into place, smoothing wrinkles.

"Whatcha got in there?" one of his companions calls. "Anything as fine as the outside?"

"It's all junk. See for yourself." He points to the wagon, and Isolde stifles a slightly hysterical giggle, wiping blood off her cheek absently. It leaves a gruesome streak from her ear to her jaw, which looks much worse than it did before.

"Doesn't matter," the third taunts. "Look at these wheels. We can sell the rest easy enough."

The second man peeks inside, swinging the door wide and letting it hang there. I hear our things clatter around as he tosses them aside.

"Why have we stopped?" Olani demands, too distracted by the crowd and our pursuers to notice the Destiny. She's still holding Raze up with their arms draped around each other's shoulders, and he's staring very hard at the cobblestones as if he can will himself to stop feeling sick.

"That's *our* wagon!" I manage, through stiff indignation. Those things they're putting their hands all over aren't theirs.

As if in response, crashing sounds from inside the Destiny again. I wince, imagining my dishes breaking. It's quickly followed by what I would think is the angry wailing of a cat if I didn't know better, then a long string of increasingly colorful curses.

I only hear snatches of the man's cry of alarm, mingled with shattering and thumping. "Horrible little—a *cat*! Listen here, you, this is *our* wagon now— Ha!"

Another, angrier meow fills the air, and he steps out onto the platform again. This time, he holds an enraged blur of black fluff at arm's length, ignoring its sharp claws as it does its very best to shred his sleeves to ribbons.

"Give it here!" the third man says, grabbing Birch by the scruff and waving him high in the air like an absolutely furious flag.

A thought strikes me that, in different circumstances, would be funny…

They don't know what Birch is. If they did, they wouldn't have entered the wagon without iron and salt and a banishment spell, at the very least.

"What's he doing with your cat?" Olani whispers. "Should we do something?"

A mischievous smile that I don't think Isolde would be able to stop if she tried beams back. She's leaning on me more heavily now, not quite steady on her feet. "We don't have a cat."

"Disgusting creature," the man says, wrinkling his nose. "Go on, get!"

And then he makes his worst mistake yet.

He throws Birch to the ground, no doubt expecting him to twist in the air, land on all four paws, and slink off sulkily into the streets, evicted from his humble domain.

Instead, the second his hands leave Birch's coat, the catlike creature hovers in midair. He bares his rows of too many tiny white teeth, and his eyes glow bright green.

It's unnerving, to say the least.

"*What—?*" the cat-thrower chokes, fury and confusion thickening his voice.

A murmur goes up through the people still hanging around

the square—shock and alarm, tinged with fear. The sound is joined by a growl from the back of Birch's throat as the brownie writhes in the air, his eyes flashing as he takes in his foes, the poor fools who would attempt to drive him from his home.

"Does your cat normally do that?" Raze sounds queasy.

"Not a cat," Isolde asserts again in a mumble, watching intently as the prickling sensation of faerie magic tingles in the air.

Even though my heart is pounding against my ribs, I'm not nearly as terrified as I should be. Instead, I can't help cheering Birch on silently, like a spectator at a tournament.

The noise Birch makes isn't animal *or* human. It's like chunks of ice melting in a stream, like the anger of a swarm of wasps, like the crunch of a snapping branch. I clap my hands over my ears, but there's no need. All his fury is turned on the three men trying to steal the Destiny.

Everyone else is clearing away from them, fear rippling through the square. I'm almost glad for the thieves, because they're making such a scene that the chances of anyone spotting us are getting slimmer by the second. Their eyes go wide, and the first one makes a choking sound. He bends at the waist in an awkward bow.

For a terrible second, I think Birch is going to kill him.

And then the man starts to dance.

His arms wave wildly, still fighting the enchantment, even as his knees jerk up and down merrily to a nonexistent beat. He's incredibly light on his feet, even as he shouts and curses and goes red. His friends join in, ankles twisting this way and that, carrying them all in a smooth jig down the platform's stairs. People clear out of their path, pointing and snickering as they make their merry way to the center of the square.

Birch's eyes go back to their normal degree of unsettling. He drops from the air and pads back inside the wagon, tail twitching indignantly behind him.

"There they are!" a distant voice calls.

The crowd's mockery is getting louder and more open now, and no one notices the fast approach of several very dangerous-looking people dressed in blue, now sprinting in our direction from down one of the narrow streets.

"I think that's our cue," Isolde says, flashing a brilliant grin. "Come on!"

chapter seventeen

I bound into the wagon ahead of everyone else, running my hand appreciatively over the sleek green varnish as I slip inside.

Olani sighs, eyes flicking between us briefly before giving in with an unhappy sound of resignation. "Seelie, get us *out of here*, fast as you can. Come on, Raze." She practically has to drag him up the steps.

Without protest, I settle into the driver's seat, checking every lever and wheel with automatic, practiced swiftness. Isolde swings in last, slamming the door behind her.

The second the door shuts, I throw back the lever and send the wheels spinning. We screech through the crowd, narrowly missing a few people, and tear down the street.

My sister peers nervously out the window, but our pursuers didn't bring their horses or wagons when they followed us. They're already choking on our dust.

Curses. I've never actually maneuvered the Destiny through a town this small before. It's…tricky. Luckily, it's still early enough that the streets are mostly empty of wagons, though I do send a few pedestrians and unlucky goats diving for cover. I can finally breathe again when we turn onto the straight, wide strip of the main road.

Finally, I look around. The wagon's interior is disordered, with things strewn over the floor where they'd been thrown or knocked over. Bits of broken glass sparkle in one corner. Overall, it's a disaster, but I'm relieved. It could have been much worse.

Once he's decided that our new companions are not a threat, Birch pretends to nap in a corner as if nothing had happened. His eyes are calm slits, and his pink tongue pokes slightly out of his mouth, like he's a cat and not a faerie creature that has just viciously hexed people—people completely deserving of hexes, but still.

"Birch!" I exclaim, realizing just how worried I'd been about the brownie and how attached I've grown to him. "You clever thing. What a good kitty."

"What is *that*?" Olani and Raze look out of place in the cramped wagon, cringing as far from the faerie creature as they can manage.

"Our brownie. How's it looking back there?" I call to Isolde, who is still peering intensely out the window.

"Good so far."

Good. I jerk the wheel to the side, rumbling off the road in a sharp turn.

My ears fill with overlapping protests as Isolde, Olani, and Raze all jolt with the sudden movement. Ignoring them, I yank on the brake.

The Destiny rolls to a stop in the grass.

"Seelie, what are you *doing*?" Isolde struggles to her feet. She has a split lip and an impressive collection of bruises blooming under her skin, along with the blood smeared over her face and the stab wound that has reopened in her arm. Aside from all that, she looks great. At least none of it will kill her.

I meet her eyes, and understanding lights there quickly. She agrees with me. This is shaping up to be *way* more than we signed up for, and we're not moving until we get some kind of explanation.

Olani somehow managed to stay planted on the bench. Raze slumps with his back against it. He still has a relatively feral look in his eyes as he takes in his surroundings. He trembles as he struggles to overcome his nausea enough to speak. Finally, he coughs and manages, "Nice place you got here."

Well, that's not what I expected. Isolde's eyebrows rise, and Olani looks like she's trying very hard not to get mad. She takes the deep breath of a parent dealing with a particularly difficult toddler. "How did they find us, Raze?"

He looks at her, then Isolde, then me. His easy charisma drops like a badly made mask, and he buries his head in his hands. Limp strands of hair ruffle around his fingers. "I don't know. We need to keep moving."

"Stop," Isolde cuts in. "We're not going anywhere until you tell us what is going on."

A look passes between Raze and Olani that I can't read.

"Let's start simple," I say, pleased to find I sound much

calmer than I feel. "Those were Leira's people. Why did they seem to personally know you?"

A long moment of shuffling silence, like they're hoping Isolde and I will suddenly develop short-term memory loss.

When that doesn't happen, Raze lets out a breath. "They, uh…they work for my aunt." He says it as if we're supposed to know who that is.

We stare blankly. Finally, Isolde prompts, "Your aunt?"

He blinks, as if surprised we don't know who he's talking about. "Leira Wildfall."

Oh. I picture the woman standing before the crowd at Revelnox, shimmering with power. I knew they were related, but I didn't think of them as *family*.

Before I can respond, he adds quickly, "Well, she's more like my…second cousin, once removed, I think. I mean, she kind of raised me, but I'm not—" this sentence could end in a variety of ways, but he chooses the one I expect least "—important."

No. He is *not* going to make me feel bad for him. Even if his face *does* briefly resemble a very sad puppy. "Ah," I say uncomfortably.

"I used to work for her," Olani says. "Kind of. She prefers to keep…the sort of work I do off the official record."

"Oh," Isolde says. "You're a mercenary—"

"I *was*," Olani interrupts firmly. "I did some work for Leira for a bit. It was supposed to be a first step, but… I got kind of stuck there. Following orders. I kept thinking if I could just impress her, she'd give me a real job adventuring. You know— finding treasure, slaying monsters, defending people. Took me too long to realize that was pointless. So I created my own opportunity."

I'm still buzzing, and none of this really makes sense, and we need to get going again before they find us. I fight to not let my limbs swing around in place to burn off the nervous energy. "What about that enchanter?" I ask. "What does she know about the compass?"

"Aris…" Raze turns to meet Olani's eyes in a silent plea for help.

Her jaw clenches, and then she finishes his sentence. "Aris is Leira's favorite pet."

Raze grimaces. "Aris is another distant cousin who hates me. We grew up together, taken in by Leira because of our abilities. But I'm not *gifted* like she is. I could never live up to her magic. And now she's tracking me down like an animal. Funny, isn't it?"

No. It's not.

"She hates everyone," Olani breaks in.

"I mean, yes, but *especially* me. She can't stand that I can shapeshift and she can't. Not that it matters. I didn't think we were bad enough for Aunt Leira to send *her*."

"I told you this was a terrible idea," Olani grumbles.

Isolde groans impatiently. "What is *this*? Why did you have to break into the manor in the first place?"

"We should get back on the road before they start following us," Raze says quickly. He's right. But one of us is going to have to give in eventually—and it isn't going to be me.

Olani seems to realize that if she doesn't intervene, we'll stand here in silence until it's too late and we've lost our head start. She speaks first. "Three months ago, I caught Raze trying to break into Leira's locked room. I was working for her on commission, but she was considering me for a more permanent position, and turning him in would have put me in her favor."

"But you didn't," I say, looking between them. Raze's face is turning redder again.

"No," she agrees.

Isolde is getting impatient. "Why?"

Olani smiles a little bit, and I can see the easy friendship between her and Raze, something warmer and deeper than simple alliance. A twinge of envy gnaws at the pit of my stomach—I've never understood how people just *become* friends. "He offered me something better. And besides, I already kind of knew Raze from—" She glances at him and stumbles over the end of the sentence, making me think there's more there. "From before."

There's a pause. Raze cringes, takes a deep breath, and says, "Leira kicked me out at the beginning of the year. I wasn't the heir she wanted, so she decided I wasn't worth the effort. Threw me out on the street with nothing. I knew that room was important to Leira. To our family. But she wouldn't tell me what was in there, and once...once I realized that I was never going to earn my way in, I decided to...you know."

"So I let him go, and we started planning a smoother heist. It would have gone perfectly," Olani adds, a little bitterly.

"But you wouldn't have had a changeling to activate it," Isolde points out.

"Right," Raze says in a flat voice that's hard to read, glancing at me.

I look down at the compass in my palm. It trembles slightly, as if it's straining to point to the road, reminding me to *get going!*

There's a long, heavy silence.

Isolde scowls, crinkling the blood starting to dry on her face. "So what now?"

"We find this fortress or whatever it is," Raze says confidently. "I reclaim the Mortal's Keep and my place in the Wild line. You take your share of the treasure. Leira gets knocked down a peg. Everybody wins." He grins, head tilted, and I can see the fantasy playing out behind his eyes. "Well, everyone except Leira."

I've been mostly silent, trying to file all this information away, but now I speak. My voice is quiet, so I'm surprised when it makes everyone turn to look at me. "You expect us to just go along with all this? Being hunted like prey wasn't part of the agreement."

Raze shrugs. He's starting to look like himself again, humor creeping back to the corners of his eyes. "The agreement doesn't matter. You need this as much as we do."

I want to say no. I want to say no *so badly*. There's still so much unexplained, and when we started this, no one said anything about running for our lives. I want to walk away and pretend none of this ever happened.

Then I think of home again, of our parents, of plucking flowers from yarrow plants at my mother's side, of the warm-earth smell of my father's studio, of golden afternoon light streaming in the cottage windows. Of all four of our voices, mingling in laughter as we swap stories.

If that wasn't enough, I know I can't run now. I used so much magic earlier, and I don't feel anything more than a slight ringing in my ears. The enchantment is woven in ink into my skin, magic seeping into my blood faster than I can get rid of it, and this is my only chance of freeing myself.

"If this gets us killed," I manage, stumbling a little on the forced confidence in my voice, "I expect double payment." Isolde reaches for my hand and squeezes it in her cold fingers, eyes shining with excitement. I try not to wince at the pain of my blistered skin crackling in her grip.

I meet Raze's eyes briefly before mine flit away to somewhere that doesn't hurt to focus on, at the tip of his nose. It twitches as a smile curves his mouth. "Sounds fair. So where to, Iselia?"

I glance at the compass again, even though I already know what I'll see. The arrow is steady, but I sense its impatience. "West," I say. "We head west. At least for now."

Beneath my skin, the enchantment relaxes a little, reassured that I haven't forgotten it.

chapter eighteen

The thing about eighty-four square feet is that it doesn't fit four people—plus a brownie—comfortably. If you do the math, it evens out to about twenty-one square feet each, which might sound like plenty, but let me assure you, it isn't.

Especially when two of the four people can barely stand without bumping their heads, and the limited square footage is also shared with everything you own.

Especially, *especially* when the four people don't really get along.

Well, some more than others. Isolde and Olani quickly form a tentative friendship that mostly revolves around talking about creative ways to beat the stuffing out of people and long-buried, probably fictional, treasure. Raze, for once, is thoughtfully silent, which is fine by me.

Eventually, we have to stop for the night. We pull off the road into a little stand of trees. I don't think Leira's people will be able to catch up to us so quickly, but slipping into the shelter of the branches makes me breathe a little easier.

"Hey, Feathers, why don't you find somewhere we can nest?" Olani says, shoving both of their bedrolls into Raze's arms. Even though it's framed as a question, it isn't one.

"Olani," he protests, blushing at the nickname. The hawk must be the form he favors most, besides human. I don't know exactly why, but she's finally managed to knock the good humor out of him with a little teasing.

"Thanks." She turns to me. "We need to talk."

I groan. I was looking forward to a calm evening of sweeping up broken glass and trying to put everything that got thrown around back where it belongs. I'd thought that Isolde and I might finally have a chance to talk unobserved.

But even my twin is giving me a strange look as the door slams behind Raze. She's not on my side this time.

I grit my teeth, propping the door open to let fresh air circulate through the cramped space. I start with the biggest things first—the cooking pot, the trunk of spare clothes, all the books that flew off the shelves. The space between my shoulder blades itches with the discomfort of being watched. Once the big stuff is back in place, I reach for a broom.

"Your sister said you needed time to process." Olani picks up the overturned basin. "But Seelie, we need to talk about your magic."

I've been here the whole time. I have no idea when they had *that* conversation. It feels like Isolde is exposing my weaknesses. It feels like a betrayal. "When were you two talking about me?"

Isolde steps toward me. "Don't try to deflect. You can't keep pretending this isn't a problem."

I ignore her. So far, it seems the more I think about magic, the more it grows into something I can't stuff down.

"Okay," Olani says, undeterred. "We can start simple. What kind of spell was that you used on Aris back there? What's your focus?" Silence. "Aris does some kind of light manipulation. I do healing magic, and the shield thing is an extension of it—sorry about that. Leira's a little all over the place, but she's such a powerful shapeshifter that none of the others really matter that much. So far, I've seen you do that lightning thing, fire, and then...the, um...the wind." She stumbles for the first time, like she's remembering Aris's face as I ripped the air from her lungs. I shiver. "So what is it? You study elemental magic?"

"Elemental?" I repeat, bending down to make sure I didn't miss any tiny shards. "Would you light that lantern?" There's a click, and the dark corner is flooded with light. I reach my broom under the stove and drag out glittering dust bunnies flecked with broken glass.

I focus very hard on my dustpan, but Olani must turn to Isolde, because my sister says, "We don't know anything about magic. This is...mostly new."

"Seelie, where did you learn that?" Olani says, patience straining in her voice.

"I didn't," I snap. "I never learned how to use magic. It just...*happens*."

There's a long pause. Finally, Isolde says, "Well, maybe you need to."

"Sol—"

She interrupts, and there it is again—that feeling that something has changed. That *we've* changed. "Don't argue with me! Your magic is *dangerous*, Seelie. You saw what it did back there…what it did to *you*! How many times do we have to have this fight before someone else gets hurt? Or worse?"

Pain twists in my gut, sparking anger almost hot enough to burn away the guilt. I stand, turning to face her with the broom gripped tight in white-knuckled fists. "I don't *want* this magic! I don't want any of this!"

"Your sister's right," Olani says, stepping between us. "You need to start practicing how to control it, or else you're putting all of us in danger. Personally, I'd rather not die an agonizing, fiery death just because *you're* emotionally repressed."

I'm stiff and silent, but my mind is racing. I don't want what she's saying to be true. All I want is to be left alone.

"I'll help you," Olani says. "I may not be the best at magic, but I know a little. Raze knows a little more. Together—"

"You have no idea what it's like trying to control my magic," I manage, through gritted teeth. I know that my magic is violent and unpredictable, and that's exactly why I want nothing to do with it.

Yes, you do. You want to seize it, and wring it out for all it's worth. You know you do.

"I know you don't want to deal with this…" Isolde starts, a little more gently. She reaches for my arm and gives it a comforting squeeze. "But you have to. You're strong enough to handle it, Seelie. I believe in you."

I let out a long exhale, shaking her off so I can sweep my dust pile out the door. I watch Isolde from the corner of my eye. There's hurt in her face, but she hesitates to reach out to

me again. Maybe she's remembering the wave of fire that de-
voured the tree, flickering blue light playing on my enraged
face as it swept out from me. She wasn't in its path, but what
if she is next time?

I don't want Isolde to be scared of me. I don't want to be
scared of *myself*.

Something squeezes tight around me. Deep in my chest,
magic surges hopefully, and I nearly choke on it. "I-I need
some air," I mutter, throwing down the broom and stomping out into the night.

Luckily, they don't follow.

Less luckily, Raze is lying in wait for me in the trees. I
don't think he's actually trying to trap me, but that doesn't
stop me from tripping over him in the darkness and tumbling
to the ground. Pine needles stab into my hands as I let out
an undignified grunt.

"We *have* to stop meeting like this," he says from the ground,
just a few inches from my head. I think this is the third time
we've tripped over each other, and at this point, I'm not sure
he isn't doing it on purpose. At least he's a soft person to fall
on—no hard edges or sharp lines.

"Shut up." I push awkwardly away from him, sitting in a
shameless heap of dirty skirts on the ground.

He sits up a little straighter but doesn't listen to me. "So
what happened in there? Any time Olani ambushes you for
a Real Talk, it can't be good."

Absently, my hands gather clusters of pine needles and start
stripping them apart. We're moving away from the mountains slowly, into the space between the Eastern and Western
Mountains that is mostly uninhabited. Overhead, the stars

are as bright as they were back home, unobscured by the late-burning lanterns of the cities. The air is sharp and clear, like we're the only people for miles. I stare into the darkness for a long time, before finally saying, "She wanted to talk about my magic."

"That...makes sense." He sounds a little hesitant, like he knows he's treading on fragile ground. "You're...very powerful. I'm lucky we're on the same team." I should be horrified that he just used the same words Isolde said last night, but what he says next is even worse. "You do have practice *not* blowing things up, right?"

My fingers ball tight around the pine needles as I breathe in their sharp, sweet smell. "I don't use my magic unless I have no other choice. And I don't want to talk about it."

Raze is, surprisingly, thoughtfully quiet. When he speaks again, his tone is gentle. "No one should be forced to use magic if they don't want to. I should know."

I have to fight not to do a double take at him. There's real pain in his voice, and real sympathy, too. Raze was the absolute last person I expected to have on my side.

"Thank you." I hesitate, brushing the crumbled greenery away from the design in my palm. "I didn't mean to steal this, you know. I don't understand why it had to be me."

"Told you, I'm *lucky*." He laughs, surprising me again. Why isn't he taking this seriously? "No one knew it had to be a changeling, not even Leira. You just happened to be the only one there, and now you're stuck taking *this* shapeshifting idiot to the Fate-forsaken fortress my ancestors clearly didn't think through. Maybe by the time we get there I'll have decided whether I want to redeem my family legacy or burn it all to the ground."

I let his words settle over me. He clearly has a complicated connection to his family, and it doesn't seem like any of my business. I shouldn't say anything, because if I care about what he does in the end, then I'm going to have to start considering if we're doing the right thing.

Amusement lights his face. "What is it, Iselia? What are you thinking?"

I don't think he really cares what I'm thinking, because my opinion doesn't matter. I'm just a pawn—a pawn who is going to be handsomely rewarded when this whole cursed ordeal is over. I'm thinking I can't wait until Isolde and I have the Destiny to ourselves, because I just want everything to go back to normal. I'm thinking he's right, he *is* an idiot. In the end, I decide on, "Why would you tell me that?"

Raze actually pauses to think about it, and the only sound is the insects settling in for the night. "Because you can't possibly like me any less than you already do," he says eventually, still attempting to buoy his words with a lightness that feels forced. "So what do I have to lose?"

My face is turned from him, but I can sense how close he is now. I don't know whether to move away or pretend I don't care.

At least he isn't talking about my magic. *Dangerous*, I hear Isolde's voice say in the back of my mind, over and over. *Dangerous, dangerous, dangerous.*

Then another voice: *Good.*

I rub my hands together, pressing into the center of the compass to focus myself again.

Raze extends a hand toward me, like a question. Hesitantly, I place my left hand in his. He holds it carefully to the faint moonlight, like he's scared he'll break it. This is his first time really studying the compass, I realize.

I stare at my hand in his. "But why a changeling?"

"I don't know." Raze lets out a soft breath. "But I'd bet it has something to do with your magic. Maybe my ancestors wanted their descendants to have to work together with a faerie if they needed to access the treasure, for some reason. It seems...fair enough."

"It's not fair," I say, without thinking. But I don't pull away. I glare up at him, wanting him to see the damage all this has done to me. For the first time, I notice the faint splash of freckles on his nose and peppering his cheeks. "Not for me."

"No," he agrees softly, tracing the silvery design with featherlight fingertips. "Getting you involved was definitely a mistake." He gives me another diagonal half smile before letting my hand drop.

It's nice to agree on something for once.

chapter nineteen

That night, when I come inside and face Isolde, her jaw is clenched tight.

"Sol," I say quietly. They're right outside and probably not asleep yet. "I'm sor—"

"I know."

And that's the end of that conversation. Her tone is like scissors snipping through cloth, and everything I could have said to apologize, to beg her to try to understand, to seek comfort, is the frayed edge that unravels in its wake.

I manage to make it through most of the next day without talking about or using magic, though I can sense the conversation brewing at the back of Isolde's throat. She keeps giving me weird looks, like I'm a lock she'll be able to pry open if she just approaches from the right angle.

When we stop for the night, Olani gathers her things. Isolde's eyes go to the quarterstaff, and I think she's remembering their fight in the rain—how many close calls there were. But instead of flinching back, she says, "Do you think you could teach me a little? I've never fought anyone with a quarterstaff before."

Olani is all too eager to agree.

Raze and I sit as far as we can get from each other, watching Isolde and Olani spar. It's dusk with barely a sliver of yellow moon rising, but they seem to enjoy the extra challenge that comes with the darkness. This time, we've stopped in a field of heather, and I can still smell traces of the blooms long after their bright purple petals fade into the night. Autumn is finally allowing its cool breezes to be coaxed into the stuffy late-summer days, and it's actually chilly when the sun sets.

I can feel bumps rising on my skin and stiffness settling in. I shiver, wishing the fire was just a little warmer.

A rush of heat startles me. Bright yellow flames sear into the night, flaring up so high in response to my accidental call for warmth that, for a moment, it looks like Raze's whole face is encased in flame.

He shouts in alarm and throws himself back, landing hard on the ground with his arms and legs in the air like an overturned beetle.

"I'm so sorry!" Horror and surprise flood me, making my hands shake. I focus, and the fire goes back to tamely licking at the cool air. I swoop over him, heart in my throat, eyes wide. "I didn't mean to. I can't—" I stop. I'm not about to explain my problems with magic to an enchanter from one of the most famous magical families in the world. My heart pounds, waiting for him to move. I don't like Raze, but I'm not trying to burn him alive.

Thankfully, he's fine. His messy red hair flops over his face as he pushes himself back up, trying to look collected and dignified. Except—

Oh, Fate.

Oh, no.

The flames didn't burn his skin or hair, but they singed his eyebrows badly enough for it to be noticeable. They aren't... *completely* burned off, but the auburn hairs are definitely more sparse and missing in patches. It makes him look even more surprised.

I can't help it. I start to laugh.

Raze looks offended, and I can easily picture him as a hawk with his feathers ruffled around round eyes. I laugh harder.

"I'm sorry," I repeat through giggles. "Your...your eyebrows, Raze."

His hand flies to his face, fear widening his eyes. "My *eyebrows*?"

I can't help it. I howl with laughter, shaking so hard I almost fall over. "That's the best thing that's happened to me all week." A cough rattles my chest as I try to control myself. "It's—" I crack a smile, snorting. When I try to speak again, my voice pitches up higher with every word as I try not to laugh. "It's not *that* bad."

"Iselia, you better be joking."

"It was an accident!" I cry.

He narrows his eyes at me suspiciously, but a flickering smile plays across his face. *"Sure,"* he says, drawing the word out for a comically long time.

Another round of cackles shakes my chest. "I swear!"

A smile cracks his annoyed facade, and then he's laughing

with me. "Just tell me my dashing good looks aren't ruined. It's all I have left."

A snort breaks through the laughter, and I roll my eyes. "Trust me," I say, "you're *exactly* as attractive as you've ever been."

He pulls an exaggerated offended face, clutching at his chest. "Maybe give me a little warning before the next time you try to kill me. It would be appreciated." But then he's laughing, too, blushing as his hands run over the place where his eyebrows used to be.

Once we've ebbed back into silence, he gives me a measured look, like he's trying to decide whether to say something or not.

"Go ahead, Raze," I say with a sigh, a grin still twitching the corners of my mouth. "I'm not completely clueless. I can tell you're thinking something."

He still hesitates, lips quirking like he can't decide whether he's amused or not. Just when I think he's going to ignore me, he says, "You really can't control it?"

I stare into the fire until my eyes start to water, mouth pressed tightly shut. A crack in the distance draws my eyes up to the faint silhouettes of Isolde and Olani, attacking each other furiously.

"You're...very good," Raze says, more genuinely than he's ever spoken to me before. "It flows through you so easily."

I tilt my head. "What does?"

He seems surprised. "Magic. It... What *do* you know about it?"

My eyes slide over to him then, glowering. Paired with the shine reflecting off them, I imagine it's a very spooky effect. "I don't really *need* to be insulted, you know."

"No! I didn't mean..." He reaches out and touches my arm gently. I jerk away immediately. "I was actually asking."

"You just really sound like such an *ass*, Raze. Without even trying." I mean it, but a smile still finds its way briefly onto my face.

He scoffs, but I swear so rarely that he can't help the surprised delight creeping over his face. "Yes, and you'd never do anything to offend anyone."

This actually does feel like friendly teasing. I don't know where to go from there. In the silence, I scoot closer to the fire, hands held out to warm my stiff fingers.

"Enchanters aren't the source of our own magic," Raze says abruptly. "Just so you know. We're just able to…sort of…channel power. It comes from the faerie realms. Seelie or Unseelie. Depends which well you prefer to draw from."

"Oh." I keep staring at my fingertips, outlined by blazing orange light. I can almost imagine my left palm burning like a brand, even though I know it isn't any hotter than the other hand. "Good to know."

"Yours seems to come from the Seelie Realm naturally, but it's like your pull is so strong, both realms want to answer at once," he adds. I think I detect a hint of envy in his voice, but that can't be right. "There's only a certain amount of power anyone can draw on before they start to strain themselves, stealing magic they aren't meant to have. That's when the really nasty prices usually kick in. But you… It's like…it jumps to meet you, before you even have to call."

How could he possibly know that's what it feels like? "That's right," I say, surprised. "It's awful. I don't know…what I'm capable of. And it's terrifying."

A line of golden firelight cups Raze's face, outlining the soft, round form of his broad shoulders and torso, flickering in unison with his expression before he speaks. "I could teach you a little," he offers. "At least, the theory of it."

I meet his eyes briefly before tearing mine away. "No, thanks."

He leans forward a little. "I don't want to push you. I just thought, if you knew, maybe you wouldn't be so—"

I don't want to learn about this. I don't want to *be* this. Opening up to Raze, even a little, was a mistake. He'll never understand. I cut him off, voice sharper this time and barbed with sarcasm. "I really don't need you to tell me what to do, Raze. Thanks anyway."

After a disbelieving pause, he coughs out a humorless laugh. "Sure you don't. I'm sure you already know more about magic than we *mere mortals* ever could."

He's right.

The fire flares up again, but not because of the cold. That makes me even angrier. I get to my feet, fists clenched. "Have you ever stopped to think that maybe, *just maybe*, the reason I don't like you isn't because I'm a changeling but because *you're* unbearable?"

"Oh, you're one to talk about unbearable." His voice doesn't change much, but I can tell I've hit a nerve. There's something so infuriating about the way he remains seated, body relaxed even as we argue. Meanwhile, I feel like an instrument that's been strung too tight, screechy and about to snap.

"Is there a reason you think you're so much better than me?" I demand, not wanting to hear the answer. I already know.

Raze rolls his eyes. "I'm just trying to *help* you, Iselia."

"I don't need your help," I snap. "And I never will. Stop trying to be *nice* to me, Raze. It doesn't suit you."

"At least *I'm* trying!"

Raze and I exchange a glare hotter than the campfire between us, which is burning as furiously as it can despite almost being out of fuel. A wave of something angry and malicious comes over me, sweeping in a suspicion I've quietly been stewing over since yesterday, since Olani's teasing and the worried looks they exchanged over the limits of Raze's magic.

"You know what? I'd actually love for you to teach me."

"Oh?"

"Yeah. I'll do whatever you tell me, too. Just do one thing for me first. Shapeshift."

He frowns, sparks reflecting in his eyes. "What—?"

"Into anything except a bird."

Raze freezes. Suddenly, he seems like he doesn't know what to do with his hands.

"Go ahead," I say, already feeling guilty about the stinging words, but it's too late to stuff them back in. "A fox. A horse. Anything. Except. A. Bird."

Raze shakes his head and turns away from me, one hand reaching up to tug at his hair. His voice wavers with a laugh that isn't really a laugh. "You're really something, Iselia."

Without another word, his shape blurs into streaks of color. He shapeshifts into a hawk and takes flight. I watch the bird until it's swallowed up by the star-studded darkness.

"What's going on here?" says Isolde's voice behind me. In my anger, my vision and attention had narrowed to a spotlight on the object of my frustration, and I didn't even see her and Olani approach.

"Nothing," I spit. In response, the fire snuffs out, plunging us all into darkness, and I curse myself. "He'll be back eventually."

chapter twenty

Raze is still a hawk the next morning.

From the window, I can see him perched high above the Destiny in a crooked pine tree, wings tucked in comfortably. He doesn't look like he plans on coming down and joining us anytime soon.

Since no one wants to be the one to march up to a tree and start yelling at a bird, Isolde and I sit in the wagon, trying to seem like we aren't waiting for him. Olani, always restless, crouches just outside, next to the faded ashes of the fire. She's removed everything from her medicine bag and is reorganizing it, even though it was perfectly organized before.

I sit in my bunk silently with my back propped up against the wall, my bare feet skimming the floorboards, and my mind bubbling like an unwatched pot.

Who does Raze think he is? I don't need anyone to teach me anything about magic, least of all him. Despite the chaos my life has been thrown into recently, I don't plan to keep bouncing between life-threatening situations, and I don't want to rely on it.

"Did Raze say something to you?" Isolde asks eventually. She isn't pretending to polish her knives anymore—she's looking at me, trying to decipher my face.

I roll my eyes, glancing at the bird. "He's arrogant and obnoxious and thinks he's better than everyone else. Isn't that enough?"

My sister's mouth presses into a diagonal slash. "Okay… I just thought that…you know, you don't always understand people or what they're thinking. Oh, don't look at me like that. You know I'm right. Maybe if you let me help you, we can make this journey a little less painful for everyone."

My mouth drops open. "Help me? Why does everyone think I need help? Am I really that useless?"

"No one said you were useless. You're being difficult, Seelie." I wish she would sound angry, would match my rising pitch, but she just sounds resigned. It takes all the joy out of fighting with her.

My hands bunch the blankets into tight knots. "He wanted to talk about my magic. Just like everyone else. I know you've been waiting for the moment to strike."

Isolde makes a noise of disbelief, finally showing emotion in the curl of her lip. "Stop acting like a baby. You're being selfish and ridiculous, and honestly, even I don't know how to deal with you right now." Finally, she sounds angry. It… isn't what I hoped it would be.

"Then, don't!" I say, too quickly. I don't know *why* I'm

doing this. I just know that I don't feel like me, and I haven't for days now. A frustrated groan tears from between my teeth. "I hate this. I hate all of it. Why can't everyone just *leave me alone?*"

Her eyebrows draw together a little. When she speaks, it's slow and careful. "I care about you too much to let you hurt yourself by ignoring the problem we all know is there. We're all just trying to—"

"Let me guess," I interrupt, bitterness coating my tongue. *"Help me."*

Isolde takes a long, deep breath, as if to remind me how much patience it takes to put up with me. More angry words bubble up in my mind, but they can't find their way out. My mouth has forgotten how to let them. I stand, flick my braid over my shoulder, and step out to retrieve Raze without another look back at my sister.

The weather is infuriatingly lovely, the sky a dreamy, cloudless blue, and the sun kissing the earth with just the right amount of warmth. It settles golden on my skin, clashing with my gray mood.

"Good morning." Olani doesn't look up. She's settling the last glass vial into its carefully formed leather case, her touch incredibly gentle.

She must be getting used to me, because it doesn't seem to bother her that I don't reply.

Finally, as she rolls her medicine case up into its neat coil, she tilts her head up to meet my eyes. I look away quickly. She follows my gaze to the distant shape of Raze, nestled in the pine needles.

After a moment, Olani speaks again. "I've never seen him be a bird for this long."

"Hm."

"Someone should probably do something before he starts trying to eat raw mice."

I shrug. Maybe raw mice will do him some good.

She looks me over, then stands with a long, lazy stretch, pushing herself up with one hand on her quarterstaff. "I don't know you very well, but I'm pretty sure you're better than this."

That startles an offended sound from me. She's right—she *doesn't* know me.

Olani studies me in that odd, still way, like a big cat. The intensity of her gaze makes me squirm. "Listen, I don't care what you want. I've tried to be nice, your sister tried to help, and I don't know what happened with you and Raze last night, but he's doing his best, too. He probably understands how you feel about all this better than anyone. So you need to stop fighting everyone—and yourself—and try as hard as the rest of us to make this work."

I think that's the most I've heard Olani say at once, and it catches me so off guard it actually makes sense. I let out a sharp breath, willing myself not to burst into tears. I *have* been acting like a child, defiantly refusing help. I don't have to like my magic: I just have to coexist with it enough to guarantee I'm not going to catch anyone else on fire. What if it was Isolde next time? What if it was more than just Raze's eyebrows?

I've been treating them all like a cornered, snapping animal, ignoring the fact that my bites still bleed. I feel so flushed with shame it sends chills down my scarred arms.

Finally, I find my voice, quiet and raw. "Fine," I whisper.

"Great." Olani swings her staff through the air, letting it

rest at her side. Her whole face lightens, and just like that, I'm forgiven. "Lessons start today. Now, go apologize to Raze for whatever idiotic thing you said to him, so he can apologize for whatever idiotic thing he said to you." I let out a small protest, but she cuts me off. "You know, there's something I always used to do when my brothers fought."

"What?"

The corner of her mouth twitches up. "I told them they'd have to fistfight each other if they didn't sort it out."

Confusion scrunches my face. "Did they?"

"Hmm." Olani's mouth tilts in a rare smile. Then, without another word, she brushes past me and goes inside. She's joking. She must be joking—right?

A cool, silky breeze skims my face, teasing through the hair that always slips out of my braid to frame my face. I'm not sure if Olani was serious or not, but if it comes down to it, in a fistfight between me and a hawk, the hawk will win. For sure.

I ball up my hands and stare up at the hawk, willing him to come down.

He doesn't.

"Come on," I mutter, letting another long moment stretch. Eventually, I give in. My boots crunch in the grass as I march up to the base of the tree, already feeling absurd.

"Get down from there, Raze!" I shout.

The hawk ruffles its feathers, head swiveling to peer at me with bright yellow eyes.

"Come on, we need to get going! We don't have time for this right now!"

I really, really hope that this is Raze, and I'm not just shouting at an innocent hawk, but it's hard to tell. All birds kind of look alike. Or maybe he's overextended himself, and he's stuck like this now.

"You...you *can* still turn into a person, right?"

The hawk lifts its wings, shaking them with an indignant screech.

Okay, then.

This boy is going to be the end of me. My patience can't take much more of this. He's slowing us all down with his petty spite, and I can feel impatience bubbling just under the surface in the enchantment again. The wind kicks up around me, and I think back to our conversation last night.

There's a chance that I was being petty and spiteful, too. I'd taunted him the same way I've been taunted all my life for the seemingly simple things I just can't do. And even though Raze might be the actual bane of my existence, he doesn't deserve to be treated like that.

No one does.

I sigh, almost choking on my words. "Raze, I'm...sorry." My teeth grind together, but I keep going. "I had no right to say that to you. Will you *please* come down now?"

For a second, I think he's ignoring me. Or maybe this really is just a regular hawk. Then he swoops to the ground, transforming back into himself just in time to land with a solid thump.

He studies me thoughtfully, and I study him back. I have to tilt my chin to look up at him, but I stand there, unflinching as I meet his eyes in half-second intervals.

There are leaves in his hair, I think as I wait for him to speak.

Which, it's starting to seem, will never happen. Maybe he was a hawk so long he's forgotten how.

Fate, I can only hope.

"Me...also," he rasps, crushing my dreams.

"What?"

Raze clears his throat, settling his weight onto his other foot. "I am also...that. Sorry. For...what I said to you."

I stare at him, waiting for the *but*...

When it doesn't come, I nod once. "Accepted."

"Likewise."

We stand facing each other for another moment, just barely close enough for me to feel his presence in an uncomfortable prickle on my skin. Is he going to say something else? What is he waiting for?

"We should go," I say sharply, turning away. "We don't want to lose our lead. I promised Olani I'd start magic lessons today."

I'm already walking, but with his much longer stride, he catches up easily. "Iselia?"

What is it *now*? Wasn't one apology enough? My eyes flick over to him in response.

Just in time to catch a grin slipping over his weary features. "Did you miss me?"

I roll my eyes. "Shut up."

But this time, I smile, too.

The magic lessons aren't that bad at first.

The first day, it feels almost like we're having a normal conversation while Isolde fidgets behind the wheel. They tell me about how they tap into their magic, about what they do with it, and what it feels like for them to channel it. At first, just talking about magic makes it jump within me, so I get quiet and stiff and try to focus on pushing it back down.

After a while, it settles down a little. I can talk about it in short, awkward bursts, interrupted occasionally by a terrible joke from Raze—who, unfortunately, finds himself hilarious. No one else laughs.

Three days pass before I have to actually start using my magic. We drive long into the night at a punishing pace, trying to keep our lead, and when I crawl out from refueling the Destiny, Isolde and the others ambush me. They sit me down by our small campfire and tell me to let the magic still pulsing under my skin bubble up. Not to summon it, but to calmly wait for it and see what form it takes. It's too much to ask of me.

That night, I dream of a pale, faraway form beckoning me closer. His face is blurred, but I know him: the guide, he called himself, the voice of whatever magic transferred from the compass to me. I try to approach, but he never gets any closer. The wind whispers something in a voice that chills me to my core, words I can't remember the next morning.

I do my best to forget about all of it.

Each day is a little less quiet than the last as my sister slips into familiarity with our traveling companions, even as the uneasy awareness that we're most likely still being followed hangs over all of us. I add to the conversation when I have to, and I faithfully allow myself to be ordered around during my lessons, but getting along isn't easy for me like it is for Isolde. She and Olani can swap stories for hours, and before long, she's laughing along with Raze's horrible jokes and trying to one-up them.

Isolde and I take turns at the wheel, and when she isn't driving, she and Raze take to playing cards. Their games always last either a suspiciously long or suspiciously short time, which leads me to believe they're both cheating.

Sometimes, Raze shapeshifts so we all have a little more space. The hawk seems to be his favorite form, but he also takes turns as a raven, a sparrow, and, on one memorable night when he and Isolde have passed around the flask a few too many times, something called a *toucan*. I quietly note that each time he switches back and forth between animal and human form, it seems to wear him out.

As we travel farther inland, the terrain smooths into rolling hills, and the trees around the roads and towns grow taller and closer together. We do our best to skirt around civilization and avoid notice as much as possible.

Just as she promised, Olani gives me an ointment that I rub over the marks on my arms every night after I've practiced my magic enough to satisfy them. She even seems truly sorry that it doesn't seem to help. If anything, the marks get worse, and eventually I just have disgusting blisters that my dress doesn't quite cover, tracing over my arms and chest from fingertip to fingertip. By then, I'm *hoping* for scars.

"Do you think you could teach me to do that shield thing?" I ask tentatively one day, watching the scars move and flex with my arms. It's just the three of us in the Destiny, Raze kicked out to give us a moment of privacy.

Olani seems surprised that I asked. Her lips press together as she finishes screwing the top on a jar, thinking. "I don't know… I couldn't figure it out until I'd mastered most of my healing spells."

Isolde leans in from her spot on her bunk, feet kicking in the air. "So it's healing magic?"

"Same principles." She pauses, as if she wants to say more

but isn't sure how much. Eventually, she settles on, "My old-est brother invented the technique."

Olani talks about her family so rarely. I know it's a tender wound, but I can't help asking, "And...he's a healer?"

She nods. "The only one who could get me to practice. He and I are the most similar. It made lessons bearable."

Isolde springs down from the bunk, lands lightly, and starts to carefully wind up a roll of freshly washed bandages. "What was so wrong with your lessons?"

"I just don't like magic. Sitting still. Being thoughtful and precise all the time. It doesn't suit me. And healing—it's kind of my family's whole deal. My parents literally met as appren-tices to the same apothecary. Then my brothers all took after them. And then...there was me."

I nod. "I know how it feels to be the odd one out."

Olani's mouth tilts. "They tried not to make me feel that way. Not that they really succeeded, but they did try."

Isolde pauses, placing the bandages in Olani's hand as deli-cately as a butterfly finding a spot to land. "Is that why you left?"

Olani's fingers close around the bandages, and she lets out a deep sigh. "No. Yes. Kind of." She holds Isolde's gaze for a moment before her attention returns to stocking her medi-cine bag. "I had to choose an apprenticeship. I sort of...told them that I did. As far as they're concerned, I'm still under the wing of a healer back in Auremore."

My jaw drops.

Isolde gasps. "Wait, they don't know what you do?"

"Well...not exactly. I'm going to tell them! After I..." She hesitates, breathing slowly. "...Make it. I know if I told them the truth now, they'd just say that adventuring isn't a career."

Isolde's head tilts. "Is it?"

Olani laughs, a short, musical sound. Her eyes roam the Destiny, the misty landscape outside. "You tell me."

Every evening before my lessons, Olani and Isolde spar until they're either too bruised or too exhausted to keep going, and Raze and I bicker around a fire. We can't seem to help it; even when we try to get along, everything I say rubs him the wrong way, and his personality is just as naturally irritating to me.

For the first time in my life, there's distance between Isolde and me. The only time I feel like I can speak freely with her is immediately before we go to bed and I collapse into my bunk for a few restless hours of sleep riddled with bizarre dreams of the same pale figure. Even then, I hold back. I'm exhausted from the nervousness that comes with nonstop human contact and the constant effort it takes to rein in the magic that wants so badly to run me over.

I even miss Birch, who overcomes his initial shyness to let both of them pet his sleek fur. He's never let anyone but Isolde and me do that before. The injustice is staggering.

I whisper all of this into the blackness as I lie awake, tracing circles in my left palm and staring sightlessly up at the underside of her bunk.

After a pause, I feel a light *thump* against my shoulder. Isolde reaches down and takes my hand in hers.

"Once you get through this, you can start over," she whispers. "You can make it back to Mami and Papa."

I squeeze her hand back, but I'm not so sure. Isolde just takes all this in stride. Why can't I?

It isn't fair.

The autumn rain returns with a vengeance, dumping

oceans of water on the foothills as we make our way closer
to the Western Range. I've never been this far from home before, and I don't know if it's unfamiliarity in the air or some
sort of lingering magic. It *feels* different here, somehow. Instead of being rounded and soft, the mountains are hard and
sharp, staring down from imposing white peaks. I notice the
shape of a town on the horizon, and since I've never been
here before, it's not until we get closer that I realize that it's
crumbling and abandoned.

The energy within the wagon changes as we all realize that
the road cuts straight through the ghost town, and then again
when we realize that it's not just a ghost town, it's a ghost
city that was once the size of Auremore, and then yet again as
night starts to fall and we're still rumbling past empty stone
husks of buildings overgrown with weeds.

It doesn't feel like Revelnox, like the veil between worlds
is thin here. Whatever happened in this place happened a
long time ago, so long that rabbits scamper around fearlessly
through the pouring rain and deer swivel their heads to watch
us pass.

If they feel safe here, we probably are, too.

"See that building up ahead?" Isolde asks. Even though
we're surrounded by buildings, none of us can be snarky about
it, because we all know which one she means. It's a soaring
outline with most of a roof still intact over the empty shells
of high, arching windows, big enough to fit several houses
inside. "I vote we stop for the night in there. It'll give us shelter from the rain, so we're not all crammed in here all night."

Olani's lips tighten. "Doesn't this place creep you out?"

"No, I'm with Isolde," Raze says, so quickly his words clip

the end of hers. His arms are crossed over his chest, and he's staring very hard out the window.

Olani's eyes meet mine, which dart away to focus on the hair piled on top of her head. If I agree with her, we'll have to figure out a tiebreaker of some kind, and I don't like our odds against my sister and Raze. Besides, even though it's a little eerie, I don't think there's anything here that can harm us. "It's safe," I say, and that decides it.

The building is just as beautiful close-up as from a distance, even in the fading light. There were probably heavy wooden doors in the front once, but they're long gone, so we can easily drive right through the enormous entrance. There's enough space to park at least a dozen Destinys on a floor that was once stone but is now claimed by moss and errant wildflowers peeking between the cracks. A staircase to one side leads up to a balcony, but it's missing several steps near the top, which sit in a crumbled heap underneath.

I can still faintly hear the rain landing on the roof at least a hundred feet above us, drawing my eye up to rafters draped with climbing plants. The roof is solid enough to shelter our campfire but riddled with plenty of holes to let the smoke out. As Isolde builds a fire and Olani and I work on preparing food, I start to worry about just how long our supplies will last. We make an incredibly generic-tasting stew that is mostly cabbage and potatoes, with a bit of leftover bacon fat to keep it from being so sad we have to season it with our tears. At least we still have leftover bread from yesterday to make it stretch a little further.

"This is nice," Isolde says, blowing softly on her steaming bowl. The words seem a little too generous.

Raze looks around, tilting his head back to the shadowy

roof over our heads. "I wonder what this place used to be," he says, voice surprisingly solemn and thoughtful through a mouthful of bread.

The rest of us go quiet, but it's different from the companionable dinner-munching quiet it was a second ago. *What this place used to be?*

Maybe it's silly, but empty, crumbling buildings like this have been a part of my world my entire life. They're so long-abandoned, so lifeless, that I've never thought about them as places where people once lived. But, of course, people must have lived here. People who built this place, spent their days here, and, at some point, fled as it was destroyed.

I think that Isolde and Olani are having the same moment of self-reflection. How could we have never wondered this before? And what does Raze know that we don't?

"Is it really awful that I've never thought about that before?" Isolde asks, head tilting.

Raze wipes his mouth with the back of his hand. "Thought about what?"

"What places like this used to be," Olani says, head tipping back to follow the curve of the ceiling. It's dark enough now that we can't really see all the way into the eaves.

"And what happened to them," I add, staring down at my plate.

Isolde stretches both legs out in front of her, leaning back. "I mean, this place has obviously been empty since before our great-great-grandparents were born, but still. You'd think someone would talk about it."

Raze looks genuinely confused now. "People don't talk about it?" It takes me a second to remember that he was raised by Leira Wildfall, in Wildline Manor, and probably had a vastly different upbringing from the rest of us simple small-town folk, including education.

"What is there they should be talking about?" Olani says.

"The War of the Realms?" Raze says, as if that should be obvious. We all just keep looking at him blankly. "Five hundred years ago? No, maybe six hundred? Somewhere in there."

Isolde makes a *No, obviously not, dummy* kind of expression with her face, which is a genuinely impressive use of nonverbal communication.

"Spill," Olani commands, leaning in like she's waiting for Raze to tell a story.

He still looks puzzled, but he's back to munching on bread again. "Huh. Maybe we spent extra time on it because of my family's…heavy involvement. And also because the kinds of places that would have kept records on this kind of thing were destroyed."

"By *what*?" I push, because honestly, he could talk forever without getting to the point.

Raze takes a deep breath and settles back, eyes focusing on a distant point like he's trying to figure out where to start. "Okay," he says eventually. "So way back when, cities like Auremore belonged to larger territories, which had superpowerful monarchs and alliances and trade deals and all that good stuff. Which, I mean, you probably knew. And people and faeries could go back and forth between worlds without it being a huge deal, and faeries were generally way more involved in our world.

"Um, then there was this rogue faerie who got a bunch of supporters together and rebelled against the Unseelie and Seelie Courts. They were going to take over the Mortal Realm, so they tried to force magic to flow through our world, and it tore apart cities with pure Unseelie chaos instead. All over, there were storms and earthquakes and fires and whatnot. Neither of the faerie courts liked that—and neither did the people who, you know, lived here. So finally, the humans and faeries ended up allying to defeat them." His face colors a little. "My ancestors, apparently, led the charge. On the human side, at least."

"And then what happened?"

He shrugs. "I guess we won, since we're still here. They tried to put things back the way they were, but...the world was never the same after that. Therefore...places like this." He finishes with a grand gesture that encompasses everything in our surroundings.

"And that's when the worlds were sealed off from each other," Isolde says, understanding dawning in her voice.

"Well, mostly," I add, thinking of the spots where it's all too easy to slip between one realm and another.

"Basically," Raze says. "I got a variation of that lesson every year, except it always lasted, like, a week, and I never paid that close attention. So yeah. Something like that."

I feel my brows scrunch together as I look up at him. "Why doesn't everyone know about this?"

"That's what I'm saying!" he laughs, in a way that is directed specifically at me and makes me feel uncomfortably close. I don't like agreeing with Raze on anything.

"The world moves on," Olani says with a shrug. "Things that happened five hundred years ago leave an imprint on the world, but does knowing what left the imprint really change anything?"

No, I suppose it doesn't. It's strange to think about a world I never lived in, a world destroyed so thoroughly that its remains are unquestioned and ordinary. But knowing doesn't change anything.

"Fate, Olani, that's heavy," Isolde complains.

Olani points at Raze. "*He's* the one talking about the destruction of civilizations like it's last week's gossip!"

"It's something everyone should know!" he says defensively.

Isolde laughs, throwing her head back. "I would like to formally recommend that we all start bullying Raze for being a spoiled little rich boy, just to keep him humble."

"Recommendation noted and seconded," I say quickly, giggling a little at Raze's betrayed expression.

"Then, I guess we're all agreed." Olani nods.

"Hey!" We all make a big show of pretending to ignore him, which is very funny until he stands and stretches and says, "Iselia, this is your most blatant attempt to get out of magic lessons yet, and frankly, I'm disappointed in you two for falling for it." Suddenly, they all turn on me, in the same joking way we were allied against Raze, but less fun now that I'm on the other end of it.

"I'm not trying to—" I cut myself off, because that would be a lie.

"Enough stalling," Olani says, collecting our empty bowls one by one into a wobbly stack. "I'll handle all the dishes if you just do it without complaining."

I'm not going to get a better bargain than that, so I accept my fate.

Olani worked with me first, but her use of magic was mostly limited to healing, which I didn't have the talent for. I was too scared to really try, in case I accidentally caused *more* damage while trying to mend a small cut on my sister's knuckles.

After that, Raze took over. We haven't made much progress, but he's a better teacher than Olani, who (despite all her virtues) lost patience with me almost immediately.

He tries coaching me through a series of exercises that mostly involve deep breathing and guiding the wind around the building's echoing interior, but I'm too afraid of blasting a hurricane-level gale that will send this whole thing crashing down around us. Each of my breezes snuffs out before making a full lap around the room, but he won't let me stop, won't stop being relentlessly enthusiastic and encouraging.

Finally, when I can barely hear anything except the blood rushing in my ears, I let the wind slam into his face as I release it with a frustrated sound. He tries to say something to make it okay, but I just turn my back and sit heavily on the Destiny's steps. Isolde and Olani have been watching this whole ordeal from the stage, and they both stare down at me with similar worried expressions.

"This isn't working," Isolde says.

I don't say anything but look up slowly and blink in what I hope is a sarcastic way. Of course it isn't working. I'm not *meant* for this.

Raze puts one hand on his hip. The other scratches his head with complete disregard for the mess it makes of his hair. "Maybe we should try another approach. Look at her, she's miserable."

I don't appreciate being talked about in the third person when I'm right here, but he has a point. I've never been able to learn anything when I'm upset, and it seems that slinging balls of fire is no different from addition or lacing my boots.

Olani leans back, giving me space to breathe as she folds her arms over her chest. "When I was learning how to heal, my parents—" She breaks off for a moment, measuring her words like she always does when speaking of her family. "They used to make me focus on happy memories. What about you, Raze?"

His eyes glaze over for a second—less than a second—and then he's back. "I used to sing." A smile steals over his face, but his eyes go distant, like he can see the memory playing out in front of him. "When I was really young, I had to sing to shape-shift. The first time I did it, I didn't even know I could. One moment I was inventing a song about the creek I was jumping over, and the next I was a sparrow. It was very disorienting."

Laughter erupts in the echoing space, and even I giggle along at the thought of a little rosy-cheeked, ginger-haired boy suddenly finding himself a very confused and upset songbird.

"What about you, Seelie?" Olani asks, before the warmth of our laughter fades. "What makes you happy?"

I have to think a second, to push aside the past few weeks, months, years. It's all so heavy, so hard to fight through to find the moments of light.

Moments of light.

"Baking," I announce, surprising even myself a little. "I used to bake with my father all the time. And then…just for Isolde and myself. It's relaxing."

Isolde and Olani clear a path for Raze to gently steer me up the stairs, through the open door. "Then, go do that."

I freeze, stiff, with all my muscles locked, so he can't push me. "And then you'll make me do more magic?"

"Then we can talk."

We have everything I need—well, not everything, but I

can make do. Birch has deigned to provide me with a block of chocolate the size of my head, half a dozen fresh eggs, and a cold bottle of milk. I say a silent apology to whoever's pantry they've disappeared from, but it's hard to feel too sorry for them with all the possibilities racing through my head.

Chocolate's a given. But should I swirl it into a bread, melt it into a mousse, or chop it up and fold it into little biscuits? No, something else. Something new. The recipe comes to me like a burst of sunlight through the clouds, the clearest my head has felt in ages. I can combine a few recipes I've made in the past into something totally new and experimental and delicious. Something that feels as warm and cozy as the inside of the Destiny when it's glowing with firelight and friendly chatter.

I busy myself setting out the ingredients and preparing the oven, letting the noise of the others fade into the background behind me.

At least, until Raze's voice breaks through, and I realize he's standing over me. "Can I help?"

"That's really not necessary."

"Then, I guess I'll just watch," he says, leaning his forearms on the counter. With him bent in half like this, we're at eye level. But also, he's in my way.

"You know, I don't need you looking over my shoulder." The warmth in my tone takes the bite out of the words, and I elbow him out of my workspace. Most of the rare occasions that we've touched have been in training or by accident. This is casual and unnecessary, and he humors me by moving at the slight nudge. Oh, Fate, I guess we *have* somehow evolved to friendly teasing.

"I won't get in the way," he promises. I don't believe him.

His head tilts as he surveys the ingredients I've pulled out. "Don't you need the flour? I can get it down for you if Birch put it up too high."

"We'll probably need it more when we're farther up in the mountains. The cocoa powder and whipped eggs should give it enough structure without wasting flour, anyway." I line everything up parallel, adjusting corners and distances until they're all evenly spaced in the order I'm going to need them.

Before Raze can say anything else, the door opens. Olani's head pokes in, braids that have fallen loose from the knot on top of her head swinging. "Raze, can you come outside for a moment?" she asks, gaze switching quickly between the two of us.

"Why? I told you I don't want to be target practice again. Or a demonstrating-where-pressure-points-are dummy, or—"

"We need you to settle an argument," Isolde's voice calls from outside, in the rhythm of when she's telling a lie. My senses go on alert. Are we in danger? Has Leira caught up? But then I realize how relaxed Olani looks, and as if that isn't enough, she winks at me with most of her face: it's a harmless lie, just to get him outside. To give me a moment to myself.

Raze sighs, pushing himself up and ruffling his hair through his fingers with a stretch. "Well, if you insist." His gaze meets mine one more time before he scoots past Olani, and he smiles.

The returning smile on my lips doesn't fade as my eyes drop to Olani's. *Thank you*, I mouth.

You're welcome, she replies, and when the door closes after her, I feel like we've formed some kind of alliance.

I settle into the rhythm of baking—wet then dry, whisk then fold—and the rain outside and the fire in the hearth form a soothing blankness. My mind clears.

And then I have to light the stove to melt the chocolate, and as the fire sparks, I'm thinking about my magic again. I could do that with magic. I *should* do that with magic. I should be practicing every chance I get, since I promised to get this thing within me under control.

But I don't want to. I don't want to be the changeling enchanter who summons storms and flings fireballs. I just want to make my parents proud, to feel the comfort of family and home. I want to make cakes somewhere cozy, where no one has any expectations of me, and be left alone.

My feelings get the better of me, and I don't even realize that my magic is flaring up until the flame under the pot of water my bowl of chocolate is nestled in turns bright blue and blazing hot. The water boils quickly, bubbling over the sides. I jump back and pull my chocolate away, cursing quietly as I fight to get the burner back under control.

Maybe magic is what I'm meant to do. It's getting warm in the cramped wagon, and I wipe tiny beads of sweat away from my face with a forearm that may or may not be smeared with chocolate. Maybe I'm only fooling myself, thinking that I could ever do anything else, when my magic is such a deeply woven part of myself.

But if this is what I'm meant for, *why can't I control it?*

At least I can control my cake. Once the chocolate is silky smooth, I set it aside to cool down for a moment so it doesn't cook the eggs I'm whisking into the sugar. There's a little coffee leftover from this morning, and I add it to the mixture in place of water or milk, for a little extra depth. At least with this, I know what I'm doing. Which makes sense, since I've been practicing my baking skills since I was too small to see above the counter without standing on a chair.

Something clicks into place so suddenly that I gasp just as a puff of cocoa lands in the wet ingredients. I stand perfectly still over the bowl for a moment, mind racing. I've been practicing baking my whole life. When I was young, I wanted to add things out of order, to throw together ingredients that I know now would never work. Papa guided me through, letting me ruin it when I had to, but always giving me the chance to try again. Eventually, I figured out which flavors went with which, and the common kind of alchemy that makes a cake rise or go flat. Once I knew the rules, I could experiment again.

Just like I'm doing now. The batter already smells wonderful, thanks mostly to the melted chocolate. I keep folding it together automatically.

What if magic isn't something that's been forced on me but something I need to develop? What if magic is like baking, and I have to do it again and again and let myself mess up before it's something I can control and predict?

What if I've been looking at this all wrong?

chapter twenty-one

After another week, the ground starts sloping up again, soft meadows and forest giving way to sharp, cold rock.

When I study the compass for direction, it seems to sense that I'm looking at it. Every once in a while, it spins, just for attention, before continuing to point to its target. We're getting close—and I still don't really know what that means.

The Destiny rumbles over the stony road, shaking everything inside and making our teeth chatter. It already feels like fall in the mountains, with the occasional hot, dry wind to remind us what lies on the other side of the peaks. Sunlight filters through leafy stained-glass windows, turning green and gold and red as it strikes the path. Even the air smells different.

The first time we pass one of the signs, it's a shock: a hand-painted wooden post warning us to turn back, that we're entering active faerie territory. Everything falls silent until we're no longer in its shadow.

Soon, the fiery-hued leaves give way to bristly pine needles. The evergreens are so tall I have to tilt my head all the way back to see where they brush the sky.

I wring my hands, massaging my left palm, a new habit I can't seem to help.

"How much longer?" Olani asks, looking up from a game of cards at which Isolde is now openly cheating.

I don't turn, keeping my eyes on the road, my hands on the wheel. "I don't know." I've tried not to think about it. There's so much unknown—so many dangerous possibilities—that it might be better to be blindsided. Or maybe we should just talk about it. "You really don't know anything else about where we're going, do you?"

Raze waves his hand aristocratically. "Depends what you mean by *know*."

"I mean *know*."

"Ah. Well, in that case—no. We don't exactly *know*." He's standing over my shoulder, studying a map on which we've tried to replicate Leira's scrawls from memory, and his shadow is starting to make me uncomfortable.

"Delightful," I say lightly, offering him a sideways glance with my lips pinched tight together, curving less than one degree up at the corner.

We've reached a fragile understanding of one another, and even though he still makes me want to pull my hair out, it makes me feel a little better to know that it isn't intentional. Not usually, at least. We've even managed to cut the squabbling down to one good fight a day or so.

We park the Destiny next to one of the hand-painted warning signs when the sky is still pink and orange, indigo-dipped at the edges. It feels like the sign is staring at me with its drips of faded paint reading *TRAVELER BEWARE: FAERIE CIRCLE*, accompanied by an arrow pointing into the forest.

I breathe in the sweet, sharp smell of pine as we build a fire and make camp.

We don't have enough room to store enough food to feed four people for very long, especially since two of them are twice Isolde's and my size. We're down to the last of the dried foods, and that would worry me if I didn't have so many bigger worries on my plate. As Olani scrapes a second serving of spiced rice and beans from the bottom of our biggest pot, I hand the last of my bowl to Isolde. She's been hungrily watching me push it unenthusiastically around the bottom of my bowl, and I've lost my appetite, anyway.

"Are you sure?" she says, even though she's already digging her spoon in. We're pretending everything's fine, but I can feel the distance between us like a pebble in my shoe.

I don't respond. Instead, I watch Raze trying to set up a makeshift target on the other side of the fire. "Is this really necessary?" I sigh, pulling my knees up to my chest.

"You promised to practice," Isolde says with her mouth full.

Raze looks over from where he's attempting to balance a wobbly empty bottle on a not-quite-flat rock. Despite the chill in the air up here, he's shed his coat, and his shirt sleeves are rolled up to his elbows, showing off his freckly forearms. "Practice doesn't end until we're all sure you can fight off whatever enchanter Leira sends next without blowing the rest of us off the face of the mountain, Iselia," he calls. "Now, get over here so we can get started."

I've become used to the way he calls me by my full name. It was annoying at first, but now it feels an inside joke—a reverse nickname. One I don't really like but don't resent enough to fight with him about stopping. Now that I think about it, though, I don't think I've ever actually heard Raze use my chosen name.

"I have everything under control," I whine, even though I'm already standing, brushing invisible dust off my rust-orange skirt.

"You're a terrible liar," Olani says through a mouthful of rice, watching me smugly from her comfortable spot by the fire.

"You're a terrible *person*," I shoot back, grinning.

Isolde snorts. "She's not *wrong*, Seelie. You were always getting us in trouble."

"*You?* In trouble?" Raze meets me halfway, pointing out the spot where he wants me to stand to take aim at the bottle. "Now, *that* I find hard to believe." He folds his arms. "So what'll it be?"

I stand at his mark in an imitation of the fighting stance Isolde taught me, hands reaching in front of me, palms-out. "I told you," I say. "I'm not doing lightning. Not unless I have to. It's too dangerous." A cold breeze snakes over my exposed skin, chilling the branched, pink scars and raising goose bumps, as if to prove my point. "And I don't see why we have to do this at all. Once we find the Mortal's Keep, I'm never going to need to use magic again."

"Never took you for an optimist," Olani says.

Isolde sighs, launching into the same speech I've already memorized. "We don't know what we're going to find in there, and we need to be prepared. And if Leira's people catch up with us—"

I can't even entertain that thought without getting light-headed. "That's not going to happen. And besides, Raze, *you* can't do any of this stuff, and you're fine. Why should I?"

He scowls, mouth opening to offer a vicious retort. Then he pauses, and his face changes. "Excellent attempt to change the subject. You almost had me there. Go ahead, then, and remember what we talked about."

What we talked about, I repeat silently, face scrunching in disgust. Raze had gone on and on about how he manages to coax magic to flow to him, but that isn't my problem. I *wish* I had a hard time tapping into my power.

The real problem is that it's overeager, and I overcompensate for that by shoving it down, and when the magic finally does boil over into the Mortal Realm, it's already beyond my control. It works better when I'm fighting, but I have to find some way to control it before it'll be remotely safe for anyone to even attempt sparring with me.

I take a deep, slow breath, letting my world narrow to the bottle several paces away. Smudged green glass, bouncing an emerald-colored shadow onto the rock beneath. Unsurprisingly, it makes me feel nothing.

It's harder to sense my magic when I'm not emotional. I reach blindly, hoping I won't pull too deep and release a flood of enchantment.

There. It tugs in my chest, and I feel a burst of energy. I coax out the part of myself that responds when I call, desperate for a gasp of air after so long below the surface. For any release.

Yes!

No, I tell my magic, reining it back to the tips of my fingers. *Less.* I ball my hands into fists and then stretch out my fingers again, sliding the magic into balance. Into a focused concentration of what *I* want it to be.

I'll start with a breeze. I'll try not to remember Aris's green eyes going glassy as the breath left her lungs. This time, instead of a raging storm, I'll make it something precise, wielded as intentionally as Isolde wields her blades. A burst of wind rushes forward, skimming happily under my palms.

On the rock, the bottle wobbles, but it doesn't explode or crash over or anything exciting that would have us picking fragments of glass out of our faces for weeks.

I let out a cry of triumph, pumping my fist in the air. Everyone else cheers half-heartedly. I mean, I know it wasn't spectacular, but I thought that was better than actually smashing the bottle. It was *control.*

"What's wrong?" I turn to my audience—Raze less than half a step behind me, Isolde and Olani still sitting by the fire.

They all hesitate, meeting each other's eyes, then mine, then the rocks behind me.

Finally, Isolde speaks. "I think we just expected a little... *more.*"

Olani scrapes the bottom of her bowl, her face scrunched with concentration. "You're a very powerful enchanter, Seelie."

Raze frowns. "A refreshing breeze is nice and all, Iselia, but...it's not going to help anyone in a fight. I can tell you're holding back. You're still scared of your power."

My left hand curls in the folds of my skirt, and my jaw clenches tight. "Well, wouldn't *you* be?"

He studies me carefully, pushing his messy hair away from his face. "You have no idea what I'd give to have what you do." His words are bitter and jealous but delivered in a dissolving package of sugary cheerfulness, which strikes me harder than if he'd yelled at me.

My face warms, and I hope the blush won't show up in the dark. "I don't want to *hurt* anyone."

Isolde crosses her arms, leaning forward. "Well, you might have to."

"Especially not any of you." I stare at my sister as the words escape, refusing to even glance at Olani or Raze. I don't care how they react. "For Fate's sake, look at me." I hold my arms out and pull up a sleeve to reveal more of my scarred skin. It's still sinking in for me that this isn't going to heal, not the way it was before, and the sight makes my stomach turn. "It's all fun and games, knocking over bottles and trying to bend magic to my will, until something like *this* happens to one of you. It's not—" My voice breaks. I take a deep breath, swallowing the heavy silence, and try again. "It's not worth it. *I'm* not worth it."

Silence. The howling of the wind between the peaks is growing more inhuman with each inch the sun falls in the sky.

Olani is the first to speak. "Is that really what you think?"

I'm not like her or Isolde. I'm not a warrior, and I never will be. What I am is a danger, just as much to myself and everyone I want to defend as to our enemies. Besides, I remind myself, I don't *want* to be a warrior. I don't want to hurt anyone.

Too late for that.

I bury my face in my hands, blinking away tears that rudely try to force their way up my throat. I just want all this to be over.

But I've already said that so many times, I don't want to hear it again.

Raze sighs, and I feel a brush of warmth as he edges closer. Gently, he pulls my hands away from my face, forcing me to look up at him.

"Look," he says, bending down so I won't have to stretch my neck to see his face. I can't meet his eyes, so I alternate between his almost-grown-back-in eyebrows and over his shoulder. "You're doing fine. We shouldn't have put so much pressure on you. Just…try it again." He gives my hands a squeeze before releasing them. "We're all here for you. You don't have to be afraid."

I look into his eyes for the space of a heartbeat. "That's exactly what I'm afraid of," I reply. But I turn around, focusing once more on the bottle.

"You've got this!" Olani encourages.

"Yeah!" Isolde whoops, voice echoing off the rocks. "That's my *sister*!"

I breathe out a shaky laugh, reaching for my magic. This time, I don't try telling it exactly what to be. I don't pull it back as it rushes forward. I just give it direction, a nudge.

Heat washes over my hands. The force of it almost knocks me down, but I push back against it. My magic is free to go, but it is *not* free to rule over me.

This time, my enchantment takes the form of a small, bright yellow ball of flame that envelops the bottle before extinguishing in a flash behind it.

The glass cracks, bursting in on itself with a *crunch* and a whine.

I let my hands flop to my sides, small drops of cold sweat breaking out on my brow. I'm shaking, but I'm fine. We're all fine. For once, I mastered my magic and not the other way around.

So why is there a coil of disappointment lingering at the back of my neck, the impulse to set the forest ablaze lingering in my outstretched fingertips? I pull my hands back to my sides quickly, even as that voice whispers, *Do it. Stop this farce of* control *and embrace it.*

Everyone stares at me in varying degrees of shock.

"Better?" I say pointedly, ignoring the tremble of my voice.

The tide of their excitement washes over me, covering the eerie sound of the wind and floating my anxieties away. I know I can't afford to lose my worries forever. My cautious streak is the only thing that's kept me alive this long. But for a moment, it feels good to pretend.

chapter twenty-two

Once I finish practice for the night, Raze and Olani head off in the opposite direction of the warning sign to look for somewhere they can refill our dwindling water supplies, leaving me and Isolde alone for the first time in what feels like forever. She sits thoughtfully on the Destiny's steps, knees curled up to her chin, and I crawl below to refuel its magic.

I unlatch the box carefully, letting my fingertips linger over its lovingly detailed brass. There isn't an inch of the wagon, even down here where no one can see, where effort was spared. I can't wait to show it to my father one day.

The thought surprises me, even though it's not the first time I've had it. Papa loves beautiful, well-made things—the more practical, the better. He could wax poetic about a perfectly made bowl for hours. But I stopped daydreaming about what it would be like to be reunited over a year ago, because it felt too distant and it hurt too much.

"I'm excited," I blurt, voice muffled by the wagon's underside. "I… I still hate all of this. But it's starting to feel real. Like we can really do this."

Isolde lets out a short, surprised laugh. "Who are you, and what have you done with my sister?"

"I'm serious!" I laugh back. "I forgot what it's like to feel *good* about the future. But, Sol, if we do this—and I know that's a big *if*—it's not just going to be a daydream. It's going to be real. I can't wait to show Papa the Destiny. We'll have to find a house with a stable or something where we can keep it, and hopefully it won't get too mad at us for not living in it full-time, but he'll be *so excited*. He'll want to take the whole thing apart and figure out how it works, but also be too scared to mess with any of the detail. We can take it out for trips." I pause, realizing how long that string of words was, and that I somehow got through all of it without her interrupting.

Isolde still doesn't respond. A nightingale, late for the season, sings in the silence.

"Won't that be perfect?" I add, trying to mask the uncertainty creeping over my face. Not that she can see more than my boots, anyway, with the rest of me tucked in the dark space beneath the wagon.

"He'll love it," she says, finally.

I crawl out from under the Destiny, my fingertips still tingling from the refueling. At the pace we've been guzzling magic, it's become part of my routine every other night, but no matter how much magic I pour into the mechanism, there's still more waiting. One side of Isolde's face is sharply lit by the dying fire, leaving the other in stark black shadow.

"What's wrong with you?" I ask, propping myself up on the ground. "I'm excited. You should be excited that I'm excited."

She rolls her eyes and holds out a hand to help me up, which I accept reluctantly, brushing dust off my skirt. "There's nothing wrong with me. I'm just worried…"

My heart hammers. I have no idea what she's talking about, but I imagine it's a conversation I'd rather avoid indefinitely. "You know I hate it when people do this." I need to look anywhere but at her, so I roughly pull the tie from the end of my braid and start undoing it. "Just spit out whatever it is so we can move on."

"Well…" It isn't like Isolde to dodge this much. I can't stand this. "Well… We're almost there, aren't we?"

I shake the last of my hair loose and self-consciously glance at the palm of my hand. The compass points steadfastly at the Western Range looming just over my shoulder. It's hard to explain the feeling, but I imagine it's how birds feel when they fly south for the winter. They know where they're supposed to land. "Yes," I say, finally. "I think we are."

"And then we get paid." Her eyes flick to the leather cord at my throat.

"Yes," I say again, wishing she'd just get to the point. "And then we can go home."

"Yeah," she says, flashing a brief smile. "But then what?"

"Then we'll go buy ourselves a magnificent new home, and I'll figure out how to restore Mami and Papa's memories, and—"

"Seelie." Isolde's voice is soft but insistent. *"Then what?"*

I tilt my head. I don't understand the question. That's it. That's where the plan ends. That's *happily ever after.*

She sighs, fixing me with a look I'd rather not be fixed by, and for the first time, I think I start to understand what she means. When we ran away, we were fourteen. We always planned to go back to our parents, to make a new home, but we were children. We didn't *need* a plan after that. We're practically grown now. But the plan is the plan. She can't mean...

"Seelie... I don't want to go back."

I don't scream or sigh or jump back. I don't even blink. I turn to stone. My heart is a chunk of rock that drops from my chest, and it takes me a second to remember how to speak. When I do, the only word I can squeak out is, "No?"

"I mean," she corrects herself quickly, wincing. Like she's still waiting for me to react. "I mean, I'll go back. I want to see Mami and Papa, so we can all be a family again. But... I like this." She gestures around us, to nothing in particular. "I don't want it to be over. I don't want to stay in one place forever."

I understand each word she's saying individually, but I can't comprehend them together. There's no version of my future without Isolde. There's no *home* without her. "Wh-wh—" I stammer, struggling to form one question that makes sense. "And wh-what then?"

Isolde looks into the fire, and sharp shadows carve out her profile as a strange smile curves her mouth. "I want to be an adventurer," she says. "I think I'd be good at it. I wouldn't have to keep stealing. I'd be hunting treasure, slaying monsters, rescuing people. Olani was telling me about what she wanted to do when she left her parents, before she started working for Leira Wildfall. If we pull off this quest, anyone would hire me. And…you could come, too."

I finally lean back, shaking my head. It feels too light, and Isolde's words ring around, echoing over and over and not making any more sense. "Sol…" I say weakly, "…the plan."

"You can't mean you want to stay tied down for the rest of your life. What, to be a midwife, like Mami? With magic like yours?" She's pleading now. She knew how this would go. "Just think about it, Seelie. We wouldn't have to say goodbye."

Anger flares, but I'm still too frozen to really feel it. "I'm not doing it," I spit. "I'm not—whatever stupid thing—you can't drag me into it this time. This, this is too far. My magic—" I can't talk about magic right now. My jaw trembles, and I will my voice not to break with a sob. "If you leave, you're leaving me, too."

"I'm not leaving," she soothes, reaching for my arm.

I pull back harshly. "But you're not staying?"

The firelight makes Isolde's eyes look as dark and shiny as puddles of ink. If she wants to run away from home again, to risk her life again and again, to leave her family and her twin behind, then maybe I don't know her like I thought I did. I thought we understood each other. I thought we wanted the same thing. "I can't," she says softly. "You have to understand—"

"No!" I sound like a wounded animal, snarling at her to back off. "I don't understand. I'll *never* understand."

She finally snaps. I see the anger in the set of her jaw, the tightening of her fists. "Well, what did *you* think was going to happen, Seelie? That we'd go home, and everything would be exactly like it was when we were kids, forever?"

"I—"

"Just because you didn't think any further ahead doesn't mean that's where everything *ends*. You're not going to be happy just because you made everything go back to how it was. You weren't even that happy *then*."

"Don't tell me what makes me happy," I snap, all in one low, furious rush.

"Why?" Isolde laughs bitterly. "Because it'll make you confront reality? Seelie, you were never happy because you could never be yourself. You've always been trapped. You think just when you're actually starting to understand your magic, you're suddenly going to be okay stuffing it back down and pretending to be what you think everyone wants you to be?"

Grief and anger both burn in my chest, in my voice, in my head, warring with each other. "No one wants me to be myself."

She throws her head back dramatically. "*I* want you to be yourself!"

"You want me to be who you want me to be." I start stomping away, even though I have nowhere to go. "*You*, but *magic*. If you had my powers, you wouldn't even need me!" The fire flares when I pass it, then dies away completely, plunging us into darkness. I keep walking.

"Don't be ridiculous." Isolde isn't about to let me get away that easily. "You're just trying to change the subject."

"Well, *you're* just trying to leave me." I crash into a low branch and swear, but I don't stop moving. My hands are shaking. I can't stop moving. I have to get away. But the memory of the faerie-ring warning sign still lingers at the back of my mind, and I'm scared to stray too far, so I end up just circling the dark campsite.

"I'm literally following you so you can't run away!"

I whirl around to the sound of her voice. "Shut *up!*" I scream. "Just shut up, Sol. You don't have all the answers. I don't want to hear your excuses. I'm not going to talk about this anymore, now or ever, and I'm not running away. Leave, if you want. See if I can stop you. I don't care."

Clearly, I don't care. That's why hot tears are streaming uncontrollably down my face as I scrape my voice raw snarling at her. I'm almost where I started now, smoke from the extinguished fire filling my nose.

"Seelie."

I ignore her. I'm done talking. That part, at least, was true.

"Seelie, stop!"

I'm barely listening anymore, but something else pulls me up short.

"Oh," says a voice from behind me, between us, a voice that I recognize somehow but can't place. "Am I interrupting something?"

The sound sends a chill up my spine and turns my stomach. I twist in place, slowly, to face Leira Wildfall.

chapter twenty-three

The first thing I notice is that Leira is just as finely dressed as she was on Revelnox, without so much as a dried leaf clinging to her long embroidered skirts. Threads of smoke trail into the sky from the smoldering campfire between us. My hands automatically jump to the same position I held them in while training, magic sparking along my nerves.

Isolde's blade glints in the moonlight. "How long have you been there?"

Leira smiles calmly, like she's indulging a misbehaving child. "As a nightingale? Long enough. What a delight to finally meet the company my nephew's been keeping these days. I'm Leira Wildfall—but you already knew that, didn't you, changeling?"

I'm so used to hearing the word said casually, without judgment, that it stings twice as hard to hear it in Leira's smug, sneering tone.

Where are Raze and Olani? I don't know if I want them to show up and rescue us or to run so they aren't caught. I realize I'm still holding my hands up defensively, but I have no idea what to do with them. I've seen what kind of magic she can do. There's no point starting a fight I know I can't win.

Leira's face doesn't change as she takes me in. "Go ahead and roast me alive if you'd like," she says mildly. "But Aris and the others won't be far behind. I just thought I'd fly ahead of them and demand surrender now, to make things simpler. There's no need for a high-speed chase or overdramatic fight scene. You may be powerful, changeling, but I do have numbers on my side."

Isolde laughs, harsh and humorless. "We're not going to surrender to you."

The trees behind her rustle, and for a second, I think they've already caught up to us, and all is lost. Despite myself, I'm relieved when a disheveled Raze and Olani burst out of the brush instead, gasping for air.

"Aris," Raze gasps. "Right behind us."

Then he looks up and sees who we're talking to. All the blood drains from his face.

In the moment their eyes lock, while Leira is distracted, Isolde springs forward. I can't see exactly what happens in the darkness; I just feel her moving, sense the gleam of a blade thrown in Leira's direction, and then the sharp jerk as Leira turns from Raze to the knife and knocks it aside with a gust of wind.

For a second, it spins out of control, speeding mercilessly

straight for Raze's heart, before she flicks her fingers again and the knife comes to a sudden, dead halt, hovering in the air just a breath away from his chest. He hadn't even had time to cry out, but now he flinches.

"Careful," Leira chides Isolde, letting the blade drop with an anticlimactic *thunk*.

Raze grits his teeth, looking a little like he wished the knife had finished the job. When he speaks, it sounds like someone trying to be polite to the hangman, even as the noose chokes them.

"Hello, Aunt Leira."

The head of the Wild line, most powerful enchanter in the land, adjusts her bodice and smiles, sugar-sweet. "Nephew," she says, in a mathematically measured voice, "I think you and I have some things we need to discuss."

"What are you doing here?" He tries to sound angry, but there's a faint shake in his voice.

She looks disappointed in him for asking such an obvious question. "I'm just trying to take back what belongs to me. So what'll it be, changeling? Are you going to come willingly and spare your friends? Or would you like to make this more interesting?"

I feel frozen. I should run. I should use magic. I should do *something*. But she's standing between me and everyone else. I'm alone, and I can't do anything except stand here, coldly rooted to the spot, thinking about how impossible it is that this is happening.

"Seelie," Isolde prompts, clearly meaning for me to blast Leira with fire. When I don't respond, she turns to Leira. "What do you want with her?"

Leira again looks disappointed, like she's teaching a class we're all failing. "The same thing Raze wants. Access to the Mortal's Keep. I'll hand it to you, nephew, using a changeling to activate the compass is something I never thought of. But your little adventure ends now, one way or another." Her head tilts as she looks at me. "Shall we?"

I shake my head. She makes it sound simple, but I don't want to go with her. I feel heavy with dread, and not just because we're about to be surrounded. The Destiny is right behind us. If I can just figure out a clever way to distract her, to get inside, we might still be able to outrun them.

I realize, suddenly, that it's not as dark as it was a moment ago. I can see the outlines of things, dark gray on black. But the sun only just set; it can't be rising again. I turn, eyes brushing past everyone and the trees surrounding us, catching on a far-off pinprick of light. The familiarity of the magic washes over me with recognition.

Aris.

If we're going to be clever, we have to do it soon.

"I mean, really, Raze, did you think I wouldn't catch up?" She turns back to him conversationally. "Even if Aris hadn't caught you and your accomplices in the act of breaking in, you left this behind at the scene of the crime."

She reaches into a pocket and pulls out something that shines a dull, corroded silvery color. His ring, abandoned on the plush carpet as he and Isolde wrestled each other for the compass in the vault. As soon as it hits the moonlight, his eyes grow even wider, and his mouth tightens into a sharp slash.

Leira examines it, bored. "If you'd just come to me with your ideas, maybe we could have worked together."

"I'm never going to work with you," he snaps. His eyes meet mine over her shoulder, then flick back to her quickly, trying to tell me something. I shake my head. I don't understand. Without looking at me again, Raze rubs a nervous hand over his eyebrows. Then he wraps his arms around himself, like he's cold.

The memory of the campfire flaring up in response to my own shivering comes flooding back with absolute clarity.

"Well, while we wait for Aris to catch up, why don't you at least let me take a look at that fascinating enchantment?" Leira looks at me with bright eyes, reaching a hand out as if she expects me to walk over and tamely give her mine.

I take one faltering step forward, jaw clenched tight. This is almost certainly a terrible idea. The crisp mountain wind raises chills up my arms as I slowly extend my left hand to Leira.

I inhale sharply, and all the magic I've been forcing into a tight, churning ball in my stomach flares into the night air—not into a direct attack that she could deflect but into the cooling ashes of the campfire. The fire roars back to life in shades of bright white and gold, and Leira, who was standing the closest to it, recoils with a shriek. She stumbles back with her arm held protectively over her face, and even my eyes are dazzled.

"Run!" Olani yells, before the fire's even receded.

I make it to the Destiny first, and she and Isolde aren't far behind. As Raze passes Leira, who's still dizzily trying to recover her senses but doesn't seem horribly burned, he snatches something from her raised hand.

"Thanks for returning this." Silver gleams in the moonlight as he barrels for the Destiny, ring already slipped back into place on his finger.

Leira is screaming something. Everyone is screaming something. It all blends into a crash of words that doesn't make any sense, but I hear the door slam shut as I throw myself into the driver's seat, gripping the wheel with white knuckles.

The Destiny roars to life, and we lurch forward. Birch, who managed to sleep through everything until this point, complains loudly. We leave Leira in the dust, but we can't just keep going down this same road her reinforcements are already on. We need to go somewhere they won't follow.

I have another awful idea.

"Seelie." Isolde's voice breaks away from the others with the warning sound of my name. "Don't."

Well, that settles it. I grit my teeth and turn the wheel sharply, slamming the wagon to top speed.

The arguing harmonizes into a chorus of screams as I send us tumbling off the road into the forest, smashing straight through the *TRAVELER BEWARE: FAERIE CIRCLE* warning sign in a cloud of splinters.

We bump along the uneven road hard enough to jolt us all up and down, to make the wheels crack under the weight. I push the Destiny as fast as she can go, ignoring the feeling of bolts shaking out of place and wood cracking. Branches smack and snap against the sides as we tumble through the darkness, lit only by the approaching light of Aris's magic.

Glancing behind us, I see dozens of cloaked figures on horseback weaving between the tress, one with her hand raised to a ball of light. It gleams on what I can barely make out as dragon scales, but the green hides blend in with the trees so well I can't see how many guard dragons they've brought with them. The tawny wings of a nightingale weave between them, skimming the leaves. Ahead, an eerily tranquil clearing, trunks bowing away from a wide circle of pale mushroom caps.

"What are you doing?" Isolde manages to break through the clouds in my head.

Words scramble in my head, so I reach for the only one at the tip of my tongue. "Shortcut!"

The horses sense the faerie circle before their riders see it, and they shy away, bucking and neighing, which sets off the dragons. The nightingale soars straight upward with a rapid-fire angry clicking sound, turning in the air to pull up beside Aris's ball of light. For a second, I think I see her green eyes, angry and surprised.

"Slow down!" Olani shouts. But I can't slow down: it feels like we're going down a forty-five degree incline, totally out of control, gaining speed with each second.

Raze adds, "We're going to—"

And then everything explodes and implodes and turns upside down all at once. I feel weightless, tense with the anticipation of the pain of landing.

But I don't remember landing. I don't remember anything after the dizzy feeling of falling and falling and falling, set to the sound of all of our screams.

chapter twenty-four

I'm sure I haven't heard this song before, but somehow I know it.

That's strange—I hum the next few notes as they rise and fall and float lazily through the air, like fireflies. I don't know how I know it, but it's the most beautiful song I've ever heard. I can't help but sway in time. My skirts sway with me, swirling around my legs in a shimmering pool of pale gold and silver, light and frothy as sparkling wine.

The sound of laughter joins the music. Above me, stars are scattered across an ink-blue sky, but it's bright as day with all the lanterns. They swing from the trees—such beautiful trees, taller than any I've ever seen before—along with natural garlands of flowering vines. I'm on the outskirts of the party, just outside a scattering of people picnicking in the lush green grass, but the dancers at the center of the clearing look so beautiful. *Everyone* looks so beautiful that for the first time, I wonder what I'm doing here. This dress is so low-cut, barely hanging onto my shoulders by lacy embroidery, leaving too much of my chest and arms bare.

All my scars, exposed to the still night air.

Panic rises in my throat. Any second now, they're going to realize that I don't belong here.

I start to stumble away. There's nowhere to go but the trees, but that will have to do. I can hide in their shadows until I figure out what to do.

Fireflies drift in front of me, yellow lights flickering on and off in a gentle rhythm. One lands on my nose and I stop, cross-eyed. Then it takes flight again. I reach out for it, but it slips through my fingers. Another lights on top of my outstretched fingertips, but as soon as I try to bring it closer, it flits away, too.

I laugh, and the sound is high and clear as it rings in my ears. I feel light and confused and a little drunk, but I don't remember drinking anything. I hop forward with a commotion of swishing skirts, but the fireflies keep evading every swipe I make at them. I can't remember why I was so upset a moment ago. How could anyone be upset in a place as beautiful as this? It smells like warm grass and honeysuckle.

The fireflies tickle my skin, but I can't seem to catch them. I twirl in place and skip forward, reaching for them, and suddenly I realize I've stumbled into the circle of dancers. I'm about to protest that I don't know the steps, but they're already linking arms with me, and I'm pulled along.

It's like when I was a small child and my father used to toss me into the air. The sudden rush of movement startles another laugh from my throat, and I let my head fall back.

The other dancers seem to know the steps well enough to guide me through, and soon enough I'm matching their pace, even if I'm doing it all wrong. I pass from partner to partner, and each seems equally delighted to take my hand—

A man with smooth, perfect skin darker than the new moon laughs. "Hello!"

A little girl, with hair so long it reaches her ankles, giggles so hard she snorts, and I laugh along, not knowing why.

A young woman with eyes as pale as a moth's wings shows all her teeth in a wide grin.

Some of them greet me silently. A few call me Changeling. I don't ask how they know what I am. I don't care.

I've never been able to dance without feeling like I'm missing something, like my arms and legs aren't quite moving to the same beat, but this is as natural as breathing. I dance and dance until I can barely breathe, and then I keep dancing. I can't stop. I've never had this much fun before, and I don't want to disappoint anyone by leaving.

It feels good not to worry. Not to wonder what I'm doing wrong or what's going to go bad next. I know I used to do all those things, but it all seems so silly now. I am beautiful and timeless and weightless.

I'm happy.

Even when my muscles start to burn, and my breath hitches sharply. I feel the pain of each step, each uncontrollable swirl as I move from hand to hand, but I can't remember why pain used to upset me.

The lanterns blur, their flames streaking by like golden

comets. I gasp in the flower-perfumed air, but I can't get enough. My head is light and soft, like dandelion fluff. I just beam brighter. It's strange, though: none of the other dancers ever seem to tire. There must be something wrong with me.

The spots swimming in front of my vision are so beautiful, like the fireflies, only more colorful. A man with deer legs and antlers takes my hand and spins me around, and the world spins round and round and—

I stumble.

I'm falling, and even when I hit the ground, I keep falling. Something tugs in my chest, startling me into clarity. It's like when you're right on the edge of sleep, and suddenly your stomach drops and you're wide awake, heart pounding. One thought, bright and cold, breaks through the rest.

That's enough of that. Wake up.

The dance continues around me as I gasp for breath face-down in the sweet-smelling grass. My feet ache, sending sharp bolts of pain up my legs, which feel like jelly. I don't know if I can stand. My fingers dig into the grass, into the soil.

Where am I? How did I get here? When I open my eyes, I see my dress glittering like dewdrops. Where did this *dress* come from?

I miss the pleasant fog in my head, because all these thoughts are sharp and bitter and painful, and my mind won't slip gently away from the truth anymore. It doesn't take long to put the pieces together: I actually managed to drive us into a faerie realm.

This can't be happening, but it is. My head drops, landing hard in the grass again as I try to collect my thoughts, breathing so hard my chest aches. I'm so thirsty. It's so lovely here, and nothing has tried to kill me, so it must be an enchanted wood somewhere deep in the Seelie Realm.

That doesn't explain where my sister is, or our companions, or how we got separated from the Destiny and each other. That doesn't explain why I'm wearing a silly, beautiful dress, dancing at a faerie ball.

I didn't think about what would happen when we drove through the faerie circle. All I was thinking about was getting away, somewhere I knew they wouldn't follow. I thought of it like driving through a dangerous stretch of road: not the best idea, but as long as we stayed in the wagon and didn't stop until we found our way out, we'd be okay. Now I have no idea how long I've been here. Everything blurred together while I was under whatever spell possessed me. For all I know, a hundred years could have passed.

Oh, Fate, I can't breathe.

I can't deal with that possibility, so I'm going to ignore it for now. I need to focus. The faerie glamour has worn off, but my panic is just as effective at making me useless. I need to figure out if my sister is at this ball, and Raze and Olani. If they are, they're probably under the same spell I was, and I'm going to have to find a way to wake them.

Which is harder than it sounds, because I don't know how *I* managed to shake the spell off. It doesn't make sense. I've heard the stories. I should have danced myself to death, or at least until I fainted.

I grind my hands into the dirt, forcing my head to lift slowly. White petals shower around me, sticking in my loose hair, and for the first time I feel the weight of a circlet of flowers on my head. My arms shake with the effort it takes to push myself up, and I check the compass in my left palm. The arrow spins unhelpfully in endless circles. I need to find the others. I need them to be here, because I don't know how I'm going to get out if I'm all alone.

My teeth grind together as I force myself to stand again. I try to turn it into a smile. The faeries—I was dancing with *faeries*—seem oblivious to me, but I don't know what they'll do if they suspect I'm no longer under their enchantment. I wonder how many of the other people here are captured mortals, empty-eyed and eerily placid.

Focus.

I try to think light and airy thoughts even as I move stiffly, lifting my voluminous skirts in a sweep. They're *heavy*, especially for something that might be an illusion. I have no idea how I'm going to find anyone. This party could go on for miles—if they're even here. An instinct I didn't know I had reaches for my magic, for the reassurance that it's still there, that I can defend myself if I have to. It rises like a riptide, like it's fighting against itself within me, and it takes several gasping breaths to keep my head above the water, to calm it back into a subdued current. I should be relieved that it's still there, but I don't know how useful it is in this state.

The gentle babbling of a creek turns my head. There, at the edge of the clearing, a gentle little stream bounces happily along mossy rocks. Every other thought fades away as I take one shaky step and then another. I need water so badly, I still might faint. By the time I make it to the creek, I just drop, letting myself fall onto the springy moss of its banks. I scoop water with my hands, splashing it all over myself.

After a few moments, I come to my senses enough to wonder if faerie water is safe to drink, but if it isn't, it's too late anyway. I keep drinking.

Finally, I push myself back onto my haunches like a wild creature, panting heavily, crystal-clear drops of water streaking down my face and staining the delicate silk of my bodice.

That's when my eye catches on a flash of bright red hair.

Raze is easy to pick out of a crowd, even the just-slightly-not-human faerie crowd. My heart rises, then falls so quickly I think I might have bruised it. If Raze is here, Isolde probably is, too—and Olani. Just my luck to find *him* first. He's still under the enchantment, lounging at a picnic on the other side of the creek with several faerie girls fawning over him. Worry settles over me—faerie food is definitely bad news. But if it's affecting him, besides making him silly and thoughtless, I can't see how.

I wipe an arm roughly across my mouth, and I feel the bumps of the scars on my face. It's strange, having so much bare skin. Raze doesn't notice me staring. Then again, I could have stepped on him while chasing fireflies, and I doubt either of us would have noticed each other. One of the faeries, a girl with amber-colored skin and a halo of golden coils around her head, wraps her arms around his neck, draping herself over him. Raze blinks down at her with a dreamy, idiotic smile. Then he leans down and kisses her nose. She catches his lips with hers, pulling him closer.

It's disgusting. I want to run in the opposite direction, but I should probably go save him from himself.

Sighing, I splash through the creek. My feet are bare—I don't know if there were shoes to go with the dress that I kicked off while dancing, or if this is part of the look—and the hem of my ridiculous dress soaks up water, even though I try to bunch it up above the shallow current.

I don't know what I plan to do. I march unnoticed past dreamy-eyed faeries until I'm standing, in a mud puddle of my own making, in front of Raze.

"You taste...like honey..." he mumbles, because even though his mouth is occupied, he can never shut up.

The faerie girl chuckles into another kiss. "You taste like desperation," she says. "Or is it loneliness? It's so *mortal*."

In all of time, there has never been an awkward throat-clearing as awkward as the one I give then.

The uninvolved faeries notice me first. They look almost like startled deer—curious, but motionless. Waiting to see what I do next.

What *do* I do next?

"Shoo." It comes out of my mouth without passing my brain. You can't just *shoo* faeries like they're mosquitos buzzing a little too close, but I do. "Go on, shoo. Go dance an eternal waltz or something."

They just keep staring at me. It's strange, like they're looking *through* me at something else. I have to fight to keep from checking over my shoulder for someone bigger and scarier. A surge of confidence pushes me forward, and I think maybe it's coming from the same place as the tide of magic.

"Shoo!" I repeat, this time with a hand motion and a step forward. They pause for a moment, then scramble to their feet. I wait for them to turn me into a chipmunk or something, but then they dash past me, leaving behind a breeze that smells like wildflowers.

Okay, that just leaves me and Raze and one more faerie.

This shouldn't be that hard. Then again, they haven't even looked up at me once.

I clear my throat again. I'm trying not to stare but also trying to catch his eye, and this is the most uncomfortable I can ever remember being in my life. I don't want to watch Raze kiss some other girl—

I mean, *any* girl. Anyone. I'm not *jealous*, because in order to be jealous of something, *you* have to want it yourself, and I *definitely* do *not* want…

"Raze," I snap. That works. His breath hitches when their lips part.

I grit my teeth.

The faerie girl looks up at me through long eyelashes. Her eyes are the same luminous gold as her hair, so rich I feel like I'm sinking in them.

"I-I…" I stammer. Raze gives me a confused pout. I can't tell if he recognizes me or not. His eyes are peaceful and vacant and a little sleepy. "I-I need to steal you away? For…just a moment."

The faerie girl's head rolls back lazily. "Ugh, leave him alone. He's having fun."

Raze seems to agree with that. He leans back towards her.

"Raze!" I crouch down, groaning. "Raze, I need you to wake up. Come on, *please*."

The girl's eyes narrow at me. "What *are* you?"

"Changeling," Raze mumbles. I don't know if he's answering her or finally recognizing me. "Iselia."

"Yes," I say, surprised by the way the sound of my full name makes my heart cram into my throat.

The girl's nose wrinkles. "Changelings aren't *real* faeries. Go find your own mortal. I saw him first."

I can't shake Raze out of this enchantment until I get rid of *her*—and I don't think I can shoo this one away. "Oh, you don't want *this* one," I say, not sure where I'm going with this. "I mean, look at him. He's so…*meh*."

The faerie trails a long, delicate finger down Raze's cheek. "I know," she says. "Isn't it funny? He wants attention *so badly*." He doesn't seem to notice her words. He's too busy gazing at her like she's the moon in the sky, gently brushing golden curls behind her ear.

My face gets a little warm on his behalf. "You can do better," I insist. "It's my turn with him now."

She frowns. "What do you want him for?"

"I—" I put my hands on my hips, trying to look like…not myself. "I, um… Same thing as you. Just…you know, toying with him. I love toying with mortals. This one is way too easy for you. You need someone who actually appreciates your beauty. This one?" I snort. I'm no good at manipulation. I need to pull this together into some conclusion that makes sense. "I mean, he's so desperate, he'd probably even be enchanted by *me*." I gesture to my scars for emphasis. "Me!"

For the first time, Raze looks at me and seems to actually *see* me. He takes in my appearance and frowns, and after weeks of travel together and dozens of arguments, I can sense the impulse to automatically disagree with me coming over him. He opens his mouth to speak.

Oh, no. I need to stop him before he unravels this whole lie around me. I panic, and I do the only thing I know will keep him silent. I grab his collar, turning him to face me. He moves easily, like a liquid, and I keep pulling, begging him to snap out of it. Our eyes meet, and for just a second I see a flicker of clarity as he starts to come back to himself. As he realizes what's going on.

I'm honestly not sure which one of us moves after that, but it ends with our lips smashed together.

As far as kisses go, it's terrible. As far as kisses *I've* experienced go, it's not all that bad. It's certainly...

Damp. And there is a solid amount of pressure.

I hold his face against mine as long as I can stand it, listening to my heart beat in my ears, and when I can't take it any longer, I hold it for another moment more. One of my hands cups his face, and the other tugs him toward me with a fistful of hair. Raze lets out a surprised sound but relaxes into me embarrassingly quickly. His breath is warm, but his hands are even warmer as they slide around me: one at my waist, gentle but firm; one at the base of my neck, brushing the bare skin under my loose hair.

Finally, after the longest minute of my life, I pull back from him. He sways forward with me, and I have to prop him up, with *my* arms around his neck this time. I wipe my mouth with the back of one hand, glaring at the faerie, who's backed off a few inches.

She looks the same way I feel: confused, and a little nauseous.

"Iselia," Raze says again, this time in a *completely* different tone. He blinks like someone waking up from a nap, this time gazing at *me* like *I'm* some mysterious wonder.

"See?" I say to the faerie. "Too easy. You're wasting your talents here. Go find someone else."

And to my enormous surprise and relief, she *does.*

"Ugh!" As soon as her back turns, I remove my arms from

Raze's neck and shake him roughly by the shoulders. "Raze, snap out of it. Now!"

He shakes his head, pushing me away gently. His hands run through his already-messed hair, making it even messier. "I-I think the magic's gone now. Where *are* we?"

For the first time, I notice his clothes. He's as dressed up as I am, in a billowy white shirt as fine as spider silk with embroidery all along the low neckline, a belt with an intricately crafted gold buckle, velvet breeches, and shiny boots that come all the way up to his knees. The only thing that hasn't changed is the simple, silvery ring he took back from Leira, which now rests on his right pointer finger.

"Where do you *think*?" I say, wiping my mouth again for good measure.

He's still dazed, looking at the forest around us like he's seeing everything for the first time. "Where are the others?"

I glare at him. "If I knew, do you *really* think *that* would have been the first thing I did?" The reality of the situation is settling in now, curling in my chest. Isolde could be in terrible danger. She could be dancing herself to exhaustion somewhere. We need to find her and Olani as soon as possible and figure out what the faeries did with our wagon so we can get back on the road. I don't have time for his questions.

"You saved me," Raze says. He stands, stretching. I wonder how long he's been sitting here. I wonder how long he would have stayed, if I hadn't come along.

He offers a hand down to me, but I ignore it, creaking unsteadily back to my feet. "If you die here, you can't pay me."

"And if I live?" he says, looking at me. I've lost whatever shine he saw in the moments the enchantment dissolved, but his expression still seems weird. Maybe he's just noticing how bad my scars are for the first time. I cross my arms.

"If we live," I say, "I want an extra *fifty* percent. And for you to promise you'll never make me kiss you again."

Raze reaches for my hand, closing it in his before I can dart away. I look up at him, heart leaping in confusion and alarm. *He doesn't think—*

Then he gives it a firm, businesslike shake.

"All right, then, Iselia. You have yourself a deal."

I free my fingers from his clammy palm and wipe them on my skirt. "Let's go find the others."

A well-marked path leads us deeper into the forest, but there are still lanterns strung in the branches, with faeries dancing through the trees or lounging at their roots. I quickly give up on supporting my own weight with my aching legs and lean on Raze's arm as he drags us both along.

I don't even have to ask.

None of this looks familiar, but I feel like I know where I'm going. Like this is a path I've walked before. The feeling makes my skin crawl, and I keep checking the compass in my palm over and over. It guided us in the mortal world. Why not here?

But the enchantment must only work in the mortal world, because it just spins impatiently, searching for something that isn't there. I press my opposite thumb into the design, squeezing my hands painfully tight.

I need to find Isolde. I drove us here. If she's lost forever, it'll be my fault.

There's still treasure waiting for you.

I recoil from the ugly thought so suddenly that I stumble, almost knocking Raze over, and we both freeze in the middle of the path. I don't want the treasure without Isolde. There's no point in having any of it without her, and my heart will stop beating before I give up on finding her here.

Let's hurry this along, then.

I hold my hand up in front of my face, studying the design. I know I've felt a presence, faint at the edges of my consciousness, ever since the enchantment soaked into my skin. But it seemed inanimate, more like a feeling than something capable of thought.

Maybe the faerie world is making it stronger, because I don't think those thoughts were mine. Or maybe I'm just now becoming aware of it. How much of what I've done these past few weeks was *me*, and how much was influenced without my knowledge?

My knees shake, and Raze forces me to look up at him, still supporting half my weight. "What is it? What's wrong?"

I stare up at him helplessly, because I can't tell the truth without losing his trust, and right now is not a great time for division. We have to stick together if we're going to survive, to find the others.

He looks genuinely concerned, which just makes me feel worse. "Do you need to take a break? We can stop for a—"

Hurry!

I obey without thinking, taking off down the path at a hobbling run. Raze follows, trying to reason with me, but I can't listen to him and think at the same time. I let my palm curl open and see the needle pointing straight, and somehow I know it'll lead me to Isolde. Whatever guides it is in just as much of a hurry to find her as I am now, except its magic is actually useful.

I hold my hand out and let it guide me. I know it would be a mistake to leave the path, but it feels like there's something in my chest pulling me into the trees, and I follow. What do I have to lose at this point? The thorny brush stings my bare feet and tears my skirts, but I don't care. My sister is nearby. I can feel it.

"Seelie, wait!" Raze calls. "Don't leave the—" He reaches the edge of the path and hesitates for a second, and then I hear him groan and crash forward after me. "Seelie!"

I try to keep an eye on the path as it disappears behind us, one eye on him, the other on the compass. But there's no way to do all three at the same time, and I almost trip over the black fox when it streaks across my feet, so close it makes my skirts flutter.

My eyes follow it as it disappears into the brush, and even the white tip of its tail vanishes. There's something off about it, and I can't explain what. The second it takes me to process this is all Raze needs to finally catch up, and he grabs me by the arm before I can run again.

"What...are...you...doing?" he grinds out, breathing hard. He must think I've completely lost my mind.

Maybe I have. "Did you see that?" I try to twist away, to check which direction the compass points now, but he's so much stronger than me.

"The fox? Yeah, it flashed before my eyes right—"

"There was something weird about it," I insist, finally shoving him away. Leaves rustle, and I see the tip of a sleek black nose, peppered with charcoal gray. The fox. It came back.

"A *strange* fox?" Raze says sarcastically. He touches my wrist lightly, not holding me back from following but warning me. "In a *faerie forest*? No wa—"

This time, he's interrupted by the sound of a hunting horn, a sound that is somehow low and high, brassy and sweet, echoing and inviting all at once.

The fox's fur bristles, and it pants anxiously, looking torn between running away and approaching us. Ignoring Raze, I crouch, extending my hand for it to sniff.

The fox leans its pointy nose forward, barely brushing the fingertips of my open left hand.

And the compass points straight at it.

The hunting horn blows again, louder, nearer. I meet the fox's eyes right before it bolts, frightened by the sound. They aren't yellow, like I expected. They're dark, rich brown, the same color as mine.

My heart forgets how to beat, hanging frozen in my chest. *"Isolde."*

The ground trembles under my feet as I throw myself into the brush. I'd know my twin anywhere, even with four legs and pointy ears. That's no faerie fox—that's my *sister*. And she's being hunted.

"Wait!" Raze does catch my hand now, throwing me off-balance. He's still looking behind us, and the thundering of hooves is getting louder, and I'm going to lose her. I pull away viciously.

"Isolde!"

"Isolde?"

"The fox!"

I'm more than a little hysterical, and I'm about to claw him like a wild animal if he doesn't let go of me, but Raze finally puts it together as another wail from the hunting horn echoes through the forest. This time, I hear the baying and yipping of dogs as they join in.

Before I can do anything else, Raze's shape blurs and re-forms. My hair is blown back by the powerful wings of a giant owl—truly giant: its wingspan must be at least as wide as Raze's human shape is tall—with coppery-red stripes in its feathers. *What is he doing?*

Then the owl is gone, diving through the leaves on the fox's tail.

"Wait for me!" I try to scramble after them, but I trip on the hem of my dress and smash my face into the dirt.

It's probably a good thing that I do.

I'm almost flat to the ground when the first horse's hooves thunder past, narrowly missing crushing my head. I roll to the side, dodging another, and then try to scramble to my feet. I'm still stepping on my hem, trying to gather up all my skirts, and then I'm sliding down a shallow ditch, slipping in mud with brambles slashing my tender, exposed skin.

I can't imagine how it must look to the faeries. It's hard to hear them at all over the horses and the dogs baying and the horn. I think I'm safe from being trampled to death here, so I risk peeking up over the embankment.

There's so many of them, more than I would have expected, all passing in a tempest of movement, flashing too-sharp teeth in their fierce grimaces of excitement. They're mostly dressed in golds and greens that blend in with the forest's summer decadence, on top of horses that gleam in every natural (and unnatural) color. A few of the horses' manes spray water in an endless stream, and some have fangs—because that's what mortal horses were missing, scarier teeth.

It's so deafeningly loud that the noises splinter, and instead of a cacophony, I hear each individual sound, all layered on top of each other: the thundering of the horses, the barking of the hounds, the chatter and whoops of excitement of the faeries…

And a familiar laugh. I search for the source, but everything is moving too fast. Olani is a blur on a silvery horse, head thrown back with laughter like she *belongs* with them.

"Olani!" I scramble to my feet successfully this time, piling my skirts in my arms and leaving my legs exposed.

But if she's part of the hunt…

I go from relief at finding her to panic more quickly than I would have thought possible. I have to stop Olani from killing Isolde. Cursing with each slow, shuffling step, I try to throw myself in her path and hope she sees me. "Olani!"

Something pulls my arm hard, and then I'm flying through the air, a scream torn from my throat. After a long second of weightlessness, I land so hard I'm afraid my backside may be permanently damaged.

I'm still screaming, but now it's into Olani's ear, thrown onto her horse in the seat behind her. I stop screaming, but I cling to her with shaking arms. This faerie horse gallops so fast I don't want to think about what would happen if I landed under its hooves.

When I catch my breath, I say, "Olani!" again. An unfamiliar feeling rises in my chest: hope. Maybe she's already broken the spell on herself, maybe she recognized me, maybe she's riding with the hunt so she can protect Isolde.

"You joined the hunt at the right time! We've almost got it!"

Or maybe not.

"Olani!" I try again, desperately. My arms dig into her ribs so tight I'm sure she can hardly breathe, and my face is buried in her shoulder. She's wearing a forest-green doublet so thick with embroidery of flowers and leaves and little birds that it practically counts as armor. In her other hand, she holds a spear with a wickedly sharp point. "It's me! Olani! Don't you recognize me?"

Apparently, she doesn't. We overtake a faerie with pale green skin on an emerald-colored horse, and Olani throws back her head with a laugh.

I want to stop her. I want to shake her so hard she wakes up, to snatch the reins out of her hands. But that won't do any good because this horse is the only way I have of possibly catching up with Isolde. Still, I shout Olani's name over and over, until my throat is raw, because there's nothing else I can do. I can't help but feel that trying to use magic to stop her would just make everything worse.

For the first time, faeries are paying attention to me. I didn't matter to them when I was just some glamoured changeling or when I was pretending to be one of them, but now that I'm starting to ruin the game, I'm making myself a target.

I imagine two identical black foxes, bleeding crimson into the impossibly green grass, and shudder. It won't come to that.

Olani urges her horse faster and faster. I watch the faeries' blurry faces as we pass them. A few look jealous, but most cheer her on. They want *her* to kill Isolde, I realize. The thought turns my stomach. And she *wants* to do it. She leans forward in the saddle eagerly, spear raised.

And there's nothing I can do about it. My arms shake with the effort it takes to hold on. Everything hurts, and I'm taking in breaths in ragged gasps I can't seem to control. My heart beats faster than the horses' hooves, frantic and desperate. I scan the ground in front of us desperately, wishing for my eyes to be sharper than hers, sharper than the faeries'. I need to be the one who sees the fox first.

I wonder if Isolde knows what's going on or if she's lost somewhere under layers of the fox's fear. I wonder if she's still herself.

We pull in front of the other hunters, in front of the faerie with the hunting horn, in front of the hounds. They bark excitedly and nip at the horses' heels, but we don't slow or falter. We're just barely at the front of the pack now, still close enough to hear the excited howls and yips and cheers of faeries and hounds alike. Still close enough for them to catch us.

A streak of shadow flickers across our path, slipping under a fallen branch without slowing. Behind us, the faerie horn blows again.

Our horse thunders on, now hot on Isolde's heels. She's so close I can see the pads of her little paws as she scurries into the brush, her sharp teeth flashing as she pants for breath, the whites of her eyes blown wide in fear.

"Isolde!" I shout, on the wild chance hearing her name will break the spell. "It's me! I'm here!" I want to promise I won't let them hurt her—but that would be lying.

I feel the tension in Olani's muscles, straining forward as if that can make the horse catch up. If I'm going to break the spell on her, now is the time. I reach for my magic, trying to focus.

Yeah, that's not happening.

I can't close my eyes because I have to keep them on Isolde. I can't filter out the noise around me because I need every cue, every clue to what will happen next. I can't...

Suddenly, I realize we've come around a curve to face a wall of brambles, and for a second, a glimmer of hope lights in my chest. She sprints straight for the thorns, headfirst. In fox form, Isolde is small enough to slip through. I'll lose her, but so will the hunt.

Then a high-pitched yelp splits the air. Isolde's paws scrabble in the dirt uselessly, crying and wailing.

She's stuck.

Stuck in the thorns, Isolde turns toward us, fear in her eyes. We're getting closer with every frantic heartbeat, every desperate twitch of her tail. She shrieks in pain and terror, and I join in.

Olani draws back with her spear, determination in her smooth movements. This is it, my last chance to do something—anything—to save my sister.

I throw myself off the horse.

I don't let go of Olani. Instead, I scrabble to hold onto her arms, her sleeves, her hair, anything. I land in a puff of skirts and curses, and a fresh bolt of pain spikes through me.

The fox is still screaming. Olani is still on the horse, but crooked and off-balance. As she falls, she throws the spear in one last desperate attempt, her teeth clenched in determination.

I expect myself to scream, but I'm choking, and all I can hear is the rushing of my own blood. I can't scream. I can't move. I can't believe this is real.

A sudden wind rustles the grass with a flash of russet wings, knocking the spear aside. It's such a close call that the spear grazes the tip of Isolde's tail as it crashes into the brambles. Raze swoops lower, circling above us.

Olani groans in the dirt beside me. She rolled as she fell, and I'll be amazed if she hasn't broken something. She must have hit her head, because she's rubbing it in her hands, squinting at me as if through a heavy fog.

"Olani?" I try tentatively. "Please be you again."

She lets out a quiet, pained curse, which I take as a sign that she is. The faerie riders behind us are calling out to each other in dismay, and something like the smell of rain tingles in the air.

I want to ask if she's okay, if she remembers anything, but there's no time. "Can you walk?"

Olani pulls a face, stretching. "I think so."

"Good." I push myself to my feet and offer her a hand. "We can talk about you trying to kill my sister later. Now, get up."

Her dark skin goes a little gray. "Isolde?"

"I said *get up*!"

"I'm sorry," Olani says. "I don't know what came over me. I… I wanted to…"

She isn't usually the type for tearful confessions, and now really isn't the time to start. "Olani," I say, anger and urgency battling in my tone, "you were glamoured. We all were. We just need to make it out of here."

We can't squeeze into the brambles with Isolde. The thorns are as long as my fingers and probably poisoned or something, but the hounds are closing in, and more spears are sure to follow.

The horn bellows behind us again, making my skin crawl. The hunt isn't over yet.

I can hear the trees, humming so low with magic it's more a feeling than a sound. I can hear the lanterns still adorning the branches, all the way out here, crackling with cheerful little flames. I can hear Olani's labored breath layered over my own. I can hear—

Meowing.

A tangle of leaves parts, and a familiar, glossy black shape slinks out, ears back. The relief I feel at seeing Birch is so powerful that I have to hold back the tears that spring into my eyes, but it only lasts a second. He has something green and glimmering in his mouth, which Olani reaches for, urging him closer.

A faerie hound's howl splits the air, followed by a chorus of barking. Birch startles, leaping straight up into the air. His fur puffs up with terror as he scrambles mid-jump, and then he takes off like an arrow back into the forest before Olani can grab him.

"No!" I shout uselessly, knowing I can't do anything but watch the forest close in around his path. We have more immediate problems.

Raze circles overhead again, and then he drops, human before he hits the ground.

"Please tell me you have a plan," Olani says, scowling at the spot where Birch was a second ago.

"I have a plan," he says, scanning the trees around us.

"Say it without lying."

He doesn't respond.

I crouch and reach my arm as far into the brambles as I can, pushing the tangle up to free the fox. Isolde doesn't run this time. Her round eyes lock on mine. "Come on," I say softly. "I'm sorry we fought."

I don't know if it's the words or if she suddenly catches my familiar scent, but slowly, shaking, the fox limps out from the thorns, favoring one of her back paws. She curls close to me, compressing the layers of my dress until she's pressed against my ankles. I can feel the frantic thrum of her tiny heartbeat through her fur.

Another spear whistles in the air, landing far to our right. We're running out of time, I realize, as a shower of arrows follows. Most of them go wide, *thunking* into tree trunks or sailing past, but one finds its mark.

Olani cries out, buckling with pain. Her hands go to her hip, to the quickly spreading red stain soaking through her trousers.

Raze catches her as she staggers, supporting her weight. Fear makes his voice crack. "Olani!"

"I'm fine," she grits out. "Just…get us out of here."

I have *magic*. There must be something I can do to get us out of this, but I don't think summoning fire or lightning will have much effect. After all, the faeries have magic, too. I wish I could just step into the Mortal Realm, tie a line around us all, and pull until we're back where we're supposed to be—but even I know only faeries can walk between the worlds at will.

We press tightly together. Raze is at my back, mumbling something encouraging to Olani, who breathes unevenly through the pain. Isolde shivers anxiously at my feet. We don't have a way out, but at least we'll all be together as we face down the hunt.

I can fix this.

The thought is sudden and clear and not *quite* mine. It comes from something deeper, something icy running deep below the surface of my mind. Something that's getting more and more familiar. It doesn't matter where it comes from, not when we're this close to death. It doesn't matter what price it demands from me later, because if I do nothing, there won't *be* a later.

I accept. I open the door to that thought, let it trickle up from its deep, dark hiding place. I have a sudden, vivid image of myself, twisting my own magic together with that in the trees, shaping it into the form I need. Making a portal.

My heart is so worn out from all the terror and anxiety and *running*, but it still skips a beat with traitorous anticipation.

Normally, I close my eyes to focus, but this time I watch every movement as I hold my hands out. The movements are unfamiliar, sweeping, like conducting an orchestra, but somehow I feel like I've done this a thousand times before. I let out a breath, and the magic rises in my blood, sings at my fingertips, flows into the trees. I pull it back to me, drawing magic from the trees with it. Twining them together. Shaping them, just like I saw in my head moments ago.

I think of the Mortal's Keep and the mysterious ruins that hide it, of the Western Range's sharp peaks, and of our mission. Something tugs in my chest, straining, and for a second I think I'm not going to be able to do it.

The hounds howl behind me. Everyone else has gone silent with tension, so there's nothing but unearthly echoes and my pulse rushing in my ears.

I pull harder. Something sharp and cold shudders through me and, with a gasp, the tension releases.

Magic simmers in the air, bright and stinging, so strong I can smell it. Everything looks exactly the same as it did a second ago, but the cord in my chest winds from me to the space between two trees.

"What did you—?" Olani starts, looking at me with something a little like fear, but I don't let her finish.

"Go!" I point. She takes one look at the fast-approaching faerie mob behind me and obeys. The moment she passes between the trees, she winks out of existence. Raze throws himself into the portal, reaching his hand out in an unsuccessful attempt to pull me with him as Isolde freezes uncertainly in place. He disappears instantly, leaving me, my fox-sister, and the faeries. I bend to scoop Isolde up, holding her tight to my chest as I risk one last glance over my shoulder.

Fate, I hope I did this right.

Something whistles behind me, but I don't allow myself to flinch, even when it buries itself into the bark of one of my trees.

I dive into the mortal world, faerie hounds snapping at my heels.

PART THREE

chapter twenty-five

The portal shatters like a mirror behind me, and not a second too soon. I'm braced to land on soft grass, and the shock of my weight on smooth stone echoes up my legs.

Isolde transforms in an instant, as if her body is catching up with the human world. I can't hold her like this at her normal size, and she lets out a thoroughly human scream as she plummets to the ground. Her bright eyes meet mine, filling quickly with tears.

"Sol!" I throw myself forward, wrapping her in my arms. In my mind, she was already half-dead, but she's not dead at all. She's alive, she's human, she's going to be okay. We're all still in our faerie clothes, so they must be more than just glamour, and Isolde wears a strange gown of sheer black gauze over a tight-fitting shirt and leggings.

She hugs me back, clinging to me like I'm a lifeline. She's shaking.

"I'm *so sorry*," Olani and I say at once, voices overlapping.

"Are you okay?" Raze adds, which is a stupid question and very on-brand for him. *No*, obviously, she's *not*.

I draw back, trying to take in everything at once: the tear Isolde wipes quickly off her cheek. My own shaking hands. Dark drops of Olani's blood on the ground. The moon-bathed courtyard we've found ourselves in, smooth white stone in a stretch at least the size of the village where I grew up.

We're in some kind of valley circled by the mountains, with dark cliffs rising up on all sides high enough to block all but a patch of sky. The Western Range, I think. I've never seen these peaks before, but where else could we be?

An enormous building stands high up on the cliff behind us, built into the mountain itself. Brushed gold adorns its arches, and a light breeze whispers through the hollows of the stone. My gaze wanders down the cliff to our level, where a jagged crack just large enough to be an entrance yawns into the darkness of the mountain's heart.

The compass points steady and sure and calm, and I can sense, with every fiber of my being, that this is where our journey ends.

"I... I think I twisted my ankle," Isolde says. Her voice trembles but comes out stronger than I expected. "When I was... running away."

Olani switches into healer mode instantly. "Move," she tells me. Against all my instincts, I ease back, letting Isolde slowly, gingerly stretch her legs out straight in front of her. I don't let go of her hand, even when it crushes mine so hard it hurts.

Olani doesn't look so good herself. She took a pretty bad fall from that horse, and if she was riding as long as I was dancing, she must be exhausted. There's still an arrow poking out from her hip at a sickening angle, and I have no idea how she's still on her feet. Her face is even more grim than usual, her practiced movements just a bit too tight. Like she's scared to even touch Isolde.

"I'm sorry," she says again, easing herself onto the ground to examine Isolde's awkwardly bent ankle. "I'm *so sorry*, Isolde, I didn't—" She stops, voice taut. "I should have stopped it."

"Wasn't your fault," Isolde says, gentle and ragged and final. Then she seems to notice the arrow for the first time. "Are you okay?"

"Never better," Olani grunts. Raze hovers over her, looking like he might pass out if he doesn't find something to do with his hands very soon. "It was a lucky shot." She turns from me to Raze, waving him away with irritation clear on her face. "I can handle it."

Olani reaches for her bag, and I silently thank Fate that the faeries didn't take it when they swapped our clothes. Her face crinkles in pain as she flips the bag open, but her eyes move with the steady sweep of a physician assessing a wound. I watch in mingled disgust and amazement as she takes a deep breath.

Releases it.

Her strong, well-practiced fingers wrap around the arrow, knuckles turning pale as her hand flexes. And then she pulls the arrow out of her own flesh with barely a sound, nothing more than a sharp hiss of breath through her teeth.

My stomach churns. Isolde and Raze both stare determinedly anywhere but at the arrow.

"Won't kill me," Olani says, reaching for a compress to stop the gush of blood that has already poured out onto the stone. "Probably."

"Probably?"

But she's already moved on, ignoring me. "Let me see that ankle."

Isolde downplayed the damage—of course. It must be worse than a sprain. Her nails dig into my palm as Olani gently removes her fitted, pointy-toed boot. Her ankle hangs uselessly, at an angle that looks wrong even to my untrained eyes.

I force myself to look down and watch Olani assess the damage, and I don't think I do a very good job of hiding my wince of sympathetic pain.

"How bad is it?" Isolde asks. I can see the white of her teeth against the dark, bared in a grimace.

Olani is so much better at staying collected than I am. "It's broken," she says gently, settling into herself again. "In a few places."

Raze finally speaks. "This is all my fault. I should have—"

Isolde interrupts him. "It's not your fault. It's the cursed faeries'. Ow!" She pins Olani, who's wrapping her ankle and splint in bandages, with an accusing glare. "Are you trying to snap it off?"

"Stop whining, or I will." Olani looks up at her for less than a heartbeat before going back to work.

Isolde groans, this time in frustration. "Well, can you fix it?"

Olani is already digging through her bag again. "Not quickly." She pulls out a few things and keeps talking steadily as she tends to the wound. "I can set it, no problem. Getting the bone to mend itself, though—that's…more than I can do. I can probably speed up the process, but it's going to take… at least a few days, I think."

"We don't have a few days," Isolde says. "The Destiny is gone. Our supplies are gone. We don't even know where we are."

And then everyone looks at me, as if they're just remembering that I'm the one who dropped us here. I'm the one responsible for leaving the Destiny, and all our things, and poor Birch behind in the faerie forest.

"Seelie…" Olani says, but then she doesn't seem to know how to follow it.

"*How* did you do that?" I realize Raze has been anxiously pacing this whole time. Like the rest of us, his faerie finery looks strangely out of place. He paces with his arms crossed, and now that I'm aware of the tapping of his boots, it's incredibly distracting.

I tapped into some strange kind of magic in the faerie world, made some kind of bargain that I don't fully understand. But I can't tell them that, so I just say, half truthfully, "I… I don't know."

"Mortals can't create passage between the worlds," he insists. "This is…*home*, right?"

That, at least, is a question I can answer. I might not know where we are, but I can feel the difference between the Seelie Realm and the mortal world. I'm surprised he can't. "Yes."

"How?" Isolde says softly. Her eyes are round and still vulnerable with pain, and the thought that they might reflect me differently now makes me feel sick.

Olani studies me with a hard, unreadable expression. "You are mortal, aren't you?"

"Yes!" I repeat, at the same time Isolde says, "Of course she is!"

Silence falls for a beat, and whatever it is that passes between the four of us makes me feel unsteady. Finally, I break it. "I don't know how I did it. I just—I had to save us. I don't know how any of this works. You have to trust me."

Raze and Olani lock eyes for a long time, having some kind of silent conversation. Then she nods once.

"We do," Raze says. "So where are we?"

A sudden shiver runs over my skin, and not just because of the cool breeze on my exposed arms. Something compels me to look down at my left hand. I can see the arrow clearly in the moonlight. It points straight, unwavering, to the hollow in the cliffside.

There. Now hurry.

"We're here," I say simply. "And we're trying to get there."

Everyone's eyes follow where I'm pointing, taking in the silhouette high over our heads. We're *here*, just a short walk away from our final destination, from the treasure, from Raze's family legacy, from everything. It should be exciting, but instead, it just makes me feel like there are weights tied to my legs, like I can't take another step.

"We should get moving," Isolde says, voice tight with pain. She looks ready to jump up and test the splint out, and I'm going to have to tackle her if she does. "We don't know if your aunt's still on our trail. A few days might be exactly what they need to catch up to us. I can walk."

Olani is still crouched over Isolde's ankle, trying to focus on weaving an enchantment to manage the pain. "No," she says, cutting off Isolde's protests. "Not if you want it to heal right and be of any use to you in the future."

Silence falls. All eyes turn to the building in the distance.

Raze plops down on the stone with the rest of us. "Not tonight." He looks so tired. The absence of charisma and humor leaves him looking as threadbare as I feel. "We need to rest."

I want to argue, but I can't. My back is on fire, and my legs are painfully numb from overuse. Once we've made the decision to rest, everything catches up with me all at once, and I can't even remember putting my head down on the stone before I fall asleep.

When I wake, it's to total darkness and the murmur of Isolde's voice.

"...how she did it," she says. "It's so different, seeing her use her magic. But it suits her, somehow. Like she's always been this way."

It feels like there are ants in my clothes with the image of both their eyes trained on my still, small shape in the darkness. Watching me. I dig my nails into my palms hard enough to leave behind crescent-shaped marks.

Raze clears his throat. "Has she ever..." He pauses. "I mean, is that—new?"

I'm not sure what he's asking, but after a pause, Isolde answers anyway. "Before we left home," she says, in a voice that sounds emotionally rusty from disuse, "she never... Our parents weren't enchanters, and we didn't want anyone to know what she was. It happened a few times, when we were really little. Things flying across the room, stuff like that. She'd cry and cry and apologize and say she didn't want to get taken away. Then we got older, and she just stopped using magic completely."

My heart hammers in my chest. Part of me wants to pretend to wake up, to stop Isolde from baring this part of my history.

But I want too badly to hear her true, unfiltered thoughts about me to do that.

I stay as still as I can, trying to force my breathing into a slow, even pattern.

"There were a few times—" Isolde swallows hard, then starts again. Carefully. "The night that we left...we wanted to protect our parents. Maybe that was a bad idea, but it seemed like our only choice at the time."

My arms are pulled tight to my chest and tug at my necklace. This dress is too low-cut to cover it, and I'd almost forgotten about it in all the chaos. But it's still there. Still smooth and whole, still familiar between my restless, wringing fingers.

"So, no," Isolde says. Her hands scrape over the stone as she shifts. "I've never seen her blast anyone with fire or summon a portal between worlds before. And I don't know how using that kind of power didn't do something worse to her. I mean, I'm glad it didn't. I can't stand seeing her hurt. But..."

She lets the unfinished thought hang in the air. Something between being fearing *for* me...and fearing me.

There's more shuffling and rustling as Raze says, "You should rest."

"But—"

"I'll take watch." Isolde must hesitate after that, because when he speaks again, I can hear the infuriating grin on his face. "Don't be a pain in the ass."

Isolde snorts but doesn't argue. A moment later, I feel her warmth as she settles onto the stone a few inches away, hear the sound of her steady breathing. We catch a few restless hours of rest on the flat, cold stones, huddled together for warmth.

I wake early enough to watch the sun rise and see the sky slowly shift from pink to silver to forget-me-not blue.

In the daylight, the courtyard isn't any less unsettling. We're at the bottom of a deep fissure, with smooth white stone in every direction. After centuries of abandonment, gray streaks and ivy are trying to reclaim the mountain's heart, but it's still bright enough to dazzle my eyes.

Eventually, Isolde stirs. Olani, who's usually up before the sun, wakes next, struggling to slip from sleep's grip. "Raze! You didn't wake me," she accuses hoarsely as she shoves herself up with a grunt of pain.

He's still sprawled on the rock several feet away, head pillowed in his arms. "Hm?"

"You're still hurt," I point out. "I thought I'd let you all sleep."

She yawns. "So you think I want to slack off, just because of one little arrow wound?" Her head tilts to look at Isolde. My sister is pretending very hard that she isn't also slowly waking, trying to bury her face in her short hair without much luck. Olani pokes her in the side.

"Don't care what you want," Isolde mumbles. Moving sluggishly, she stretches.

"Sol." I don't know what to say. I want to say, *I'm sorry we got separated. I'm sorry you were turned into a fox. I'm sorry I scared you. I'm sorry for making you worry. I'm sorry I have to fin-ish this for us.*

But I can't make any of those words come out, so instead, I say, "How's your ankle?"

Our two identical sets of wide, dark eyes trace down her leggings to the swollen, bandaged, vaguely ankle-shaped lump at the bottom. "Better," she lies, forcing a smile.

With a quiet groan, Olani leans in, pressing one hand firmly over Isolde's shin. It's almost big enough to wrap all the way around her slender leg. "Liar," the healer mutters. "It hurts like hexes."

Isolde pouts, glancing at me. "I was trying to put on a brave face."

Olani sighs. I watch her breathe slowly and deeply, eyes closing as her face crinkles with concentration.

"Wait," I say, one hand hovering over hers. "Are you strong enough for this?"

She just glares at me. "Let me help."

It doesn't escape me that she didn't answer the question.

Suddenly, Raze is behind us, still stretching. "Good morn-ing," he yawns, putting more effort into sounding cheerful than is necessary or wanted.

I take Isolde's hand. She squeezes tight as the sensation of Olani's healing flows to the pain in her ankle, then relaxes. "That's better."

Olani smiles, pushing back escaped locks of hair from her forehead. "You're still not going anywhere fast."

We split a meager, pitiful breakfast of the few edible herbs from Olani's medicine bag and discuss what we already know has to happen.

"So Raze and I will go," I conclude, folding my arms over my chest. This takes some arranging, since I'm wearing his utterly impractical shirt over my dress to cover my arms and shoulders, tied at the waist and rolled up at the sleeves. He's down to just a long-sleeved undershirt, cut low to accommodate the billowy shirt, and Isolde is barefoot, since I needed her soft faerie boots more than she does. "You're both hurt, and I hate leaving you alone, but—"

Isolde nods. "We need to make this as quick as possible, whether I like it or not."

I don't know what to say. This was always supposed to be her adventure, and now we're so close to the end of it. I should feel relieved, but I'm more anxious than ever.

Olani lets out a deep sigh. "You're right." Despite the toll exhaustion and injury have taken, her dark brown skin still catches the light as she folds her arms across her chest. "I'll see what I can do to speed up the healing. You two go find the Keep."

Raze nods, but guilt shades his face as his eyes fall on the dark blood staining her clothes. "Olani, I am so sorry. This is all my fault. I shouldn't have let you get involved in this."

She raises an eyebrow at him. "Let me?"

"I... You know what I mean." He looks away.

"Raze." She leans in, elbowing him gently until he finally looks back at her face. "I didn't make a mistake. I chose your side because I wanted to be here."

"Here?"

She takes a second to observe our bleak surroundings before an ironic smile tilts her mouth ever so slightly. "You know what I mean," she says.

Raze's shoulders are still hunched. "But Leira…"

"Is a power-hungry murderer who needs to go down. I want to be a part of that."

"And the treasure?"

"Well, the treasure doesn't hurt." She leans her head onto his shoulder in a brief almost-hug that reminds me starkly of Isolde and me doing the same thing. Finally, Raze relaxes, allowing himself to smile back at her.

Isolde stares daggers at her splinted ankle, as if pure anger might be able to heal it faster. I know she's taking the injury hard. I know there's nothing she'd like more than to spring into action as the protector, the hero. "On my next quest, I'll just have to try harder not to get hurt right as it's getting good."

"I—" I start to reply, but I can't. Her *next quest*? She can't be serious. That argument we had—that was just an impulse, like every other decision she's ever made. That was before the faerie world, before she was turned into a fox, before her broken ankle, before we almost *died*. She can't possibly still mean to turn her back on home. "W-we're going home," I stammer, eventually.

"What's wrong?" Raze says.

Isolde ignores him. "Yes, we're going home. But…after that. We talked about this, Seelie." She pushes against the ground to force herself to her feet, too, gritting her teeth.

"No." My voice shakes. "No, no, no. This was supposed to be fixed. I… I tried so hard." I've tried to keep her safe, to finish the mission, to do everything I was supposed to do. To be the sister she wants me to be, so she won't need to go. "And you still want to leave me?"

Isolde sighs, and I can hear the frustration in it. Pain and exhaustion are wearing on her usual patience. "It's not about *you*, Seelie. Sometimes, things aren't about *you*. Did you ever consider that?"

I'm stunned. Even Raze and Olani flinch, averting their eyes. Isolde never talks to me like that. I mean, we've fought before, plenty of times. But every time, it stings. My throat feels tight, and I have to focus very hard on shutting up, on not crying, on not embarrassing myself in front of my new friends.

"Maybe—" Raze tries.

"And it's not like I said you couldn't come along!" Isolde interrupts. She's getting loud now, her voice magnified in echoes that crash down on me one after the other. "I asked you to. All the things you can do, and you just want to hide behind me like you can't—behind Mami—behind any excuse."

She seems angry about something else. I don't know why she's angry at me. It's too warm in the morning air, it's too uncomfortable in my own skin, and I'm squeezing my hands tight into fists and forcing down magic and tears and—

Isolde limps closer, and I flinch. She stands right in front of me, and since we're the same height, it's hard to avoid her eyes. "Look at me," she says, voice lowering. *"Look at me!"*

"I don't understand." It comes out as a sob. I don't know what she wants from me. "I just—I just—I just don't want you to go."

"You just want everything to be exactly the same way it was before we left." Isolde isn't yelling anymore, but her voice holds a note of something hard and unfamiliar. "But it's not,

Seelie. It can't be. You're a changeling. You can summon
lightning out of the sky and walls of fire and—"

"And you're a thief!" I finally find my voice, and it's also
hard and unfamiliar, trembling with something that isn't anger
but could be. "Is that why? You're too ashamed to face Mami
and Papa? How long do you think you can go without picking pockets or threatening someone with a knife?"

Her mouth drops open, her face twisting. "I only started
stealing to take care of *you*. Fate knows you weren't doing
anything to keep us fed."

"I didn't ask you to come with me! I didn't want you to
leave home! I was trying to fix a problem that *I* caused, and
you're the one who decided you needed to be the savior. You
always have to be—"

"How long do you think you would have made it on your
own, Seelie?" Isolde's voice raises again, even as the corner of
her mouth trembles. "You wouldn't last a week without me."

"Yeah, and with you I'm doing *so well*!" I gesture around
us: at the mountains, her broken ankle, the empty space where
the Destiny *should* be, the whole cursed situation. "Oh, wait."

I'm distantly aware that Raze and Olani are still here, but
I can't make it matter when my whole existence is burning
with anger. I've never felt this angry. Not at Raze, not at
Cassius Redbrook, not at Leira Wildfall, or Fate itself. I expected all of them to hurt me. The surprise that Isolde, who
I trust, could betray me like this burns worse than anything
else ever could.

I flex my fingers and roll my neck, trying to hold back the
magic that rises up with my storm of emotion. "You always
know how to get in trouble, but you never think about get-

ting yourself out. That's what *I* have to do. And when you leave me, there won't be anyone there to save you from yourself. Now, let—"

She limps forward, cutting me off before I can brush past her. There's tension in her face, in her stance, in her hands. I wonder—for the first time since we were very young—if she's going to hit me.

I try to put distance between us, but Isolde grabs hold of my shoulder—tight. I yelp at the sudden contact, trying unsuccessfully to twist away. "Let me go," I manage, but my voice is dry and rough.

In her face, I see every time I've run away from emotions too big to hold within myself, every time she's lost me and had to track me down again. She's scared I'm going to run. She's trying to protect me.

Well, maybe it's time to protect myself.

It's a treacherous thought, too cold and slick with anger to untangle whether it's truly mine. But Isolde's half-right. I have magic.

I have power.

Just the thought is enough to make it spark up without permission, and a shock jumps across my skin. A burst of lightning pushes against Isolde's grip on my shoulder, and she jumps away with a cry.

"Seelie!" There's pain in her voice, an arrow straight to my heart. It's not enough. Not enough to calm me down, to settle my magic. I can feel the sparks dancing up and down my fists, and I don't want to hurt her—but I don't want to stop.

The thought scares me enough to make me tumble a step back, away from her. I shake with the effort it takes to breathe, to try to rein myself in. It's just the enchantment, just the presence at the edges of my consciousness. Thoughts like that aren't *mine*.

They can't be.

Isolde retaliates, her hands reaching desperately for some way to keep me from running. She grabs the only thing she can—my necklace—and pulls *hard* before she realizes what she's got.

The cord snaps, leaving her clutching the vial in white knuckles. We both stare at each other with wide eyes, breathing hard.

"Seelie," she tries again, but I don't want to hear it.

"Why don't you hold onto that?" I say, pain raw in my voice, because that vial represents our family—everything she's decided she's ready to let go of. "For safekeeping."

Everyone is still staring in silence when I turn and walk straight into the tunnel opening, disappearing into the mountain. This time, she doesn't try to stop me.

chapter twenty-six

I hear my name, called in three different voices, echo behind me, and I don't stop walking until the sound fades away. I don't make it much farther before I can't hold up the weight of my emotions another second. My chest aches. I stumble and catch myself on one rough stone wall before sliding to the floor. I can't make myself get up. I can't keep going.

Isolde and I never fight like that. When I remember the anger that simmered in her eyes, the fear not far behind, I feel dizzy and unsteady. What if that's secretly how she's always felt about me and she's just now saying it? No wonder she wants to leave our shared life behind, if I've really always been such a burden to her.

I thought we were a team. I thought that, together, we could make it through anything.

But we're not together anymore.

Eventually, I hear footsteps, tapping on the stone faster than I thought Isolde could walk with her broken ankle. I feel like I should be crying, but instead I'm a dull, frozen lump.

I don't know what I'm going to say to her.

But it isn't her.

"Seelie," Raze breathes. Hearing my chosen name in his voice is jarring, and not just because he sounds so relieved.

"Go away," I say, not looking back at him. "I know you're scared of me."

I hear him stop, standing just behind me. He wants me to turn and look at him, but I can't face anyone right now. "Okay," he admits. "But what else is new?"

I stare straight ahead, jaw clenched. There's only a faint trace of light left, barely enough to make out the path ahead.

"Isolde is sorry," he says, after a long moment.

Each word feels like struggling to lift a heavy weight. "You don't understand."

"I do." He ignores my glare, leaning against the wall at my side. "Isolde explained what that necklace meant to you. What it holds. I'm sure she'd come beg for your forgiveness herself, but I wasn't going to pick her up and carry her."

I picture Raze running after me with my sister bouncing up and down on his back, and a small laugh breaks through the knot in my throat. I let my back relax a little, let myself catch his eye out of the corner of mine. "You don't think… you don't think she…?"

I can't make myself ask if he thinks she thinks I'm a monster. I don't want to know the answer.

Raze takes a long, measured breath, and I repeat it. A little of the tension wound around my chest loosens. "You're both under a lot of stress. You'll figure out how to forgive each other."

I wonder how he can be so sure.

"But you don't have to go back and sort it out now if you don't want to."

I'm still angry, but it's deeper down, not burning through me. I feel bare without my necklace, but maybe Isolde breaking the cord is a good thing. Maybe it'll make her actually *think* about what she's planning to do to us. Maybe it'll change her mind.

Maybe everything will be okay.

I repeat that in my mind, silently forming the words with my lips, until I force myself to believe it. Everything will be okay. I didn't actually hurt her, just zapped her a little. I can control this. I'm not dangerous. Isolde will realize she's in the wrong. When I return, triumphant and buried in gold, she'll apologize, and *everything will be okay.*

The anger subsides into something hard and small, something I can tuck away for now but not get rid of completely. "What now?" I ask, after a long silence. I turn my attention ahead, to the immediate task, instead of my jagged past and nebulous future.

Raze stands, offering me his hand, and I let him help me to my feet. We stare into the darkness of the tunnel ahead, uncertain. I'm still tired and stiff and achy. Olani's healing helped, but I still feel wrung-out. And not quite like myself.

The compass seemed to be urging me forward, but I don't know how far this tunnel winds before it eventually slopes up to the building—if it slopes up at all. I can sense the same hesitation in Raze, in his held breath and nervous glances backward. But back is the only other way we can go, and that is *not* happening right now.

I release him, allowing myself one more look at the compass in my palm. One last brush over the needle with my opposite thumb. "Let's get this over with."

Raze won't stop talking, and I think I'm going to kill him. Luckily for him, he has yet to bring up what happened between us in the faerie realm—though all those memories are hazy now, dissolving in my mind like a dream. Maybe he's forgotten about that.

As if I could be that lucky.

After the fourth apology about Isolde's ankle, I snap. He's gripping my arm in the half light, helping me climb over a steep boulder that blocks the whole narrow tunnel.

I shove him away, hopping down by myself and praying I don't break *my* ankle, too. "So you mean all this *wasn't* your master plan to get me alone in a cave with you?"

"As if you haven't been *dying* for some more time alone." His voice echoes off the stone, magnifying its smugness. "I thought changelings didn't lie?"

"Not like—" I cut myself off with a sharp breath. "We're perfectly capable of lying. I didn't mean it like that. I meant to kill me off or something. So you wouldn't have to pay us."

He looks at me like he isn't sure if I'm joking. I can see the exact moment he decides I am, in the slight wrinkle at the corners of his eyes. "Well, now that you mention it..."

I relax a bit. "I'd like to see you try, Wildborn."

He seems offended. "You haven't seen me as a goose yet. Have you ever tried fighting a goose? They're bloodthirsty."

That actually makes me laugh out loud. "Is that a threat?"

"Wouldn't you like to know?"

The relaxed air between us fades as soon as the last of the light does. Raze goes strangely quiet, and I can hear his breathing turn shallow and rapid, as if he's frightened.

I try to feel my way along the wall until my toe catches on an uneven spot. I hear myself cry out as I sprawl forward, stumbling to try to avoid falling flat on my face, and then a tight grip closes around my arm. Raze pulls me back onto my feet, holding on until I'm steady again. After that, we walk through the darkness hand in hand, keeping each other steady. From the way Raze's sweaty hand clamps around mine, it seems like he needs that.

Light returns so slowly that I don't even notice it until I realize that I can see my hand in front of me.

"Look!" I say, pulling free. Suddenly, we turn a corner, and a corona of light blazes in front of us, pouring through a tall, arched doorway at the top of a smooth set of white stone steps. Our steps speed with excitement until we're practically running up the stairs, but at the top, I stop. Chills run over my arms. I don't know what's up there. I don't know if I'm ready.

"What are you waiting for?" Raze calls tightly, passing me. His broad shoulders relax with relief at being back in the open air.

As soon as I cross through the arch, sunlight blazes on my skin again. The wind, unsure if it's summer or autumn, brushes over me, filling my lungs with a refreshing breath.

Once my eyes adjust, I gasp. Raze stands frozen, too, his eyes moving over everything hungrily.

I press my left hand to my chest and feel the pounding of my heart. We're *so close*. So close to the end of all this.

We've ascended into an atrium facing five floors of balconies, each with stone floors and walls and railings carved to look like vines. The domed ceiling of the atrium opens to the sky in a huge circle that floods the whole place with sunlight. Rows of shelves extend back on each floor as far as I can see. Swooping spiral staircases, suspended by supports that look too slender to hold anything up at all, curl on each side of the balconies, leading from one floor to the next. It looks like it was all carved straight into the mountain.

There's a noticeable lack of gold.

The Mortal's Keep. But…

"It looks like some kind of library," I whisper, wrinkling my nose. I try to imagine treasure in the back rooms, piles of gold and whatever *legacy* Raze is looking for just beyond the extremely drab reality of what we can actually see. I check the compass in my palm for guidance. It points, unwaveringly, to me.

I hide my hand behind my back before Raze can snatch a glance. I'm sure that doesn't mean anything. Now that we're here and the enchantment has served its purpose, it's probably just a little broken. I'm surprised it hasn't dissolved away altogether yet. Maybe this is the first step to that.

Raze ignores me. "Hello?" He calls, at the top of his very loud voice.

"*Shhh!*" I whip around, crushing a hand over his lips. "What is *wrong* with you?"

He raises his eyebrows, and I realize I can feel his warm skin molding into a smile under my hand.

"Can you be serious for just one second?" I whisper angrily.

He just stares at me, amused, his breath hot and damp against my palm. Disgusting.

I relent, lowering my hand and wiping it viciously on my skirt. Raze smirks, squeezing every last drop of enjoyment out of my irritation. "I thought if there was anything spooky hanging around, it might be better to confront it first, rather than get ambushed. I don't know—Olani usually handles this sort of thing."

I can't really argue with that line of logic, but it still seems flawed. I settle for rolling my eyes with a long-suffering sigh.

When no monsters appear, I look back to Raze. "Are you sure we're in the right place?"

He looks a little uncomfortable. "This is it, all right. I expected more of a fortress or vault, and less enchanted library, but I guess knowledge is power, right?" The awkward look deflects easily into his cocky grin. "The good stuff must be hidden in here somewhere."

"Enchanted?" I say, catching on to the one relevant detail. "Does that mean that this is a library of books on magic, or enchanted books? Or other enchanted items?" The push and pull of awe and fear within me is going to wreck my nerves.

"How should I know? Just…try not to touch anything. To be on the safe side."

"Really?" I reply. "I was planning on licking everything, just to make sure."

Raze tilts his head up, squinting. "That might take a while.

We're going to have to search every inch of every floor, aren't we?"

"I don't know." I'd ask the compass, but it's still pointing to me, which is unhelpful.

"Where should we start?"

I pause. My rational mind screams not to take another step into this beautiful, impossible building, that there's something wrong here. Another, louder part of me is captivated, pulled, itching to explore. I take one delicate step, then another, feeling like a princess in a faerie story as the tap of Isolde's boots echoes through the atrium.

"Let's do the first floor first," I say. "Work our way up."

Raze looks around like he also senses something isn't quite right, but he agrees, extending his elbow to me like we're about to walk into a ballroom.

I ignore it and brush past him.

After that, Raze finally goes quiet for a bit. I don't know what we expected—a giant nest of gold and jewels, a brightly lit sign that says *WILDLINE LEGACY HERE*—but there's no indication of anything on the first floor.

Or the second.

All we pass is the shelves of books and cubbyholes of scrolls. Skeletons of glass cases, the panes long broken and scattered, stand over every couple of rows of shelves. Even though the building is open to the air, the books themselves don't seem rotted at all. They're dusty, some of the titles hard to make out, but after hundreds of years of abandonment, they should be totally disintegrated.

The breeze tastes of leather and paper and spoiled magic, bitter and oily. Even the air around me feels different, like the hum I felt last night in the faerie realm or at Revelnox. There's an enchantment here, I realize. One cast over the whole library to preserve its contents. One that, after so many centuries, is finally beginning to unravel.

I glare at my palm, willing the arrow to move, to point at anything but me, but apparently that enchantment is done helping.

Besides the shelves and cases, webs of halls and cavernous rooms fill each floor. Some are filled with books, some hold enormous tables surrounded by chairs, and some are completely empty. Every once in a while, the sound of the wind or fluttering of a bird's wings startles us, and we laugh nervously when we realize it's nothing.

Finally, somewhere around the middle of the third floor, I can't bear the silence. The question that's been quietly stuck in the back of my mind since Leira confronted us spills out, surprising even me.

"Why do you care about that ring so much?" Raze stiffens so obviously that even I can tell. I keep going, despite my better judgment. "You don't have to tell me. I just mean… When Leira showed it off, it seemed…important?"

Raze shakes his head, taking a step back from me. I've tried so hard not to think about last night: about his arms holding me up as we limped into the forest, about the way he looked at me as the enchantment fell away, about the brief, horrible moment when his lips were on mine, about the way he rushed in to protect Isolde without a thought for himself. It all seemed almost like a dream, but when his eyes lock on mine, everything rushes back.

Then he looks away. It's strange, not being the one to look away first. "You'll think it's silly."

I thought I hated him, but I don't. I just can't stand him, with his secrets and his scheming and his *smiles*. And now, when I've finally started to allow him to get closer, he wants to back off. "No," I say honestly. "I won't."

Raze looks like he's seriously considering shifting into a hawk and flying away. Then he shrugs, looking back at me again. His eyes are almost gray in this light, dark and deep as murky water. "It belonged to my dad," he mutters.

Belonged. I haven't thought much about Raze's parents, about his family beyond Leira, but of course he must have had one. I feel selfish for not considering that sooner or wondering why he never talked about them.

"What happened to them?" I blurt. *Great job, Seelie,* I think angrily at myself. *Dig deeper into what is obviously a very painful past for him to discuss. That will make everything better.*

Raze looks at me out of the corner of his eye, and he must decide that I'm doing my best, because he answers.

"They…died. When I was six. I don't have anything else to remember them by." Light glints off his ring. His face twitches, like his throat is going dry, and when he speaks again, his tone is low and pained. "It was right after I started shapeshifting. Leira was a distant cousin of my mother's. She took me in, raised me, gave me everything I ever asked for."

He scowls at the floor.

"At least, until she realized my magic wasn't getting any stronger. She tried everything to coax my power from me—teachers, potions, enchantments. None of it made any dif-

ference. I'm just…weak. But Aunt Leira wasn't satisfied with
that explanation. So she…she…"

He's still walking, faster now, like he's trying to outrun
the end of the sentence. I reach out and touch his arm lightly,
and when he doesn't pull away, I tug gently to slow him. We
stop in a patch of yellow sunlight between stacks of books.

"She started locking me up. Forcing me in smaller and
smaller cages. She said that if I really wanted to get out, then
I could just change my shape into something small enough
to slip through the bars. But I—" Raze's hands squeeze into
white-knuckled fists "—I *couldn't*."

My heart squeezes sickeningly. It's such a horrible thing
to do to another person, to a *child*, that I can't quite wrap my
head around it.

But Raze isn't done.

"I was old enough to know that it was *evil*. That *she* was…
But I didn't want to see it. I used to think that it was just an
accident, what happened to my parents. A coincidence. But
now…" The pause that follows is so dark and empty it makes
my chest ache. "Now I'm not so sure."

Oh.

Loud Raze, brash Raze, annoying Raze, flirtatious Raze.
All layers of paint slapped over this deep pit of sorrow and
confusion. I can't say I suddenly understand him now, or that
it makes his other sides any less *real*.

But a useless, sympathetic ache fills me anyway. Wisely, I
keep my mouth shut this time, trying to project sympathy in
my light touch on his wrist.

"You saw me under a faerie glamour," Raze laughs, after

a long pause. "I thought it couldn't possibly get more embarrassing than that."

Unwelcome memories of his dreamy expression and the warmth of his hands flash through my head. "No." I pull away, sitting up a little straighter. "It's not silly." It's what I should have said first, but now will have to do.

He hums, but whether it's in agreement or not, I don't know. For several long moments, the silence hangs empty between us with a strange new openness.

It's awkward, this friendship thing. Awkward and uncomfortable. Because now that I know more about Raze, now that he knows me, it's harder and harder to hide all the things we'd rather keep to ourselves.

The silence between us is open—but it's also vulnerable.

Finally, he cracks it.

"Maybe we should split up," Raze suggests, as we pass from a forest of tall shelves into a clearing of sunlight and smooth stone. "Cover more ground."

"Yes," I agree quickly. We're almost to the stairs again now. "Let's meet on the third floor landing just before sunset. Think you'll be okay alone?"

Raze shoots me an almost-convincing overconfident grin, all teeth and floppy red hair. "Believe me, I'm just fine on my own." Then he keeps walking, this time not waiting for my shorter pace to catch up.

chapter twenty-seven

The sound of Raze's footsteps fades, leaving me completely alone. The back of my neck prickles, like I'm being watched. I ignore the feeling, telling myself over and over that I'm not going to let some dusty old books and shadowed, cobwebby corners scare me. I'm on a mission. I'm an enchanter, and I can take care of myself.

For the first time, that thought is more of a comfort than a burden. Despite everything, some part of me feels stronger knowing I have magic at my fingertips, and I can't entirely hate it. I've been bullied and smashed down and targeted my whole life. Suddenly, I can bite back.

I shouldn't—but I can.

I wander from one room to the next, walking slowly, stopping occasionally to take a closer look at anything that sticks out. My fingertips itch with the desire to run along the spines of the books, to pluck them off the shelf and flip them open, but I'm no fool. I've read my fair share of faerie stories. Tearing my eyes away, I dig my nails into the tender skin of my palms.

Eventually, I find a staircase. My right hand skims the cool, smooth stone as I walk up, one step at a time, twisting in tight coils up to the fourth floor. Honestly, it's a miracle I don't trip and smash my head open on them.

The fourth floor is the same as all the ones below, perfect lines of shelves extending back into a series of rooms, scented with old paper and faint traces of mold and rot. Open windows along the sides let in streams of sunlight and a breeze that stirs around me, playing with my hair and tugging my skirt, like it's inviting me in.

Then I notice something different: all the books on this floor are locked in prisons of rusted chains, winding up and down the shelves.

That can't possibly be good, I think.

Part of me wants to call for Raze, just for the reassurance of having a real person at my back. Another part of me thrills: maybe this means I'm getting close. I want to prove that I can do this alone.

A shiver runs over me, leaving cold that goes down to my bones. I look down at my palm. For the first time all day, the arrow moves.

The smothering silence of the library folds around me, surprisingly calming. There's more ivy up here than below, waves of deep green claiming their territory along the wall and up the shelves.

I hold my hand out in front of me, palm-up. It points

straight ahead. I take one step onto the living green carpet. Then another. Then I'm not even looking around at where I'm going, completely absorbed in following where the arrow points. Ivy whispers softly under my boots as I move faster and faster, not quite running, the shelves passing in vague blurs.

My head feels fuzzy, and my body feels like it does when I'm using magic: mine, but not fully under my control. Like it's propelled by something deeper and stronger than my own mind.

I don't know how long I'm walking for. All I know is that when I stop, my heart flutters like a trapped moth against a window.

In front of me, a small platform is settled under a huge, arched window. The ivy has completely overtaken the three stone steps and the platform and is starting up the legs of the elaborately carved statue that stands there.

It isn't gold. It isn't whatever treasure or enchantment or artifact we're looking for.

I know that. I know I should turn and go back to looking. But I can't tear my eyes away. I *know* that face. I've seen it before, in Leira's locked room, translucent and irritated.

The form of a slender young man stands over me in white marble that blends in with the walls and floor. It's so intricately detailed that I can see the individual eyelashes of his closed eyes, resting against his high cheekbones.

My foot settles on the first step. I almost can't help myself.

The statue's long, sleek hair sweeps back from his face, and he stands relaxed, like he's fallen asleep on his feet. I know that face, those pale, perfect features. I saw him weeks ago, in

Wildline Manor. I've seen him, blurred by distance, almost every night since in my dreams.

Another step up.

A heavy iron chain wraps around him, from shoulder to foot, as if to emphasize *You really shouldn't mess with this statue.*

He said he was imprisoned here. I didn't think he meant that literally, that we would find him wrapped in iron.

That prickling feeling is there again, like drops of sweat on the back of my neck. Except I'm cold and getting colder by the second. The air buzzes around me, the whole world narrowing to just me and the statue.

You really, really shouldn't mess with this statue.

My hand lifts. The needle points straight at the statue's heart. My magic started bursting out of my control after I got the compass. And I feel certain—whatever is happening to me, this statue has the answers.

If only I could talk to him.

Just one touch.

I move slowly, feeling like I'm floating. Like someone moving underwater.

One.

I press my left hand to the statue's cool cheek. It's a strange gesture, but simple. No magic, no harm done.

Until the statue opens its eyes and smiles. "Seelie," it says on a sigh, in a voice I recognize clearly. That voice has been with me for weeks now, quiet and cool in the back of my mind. "I've been waiting for you."

I pull my hand away like I've been burned, staring at the now-rippling design in absolute horror.

The statue's smile grows a little troubled. "Are you okay?"

All I can get out is a strangled, high-pitched *"You!"* I can't catch my breath. I squeeze my hands into fists, trying to inhale slowly. "How do you know my name?"

He looks a little hurt. "Oh, come on, we've been traveling together for weeks. You don't recognize me?"

Of course I recognize him. When the compass's physical form disappeared, I thought he was gone, too, just a dreamlike shadow of himself in the back of my mind. I never connected that presence with the way my magic raged within me, the feeling of it soaking into my bones from the design in my palm. I see lightning ripping through the sky, see a gust of blue flame and fear in Aris's eyes, feel that deep fury, the urge to just give in to my power and let it destroy everything.

My heart squeezes tight, and so do my fists. "You've been messing with my magic!" I gasp, voice raw with anger. "The destruction—the scars—the *rage*—that was all *you*!"

The statue's face is perfectly still, like he's trying to understand. Then it slides into a smug, sideways smile. "No, Seelie," he says, almost pityingly. "A tiny fraction of myself was in the compass—barely a ghost, watching and waiting. I couldn't use your magic. I just helped prop open the door to it that you like to keep so tightly closed. All the rest—that was *you*."

That can't be true. I'm not violent or power-hungry. I don't want to *destroy* people. I didn't know he was there, but I was certain the compass's magic was infecting me somehow, and if it wasn't—

Then, what does that make me?

"You're lying." My tone is vicious and wounded, more like a snarl than I thought I was capable of.

The statue is unaffected. His smile doesn't slip, but he raises one delicate eyebrow. "Oh, am I?"

He isn't. The realization feels like a weight dropping on my chest, but it rings so true I can't pretend otherwise. I know in that moment, with total certainty, that this figure can't lie. The realization dawns on me with an increasing slide into horror. I'm talking to a faerie, face to stone face. And not just any faerie: the faerie that's been *living* in the enchantment under my skin for weeks.

I scratch my nails over my palm, like I can erase the past. "What do you want with me?"

"Seelie," he breathes out again. I hate it. I hate that he knows my name, when I know nothing of him. I hate the familiarity of his tone and the softness of his marble face. "I want you to free me."

I am breathless with disbelief. The *absolute nerve* of this faerie, to trick and deceive me and climb inside my head and somehow expect to be rewarded, is so dizzyingly intense that for a moment I'm not scared anymore. I'm just angry.

Flames leap unbidden to my fingertips, and this time, I don't hold them back. I circle the pedestal, taking in the statue, the thick iron chains that loop over and over. He's draped in clothes so beautifully rendered I can see the translucency of the fabric, with elfin eyes over high cheekbones and a long, sharp nose. His head can't move, but his eyes follow me around.

"I've been trapped here for a long time," he eventually says, in the same cool tone.

The fire sparks and snaps between my fingers. I know that he's stone, and it won't hurt him, but the relief of letting my magic free makes it feel like maybe I can manage my emotions without exploding. "Don't."

"A *long* time," he repeats, raising his stone brows. Like he's trying to say something, but it just isn't coming out right. "Not a long time for a mortal. A long time for a faerie. I... faded. Mortal and faerie magic together forged these chains, so they could only be undone by a changeling, someone who wields both."

I hesitate, remembering what he promised, so long ago, we'd find here. And then what Raze told us in the abandoned city, his ancestors' part in the war that ended their world and birthed ours. "Are you a prisoner?" I ask breathlessly, reaching through my memory for what Raze called that war. "From the...the War of the Realms?"

The statue laughs, a hollow sound that rings against the stone walls. "The what?"

"Who put you here?" My voice is getting shakier, desperate for answers. "Why me?"

"You," the statue replies coolly. "Seelie. Any changeling would have done the trick, but it was Fated to be *you*. I wish I could have revealed myself to you sooner. I've never seen a mortal wield magic like you do."

I've never spoken to a faerie for this long before, but no faerie I've ever spoken to has been so earnest, so willing to show vulnerability and weakness. To admit to needing anyone else.

"Get out of my head!" My hands are leaping and twisting in the air with all the anger I can't hold in. "I don't care about any of this. I just want you *gone*. From my mind—from my magic. *Now*."

"Then, it seems you and I are after the same goal." He studies my face steadily with those flat stone eyes. "All you have to do is free me from my imprisonment, and the compass's enchantment will dissolve as well."

He makes it sound so easy. Too easy. I know I'm being reckless, but I don't really care. I need him gone, and it's hard to think about anything else with the unbearable itch of that thought at the front of my mind. "And…and you won't hurt me or anyone else? You'll just go on your way?"

"I will return to my own devices the instant that I'm able to." He speaks in a rush, careful control bubbling into heady excitement.

I sigh, letting the fire out. I can't believe I'm going to do this. "What do I do?"

His face softens with relief, and a grin that looks way too much like a human boy's tugs at his mouth, revealing incisors just a little too sharp. "It has to be a bargain. Just tell me, by name, that you release me, and make your request."

I pause, watching my hand hover over the iron chains where the faerie's heart would be. My throat feels dry. A faerie bargain. When I heard stories of those cursed by dealing with faeries, I shook my head, thinking they were just fools thinking death would be easier. Now I'm in a corner with no other choice, and suddenly I understand. "What is your name?"

"Gossamer."

I place my hand against the chain, just for a second. Not long enough to burn. "Gossamer," I repeat hoarsely, "I release you. In return, I ask only for the name you've already told me." A shock of cold runs up my arm, freezing me head to toe, blinding me. I hear a click.

Then it's over, so quickly I must have imagined it.

The chains fall off, pouring onto the floor in an echoing waterfall of clanging. The statue's face transforms quickly to confusion, then surprise—and then it stops moving completely, the spark of life gone.

When I pull my palm away, it's blank: nothing but smooth, pink skin. Not a trace of the ink I've gotten used to. It feels like losing a tooth when I was a kid, feeling the space in my mouth where there should be something but there isn't anymore.

I'm left shaking uncontrollably, even though I'm not cold anymore.

chapter twenty-eight

The faerie is gone. I reach over the puddle of iron between us to brush the statue's face, but it doesn't react. It's just a statue now.

"Well, that didn't go as expected."

I jump at the voice behind me, whirling around to face Gossamer. Even freed from his stone form, he's completely colorless, from his long white hair to his bare feet. His eyes look almost blank, the irises barely tinted gray. He examines his long, pointed nails in dismay before looking up at me.

It feels like meeting eyes with a tiger through a cage, knowing the thing before you could rip you apart without any effort at all. My heart thuds against my ribs painfully. "What do you mean?" I say, trying not to look afraid. "I-I freed you."

Gossamer's mouth twists in a half smile, and he paces to

the statue, forcing me to stumble out of his way. He moves like a liquid, lazy and smooth. "I said I'd return to my own devices as soon as I was able," he murmurs, tracing his fingers over the statue. Examining it like he's looking for a hidden message. "Did I say that would make me able?"

No. He didn't say that. It was a trick—of course it was a trick. That's how faerie deals always go, and I fell for it like an ignorant child. "What—" there's a pounding in my head that's difficult to think around "—what do you mean?"

Gossamer circles the statue, twisting around at awkward angles. When his eyes return to mine, he wears an apologetic smile that doesn't look right at all on his not-quite-human face. "I don't think you're going to like this," he says.

"Like what?"

"It's hard to say." He slinks around the statue and leans back against it, which is unsettling, to say the least. His eyes sweep over my face and my strange getup, calculating. "I mean, after such a long imprisonment, so much has changed. How could I…"

I've never known a faerie to be this awkward, this indirect before. All without telling a single lie. "Just tell me!"

His face scrunches up, and he gives in. "I'm not at full strength. I don't have my own physical form to return to."

My heart drops, even though I don't fully know what that means. It's just the way he says it that makes me feel a little dizzy. "So…?"

"So I'm not truly free yet, it seems." Gossamer's form flickers, and he slips straight through the statue as though he's made of nothing but air. "Which is to say, I have a new prison." Suddenly, he's nose-to-nose with me, his icy eyes boring directly into mine. The same chill from earlier creeps over my skin like a layer of frost as he reaches up to tap my temple with one gentle finger. "In here."

My knees wobble as I try to back away. I feel like I'm going to be sick. That can't be true. "No," I say. "No, I released you. I… You can't—"

"It's not that bad," he soothes. He starts moving forward but stops short when I hold up a hand to push him away. "Not that different from the compass, and you survived that. Just until the magic can be undone."

The pain behind my eyes sharpens. This can't be happening. There's still the lack of treasure, still Isolde's broken ankle, still my own magic and Raze's aunt and the missing Destiny and—

"So it *can* be undone?" I'm shocked at how calm my voice sounds. I must be more overwhelmed than I thought.

"It shouldn't take long to figure out a way," Gossamer says. This time, when he takes a cautious step forward, I let him. I wonder, if I reached out, would my hand pass straight through him? He's not really here. I might as well be imagining him. "But you were looking for treasure first, weren't you? I could take you to it. Books talk, and I've been in this library a *long* time. I know lots of things."

He doesn't wait for a response before sweeping past me. It's weird, watching him pass without feeling the movement.

I hurry to follow.

Following Gossamer is like following the enchantment that brought me to the room with the statue. I'm breathless and light-headed, dashing to keep up, chasing the disappearing wisps of white around corners and down long hallways. His steps don't make a sound—of course they don't—but mine all run together, like rain.

He stops so suddenly that I run into him. At least, I would if he had any substance. As it is, I run straight through him and gasp so hard I choke. I wrap my arms around myself against the cold, turning over my shoulder. "Why—?"

Gossamer holds up a finger to stop me. His head is tilted, looking alert into the distance. Listening.

I listen, too. It's as quiet and still as the rest of the library. Even the stirring of the wind seems to have died out.

Then I hear a sob.

I look around wildly, forgetting everything else. We're standing in the space between the high, arched openings to several rooms, and in one of them, someone is crying.

"Raze?" I don't dare to raise my voice.

No response.

My skin crawls. It seems impossible that there could be another person here, but I know what I heard. Something is wrong here, very wrong. Still, I can't just ignore it.

I turn my back on Gossamer, running to the sound of sobbing.

I follow the sound into the darkest room. The windows are covered, shrouding the whole area in gray. I run to the shadows, not knowing why or what I'm going to find.

What I see when my eyes adjust makes me stop so suddenly I fall to my knees. The dark room is full of people—at least, it had been, once.

They're all dead now.

Draped half-standing at awkward angles over tables, sprawled in puddles of blood on the floor, slumped in chairs. I scan the faces for Raze, for a flash of red hair, but I see none. At least I think he was spared.

There's so many of them, all dressed up like they're going to a party. Musicians still holding their instruments, sitting like they might strike up the next song at any moment, if their throats weren't slit. Blood running down fine dresses and jackets, eyes open wide in horror. I thought the library had been abandoned for centuries, but they can't have been here for more than a few hours.

I feel the scream tearing out of my throat before I hear it. Its echo lingers in the high, arched ceiling like captured birdsong. My eyes burn. I clap a hand over my mouth.

What happened here?

Another high-pitched sob rings through the room. Someone in here is still alive.

I've never wanted anything in my life as much as I want to turn and run and run until I'm back with Isolde and this whole library is behind me.

But I have to do something.

"Hello?" I say quietly. My voice shakes so badly it feels like the word might break in the air. I scramble quickly from my knees back to my feet and force myself forward.

"Help," someone says weakly.

I break into a run, my eyes skimming over the corpses for some sign of life. I'm met with blank, open eyes and have to fight down a wave of sickness. I step around them, desperate in my need to find the survivor—but there's no way to avoid the puddles of blood. My boots splash in it, trailing deep crimson prints along the white stone.

Movement.

A young woman near the middle of the room raises her head, just a little. I've seen her face before. Somewhere I can't remember, not that long ago…

I run to her, crashing to my knees again. My fine-spun faerie skirts soak up the blood thirstily. "I'm here," I say. "I'll—"

Recognition hits me so hard I gasp. It's the girl from the inn, the girl Raze had flirted with, the girl with lively blue eyes and lovely black hair and cheeks flushed with life. Her face is almost bone-white now, her hair matted with blood—hers or someone else's? It doesn't matter. "I'll—"

I can't say I'm going to help her. That would be a lie.

The girl looks up at me, her chest heaving as she struggles for breath. She reaches for my hand, and I close it around her frail white fingers. A trail of blood trickles out of the corner of her mouth, and she coughs wetly. She must have been stabbed somewhere vital: it's too dark to see for sure.

Hot tears blur my vision. "What happened here?" I whisper, rippling the quiet air with the rasp of my voice.

She's fading from consciousness. Her blue eyes focus on me for a second, then float away. Her lips part as she whispers something I can't hear.

"Can you move?"

She just looks at me helplessly.

There is nothing I can do.

How did she get here? echoes in the back of my mind with a hundred other questions, but that isn't what matters now.

Lost, I reach out and stroke her hair back from her face with my free hand. Just like Mami always did when I was sick. My palm is wet with blood now, but I don't care. I shush her gently, stroking her damp hair back. "I'm sorry," I whisper. Tears track down my face. Foolish, selfish tears, brought on by the pain watching her suffer causes me. "I'm so sorry."

"Don't," she says. Her breath is even more labored now as her chest fills with blood.

There has to be a way to save her. I'm not a healer like Olani, but surely there has to be something I can do—

anything—just so this nobody from a small town on the coast, a girl who works in an inn, a girl who has no reason to be here, won't die. I press my hands over her wound, soaking my fingers in blood. My magic recoils, but I draw it forward, reaching out, like I can *force* it to heal, to suddenly know what to do with shattered bones and split veins.

But it doesn't. And I don't either.

I'm disgusted, frightened, with lightning crackling in the air and arcing over my skin.

Suddenly, Gossamer is beside me. I don't know if he followed me without me seeing or just appeared here. His face looks troubled, veering into what I'd call *sorrowful* on a human. He doesn't ask who she is or what happened. He cuts straight to the point. "You want to save her?"

I cry even harder, so hard my chest hurts. Too hard to speak or nod.

Gossamer seems to take that as a *yes* anyway. He moves like a ghost, slipping behind me and putting his arms over mine. His hands over mine. They slip right through, so when I look at my own hands, they have a pale shadow with longer fingers, sharper nails.

"I have the power to undo this," he murmurs. His lips, this close to my ear, make ice shiver at the back of my neck. "All you have to do is hand over control."

I feel myself go stiff, wary at the hint of a faerie trick.

He feels it, too. "Seelie, there isn't much time."

Under my hands, the girl struggles to breathe. She shakes uncontrollably, eyes going wide. Where Gossamer's hands meet mine, magic tingles expectantly.

"We need to work together," he urges.

I can't agree to something like that—I can't. I can't let him have all of me, all of my magic. I'm already in too deep, so deep I feel like I'm drowning.

But this girl is *dying*.

"I—" I start, not knowing how the sentence is going to end. Tears splash on the girl's cold, white skin.

"Just *give me control*. Now!" Gossamer's voice is desperate and strained.

"Seelie!" The echoing sound of footsteps down the hall makes my head snap up.

Raze's voice. Raze's footsteps.

"Help!" I scream.

"No!" Gossamer tries to hush me, but it's too late. His hands pull back from mine, and his presence leaves my skin. Everything ebbs away into shadow.

All the bodies fade away. All the puddles of blood, all my footprints, even the wetness on my hands. Everything dissolves, except the girl in my arms. And then she's gone, too.

My hands are dry, but the tears are still rolling down my face. I wipe at them viciously, turning to Gossamer in confusion. My skin tingles like it wishes it could rip away from my bones and jump out the window.

"Wh-who were those people?" I can hardly speak between ragged gasps for air. "Wh-what—?"

They weren't real people. Not a real massacre. Not real blood. Not a real girl dying in my arms. Which means…

A trick, my mind screams. *It was all a trick. A vision planted in your mind to make you give him control.*

The most frightening part is that I would have done it.

Gossamer just closes his eyes and laughs. The sound is pure and clear, like an icy mountain stream. *I'll see you soon, Seelie.*

And then he vanishes, too.

chapter twenty-nine

Raze appears in the doorway, red-faced and out of breath. I'm wiping off the memory of blood on my hands on my skirts again and again, still shocked by the sound of my name hanging in the air, by the faerie's laugh, by everything I've seen and done.

As soon as he sees me, standing numbly in the middle of an empty room, apparently uninjured, he melts with relief. "I heard you scream," he says. "What—?"

I don't think. I throw myself into his arms, his wonderfully solid, warm, flesh-and-blood arms, and bury my face in his shoulder.

For a moment, he's totally still, his question forgotten. Then he wraps his arms around my small, trembling form. My arms fold, pinned between us by his, and my hands press to his chest. I can feel his heartbeat, strong and steady, thumping against the warmed fabric of his soft undershirt.

I can feel myself shaking, unable to form words. Unable to even cry. Terrified in a way I've never been terrified before, of something I can't escape from.

"You're safe," he whispers, over and over again. It's comforting, even though I know it's not true.

I should tell him what happened.

I can't. He won't be able to look at me the same if he knows there's a faerie trapped inside my head. He won't trust me; no one would. Besides, I brought this on myself, with my own foolishness, and I'm too embarrassed to admit it.

Raze's chin tucks over my head protectively. I hate myself for letting him.

I can't remember being this close to anyone outside of my family—besides that time on the horse. I should hate it, hate the feeling of being caged.

But I don't. I'm glad he's here with me, I'm glad for his huge arms and his gentle strength, I'm glad that somehow I screwed up badly enough to let him and Olani become my friends. Which is why I have to keep this whole Gossamer thing a secret.

I cling to Raze until I can breathe again, until the tight squeeze of my lungs and the shaking subside, but he still doesn't let go. "It's okay," he says, gently relaxing his grip on me until he's still holding my shoulders, but loosely enough that he can look at my face.

"What happened?" he asks. One hand reaches for my face, like he might brush away the tears that have already dried, but then he thinks better of it. I'm not the best with social boundaries, but that seems like it might be too much.

Chest aching, I finally find my voice again. "This p-place is playing tricks on me," I say, which isn't exactly a lie. "I th-thought I saw something, b-but it was just an enchantment." Also true.

"Are you hurt?" he asks, his eyes running over me for any kind of injury.

"No," I lie, pulling away from him. "Just scared." I flash a fake smile loaded with very real embarrassment. I can't believe I let him see me fall apart. I can't believe I *ran* to him.

"Are you—?"

"I'm fine now."

I don't think he believes me, but he lets his hand run from my shoulder down my arm to my hand. He squeezes it once before letting it drop to my side.

It rises, palm-up, and he does a double take. "The enchantment," he gasps. "It's gone."

All I can do is nod, pulling my hand back to my chest defensively. "We...we must be close."

Raze hesitates, looming over me with sad blue puppy-dog eyes, like he's waiting for me to burst into tears again. When I don't, his face lightens a little. "I found something," he says, excitement creeping into his voice. "Before I heard you." He sways in place, like he wants to reach out and hold me by the shoulder again and just ends up looking like he doesn't know what to do with his hands.

I nod, sniffing one last time. "Let's go."

But before I can turn away and stiffen my shoulders and try to focus, he finally does reach out again, fingers lightly brushing the sleeve of my borrowed shirt. "Wait," he says. "It's probably not...exactly what we expected. I just want you to prepare yourself."

"What does that mean?" I snap, before I can think about how to soften the words. I don't know if I can take one more thing going wrong. We have to find the treasure. This can't all be for nothing.

"You're going to get paid," Raze promises. "I'll make sure. It's just... Well, I think you'd better see for yourself."

"So, as I already said, *let's go*." I know he's trying to be kind and I'm being unfair to him. But rudeness is the only armor I have left.

Raze blinks at me for a second before letting out a sharp breath and brushing past. He leads me down the hall, in what I think is the opposite direction from the one I came here, but it's impossible to tell. I feel numb and slightly confused, and it doesn't really matter where we are.

Fate, this has become a nightmare.

Eventually, we reach a room with nothing but an enormous window, and I'm briefly blinded as coppery late-afternoon light melts over the smooth white walls. I blink a few times. It isn't a window at all: it's a wide, open doorway that leads out to a balcony.

We're dizzyingly high up on the same side of the mountain we came in through, looking over a wide expanse of dazzling white stone. I lean over the carved railing, but I can't see Isolde and Olani from this angle, just a long drop to the smooth stone floor. To my left, a spiral staircase leads up the side of the building.

I follow Raze up the stairs.

This set winds upward in an even tighter spiral than the ones on the lower floors, with a pitifully inadequate railing. All it would take is one slip, and I'd be done. Raze, unsurprisingly, seems completely unbothered by the height. I guess being able to sprout wings on command will do that.

My heart beats rapidly, and not just from the exertion of all these stairs. We're so close to the end. Once we get the treasure, once I get paid, once I get home—then everything will be okay. I'll figure out a way to get rid of Gossamer and to keep Isolde close. I'll be safe.

"Raze," I say, an apology stalling on my lips. Then I bump headfirst into his shoulder. We're at the top of the stairs, and I didn't even realize.

Raze looks over his shoulder at me, eyes shining. The apology dries in my mouth. "Look."

I push past him—and then I almost jump right back down the stairs.

A dragon stares back at me, ivory teeth grinning across a face wide enough to swallow me whole.

Not a dragon, I realize, my heart slowly settling back where it belongs. *A dragon's skeleton.*

The tall columns of its spiked spine, bleached as white as the stones it rests on, curve in a spiral, resting on a rib cage the size of my parents' cottage. The structures that once made up its legs have disintegrated over time, but I can still tell that they're tucked under its body the same way Birch curls up when he's sleeping.

It died peacefully.

We emerge onto some kind of enclosed rooftop deck, a crescent-shaped room curved around the dome at the building's top. The only real wall is open to the air, with pointed arches that stretch its whole length. The setting sun paints the whole space in blazing orange.

But it's hard to focus on the room, what with the enormous dragon skeleton taking up its square footage.

Something glitters in the fading sunlight, glaring against my eyes. I expect a bed of gold and gems, but this dragon's hoard is bare, except for one glittering thing. It almost blended in, but once I spot the dragon egg, it seems impossible to miss.

I saw a fire opal once, embedded in a brooch Isolde lifted off someone. It looked like it was lit from within, with swirls and specks of color that sparkled and jumped as if alive. It was nothing compared to this.

The egg is tucked safely into one of the curves of the dragon's skeleton. It's melon-sized but looks tiny in comparison to the full-grown one. The surface is mostly a soft tan, with sparks of red, orange, and green so brilliant it almost hurts to look at. Light plays over the surface with the familiarity of an old friend. When there were still scales and sinew there, it would have been snug against the dragon's heartbeat.

The same enchantment that protects the books despite the lack of glass in the windows must have sheltered this little room from the elements for centuries. If you couldn't protect your baby or entrust it to anyone else, I can hardly think of a better hiding place than this rooftop.

"I won't fit in there." When Raze finally speaks, it takes me a moment to figure out what he means. He leans to me, pointing. "The ribs are all locked together. I won't fit through those spaces." He pauses, letting me work it out for myself, before finishing. "But you might."

I pull away, recoiling at the thought. "So you want me to climb in that skeleton like a kid playing in a tree house."

He barely manages to bite back the start of a frustrated sigh. "It wouldn't be my *first* choice, but I don't think there's another way."

"Doesn't it feel...disrespectful, somehow?" Even as a pile of bones, the dragon commands awe. It *radiates* magic. I've been around tame dragons my whole life, but tame dragons don't get to this size. They don't breathe fire.

They don't curl up on a rooftop to die, protectively wrapped around their only heir.

But this isn't an ordinary dragon. It's a firedrake—at least, it was. Which makes its small, glittering egg a treasure of incalculable value. What would someone pay for the last living firedrake?

Raze voices the same thought. "Wouldn't it be more disrespectful to leave it here and never give it the chance to really live? Or to leave empty-handed?"

The memory of Isolde's voice rings in my ears. *You can't mean you want to stay tied down for the rest of your life.*

"Empty-handed?" I repeat, head buzzing. "I... There must be more. There must be *something*. That's...that's just an egg."

"And this is just a library!" His voice rings on the stone, in the hollows where the dragon's eyes once were. "It's not a fortress or a treasury. We could spend weeks looking, but this is *it*, Iselia. We're not going to make something better appear just by wishing for it."

My mind races. "We...we could gather the scrolls. You said they're enchanted. Maybe they have spells. Enchantments people would pay for. We'll collect as many as we can and—"

Raze shakes his head. "Waste of time. Maybe they're worth something, maybe they're not, but there's no way to find buyers for that kind of thing without Leira's help. In our hands, it's just a bunch of old, dusty paper. This—" he gestures, and there's a light in his eyes "—this is actually worth something."

My borrowed boots grind against the stone. "You're not paying me in *eggs*, Raze. I need gold."

"You'll get it," he promises. "I'll make this right. What do you know about firedrakes?"

I sigh, but fighting him doesn't seem to be going anywhere. "They breathed pure magical energy. They liked gold and gems. The last time one was spotted was over two hundred years ago. Fate only knows how many centuries this one's been sitting here, so it's probably not even alive."

"No," Raze says, eyes sweeping past my shoulder over the skeleton. "Dragon eggs can incubate for thousands of years. They don't need a mother to tend them. No one knows exactly what it is that eventually catalyzes them to hatch."

"So it could hatch tomorrow?"

"Or never." He shrugs. "But if it's made it this long, it probably needs to be cared for in order to hatch. We can figure it out."

I cross my arms. "And then what? We sell it to the highest bidder and put a living creature in their hands like a weapon?"

I don't care. I don't care. I don't care. I'm only in this for the money, for my family. I'm not thinking about what comes after that, because none of what comes after affects me.

Raze's eyes snap back to me, studying me while mine roam anywhere but his face. "Maybe." Then he reaches for my arm again. "Or…we hatch the egg, and then the dragon is ours.

I'll take back the manor and everything from Leira. She'll be powerless against something like this. And once I'm the new head of the Wild line…" I can sense his imagination running wild without even looking up at him. "I'll give you whatever you want," he finishes softly.

Maybe it's just the infectious excitement in his voice, but the thought is tempting. I'll have to wait for however long it takes the dragon to grow powerful enough to be a weapon— maybe a year? But then the reward will be so much grander. With the influence Leira now has, Raze could pardon me. To- gether, with power like that, we could protect other change- lings like the child I once was.

He looks back at the egg over my shoulder—or maybe at the dragon skeleton protecting it. "I don't know what we'll do next. We can ask Olani and Isolde what they think when we get back. I just know we can't leave it here."

He's right, at least about that part. We've come too far to turn back empty-handed.

"Fine," I say. "We'll take it. I'll crawl into the skeleton. But you owe me one."

"I already owe you one." Just like that, lightness returns to his voice. It's comforting to know some things don't change.

"You owe me, like, five or six at this point," I say grimly, gathering up my ridiculous, muddy, torn skirts and taking a step forward.

His mouth slips into a sideways grin. "Are you counting the time you burned my eyebrows off? Because I'm pretty sure that counts for a few."

I can't argue with that.

I have to be honest—some childish part of me expects the

dragon's remains to spark to life as soon as I touch them, snarling at me as they shift into motion. Its stillness is almost as bad, coldly judging me from beyond the grave. I think of stories from my childhood of treasures that could only be claimed by the worthy, of faerie punishments and tricks.

I know I'm not a worthy hero. I'm just a changeling who happens to be small enough to slip between a dragon's ribs.

The bone is smooth and warm to the touch, as if fire still lingers within. I have to brace both hands against it to push my way in. If I didn't know it was bone, it probably wouldn't send itchy chills crawling over my hands—but I do know that.

"Sorry," I whisper, even though I'm almost completely sure it can't hear me.

I kneel in the cage of bone, reaching for the egg. I can't believe I'm really this close—to it, to the end, to the mysterious *after*.

As soon as my fingers touch the shell, a hum of life reverberates through my arm, warm and soft, the exact opposite of Gossamer's enchantments. I shiver, heaving it up into my arms like an unwieldy toddler.

My arms wobble with the weight, and fear washes over me with the image of it dropping and shattering. "You should probably hold it."

Raze looks at me sideways. "You don't think I'm going to run off with it, never to be seen again?"

"Well, *now* I do."

He reaches out, and I carefully push the egg back through the rib cage, lowering it into his large hands. "Everything will be okay," he says, cradling it to his chest like a baby. I'm not sure if he's talking to me, or the egg, or himself.

I wriggle my way back out and look over the crevice, sprawling out below us bathed in golden light.

"We need to move fast," I say, shivering. "I don't want to be here when night falls."

This is it, then. I keep waiting for something else to happen, for another faerie trick, for an ambush, but nothing happens. Of course it isn't as simple as I thought it would be, but soon enough, I'll be headed home with my ransom of gold.

I'll be losing Isolde.

I shake my head. She'll change her mind. After everything that's happened, she can't still feel the same way. Everything will be fine, and just for a second, I want all the weight off my shoulders. I want to let myself feel light-headed with relief.

I rip a long piece of fabric from my voluminous skirts, which we tie into a sling Raze straps over his shoulder. With the egg nestled in against his torso, he looks like a father carrying his newborn at the market, and I can't help a giggle at how ridiculous it is.

He glares, settling his hands protectively over the rounded lump. "Go ahead and laugh. By next summer, every gentleman is going to have an egg sling in his wardrobe."

That just makes me laugh harder, maybe a little hysterically, until I see how pleased with himself Raze looks and cut it off abruptly.

As we walk away, I let one hand press against the dragon's skull, promising silently not to let the treasure it's spent so long protecting come to harm.

We make it out of the building the same way we came. I keep looking over my shoulder, waiting for Gossamer to appear again, for a monster to jump out at us, for a curse to strike us and turn us to stone. Even as my foot crosses the threshold back down into the tunnel, I half expect some wicked faerie magic to trap us in the library's stone walls.

It's suspiciously calm.

I throw one last look over my shoulder before plunging into the darkness. Fiery orange light paints over the rows of books, streaked with sunset pink. It's eerie, lifeless, beautiful. I wonder how long it will be before this spot falls under human eyes again.

Then I remember that, no matter how human my eyes look, I'm not one of them.

No, you're not.

I flinch. I've let that same quiet voice slide past my attention so many times in the past few weeks, as if ignoring it harder would make it disappear. Is that my own worst thought, or something else?

No—*someone* else?

"Seelie, come on," Raze says gently. "They're waiting for us." He takes my hand in his—for safety in the dark tunnel, that's all—and guides me back into the mountain.

chapter thirty

It's hard to tell how long we're in the tunnel. Minutes and hours turn into a number of steps and the specific angle of a turn. I take the lead, our fingers still entwined. Raze's hands are so much bigger than mine that it almost hurts to stretch my fingers wide enough for his to fit, but I don't let go. I can feel his hands getting clammy again, hear his breath coming faster.

"Are you scared of the dark?" I ask quietly, after rolling the question around in my head so many times I can't think about anything else.

Raze hesitates, tensing. "Do you think I'm scared?"

It's slow going here, rocky and uneven. I bash my toe into a short ledge before stepping up onto it. "Step up here," I say. "Everything I've learned about human behavior suggests that rapid breathing, sweaty palms, and unusual silence are markers of fear. Right?"

I feel him try to pull away, and grip his hand tighter.

"Don't let go. I don't want you to get lost."

"My palms aren't *that* sweaty," he grumbles.

"You're trying to distract me." My toe hits something else, this time a smaller stone that rattles as it bounces out in front of us.

Raze relents. "I don't like…um…confined spaces," he admits. Which—of course. I should have realized it earlier, after what he told me about Leira and everything she put him through. I squeeze his hand tighter in mine. "Actually, I hate them. I get all sweaty and sick and… Well, if I lose my last meal all of a sudden and it gets in your hair, you've officially been warned."

I crinkle my nose in disgust, which he, of course, can't see. Still, I don't let go. "What about the Destiny?"

He snorts. "Why do you think I always shapeshift when we've been on the road a few hours? It's a huge waste of energy, but at least I can stretch my wings out. This is worse. Even your cursed wagon has windows."

How dare he? "Hey! The Destiny is the finest enchanted wagon this side of the Dragon Lands. You're lucky to travel in such luxury."

"Of course," he says and chuckles. "My mistake."

Several more minutes pass in silence, except for our steps and whispered swears every time we smash into a wall or protruding boulder.

"So," Raze says eventually. "What are you going to do with the money?"

"I—" I stop. I don't owe him any explanation. I thought I had an answer to that, but Isolde turned everything upside down. "What are *you* going to do with the firedrake?"

"I asked first," he says. "Humor me. Give me something to think about besides the imminent rockslide that will cave in this entire thing and lead to our untimely demise."

"You're so dramatic," I complain, stepping carefully as the path declines.

We're never going to see each other again once the whole firedrake thing is sorted. What can it hurt? I sigh.

"I'm going home," I say softly. It stings to admit it: *I'm* going home. Not *we're*. "Our parents...they live in a village on the northeast banks of the Harrow. I haven't seen them in three years." My free hand strays to the vial, but it's no longer there.

"Why now?"

I bite my lip, but the story comes spilling out anyway. "We kind of got...chased out of town. After everyone found out about me." I tell him about Cassius Redbrook, about the potions and charms, about my raised voice and my broken wrist and the flames. About listening to the sound of a man's dying breath. About everything.

I've never told anyone that before, I think, surprising myself with each new detail I unravel. Isolde already knew, of course. There wasn't anyone else I'd ever let close enough to wonder where I came from.

He keeps catching me with my guard down, and it feels dangerous. I just have to make it a little while longer. Then we'll never have to see each other again.

Exactly how I want it. How I've always wanted it.

A smudge of gray ahead catches my eye. "We're almost there," I say, squeezing Raze's hand.

There isn't a bright white light at the end of the tunnel this time. He doesn't let go until it's light enough to see the outline of our surroundings by the blue moonlight, and his shoulders relax with a sigh of relief. We're close enough to the outside world now that a breeze stirs, wrapping me in its cold fingers.

I'm ready to sit down for a moment. To see my sister again, show off the firedrake egg, and joke back and forth with her and Raze and Olani. For all of us to put our heads together and figure out what our next move is, and then go home.

I emerge under a canopy of sparkling stars in an indigo sky.

Something pricks at the edges of my awareness—the instinct that something is *wrong*. Even if Isolde and Olani were trying to keep a low profile, it shouldn't be this dark and still and silent. There should be some sign of their presence, not silence disturbed only by my breaths and the distant wind whistling high above us.

"Isolde?" I call cautiously.

No response.

Against the cliffs, almost out of sight, my eye catches something moving. By the time I turn to see it, it's gone.

The feeling of wrongness increases, and I push forward, picking up speed.

"Seelie, wait!" Raze hurries behind me, a protective arm around the firedrake egg in its sling.

I ignore him. "Isolde!"

That time, I think I hear a response, and I have to stop

moving to strain my ears for it. There it is again: muffled squealing, like someone trying to talk through a gag.

I turn, just as light blooms in the canyon, sparkling white on the stone. My hand flies up to protect my eyes, seared with pain after so long in darkness, but I try to squint through it. It isn't actually that bright, maybe a little lighter than it would have been around sunset, illuminated by a ball of pure white light suspended in the air.

It's plenty bright enough to see Isolde ten or fifteen yards away, sitting on a toppled column back-to-back with Olani. They're bound together around the shoulders, with another binding around each of their wrists. My sister's face is pale, a rag tied tightly over her mouth biting into the corners to silence her. Her injured leg stretches in front of her awkwardly, still pained. Olani is unconscious, and she doesn't have her quarterstaff.

Beside them, holding the staff, is someone with a delicate, angular face I hoped I'd never see again. Green eyes flash in the artificial light.

"So nice of you to finally join us, changeling," Aris purrs.

I have to fight every instinct to not run to my sister and untie her, hold her, protect her.

There are a few other people in the canyon. I think I recognize some of them from our scuffle at the inn. But here, there's no cliff, no distraction, no help from Isolde and Olani.

We're doomed.

Raze stands behind me, arms wrapped around the bundle at his chest, as if that might hide his cargo.

"Aris." He sounds disgusted, not even bothering with his usual veneer of pleasantness. "How did you find us?" His eyes dart around, and in the stiffness of his shoulders, I read his second, unspoken question: *Where's Leira?*

Aris folds her arms over her chest. "You leave a trail of incompetence and disaster everywhere you go. It's not exactly hard to trace, Raze."

My head swims. We went in and out of the faerie world and landed in a hidden spot in the deepest ruins of the Western Range. I can't imagine what she means. Even our wagon is gone, lost with Birch in the faerie forest.

I feel Raze tense. "What did you do to Olani?"

"She's not the one you need to worry about." Aris smirks. "Focus on your own feathers." The reminder of his magic's limitations doesn't sound like a friendly joke, like when Olani said it. Instead, it's a pointed jab.

"That's enough, Aris." Leira steps forward from behind one of the largest thugs, flanked by two gleaming dragons. They might be the same ones from the manor, graceful and sinewy, moving in perfect sync with her as if they've trained for this all their lives. Leira rests a hand casually on one of the dragon's heads, palm flat against its crest. In the other, she holds a compass.

It's a real compass, not an enchantment, made of metal and glass gleaming in the white light, but I can still sense the magic seeping from its case.

Olani groans, rolling her neck. She's coming to. I just thank Fate she isn't dead.

I finally find my voice, even as a tingling shiver runs up my spine. "Let them go."

Leira gives me a pitying look before her attention goes to him again. "Oh, Raze," she sighs, disappointed. "Raze,

Raze, Raze. Where did I go wrong? You could have at least made it a challenge. All I had to do was wave that ring under your nose and you snatched it up without a second thought."

Raze's fingers curl automatically around the dull ring he stole from Leira back on the mountain road—his father's ring. "You put a tracking spell on it!" I knew that they were related, I knew that she raised him, but it still strikes me how much he sounds like a defensive child.

"You managed to disappear for a few days—not bad. But the second you landed back in the mortal world, I knew exactly where to find you."

A few days? I didn't think we'd been in the faerie realm longer than a single night.

She'd wanted him to take the ring. She'd wanted us to get away. All of this—everything we sacrificed—was for nothing. "You weren't…trying to get me," I say, rubbing the spot on my palm where the enchantment used to be.

Behind Leira, Olani blinks, brow furrowed as she slowly comes to. One of the dragons sniffs, curling its lip slightly, like it's waiting for her to wake so it can attack. Isolde is still struggling weakly. Anger starts to thaw my surprise. What did they *do* to her?

Leira looks at me as if she forgot I was there for a second. There's something predatory in her green eyes, like she's a snake and I'm a tiny, delicious mouse. "Why bother? I could just let Raze and your merry gang of misfits do the hard work of retrieval and be here waiting for you at the end. Speaking of which—" she holds her hand out, just like she did to me on that night "—hand over the firedrake egg."

Raze's arms close protectively around the egg. His wide

eyes meet mine, and we share a moment of shock and confusion.

How did she know about the egg?

"Oh, come on," she snaps, smug tone finally giving way to impatience. "Why do you keep assuming that I'm as ignorant about everything as you are? I've been studying that compass for longer than you've been alive, with all the knowledge from all the Wildline matriarchs who came before me. You're way out of your depth, all of you."

Raze isn't acting like himself, and I can't figure out why. I need him to say something clever or confident or incredibly foolish, to do something unexpected and escape this whole mess. "I-I know exactly what I'm doing," he stammers instead. "And it mostly revolves around getting rid of *you*."

Leira places her hand over her heart. "How sweet." Her tone transforms in an instant, going sharp and brittle. "Grow up, Raze. If you had any sense you'd have realized a long time ago that working with me is always a better bet than working against me."

He takes a step back. His voice is thick with tightly controlled emotion, his fists clenched. "You're the one who kicked me out!"

She pauses, not so much as a twitch of emotion showing on her face. "And at what point did you decide you were too *good* to try to redeem yourself? Who raised you? Who taught you how to use your powers, no matter how—"

"You put me in a *cage*!" Raze's shout echoes over the stone, not quite a sob. Sympathy shreds my heart, and I'm almost overwhelmed with the urge to put a comforting hand on his arm.

"You learned, didn't you?" she snarls.

"Apparently I didn't learn enough. I should have seen you for what you are. I was a *child*."

"You were—are—an enchanter." Her hands twitch, and I wonder what destruction she's about to rain down on us. "You were weak. Pathetic. You would have been *nothing* without my training. It's a shame," she sniffs, tilting her head to the side. Her dragons sniff, too. "I really thought I could make some use of you. And I was *so* hoping we could resolve this without resorting to violence. Now, give me the egg, or I'll kill all your little friends."

On Leira's command, Aris draws a shimmering silver dagger and presses it to my sister's throat.

"No!" I scream. I realize I'm holding my hands out in front of me, palms raised. Tiny balls of flame flicker, dancing over my skin without leaving a mark. I hadn't meant to summon them, but I hold my hands up anyway, trying to look threatening. Trying to look like I have any idea what to do with it.

Isolde's eyes go wide, and a few of the guards around her take a step back. The dragons snarl, revealing their pointed teeth, and I see their muscles tense, waiting for permission to pounce. Aris's eyes widen, and her hand trembles almost imperceptibly. Even though she tries to hide it, I see the truth: she's still afraid of me. She covers it quickly, glancing at Leira, and holds her ground.

Leira couldn't possibly look less impressed.

"Stop!" Raze says. I meet his eyes, trying to read his face. I think I can guess what he's thinking: Leira is right. The firedrake, fully grown, *could* be a formidable weapon. The fact that there's nothing else like it in the world would make it almost unstoppable. That isn't the kind of power that some-one like Leira Wildfall should have.

And we're selfish—horribly, irredeemably selfish. Because both of us would trade the lives of thousands of faceless victims bound to suffer under Leira's thumb for Isolde and Olani.

In a heartbeat.

Raze steps forward, untying the makeshift sling from his chest. He walks slowly, deliberately, to his aunt, holding it out. The fabric slips away, uncovering the egg. It glimmers merrily in the artificial light.

I hate this. I'm sick with guilt, knowing how badly she hurt Raze, knowing she'd do it all over again to this poor creature, as long as it gets her what she wants.

But we don't have another choice.

"Thank you, Raze," Leira says mildly, like he's a disobedient child. She picks the egg up in both hands, abandoning the sling. Her eyes light with something greedy, and her dragons stretch their long, sinewy necks up, sniffing the egg curiously.

Raze says nothing. I can sense him gritting his teeth, even though his back is to me.

"Okay, now let them go." I'm surprised by the strength of my own voice. My eyes stay on Isolde, on Aris relaxing her grip and lowering her knife.

Leira lets confusion settle over her features for a brief second before wiping it away with a smile. "I'm afraid I may have stretched the truth about that one a little bit."

She lied. Of course she lied. Because she's human and she can, which makes dealing with her somehow even more dangerous than a faerie deal. We just gave up our only bargaining chip, and we have nothing left to appeal to except her mercy.

She strokes the dragon's egg like a favored pet. "Aris."

"Aris." I'm surprised to hear Raze echo his aunt, a pleading note in his low voice. They were raised together. Their history is troubled, but it runs deep between them. Maybe even deep enough to persuade her to do the right thing.

She looks as surprised to hear Raze say her name as I was, and for a second, she doesn't move. Her eyes go back and forth between him and Leira, and for a moment, hope dares to flutter in my chest.

Leira's jaw tightens, and she gives a brief turn of her head to stare at her niece. She doesn't even have to say another word.

Aris's knife flashes in the light, pressing lightly to my sister's throat. Isolde flinches, too tightly bound to do anything else, her dark eyes round and watery.

"Now," Leira says pleasantly, cradling the egg, "here's how this is going to go. We're going to leave this wretched place. You are not going to try to stop us, with magic or otherwise. I see the tiniest spark, feel the smallest rumble underfoot—Aris kills them both. I see you following us on the road back to Auremore—Aris kills them both. You try any number of terribly clever but ultimately ill-conceived plans—any guesses?"

I can feel tears building at the back of my throat, but I force the lump back. The fire in my hands goes out as they fall to my sides.

"You can't do this," Raze says hoarsely. But he's just as frozen as I am.

Leira rolls her eyes at him. She turns, letting the gold brocade of her long, trailing skirt swirl behind her. "Say your goodbyes from over there. So long, Raze." Her dragons close in behind her, an impenetrable wall of scales and twitching tails.

Everyone starts moving after that. It all happens so fast. Olani is only half-conscious, and they drag her away before any of us can say anything.

"Sol," I manage to force out through the lump of tears.

They're pulling at her now, dragging her to her feet. Isolde pulls away roughly, twisting and jerking. Not to escape, just to move on her own terms. In the flurry of movement, her gag comes loose. An exhausted half smile twists her bloodied face, just before a heavy hand claps around the back of her neck. "It'll be okay," she says, comforting me, even now. "I'll see you soon. Promise."

Something crunches under the boot of the person who drags her away. I manage to hold back my tears until they're fully swallowed by the darkness, retreating to the horses and wagons they left on the distant mountain road. Until there isn't even a pinprick of Aris's light left to illuminate the crevice.

The sobs hit me like a wave, and I collapse under their force. It's only when my knees hit the stone that I see something glittering on the ground where Isolde had been standing, where she'd fought before being taken captive.

My necklace, shattered into a thousand pieces.

The dried flowers—*our parents' memories of us*, too blue to be real among the crystal shards—are slowly dissolving. They wither into dust, then smoke, and the wind carries them away.

Something shatters and withers within me, too.

chapter thirty-one

It feels like forever that I'm curled up on my side, trembling against the stone. Raze lets me cry myself out without speaking for what feels like forever, until I'm finally so dried-out and hollow I fall silent.

"Are you hurt?" he says, startling me. How long has he been sitting beside me? "Seelie?"

I look up just long enough to shake my head before burying my face in my arms again. I can't face him right now. All the rules of human behavior I've worked so hard to learn feel wispy and impossible to grasp. I reach up automatically to fidget with my necklace, and my fingers slip through empty air.

I start crying again.

Raze doesn't say anything else. His arm brushes mine, and

then there's the pressure of his hand on my shoulder trying to hold me.

I flinch back. "No."

"Sorry," he says, quickly. This afternoon I needed to be held; now I won't even allow myself to be touched. I'm the girl who runs away, who sits on the ground and cries. He must think I'm a freak.

"Sorry," I repeat back to him, muffled through sobs. "Sorry. Sorry." I sniffle and nod. My nose is running, and it's embarrassing. I don't want Raze to see me wipe snot on my sleeve.

"Seelie." His hand hovers over my elbow, but then he pulls back again. He's used my real name twice in a minute now. That must mean something else is wrong. "Stop apologizing. It's okay. You're allowed to cry." His voice is calm, but not too syrupy, and I just want him to keep talking. He leans back, tilting his head up. I think he's avoiding staring at me on purpose, and I appreciate it.

I force my eyes to trace up his face, to meet his. They're swollen and tired, with dark shadows smudged underneath. His nose is redder than usual, as if he's been crying, too, but silently so I wouldn't know. Why would the rules of our friendship be any different the other way around? "Raze," I murmur.

He looks at me expectantly.

I don't have anything else to say. But he's trying to comfort me, and I owe him the same. Uncertainly, I reach out and let one hand rest on his shoulder. "Are you okay?"

He doesn't answer.

Well, I did everything I could. I can't force him to talk to me if he doesn't want to. "We should get some sleep," I try, instead.

"Yes," he agrees. "We should."

He seems disappointed, or maybe conflicted, and I can't figure out why. I gave him every possible chance to confide in me. With the shoulder touch and everything. I thought I'd made it clear that I would support him.

I try to push away, but then he sucks in a breath. "Seelie, wait." The soft sound makes me go perfectly still, and I stay right there, my arm brushing his. I think he's going to get mad, to turn and leave me alone on the ground. Instead, he says, "I'm not. Okay, I mean."

I've stopped crying, I realize. I can still feel sticky tear tracks on my face, though.

I uncurl a little. Then, slowly, I rest my head on Raze's shoulder.

He doesn't move away.

We sit like that until all that's left on my face is the itchy sting of salt. My thoughts turn in halting circles.

Finally, I break the silence. "You care about Olani a lot."

Raze's whole face seems to tremble, like he's trying not to start crying again. "Yes," he confirms. "I'm worried about her. She's…she's the best friend I've ever had."

That makes sense. Olani isn't exactly one for emotional speeches, but I've seen the way they interact. How they protect each other, understand each other, cheer each other up. They're so different that you'd never expect it, but they balance each other out somehow.

"Back before…" His voice breaks, and he stops, clears his throat, and tries again. "When I lived with Leira, I… We weren't allowed out of the manor much. When Olani started working for her two years ago, Leira gave us a job to do together. Nothing important, something even I couldn't screw up. It was a test."

I stare down through my lashes at our hands. He's fidgeting with his ring, twisting it on his finger.

"And I still screwed it up." He laughs bitterly. "Olani did her best to fix everything, but Leira still blamed me. Screamed at me, and locked me up in my room. That night, Olani somehow managed to unlock the door, apologize for how I was treated. Then she snuck me out of the house for the night." I can hear the smile in his voice. "We got dumplings."

I sit with that information for a moment. Leira was Olani's employer, and she still risked her wrath just to help Raze. I wonder if anyone had ever gone out of their way to be kind to him before that. No wonder he cares about her.

"We snuck out together all the time after that. I felt so free on those nights, like my world was bigger than what Leira could get from me. She acts tough but…"

But she's only human. She needs someone to protect her now as much as he did then. Just like Isolde needs me. And we're stuck here, with no way to help them.

Quiet falls again, but I can sense his short, sharp breaths: there's something else he wants to say, something he's holding back. I sigh, but my head doesn't move from his shoulder. "Tell me what else is wrong."

He struggles to hide the surprise that flickers in the corner of his mouth, the conflicting emotions that run across his face like clouds over the sun. "I thought the *losing everything to Leira, hopelessly stranded with nothing to eat and nowhere to go* thing was a good-enough excuse."

"Raze."

My eyes flick up defiantly to meet his, long enough to let him know I'm serious. Long enough to feel the discomfort of it tickle the back of my neck.

Raze sighs. "Fine. You're relentless."

The autumn breeze makes me shiver in my thin shirt, but Raze is warm. I lean in a little closer, waiting for him to speak.

He casts another miserable sideways look at me. "It's my aunt. Seeing her like that... I should have been prepared for it. But I wasn't." He holds his open hand in front of him, watching his fingers squeeze into a fist like it's suddenly very interesting. "I *know* how she is when she wants something. But I still—" He cuts himself off abruptly with a strangled sound somewhere between a sob and a chuckle.

I don't know what to do, so I reach out awkwardly with one hand. It ends up resting at a strange angle on top of one of his wrists. His head bends to study my slender fingers, then twists sideways like a hawk's to my face again.

"I feel ridiculous," he says, a hint of bitterness creeping into the edges of his tone. "You don't have to pretend it isn't."

"I'm an expert in ridiculous," I say without thinking, which is almost definitely the wrong thing.

Raze laughs anyway. "You're in good company," he says, before the grin slips from his face again. "It's just...she *raised* me. You know? It's *different*. I don't see Aunt Leira as a motherly figure or anything, but... I hardly remember my parents at all. Just her."

I'm suddenly very aware of the spot where the glass vial *should* sit at my throat. But this isn't about me. It's about Raze, and his messed-up family that tried to kill us. My voice stalls in the back of my throat before words form. "I'm so sorry, Raze. That...that must be very difficult."

It isn't enough, but I don't have anything else.

"So...what happens to those memories now?" Raze asks, after a pause.

My eyes flick to the broken glass, the snapped cord. There's nothing to salvage there. My throat tightens, and it takes me a long time to manage a reply. "I have no idea."

Leira and Isolde and Olani are long gone, but it's still too soon to follow. I don't think Leira expects us to rot here, but I don't know how long we're supposed to wait before leaving.

How long until the egg hatches? Until Leira releases her prisoners and forgets about all of us?

He studies me for a second, eyes soft and unreadable. "Listen. Your sister and Olani are two of the most capable people I've ever met. They can take care of themselves until we find a way back. You're going to see your sister again, I promise."

"That isn't something you can promise." My arms circle around my drawn-up knees, and a yawn fights its way up my throat.

"You're impossible."

I try to breathe slowly and fully, to slow down my racing mind. He's right, Isolde and Olani can take care of themselves. That awful fight we had can't be the last time I ever see my sister. It *won't* be. "I know," I say, through another yawn. "Sorry, I—"

"No, it's fine." His voice sounds weirdly flat, but I don't have the energy to investigate that further. "We should both get some sleep. We'll figure out the plan in the morning, okay?"

I should argue with him. I should insist that we make a plan *now*, and execute it as soon as possible.

But I'm already half-asleep, and all the crying took what little fight I still had left in me. I nod, curling up on the hard ground again. I can feel him settling down just a few feet away.

I toss and turn and fantasize about bread. And roasted mushrooms, and big bowls of steaming rice, and coffee, and honeyed cake, and apple cider, anything and everything. I'm almost certain that I'm not awake, that I'm only dreaming. Dreaming of food in my belly, the dry warmth of a fire or even just a blanket, the familiar sound of Isolde breathing nearby.

My eyes drift shut, and I feel like I'm sinking. Then the familiarity of the feeling strikes me, and I'm alert again, fighting my own tired body as I try not to give in to the dreams that Gossamer has haunted for weeks now. I reach out in my mind, trying to envision it as a big room, checking every dark corner for the faerie. For anything that feels foreign.

I have plenty of dark, unwelcome thoughts to go through, and by the time I give up, my fists are squeezed tight and I'm sitting all clenched up again, knees drawn to my chest.

It isn't *fair*. After everything we've been through, it *still* isn't over. At this point, it feels like Fate is just punishing us.

Or maybe laughing at us.

Anger flares in my chest, and magic surges in my veins. I rein it back in quickly, before I can cause untold destruction, sitting up as if to announce I've officially given up on falling asleep.

Not now, I beg. The magic still crawls over my skin like an itchy coat, still puddles in the restless movements of my hands. To satisfy it, I allow one fingertip to produce a flame, no bigger than the wick of a candle.

I blow it out and light the next one. Then the next.

One by one.

I can control this.

"You sound just like them," an amused voice says from behind me. "Mortals, I mean."

chapter thirty-two

I jump up and twist around, hands already out. Gossamer stands over Raze's quiet, sleeping form, looking down at him the way a small child might look at a slug wriggling at their feet, with curiosity and disgust.

I scowl at him, holding a finger to my lips. There's no way I'm about to wake Raze with angry rambling at a specter.

"*Relax*, Seelie." His lazy, aristocratic drawl grates a little bit more with each word. "Your mortal's sound asleep."

When I still hesitate, he crosses one finger in an *X* over his heart, face morphing into the very picture of innocence. With his pale skin, slightly pursed, full lips, and pleading eyes, he could be any marble statue of a romantic hero. If it weren't for those sharp teeth.

I turn my back. Maybe if I pretend he isn't there, he'll go

away. But I'm still too distracted to make my fingertips light again.

"You can't ignore me forever," the faerie teases, drawing the words out. "I have a lot to say, you know. I was trapped in that statue for—oh, no telling, centuries at least. Plenty of time to build up things to talk about. And I don't even know what your human world is like now! That mediocre shapeshifter—what was her name?—so *fearsome*, I'm sure, but wouldn't have been anything to write home about back in *my* day. You mortals change so quickly."

Strange, how his voice echoes off the stone, like it isn't all in my head. But I know better. He isn't truly here. "And why were you locked away, Gossamer?"

He tries not to flinch at the use of his name, waving an elegant hand. His nails are long and pointed and look manicured—but of course they aren't, because they're *not real*. None of him is real. Not his long hair, not his bare feet, not even the gauzy sleeve brushing my arm. "Who remembers anymore?"

I get the feeling that *he* does, but I can't force him to tell me, no matter how badly I want to. "What do you want?" I whisper angrily.

The innocent look wrinkles like a badly made backdrop at the theater, letting a hint of irritation peek through the curtain. He paces forward as smoothly as if he was made of liquid. "Didn't anyone ever bother to teach you that it's *unwise* to be rude to faeries?"

Fear surges up briefly, but I force myself to think. The truth is obvious. "If there was anything you could do to me, you would have already done it by now."

Gossamer stops short, his eyes narrowed. "You seem terribly sure of yourself, Seelie."

It would probably be a bad idea to point out that, by not outright denying what I'd said, he's as good as confirmed it.

Truth is a tricky thing that way.

I lean against a rock, watching the faerie warily. He's just a few feet away now, studying me like I'm some kind of rare butterfly he'd like to add to his collection. The chill of his pale gray gaze makes me shiver.

"But if you won't spare a thought for yourself, perhaps you should think of your annoying little friends." He casts a meaningful look behind us at Raze. "It would be a shame if anything happened to him…or the others. The one's interesting, for a mortal. The one you call your *sister*. I've never seen one like it before."

"Leave them alone," I mutter, not daring to raise my voice. "Just tell me what you want. Why you're in my head."

Gossamer sighs, almost like a human. He closes the distance between us, standing almost nose-to-nose with me before shifting to lean against the stone beside me. "When you freed me, Seelie… I tried to get away. I tried to return to my realm, where I could gain strength again. But I was tethered to you, to your magic." He turns, his face too close to mine as he leans in. "Ask all the questions you like, little changeling. I know that you can feel it, too."

My skin crawls, tingling with a magic that isn't my own. Now that he mentions it, I *can* feel the tie between us. Even if he'd been on the other side of the crevice, standing under the cliffs, I would be just as aware of his presence as I am now. As if it's a part of me, like my magic or my fingers. I swallow hard, forcing myself to form words without shaking. "You want to get away. Couldn't I just free you, then?"

"No!" Gossamer says, too quickly. The feeling of magic

on the bare skin of my neck and scarred hands turns ice-cold. "It's not that simple," he adds, a note of something dark and bitter in his tone.

I suck in a breath, my chest squeezing. My anxious fingers go to where my necklace should be. "You need me," I say on a breath. This time, I turn to look at Gossamer's face, to examine it for any sign of the truth.

He leans back against the cliff, scowling at the stars.

"You need my magic," I guess. "Because yours—"

"I couldn't end this even if I wanted to," Gossamer snaps. "Do you think I *like* being tied to a mortal body? You're so fragile. You could just drop dead at any moment, and then where would *I* be?"

For once, the faerie reeks of earnestness. He's trapped in this as much as I am, a tiger scratching at the cage of my mind. If he claws hard enough, he might just break it.

"I don't know."

He slumps, somewhere between lazy power and defeat. "I can't even fully take control of you. I might as well be a common *conjurer*."

Part of me screams to get as far away from the faerie as I can. His inability to possess me isn't exactly a good reason to pity him. But my curiosity still gets the better of me.

"So the magic you said you couldn't access before…?" I don't know enough about this to even ask questions without sounding like a fool. "*My* magic?"

"Together, we can draw on my true power," he says miserably. "Unfortunately, I can't access it alone."

"Pity," I whisper sarcastically, even as a chill runs over my skin. But my mind is racing. *We* could draw on his true power.

Together. If I use my magic now, how much will be mine, and how much his? If our magic gets tangled together, will I be able to pull myself free, or will I give a little bit more of myself over every time?

Another, quieter part asks: *What might I be able to do with his power?*

I ignore that. "So how long does this last?" I try not to sound frightened. If Gossamer was human, he probably would have noticed what a wretched job I do at that. I'm not human, and I still cringe.

His quartz eyes flash with irritation, and his lip curls to reveal those too-sharp canines. "What kind of question is that? As far as I know, *this* has never happened before. Our little *situation* is completely unique. As unique as you are, little changeling."

"Don't flatter me," I snap quietly. I don't mind being reminded of who I am. I accepted it long ago, and the word itself can't hurt me anymore. Still, the word twists out of shape in Gossamer's mouth, like there's another secret meaning to it I don't know.

Those pointed teeth gleam as Gossamer's lips stretch into a grin. "Oh, but you like it. What a number these mortals have done on you, changeling. Don't forget, I can *feel* what you *feel.* You hate me, sure—*for now*—but you still *love* my praise." His chin tilts up, white eyebrows rising. "Very mortal of you. It's almost cute."

Do I really like Gossamer's compliments? I don't think I do, but he wouldn't be able to say it if it wasn't true. I stamp out the sparks of something warm in my chest, something that had been getting hotter by the second without my attention. "You're right," I seethe. "I do hate you."

"Devastating," Gossamer deadpans. His fingernails click against the stone in a maddening rhythm. "But I'm afraid there's nothing to be done. Unless…" He stops, staring at nothing in particular.

Click.

Click.

Click.

Finally, I relent. My hands squeeze tight. "Unless…?" I prompt.

He grins triumphantly. Every inch I give him is a victory. "Well, I might be able to think of *one* way to sever this." His voice, which he hadn't bothered to hush for the benefit of my sleeping companion, dips lower as his lips move closer to my ear. "But there would, of course, be a price."

I almost laugh at that. It's so *unthinkably* absurd. "You think I'd ever make another deal with you? No way. You need this as badly as I do. I'm not giving you anything just to make you go away. There's got to be another way."

He shrugs, mouth pressing into a tight smile. As if to say *This isn't over*, even as he moves on. "Perhaps if you could return me to a faerie realm… In a land of magic, I might be able to build enough power to take my own form."

I've looked for refuge in the Seelie Realm before, and I have absolutely no intention of doing so again. I barely made it out the first time, and only because of another faerie bargain.

Still, it isn't like I have another choice. Gossamer will take everything he possibly can from me. The only way this can possibly end is with my destruction—whether it would be my mind, my magic, or my body is still to be determined. But maybe, if I play my cards just right, I can get rid of the faerie before anyone even has to know he was here. Before his games can leave lasting damage.

"Why not?" I sigh. "I've got plenty of time."

Gossamer's sudden grip around my wrist is almost a relief after the tension of standing so close, brushing sleeves so lightly I couldn't tell if I was imagining it. It's like he's been waiting this whole time to spring, to pull me close and whisper in my ear.

"I'm glad we're finally seeing eye to eye, Seelie. As long as we're stuck with each other, we might as well make the best of it. Let's just agree now not to *play games* with each other, shall we?"

"No," I say, steeling myself. Refusing to flinch, even though I can feel his torso pressing into mine, his sharpened fingernails digging into the tender skin of my wrist. *Not real, not real.* I refuse to be trapped in a faerie deal or so-called agreement by a foolish slip of the tongue. "You might not be able to lie, but that doesn't mean I'll ever trust you."

"Clever little changeling," Gossamer praises. His smile flashes like the blade of a knife right before it slices through your throat as he pushes lazily backward and dissolves into the darkness. As he retreats back into a corner of my mind.

I grip my wrist with one shaking hand and hold it close to my eyes.

The indents from Gossamer's sharpened nails are still there, pressed into the smooth brown skin.

chapter thirty-three

I don't know when I fall asleep again. It's probably hours later when I wake to the sound of "Iselia!" whispered in the half light of dawn, but it feels like I've barely closed my eyes. I try to turn over and ignore the voice in my ear, but then there's a large hand shaking my shoulder. I swat upward blindly, getting a good, solid whack to Raze's nose before I realize what's going on.

"I'm up!" I whisper, shoving him. "Go away."

"Ow," Raze says pointedly.

I sit up, yawn, and roll my shoulders. Sleeping on stone was worse on my aching—well, everything—than you'd think. And I'm still hungry.

"I haven't eaten in *days*." I ignore the fact that Raze is ignoring me, that he didn't move even when I got up, that he's so close to me I can feel the warmth of his skin. "You should know better than to mess with me in this state."

"You were talking in your sleep. Did you have a nightmare?"

I try to think back, but I truly have no idea how to answer that question without giving everything away. "I'm okay."

The sunrise tints the stone pink as we sit in silence after that. We need to find water soon, and food, too. We can't just sit here forever.

We don't know where to go.

But neither of us wants to admit that, so we just sit. My fingers fidget with the shimmering embroidery of my faerie dress, and I wish the fair folk had given me something a little more useful.

Once the egg hatches, Leira won't need Isolde and Olani anymore. She'll probably free them. I don't think she's the type to kill for no reason despite her threats. We can eventually return to Auremore and find them, once we're sure she doesn't feel like we're a risk to her plans.

But even if we do…we'll be walking away empty-handed. She'll have the firedrake egg, the Wildline legacy, the only treasure actually worth anything, which could hatch literally any day now. And then all of this will have been for nothing.

I can't stomach the thought. There has to be another way, some way to get the egg back before the dragon is in Leira's hands…or at least to get paid. But we can't risk following them, not for any amount of money.

"What if you flew there?" I ask abruptly. "Like, in the middle of the night."

He shakes his head. "I wouldn't be able to carry that thing as a bird. Even if I could, she's definitely going to have it guarded, and I'm pretty sure if a giant eagle flew off with the egg, she'd know who to suspect. And if I flew alone, you wouldn't be there to try to free Olani and Isolde." He doesn't say the last part: *and then she would hurt them.*

No, he's right. It isn't worth the risk. We need to wait until Leira is already certain that we've given up, that she's won, that the egg is safe. When she dismisses her mercenaries and lets her guard down.

Raze frowns. He still looks exhausted, and his face scrunches even more with thoughtfulness. "What if we could somehow get to the manor before them? Couldn't you make a portal?"

That might work, but I realize now that it was only because of Gossamer that I was able to create one before. His influence must have been how I did the impossible for a mortal, the invisible push that shaped my magic. Maybe we could do it again.

"It depends." I try not to react to his voice, but I still flinch, peeking over my shoulder to see that Gossamer has materialized in my periphery. He's just watching me, judging everything I do in a cold, bored tone with cold, bored eyes. "Make me an offer."

My magic bubbles up irritably, stirring a cool breeze against my already chilled skin. I usually consider myself to be a nonviolent person, but I'm considering making an exception for the faerie.

"What are you doing?" Raze asks, and I realize that he's still sitting on the ground, and at some point I rose to my feet.

I let my hands card through the air, trying to feel the threads of magic. "I might… I don't know how I did it." It's not exactly the truth, but it's not a total lie, either.

His face lights with devastating hope, and he jumps to his feet, pacing tight, anxious lines beside me. "That…that would be brilliant. We'd be there waiting for her, and it'll take them weeks to get there, so we'd have plenty of time to plan it all out. We could just wait for her to put the egg in that room, because it would definitely be in that same room, right? And then we could just grab it and free Isolde and Olani before she even noticed it was gone."

"As long as she keeps her word and doesn't harm them on the way home," I murmur. Anxiety twists in my gut at the thought of Isolde's tired, drawn face, of her wide eyes and how *frail* she looked.

"If they haven't escaped by then," Raze says with a smirk. "Which they definitely will, if they have enough time to heal."

"Okay," I say, wringing my hands. I can feel my pulse speeding, almost keeping up with my thoughts. My heart feels heavy, but it's different from the weight I've been carrying all night; this feels like it might be able to be lifted. "Okay. Okay."

There's just the tiny matter of how to convince Gossamer to help.

Raze grabs my hand and squeezes excitedly. "Seelie, we might—we might still have a chance."

I blink. He keeps using my real name. I don't know if that means anything.

But his excitement is contagious. Beyond the sick twisting worry for Isolde, there's hope. Hope that we can save them *and* get the egg. That I can have my sister *and* go home.

The glass shards sparkle in the growing sunlight. Home, or whatever's left of it.

I nod slowly—at Raze, but also at Gossamer. "I think I can."

What do you want? I reluctantly ask Gossamer in my head.

"I'm afraid it's not that simple," he says, annoyingly, out loud. I can feel him circling me, but I am *not* going to stare at him.

I grind my teeth, reconsidering. Even *if* this works, it'll still be weeks until I see Isolde. Can I really let her suffer in captivity for that long?

Can I dare to risk doing otherwise?

Can I face her disappointment when we walk away with nothing and watch her turn to riskier and riskier schemes to try to find something as valuable as what we already lost?

I need to save her from Leira and from herself. This is the only way I know how. I don't care what it costs.

"For your magic, then?" he says, all too casually. "If you really don't care the cost."

"No," I say out loud.

Raze's head tilts. "What?"

"I–I'm…thinking," I stammer, trying to ignore Gossamer's chuckles. "Shhh." I don't know which one of them I'm shushing.

I need to think of a fair price. Something he'll appreciate but that won't take too much from me. What does he want? What did I offer before?

Access to my magic, I think. *In exchange for your help with the creation of a portal spell—for the duration of the spell, and not a second longer.*

"Done," he says and disappears.

I feel the shift in the air immediately, but this time, the split between my ability and Gossamer's is more severe. My hands move less gracefully and certainly as they rise, plucking at the magic in the air, creating a tether between me and the stone.

What am I supposed to do with this? It feels like I'm holding loose threads in my hands, and I don't know where to tie them off.

I can sense Gossamer's frustration with me, almost like he's elbowing me aside in my mind to take over the enchantment. If faeries innately know how to make portals, how can he explain it? How would I explain to someone how to breathe? *Think of where you want to go. Think of what you want and what ties you there.*

I think of Isolde, of Wildline Manor's imposing stone face in the heart of Auremore, of its lavish interior, of how I need this to work because all I want is for us to be able to go *home*.

Home.

Something tugs in my chest, straining, and for a second I think I'm not going to be able to do it. I pull harder, and Gossamer pulls with me. Something sharp and cold shudders through my ribs, and with a gasp, the tension releases. That same cord I could sense in the forest is knotted around me now, the other end tied to somewhere else entirely.

Raze can sense it, too, even though there's barely a shimmer in the air around the portal. He's shaking a little. He holds out his hand, fingers spread to make room for mine. "Are you sure about this?"

No, I think, rolling my eyes, but I slip my hand into his. At least I don't have to do this alone. "On three," I say, trying to summon the confidence to make it sound like a command. Like Isolde would sound. "One…"

I exhale slowly. I don't like the way he's looking at me, awe tinged with fear, but I don't have time to think about that, because I can't hold this portal much longer. I don't have time to hope I did it right, that Gossamer isn't tricking me somehow.

None of that matters. All that matters is saving Isolde, saving the egg, saving everything.

"Two…"

Raze's hand squeezes tighter.

"Th—"

Raze jumps, pulling me with him.

We fall longer than we should, and I know instantly that we've made a mistake. For one disorienting second, I'm filling the air with my voice, flailing my arms and legs like I'm trying to fly.

I hit water instead of stone, and it swallows me whole.

My high-pitched scream cuts off abruptly, along with the low roar of the mountains that I didn't even notice until it was gone.

I can't hear.

I can't see.

I can't breathe.

Raze's hand is still wrapped around mine. Why isn't he swimming up?

Bubbles surround me with the distorted sound of his voice. I pull, but he won't let go, and he isn't rising back to the surface.

Something grabs my ankle. I try to kick it away, but it isn't alive. The water itself is coiling its current, wrapping around me.

But I'm an enchanter. I can shape the water, too.

I fight to clear my mind, to picture the water releasing us—or, better yet, pulling us up to the surface. I feel the current give, bending to my will.

So why are we still sinking?

The harder I pull, the faster the water drags me down.

Raze's grip on my hand loosens, like he's losing consciousness. I hold on tighter. I'm not sure I can drag him out of the water, but I can't just let him drown.

My magic's grip on the water slips, and we're still being yanked down, down, down.

My spine tingles as a voice slithers through my mind.

Did you think you were going to drown? Gossamer's quiet voice asks. *I won't let you die, changeling.* He's not real, and I'm not fully conscious, but I feel the trace of a finger skimming my face. *Not while I'm stuck up here. We're* bound. *You don't have to fear anything, not as long as I'm with you.*

The sensation stays there, cupping my face, for too long.

Then I break the surface. There's earth beneath me, pressed under my hands and my face, half on land and half in the water. Raze is beside me, coughing up water.

But alive. We're both alive.

It doesn't make sense. I never felt the current shift, never felt myself moving up. It was just down, down, down—

And then we were breathing again.

Soft sand presses under my palms as I push up onto my hands. I can feel more grains caking my face and hair, finding their way into my clothes.

I don't know where we are, but it isn't Wildline Manor.

I open my eyes, still coughing water from my lungs. My chest shakes with the effort. Raze's hand closes around my arm, like he's checking that I'm still here.

"Raze," I rasp through another mouthful of water, crawling until I'm peering over him. Water drips from my loose hair, drops splashing his cheeks. "Raze, look."

"Not...how I remembered home," he chokes out. His head turns, and he meets my eyes through wet lashes. Emotions flash over his face in quick succession, like a Revelnox fire-works show: confusion, relief, fear, confusion again for a grand finale.

Confusion at the blue sky behind my head and the ivory sand under our bodies. At the green grass and the wild tangle of trees, the sparkling silver water we dragged ourselves out of.

Raze props himself up on his elbows with his knees poking up at awkward angles and spits out a long stream of water.

I sit up, too, panting but finally catching my breath.

The world of smooth, sharp peaks and unforgiving stone has disappeared. In its place is a picture-perfect landscape, a large lake as smooth and bright as glass, its surface spotted with deep violet lilies, surrounded by soft, sandy shores, and rolling meadows giving way to forest on all sides.

"This is different," Raze observes, in a voice so calm it nearly circles all the way back around to absolute panic.

No cliffs.

No caves.

No way back.

The air is thick with magic like pollen in the springtime. I can feel it coating my throat, I can smell it, I can hear it on the wind. I know the truth, even before Gossamer appears in the corner of my eye, frowning like a particularly smug marble pillar.

This isn't Wildline Manor. This isn't even the mortal world. I don't know if it was my error or Gossamer's interference, but somehow, we've found ourselves in a faerie realm.

Again.

chapter thirty-four

"I suppose there's good news and there's bad news," Gossamer observes blandly.

"Where are we?" I force myself up on shaking legs, turning in a slow circle to take in the view. It looks like a vacation spot. Like there should be fancy lake houses dotting the abandoned shores.

"I don't know," Raze says, at the same time Gossamer says, "I'd tell you, but I don't think you'll like the answer."

Which confirms something I suspected and feared: even here, in a realm of magic, only I can hear or see the faerie.

But this place doesn't feel like the enchanted forest. It feels sharper, darker, wilder. The sun is hotter and brighter, the shadows cast in starker relief.

I don't know what I expected the Unseelie Realm to look like, but it wasn't *this*.

Raze can't seem to believe his eyes, either. He takes everything in with an expression of confusion and maybe frustration—it's impossible to tell. He pushes himself to his feet, standing beside me.

Maybe we can get back the same way we came. I recognize that thought when it flickers over his face, because it's the same thought I'm having. The only difference is that I know where we are, and I'm paralyzed in fear.

Raze takes a long step forward, like he's preparing to throw himself into the water, to dive in and swim until the water pulls him back to the Mortal Realm or his lungs explode.

"I wouldn't let your little pet go in there if I were you," Gossamer says lazily, leaning against a tall, silvery aspen tree.

"Raze, wait!"

He turns at my warning, jaw set with determination.

At the same exact second, a sound like breaking ice emerges from the ripples around his legs. Dozens of pale, not-quite-human hands break the surface all across the lake—reaching for him, begging him to come join them. Their nails are blackened by algae, and streaks of dark mold trail down their veins.

He lets out a surprisingly high-pitched scream, scrambling back to the shore so quickly he trips and lands at my feet. "What—what—*where?*" he chokes, breathless. The hands sink back down, leaving the lake as serene as a pool of liquid mercury. "What was *that*?"

I bite my lip and offer a hand down to him. "I..." I don't want to admit it aloud, but he needs to know. "I think..."

Raze, used to this by now, waits for me to gather my thoughts, yanking off one saturated boot and turning it upside down to let a stream of water run out.

"I think I did it wrong," I finally manage—in an impressively calm-sounding voice, if I do say so myself. "This…this is… It's a…"

But I can't make anything follow that. My voice scratches, stuck on the words. Maybe I shouldn't have patted myself on the back so soon.

"A faerie realm?" Raze finishes for me, shaking water from his hair. Soaked with water, it takes on a deeper tone, like bronze. He's taking this surprisingly well.

I nod, swallowing hard. Pushing my own dark strands of hair away from my face, shivering as the cold drops slide down my spine. "Isolde," I get out. "And Olani." It isn't a question. It's barely even a statement, but somehow, he understands.

"We'll get back to them." Raze's hand twitches, then rests at his side. "Can't you just make another portal?"

"Yes, let's," Gossamer adds. "Maybe if you offer me something tempting enough, I'll make it to your preferred destination." So he messed up the spell on purpose. Of course he did. I never trusted him, but in my desperation, I was still far too loose with my conditions.

"I can't," I tell Raze, trying to pretend I can't hear the faerie. "I could… I could send us anywhere. In the middle of the sea, the middle of Leira's camp. It's too dangerous."

And it would cost me dearly.

If our only choices are making a deal with Gossamer or wandering the Unseelie Realm forever, looking for a portal back, I'll take my chances.

Raze takes a deep breath. "Okay. We'll find another way."

I wish he would stop being so calm. This situation is fixed against us in every way. We're trapped mice, waiting to see whether it'll be the fox or the snake that snatches us up in its jaws. "But what happens until then? What if we can't make it back? Leira might hurt them, or, or anything could happen, Raze, I need to… I don't—"

"Seelie, stop." He's *looking* at me again, and I don't understand it. He should be furious with me. I've ruined everything, shattered our last chance, made everything a thousand times worse. What is wrong with him?

"Why aren't you panicking?" I blurt. I'm still soaked and cold, and I feel myself shiver through the words.

"I don't know. I mean, I'm scared, it's just… We've gotten out of worse in the past few days. And I know you won't give up until we get home. Or until you get paid." He cracks a fraction of a smile, but we both know he's only half joking about that last part. "All I'm trying to say is, well, we can figure it out together. If not, and if things get really bad, then you can try the portal again."

I nod numbly, shaken to my core by his misplaced faith in me.

"Okay, then. First things first, we have to figure out where exactly we are. I had so many lessons about magic and the faerie realms, you'd think I'd be able to tell which this is, but… I guess my tutors didn't count on me actually finding myself on the wrong side of a portal. So…"

I listen to his rambling, pushing back the tightness that makes me want to seal my lips forever. I only have to say it once. I can do anything once.

My voice is still too quiet, too tight with unshed tears, too shaky, but I manage to croak out the one word I need.

"Unseelie."

His eyes widen, and he fights to control his face. "Well," he says, slowly, carefully, like he's talking to a wild animal. "What do you want to do?"

I want to go back.

I want to go home.

I want to tell Isolde I'm sorry.

I want to eat something.

I want to sit in my bunk and listen to the clink of metal on metal as Isolde sorts whatever she stole that day and Birch purrs on the hearth.

"I want to dry off."

We back away from the shore to the aspen tree, which is taller than any tree I've ever seen back home, its leaves a brighter green. I sit at its roots, pull my knees up to my chest, and sit with my arms over my head, listening to my stomach growl, tracing the slow *drip, drip, drip* of water down my skin.

"You're never going to get dry like that."

I turn to look at Raze, ready to argue, and cut myself off. He's hung his shirt up on a branch. His boots and socks are a few feet away, stretched out in the sun, leaving him down to just his trousers.

I look away quickly, embarrassed. How could one person have *so many* freckles? They spot his shoulders, all the way down both arms and sprinkling his broad chest. Then there are all the scars—a dozen, at least, small and uneven, from one the size of my pointer finger to several tiny pebble-sized marks. I've always known Raze was strong, but now I can see his muscles, obvious even under all the softness.

He frowns at me, crossing his arms over his chest. "Not that I'm trying to get you undressed, Iselia, but you're going to start stinking like those moldy hands if you don't let all those layers dry."

I grit my teeth. He's right.

Without speaking, I stand, gently working free the knot holding my borrowed shirt in place. "Stop looking at me!"

He raises his hands in surrender and makes a big show of turning to face the lake.

I lay the shirt flat on the grass beside his socks, tugging out all the wrinkles. Then I stand with my back to the lake, even though I can still feel Gossamer's eyes on me as I peel the battered remains of my ball gown away from my skin, leaving me in the much-lighter layer of faerie underclothes.

He's a faerie, I remind myself. *To him, clothes are just a silly human construct anyway.*

It doesn't put me any more at ease.

Next come my boots, then my socks. I'd rather die than admit to Raze how good the fresh air and dazzling sunlight feels on my skin after the constricting itch of my soaked clothes.

"Okay," I say, slowly picking my way around the tree to stand beside Raze, facing out to the lake. I'm self-conscious, and the undergarments that went along with my faerie dress aren't helping. The undershirt is sleeveless and ties up the front, with short, loose pants under a strip of bare waist. It feels like my web of pink scars is shouting for attention. "Don't look at me."

A corner of Raze's mouth turns up. "Doesn't seem fair,"

he muses, risking a glance out of the corner of his eye. "Considering *you* got a pretty good look at *me*."

I punch his arm.

"Hey!" He actually faces me, looking very offended and rubbing his arm more than my feeble blow really justifies.

"You didn't warn me you were *undressing*," I say, feeling my face warm. He's not staring or anything—this isn't as bad as I expected. "And…and it was distracting. Where did you get all those scars, anyway?"

"Oh!" Raze's face lights up, despite the circumstances, despite everything, like he doesn't have a care in the world.

And despite myself I smile too.

He points to one of the smaller ones across his right shoulder. "This one is from running into a table too hard when I was four." Then to a button-sized one under his arm. "And this one is from when I tried to tame a stray cat." A shallow, silvery scratch that extends halfway down his ribs. "And this one is from falling out a window at a tavern once." A puckered mark he has to twist around awkwardly to point to. "And *this* one is from Olani trying to train me with a knife, and *this* one is from filleting a fish wrong, and *this* one is from getting knocked off a horse, and *this* one—"

"Stop!" I giggle. I can't help laughing. Maybe I'm finally cracking under the pressure, but it feels so good to stop worrying, just for a second, and let myself laugh. "I get it!"

Raze chuckles, looking pleased with himself. His crooked grin reminds me of the first night we met, unbearably self-satisfied yet genuinely delighted. "And *this* one," he says, gesturing to a small, jagged sunburst right at the crook where his shoulder meets his chest, "is from this girl I knew once who could enchant lightning from the sky."

My laugh fades. I'd know that mark anywhere. It's the smaller, fainter twin of the scars etched on my own body. It's *my* mark. "I'm sure you deserved it," I say softly, a smile still tugging at my lips.

"That's debatable."

Comfortable silence hovers in the air as the laughter ebbs, and both our eyes lock on the far horizon. A breeze I don't think is mine stirs the air, making me shiver and shift slightly closer to Raze's side—still not touching, but just barely.

My fingers twist together nervously.

"So, what next?" Raze finally asks, brushing my arm with one hand as he reaches up to push his drying hair back from his face. I'm not sure if the touch is intentional or not.

I swallow hard, turn from the lake, and tilt my head up so that I can see his face. "We have to figure out how to get back?"

He sighs. "I was hoping you had some more specific ideas."

"Personally, I'd recommend heading north, if you're absolutely dead set against bargaining with me."

My shoulders bunch. How did I almost forget about Gossamer? His voice came from behind me, but now he materializes behind Raze.

I grit my teeth, trying to keep my eyes from flickering between the faerie's face and my friend's. "I don't know," I say, not sure which of them I'm talking to.

Raze says something then about his tutors and the lessons he skipped, but it's hard to focus on what he's saying as Gossamer circles us. "I'd offer to help, changeling, I really would.

It's just…" The faerie reaches out to tuck a stray strand of damp hair behind my ear, and I flinch away. "Well, at this point, if you leave the Unseelie Realm, I go, too. Unless you want to try to make me an offer I can't refuse…"

Last night, he told me visiting a faerie realm might help him build the strength he needs to stop sharing my mind, my magic, my body. It feels strange to admit, but despite the deep, aching sense of dread I feel seeping into my skin from the earth itself, this detour might actually save us both. "So you're stalling," I blurt, before I can think better of it.

Raze tilts his head, puzzled. "Are…are you okay? You just kind of twitched—"

"You're stalling," I repeat, this time staring directly and probably too intensely at my human companion. "Because you don't know where to go." I let my gaze drift away, back to the serene lake. "What's east of here?"

"How would I know?" Raze says, confusion edging into irritation.

"The Queen's Court," Gossamer responds easily. "*You've* dropped us in the middle of nowhere, but if you can manage to *survive* until we reach civilization, I'm *sure* you could find yourself a portal back to your quaint little mortal world. Ideally, without me."

We'll head east, then. At least until we figure out a better way. Until I manage to get rid of Gossamer. The last thing I want is to visit a faerie court, but I'm running low on options.

"Seelie?" Raze has the nerve to look concerned. "What's going on with you?"

"Nothing," I say, turning from him. "I just feel like we

should head east. It's strange being here. The magic feels… different."

It's a pitiful excuse, but he seems to buy it. At least, for now. If I tell Raze the truth, I'm terrified that he won't trust me anymore. That he won't want to travel with me any longer, and we'll both die alone in the faerie world. I won't be able to keep my unwelcome faerie guest a secret for much longer if Gossamer keeps going on like this.

But I'm nothing if not stubborn.

So I stubbornly clench my hands into fists and ignore the faerie until our clothes dry in the sun.

I stubbornly walk for miles and miles at Raze's side on a narrow, worn path that cuts through the ever-changing faerie landscape.

I stubbornly brush off his concern.

And I stubbornly tell myself, over and over again, that I'm going to see my sister again. No matter what it takes.

At first, the forest seems to go on forever. My freshly dried clothes don't feel *clean*, exactly. They're still stiff, crumpling under my arms and sitting wrong on my legs. They don't stay that way for long with all the mist hanging in the air, and soon I'm chilled and damp. Again.

This. This is what I expected of the Unseelie Realm: a ghostly forest of aspenlike trees with pale bark and silver leaves, rustling like whispers overhead, half-sunken into a thick, white fog. There's something about this place that feels *wrong*, but I can't quite place it. Maybe it's the smell, magic seeping from the trees and the mist and the earth, fresh and sharp as pine sap. Maybe it's the tingle on my skin, like I'm being watched—

Something catches my eye. I *am* being watched.

I gasp and spin on my heel, hands outstretched. As soon as I notice them, all the eyes that had popped open in one of the tree's trunks—eerily human, but not quite—seal shut again.

"What?" Raze turns, too, unsheathing a knife in one fluid motion. "What is it?"

I stop, forcing my breathing to slow.

He doesn't lower his blade.

I check again, but nothing in the forest stirs except the slow swirl of fog. Hesitantly, I turn away from the tree that had been staring at me. "The trees. They…they're watching us."

Raze puffs out a breath, relaxing slightly. "Well—" despite his best attempt his voice is still a little ragged "—can't say I blame them."

We pause, letting silence seep in. Listening for a sign of anything else that might be watching in the forest.

"Seelie," Raze says eventually, turning his knife in his hand, "are you… I don't know how to say this."

Is he really getting embarrassed *now*? Every moment he wastes could be a matter of life and death. I can't hold back the exasperation in my tone. "Just say it."

He shifts uncomfortably. "Are you sensitive to iron?"

I flinch, shoving back childhood memories of the other kids back home taunting me with bits of iron, chasing me up and down the river's shore until I was too tired to run anymore. "It gives me a bit of a rash," I say, when I finally summon my voice again.

"Then, you'll need to be careful." He flips the knife smoothly, offering me its hilt.

"What?"

His arms droop in disbelief. "Take the knife. You might need it to defend yourself."

I push back, something deep within me simmering with discomfort and rage that he'd even suggest such a thing. "I have magic."

"We're in the *Unseelie Realm*, Iselia. You need iron."

"Well, what about you?" I cross my arms, tilting my chin at a stubborn angle.

Raze sighs, finally succeeding at shoving the hilt into my hand as he reaches for something on his other side. "I have another. How about *Thank you, Raze. I know you're trying to protect me, Raze. I'm so glad you're here in the nightmare forest with me, Raze?*"

My fingers wrap around the dagger's hilt. It's cool to the touch, wrapped in smooth leather, heavy despite its small size. I test the unfamiliar weight in my hand, staring down at the dull glint of the iron.

It looks strangely...familiar.

"This is the same knife you held to my throat, isn't it?"

It isn't a question; we both know it is. Raze looks stunned as I push past him, taking the lead with my new blade held out like a warning to any faerie creature that might cross our path.

chapter thirty-five

Night doesn't *fall* in the Unseelie Realm. Here, night staggers drunkenly, clawing at the blue sky with its dark fingers. Desperate and hungry.

Bright sky, dotted with puffy clouds.

Ink-black, sparkling with diamond stars.

The first time, we freeze in fright, our heads snapping up to the sky blocked out by silver leaves, but then it happens again, and again, and again. There's no streaky pink sunset or cool indigo dusk like the Seelie forest. The sky flickers back and forth like a candle guttering out. Like day and night are fighting for control.

Finally, night triumphs. A smooth, moonless expanse stretches out above the trees, swallowing us in blue shadows.

We keep walking, determined to make it as far as we can

before collapsing. Neither of us wants to sleep in the faerie forest, anyway.

If the forest is unsettling in the day, it's downright bone-chilling at night. Glowing eyes watch us in the trees, in the distance, high above. Silent and still, tracking our progress. The fog glows faintly, lighting our path, but I still summon a ball of flame to hold out like a lantern. There's no point in subtlety. The forest knows we're here. The fae must know, too.

Raze inches closer to my side, so close that our shoulders brush. The flames in my hand cast ghostly shadows up his face from below, emphasizing the hollows beneath his eyes. They don't look right in his friendly, boyish face.

Weird noises echo through the branches, the hoots of owls, the cries of foxes, the sounds bouncing around so I can never really tell how near or far the source is. Vaguely human-sounding screams and moans and laughter, slicing the night air at odd intervals. There are other sounds, too—like a low hum, like a distant wind, like a squeaking hinge—that I can't quite place.

I grip my dagger tighter.

I don't know how long we walk through the forest like that, huddled together, tense, jumping at every crack of a twig. It might be less than an hour or nearly a day. We've been in here less than a day, haven't we?

Time is already losing its shape.

But I can't think about that. I can't try to count each second as it slips away from me: that's how people go mad. I just have to keep moving forward, keep pressing in the direction I truly hope is east.

Left foot.

Right foot.

Left foot.

Right foot.

Don't count them!

Left foot.

Right—

A new sound distracts me, yanking me viciously from my thoughts. This one is definitely human, carrying from far away. Wailing? Crying? My gaze flicks to Raze to see if he has heard it, too.

He looks confused.

We keep moving.

The human voice gets closer, like it's walking toward us. It isn't *crying*, I realize.

It's *singing*.

The closer it gets, the better I can make out the tune. And the lyrics, familiar words I've heard a thousand times before on city street corners. It feels familiar—smooth and clear, bright and warm. It's the voice of a singer, someone who knows his voice and knows how to use it. Whose notes aren't hollow with perfection but rich with a faint grate and a passion that forces you to really *listen*.

"I know that voice."

I look up at Raze, startled. He's fallen behind a few steps, but he doesn't seem to notice. His eyes are focused on a point in the distance, clouded over with pain. No, with heartbreak.

His mouth drops slightly open as his face goes slack, like he doesn't understand what he's hearing—or what he's feeling.

He stumbles forward a step, as if something is pulling him. It takes me a second to find my own voice. "Raze?"

He doesn't seem to hear me. His feet shuffle again, parting the grass alongside the path. Drifting uncontrollably towards the sound of that voice.

I close the distance between us, barely remembering to extinguish the flame in my hand as I snatch at his sleeve. "Raze, stop!"

The faint feeling of security I'd felt vanishes with the dim pool of golden light.

Raze shakes his head like he's trying to clear it and blinks down at me, at my hand digging tight into the fabric of his sleeve, up my scarred arm to my eyes. His face twists like he's struggling to focus, to remember who I am.

The singing doesn't stop. The voice is like sunshine, starkly out of place here. Jarring and impossible to tune out.

I tug his sleeve again. "Raze. Stay on the path. Come on, just keep moving."

His voice sounds dull and hollow as his gaze flicks back to the deep forest. "I remember...my father's voice. He used to sing to me. Just like that."

I thought the voice's vague familiarity was a faerie trick, but it's not. It sounds familiar because it sounds like Raze. The faerie trick is darker, wrapped in a layer of the truth—but it's still a trick. His parents aren't here.

Raze tugs his sleeve from my grip. "I have to..."

"There's nothing for you to do!" Desperation is starting to fill my chest. I pull his arm, staggering backwards through the brush. "Raze, please, listen to me!"

If he can hear me, he doesn't show it. He pulls back, using

his considerable size advantage to pull me along with him into the trees.

My boots scrape in the soft, black earth as I try to dig my heels in. I shove the iron knife into my boot and reach for his face with my free hand. "Just—listen—!"

My hand cups his freckled cheek, and I force him to look back at me. The gingery scruff starting to grow along his jaw prickles against my palm.

"Listen!" I say, meeting that blank look again, begging Fate for him to come back to his senses. "I don't know who you think it is, but it's not real. It's just a trick. Come back to the path with me. *Please.*"

Something lights behind his eyes for just a second, through the curtain of red strands that fell in his face when I turned it to me. "I…"

For a moment, the singing fades. I hold my breath, letting Raze's sleeve slip from my grip.

The singer starts the same song over. The echoing voice sounds distant, yet just within reach.

And Raze is gone again.

His blue eyes glaze over, and his neck strains as he pulls away from me, frantic as a wild animal in a trap, trying to turn back to the source of the song.

But I'm not going to let him go that easily. "Raze!" I grab onto his arm, pulling in the opposite direction. "Stop!"

It's useless. He shakes me off easily, pulling his arm out of my grip with a roughness I forgot he had. I try to snag his arm again, but his elbow catches me in the ribs hard enough to knock the air from my lungs and send me falling.

My feet tangle as I stagger backward, and then I'm crashing

to the forest floor. I reach out desperately, and he stops. For a wild moment, I think he's shaken off the glamour.

Then I notice the unnatural posture, the stiffness, like an abandoned toy.

My fingers dig in the dirt as I surge back to my feet, a little off-balance. I start to stumble after him—

"You can drop the act now."

I freeze at the sound of the voice, a voice more familiar than Gossamer's. Recognition hits me like an arrow to the chest, and I forget how to breathe.

I turn slowly to face the speaker, and for a moment I forget Raze, forget the path, forget the distant singing. Forget everything except *her*.

She stands in a spot of golden light, holding up a blazing lantern that fights back the shadows. It illuminates a face almost as familiar as Isolde's or my own. In fact, it's strikingly similar to ours, with the exception of lighter, tawny skin and delicate, arched brows. Her hazel eyes light up with gold in the lantern's light when they meet mine.

The singing fades away as silence wraps around me, smothering and cold and dark. The only sound left is the blood rushing in my ears.

My heart sticks in my throat, and my hands ball into fists. I can't believe what I'm seeing, but I can't stop the trembling word from escaping my lips.

"Mami?"

chapter thirty-six

My hand flies to my throat, closing around empty air where my necklace used to be. I can't understand it. The harder I try to piece together what's wrong here, the fuzzier my head feels. How could my mother be *here*?

Then her face twists. She props her hand on her hip and studies me with a mix of triumph and disgust. "Gossamer. You have some nerve showing your face around here. Or... whatever face *this* is."

Just like that, my head clears. The faerie standing in front of me still has my mother's face, my mother's voice, her faint laugh lines, even her herbal smell. I ache to fold myself into her spindly arms, to feel her calloused hands rub my back with soothing, gentle strokes.

But she *isn't* my mother.

Anger and sadness and hurt and maybe just a *hint* of disappointment almost knock me over. The last thing I truly want is for my mother to be *here* of all places, but for the space of a heartbeat, I had the foolish, childish hope that she was here to make everything okay. She tilts her head to the light, and her eyes flash as crimson as poppies, just like they did on Revelnox. Red eyes, a cruel, knowing smile: this is the same faerie who winked at me from across the crowd, who turned the guard into a donkey.

How long has she been following us? I try to focus on the question, but I can't think clearly. It feels like being drunk. No—it feels like being *glamoured*. In the Seelie forest, I didn't know I was under a spell. The second I realized it, it broke.

Why isn't it breaking now?

I can't stop looking at the faerie. It's been *so long* since I've seen my mother...but also, my head won't turn. My eyes won't move.

My hand twitches and drops to my side without my permission.

I'm not Gossamer, I try to say, but my mouth won't form the words. I know what it's like not to be able to speak...but this is different.

Panic swells up in my throat. I feel my lips twist into a smirk.

"Briar," I hear myself say. "How unexpected."

They aren't *my* words, aren't *my* thoughts, but I know them just the same.

Oh, Fate. Oh, no.

Gossamer.

Forming every thought feels like trying to wake myself from a nightmare, sluggish and slippery.

Something is wrong. Something is letting Gossamer use *my* voice, *my* face, *my* hands.

I try to gasp, but my body won't listen. My chest constricts painfully.

Is it really even mine anymore?

The faerie's—Briar's—eyes flash red again as she drops the lantern to her side. It dissolves into mist, swallowing the yellow light with it. Even though she wears my mother's face, the expression looks totally unfamiliar.

"You were banished," she says. "And, last I heard, locked away somewhere in the mortal world. I didn't think even *you* would be bold enough to come back here after what you did. In a *mortal* body, no less." Her eyes narrow. "What are you playing at?"

I want to turn and run, but I can't so much as twitch my gaze away from her face.

"*This* is temporary, I assure you," my voice says. Gossamer tilts my—his—*our*—chin up at an disdainful angle. "I suppose thanks are in order." He has a certain cadence, a way of emphasizing words to give you the impression that each one carries layers of meaning that you're just too dull to understand. It sounds wrong in my high, thin voice.

Something like real delight lights up the faerie's borrowed face, but there's still something not-quite-Mami about the eyes. "You're trapped in there, aren't you? Oh, this is almost too easy."

In the distance, something howls. Raze lets out a soft groan, reminding me that he's still behind us, even if I can't turn to look at him. I wonder if he's awake now, or if he's still lost, hearing music in his head.

A tight smile presses on my lips, and I feel a surge of anger heat the clammy desperation in my chest. "I *was* trapped, until you did me the favor of ensnaring the changeling's mind. Now—" he lifts our right hand, examining my short, dirty nails and flexing my fingers "—now I shouldn't have any more *trouble*." The smile expands into a full grin, baring my regular human teeth.

"The mighty Gossamer." Briar glides closer with inhuman grace, stopping just short of lifting her slender, calloused fingers to our chin. "All those stolen scraps of power, and yet *you* somehow find yourself locked away by mortals and reduced to *this*. Unable to even enchant one—little— changeling's—mind." With each word, she taps our chin, our jaw, our cheek, our nose. Gentle and playful. "How does such a thing happen, I wonder?"

I flinch away from her touch. At least, I try. My body doesn't move. The icy fear and revulsion makes me lose focus, lose the little grip I have left on my mind.

I have to hold on. I have to fight back.

Now that *I'm* the one who's trapped, ensnared by enchantment in my own mind, my connection with Gossamer is stronger than before. I wonder if this was how *he* felt. Getting lost in my emotions, in fear, will make me slip away.

But I'm not the only one in here who can feel fear.

Gossamer meets the faerie's eyes—my mother's eyes. Hard and unblinking, long enough to make me feel unbalanced and queasy.

Our lips twitch, still baring our teeth. I try to swallow

the words back, but they come anyway. "I'm not too *weak* to admit my mistakes, Briar. But don't worry yourself over me. I *never* repeat them."

But under the calm surface, our stomach is turning with the effort it takes Gossamer to hold me back.

"Of course not," Briar says, unaware of the struggle being fought inches away from her. She leans back, giving me space to breathe. "I doubt you'll live long enough to get the chance. The whole Court's after you, Gossamer. From the moment you arrived, we could smell your magic, smell the mortal stink you brought with you. Whoever brings you in is in for quite the reward, it seems. And once that's done, we're going to *tear you apart*. But this time, you won't have your army of traitors to save you."

That seems to hit Gossamer hard. The sudden realization of how defenseless he is right now sinks like a stone through him, churning up anger and grief in its wake. Just long enough for me to gasp—a breath that's ragged and fully my own.

Cold claws dig into my mind, forcing me back under the surface. I struggle against them, but Briar's enchantment is still on Gossamer's side.

As long as it lasts, I won't be able to overpower him.

Briar's face splits into a grin, and her hungry eyes sweep over us like we're a puzzle she'd like to take apart. "Giving you a fight, is she? What an exquisite specimen."

Pain stabs through our chest as Gossamer fights to regain his composure, to maintain a conversation while also struggling against my clawing, screaming efforts to take back my mind and body. "One of yours?" he asks mildly. A grunt of pain manages to break the surface, and he holds our hand tight to our ribs, like he's trying to physically hold himself together.

Briar smiles politely, watching us like someone might watch the twitching limbs of a drowning fly. "Not my style," she says. "The other one, though..."

"Other—" I gasp, regaining control of our mouth even as our hand, still under Gossamer's influence, claws at our throat "—one?"

Mist swirls around Briar. Her form flickers and changes, like paint bleeding into water. It's hard to make out her new face in the dappled shadows, but I know it anyway.

It's *my* face. With shorter hair. Dressed all in black.

Briar grins with my sister's mouth. "This one is some of my finest work yet. Keeping an eye on her these past years has been entertaining, even though she still has no idea what she is. Such fine craftsmanship. So...*human.*"

I choke, flinging our hand away from our windpipe. Air rushes in as I scrabble back, making it less than two steps before Gossamer controls our feet again. Briar's meaning is still unclear, but I can't focus on fighting Gossamer *and* try to understand her.

"Well," Gossamer snaps, "it's not like I had a choice. This one—" he groans, twisting our torso with the effort of holding me back "—this one freed me."

What are they saying about my sister? I let Gossamer have the hands, the body. I need to speak more than I need anything else, even to breathe.

But he won't let go. Gossamer won't be satisfied with anything except my full self.

Darkness flickers in front of me, and I don't know if it's

magic, or the shadows of the silvery leaves, or my slipping grip on consciousness. The trees blink at us, and the sound of something tearing through the forest circles closer, howling and shrieking.

They're already here, I realize. Whatever *they* are, they're circling, waiting for Briar to finish with her prey, pacing around us. I can only see them in flashes: fangs, bright eyes, insectlike legs, gleaming claws. Raze must see them, too. He makes a sound in the back of his throat behind us, but he still can't move.

They better not touch him. I don't know what I'll do if they do, but—

The darkness plays over Briar's form, wreathing her in night, slipping in and out between her nimble fingers. She looks at us through Isolde's eyes, impassive and vaguely smug, even as we drop. Our bony knees dig into the dirt as Gossamer and I fight for control, but we ignore the jab of pebbles and twigs in our tender skin.

I don't know who's winning.

Our fingers scratch at the soft, decomposing leaves as our spine arches and twists, and I don't know who's doing what.

I just— I have to—

Finally, I find my voice. "But Isolde *is* human. *I'm* the—" I cough, and my sentence is cut off with a strangled cry.

A horrible sound fills the air. At first, I think the creatures watching from the trees are screaming, until I realize it's tearing our throat raw.

I'm getting too emotional, too desperate.

But so is Gossamer.

When we go almost quiet and our screams die down to

whimpers, Briar finally kneels, digging her fingers into our hair. I try to fight back, but Gossamer won't let me. Tears blur our vision.

"She *is*, little changeling." Briar's teeth flash in a dizzyingly familiar smile as she yanks, pulling our head back sharply. "Just as human as *you* are."

That doesn't make sense. I *know* what I am. And I know Isolde is—

Uncanny.

Inhumanly swift and graceful.

Faerie-touched.

The realization stings. All the air leaves our lungs, and I can't get them to fill again.

Isolde.

My twin.

My human half.

Not so human, after all. But not like me, either, with my magic and my eyes that gleam in the dark. *What is she?*

I'm losing my grip. With every spiral into panic, Gossamer gains more control. Our shaking body steadies as we meet Briar's eyes with a rebellious flash of our own. "What...do you want...?"

"Shh," she shushes gently, brushing a finger over the exposed skin of our throat. "I'm in the middle of a conversation."

I can control this. All I have to do is put aside my emotions, my shock and confusion and all the other, more chaotic feelings that swarm over me. Just until I can fight Gossamer off. I try to imagine squeezing it all into a ball and setting it aside.

"This," Briar says, sliding her hand under our infuriatingly limp arm, extending it its full length, "is a *human* body, with

a spark of faerie life. The other is a faerie-made body, imbued with human life. Both human. Both faerie. Both equally your mother's child and *not*. I was there when your mother played our game, you see. I made the faerie body in which your sister's human soul returned to the Mortal Realm. Or…was it your soul? I suppose not, since it never actually touched *this* body, did it?"

She's musing to herself now, as if with those casual words she hasn't shattered everything I know to be true. Isolde and I truly are two halves of a whole—or we could have been, once. After seventeen years of different lives, different experiences, we are fully and completely different people. If we were somehow one, we'd be neither of us.

Have I been in the Unseelie Realm too long, or did that actually make sense?

Briar tilts her head, still studying us. "I've never seen anything like what your mother did. Yet here you are in our realm anyway. Neither of you could ever be what she hoped of you, because you were both *real*. *Real* creatures, I find—" she confides, letting my wrist go and my hand drop back into the mulch "—are *so* much harder to control than imagined ones."

I stare helplessly into my sister's face, tears welling in my eyes. Then, the story is true: our mother *did* walk through the faerie realm, driven by her love for us.

Or maybe, by her love for the imaginary portrait of us she'd painted in her head. The expectations we could never meet.

Grief floods me, washing away any hold I had on my body. It doesn't fit into a ball or a box. It's huge and shapeless and impossible to control.

Gossamer digs our hands into the earth again, smirking even as sweat drenches our brow.

And yet he still chooses not to move.

"What," he repeats, through gritted teeth, though it comes easier now that I've been shoved further into the back of my own mind, "do you *want* with me?"

Briar blinks pleasantly, bobbing on her toes while she crouches, just like Isolde does when she's excited. "You should have stayed in the Mortal Realm you seem to love so much, Gossamer. I told you, you're coming with me to the Court. And then I'll throw your little changeling's mortal pet to the dogs." In the trees, the eager pacing and snarling seems to get louder. "I'll be well rewarded."

Our canines dig into the soft, chapped skin of my lip, almost hard enough to draw blood. "And *why* would I do that?" Despite his defiance I feel his fear.

"For the same reason you're not fighting against me now," Briar says. "I could dispel my enchantment over the mortal's mind like *that*, and then *you'd* be forced out again. Forced to manipulate and struggle to control your little changeling for even a chance at using your magic again." She leans in close, pulling our hair again for emphasis as she whispers. "And you don't want that, *do you?*"

Gossamer's frustration snarls in our throat. The faerie is right. He *won't* fight her. Not while he still has control over our body, over our magic.

But I can't stay trapped in here until Gossamer is strong enough to lock me away forever. He mentioned going to the Unseelie Court to find a portal, but this can't be what he had in mind. Maybe we were going to sneak in, or maybe he didn't realize his own court had turned on him in the long centuries he was imprisoned. It doesn't matter. All that matters is that I can't let them hurt Raze. I have to get free, no matter what.

"That's what I thought," Briar says, patting our cheek triumphantly. Her face looks like Isolde's every time she beat me at a game of cards, when she knocked over a bigger, stronger bully, when she showed me the newest shiny thing she'd collected.

I might never see that look on her face—her *real* face—again. I might never have the chance to tell her the truth about herself.

Our chest aches with hollow sorrow, followed by a flare of rage.

You promised not to let me die, I think, remembering his whisper underwater. *They'll kill us both.* I'm used to faerie deceit, but I believed that. I always knew Gossamer would hurt me—but he said he wouldn't let me die.

A flicker of remorse. My hand twitches—*my* hand.

She'll kill you, I push. *I can save you. I can make a deal with you. Let me save us.*

Teeth snap and branches rustle. The monsters are growing impatient. It's time.

The grip on my limbs loosens slightly, giving in. He can't break a promise, and he knows, despite his pride, that I'm right. His hunger to bargain with me, to taste my magic again, gnaws at our heart.

Ignoring it, I reach for the knife tucked into my boot. Briar holds us crumpled to the ground, and my skirts hide the movement. I touch the iron blade first, feel pain crack through us at just the touch of the cold metal. But Gossamer doesn't bite me back. Not yet.

Briar's Isolde-shaped dark eyes fill with confusion as we tremble and groan, as our teeth bite down hard enough on our tongue to draw blood. I don't break her gaze, even as tears fill our eyes.

We grip the leather hilt so tight our hand shakes.

Her eyes narrow, like Isolde's when I'm not telling her the full truth. Dark, messy hair frames her face. "What are you playing at *now*, Gossamer?"

Isolde's eyes, Isolde's face, Isolde's clear voice and delicate hands and strong arms.

It *isn't* Isolde.

But she looks so much like her.

The ache flares in my chest again, and this time, I allow myself to feel it. I feel anger all over again, knowing that no matter what I do, I'm going to lose her.

Not Isolde.

Not my sister.

We drag our arm up.

Not my sister.

Not real.

I raise my hand, and before I can talk myself out of it—

I stab my sister in the heart.

Not my sister.

The dagger moves with speed foreign to me, swift and vicious as a lightning strike. It lands with a sickening *crack*, slicing into the tender skin between her ribs, driving mercilessly up through skin and muscle.

We both cry out with pain in unison.

Briar's eyes widen with almost human surprise.

She releases me, both hands flying to the wound, to the magic-scented blood seeping freely from her Isolde-shaped flesh.

But it's already too late.

The knife is pure, cold iron, and no faerie could survive that.

"I'm *not* Gossamer," I hiss, as faerie blood stains my hands.

chapter thirty-seven

The faerie's eyes go blank, and her hands slip away from the knife. Then she goes limp and collapses into the ink-black soil.

Everything, even the faerie creatures and the wind, is still. For a horrible second, I'm looking down at my twin's dead body: Isolde's ashen skin, her eyes as dark and empty as a doe's, her black hair spread in a halo around her slack face. Isolde's hands and chest smeared with blood, with *my* dagger still protruding from her chest.

Then her form flickers, and Briar's magic dies with her.

The remaining fog in my head clears, and I'm staring at a dead faerie's pale skin, ruby lips, scarlet-tipped nails, wide and unseeing crimson eyes. It's all a gruesome match to the red blood that soaks her translucent white dress and streaks her skin.

My thoughts are mine again, but Gossamer's presence is closer to the surface than ever. Another tear slips down my cheek, and I wipe at it viciously. Then I remember my hand is still wet with blood, blood I just smeared all over my face.

Something snarls.

I wrap my fingers around the dagger's hilt and pull. It comes free with an effort and another gush of faerie blood, filling the air with the bitter sting of magic and pine sap.

The scent of blood in the air breaks the moment of stunned silence. I scramble back from the body as a swarm of imps with dragonfly wings buzzes out of the trees to cover the dead faerie, their hair and skin a riot of colors like oil swirled in water. Something larger and too dark to make out stalks forward, lapping at her blood.

I hear the words *Stay back!* in my voice, but I'm not sure who said them. It doesn't matter. I turn, searching for Raze where I left him. He's crumpled unconscious in the dirt. A humanoid creature with goat legs sniffs at him curiously, and I rush forward, dagger and teeth bared. *"Leave him alone!"*

It scampers back as I run to Raze. I don't stop glaring at the shadows, even as I reach down to feel if he's still breathing. A lone imp flies so close I can see its tiny, sharp teeth and gleaming black eyes. I swipe at it with my dagger, snarling.

Raze's chest rises and falls beneath my fingers. Not dead yet. But with the Unseelie creatures swarming and a bounty on the faerie living in my head, I don't think we have long.

"Gossamer!" something shrieks, far away.

I stand over Raze, turning slowly. I can't even feel my

heart beating in my chest anymore. I can't think, can't feel. My mind is still all tangled with Gossamer's, so woven together I can't pull myself free. "You didn't tell me you were an outlaw here, too."

Then Gossamer is beside me, standing protectively at my back, as if he didn't just try to kill me. "I was unaware. Things have changed in my absence." His pale skin and hair glow faintly in the dark forest, but none of the other faerie creatures seem to be able to see him. They're all swarmed around Briar's body, filling the air with the sick tearing of flesh and crunching of bone.

My stomach turns. Something in the shape of a wolf lunges at me, and I strike blindly with my knife. I don't stab it deep enough to kill it, but the burn of the iron sends it running back into the trees with its tail between its legs. Its yelp of pain sounds human.

I don't have time, I don't have time.

If Raze woke, we could run, but how far would we get? The faeries and faerie creatures know we're here and, worse, they know we're wanted.

At least, I am.

"About that deal," Gossamer says.

My head spins as I ward off attack after attack with threatening waves of my knife. I could bargain with him again. The twisted part of myself that's all mixed up with the faerie *wants* to bargain with him.

No, I tell myself. I can feel sweat starting to prick at my face. *I want to survive. I want to tell Isolde the truth.*

Gossamer grabs me by the shoulders and spins me around, plunging my knife into an oversized white raven diving at my back through the air. It falls with its claws and wings open. "Don't lie to yourself." He stands face-to-face with me, taking in the streaks of blood across my cheek. "There's no shame in seeking power."

Raze groans, drawing my eyes. Is he waking? He looks like he's in pain, but I can't see anything wrong with him.

While I'm distracted, something breaks through and slashes my leg. I kick it off, but I can feel the blood dripping into my boot. It should hurt, but I'm not thinking clearly enough to feel pain. There has to be another way out. This can't be it.

I see a flash of pale skin between the trees, and someone screams Gossamer's name again. They're closing in.

A creature with the head of a stag and the body of a man turns from Briar's corpse, blood staining its nose. Its eyes lock with mine as it sniffs the air.

I nudge Raze with my foot. "Wake up."

He doesn't stir.

"Raze, please." The sound of tears in my voice draws some of the creatures' attention, and I have to stop and take a deep breath. An imp buzzes around my head, dodging every swipe of my knife, tugging my hair and nipping at my shoulders.

Another small, spidery creature crawls up Raze's leg and over his back.

"That one's venomous," Gossamer says. His voice is lazy, but I can see the way his eyes scan the trees, watching for more Unseelie knights. "Better not... Ooh, too late."

I kick the spider away, and blood sprays from where it's already bitten Raze. His eyes fly open and he gasps for breath, struggling to sit up.

A faerie on horseback charges toward us through the trees.

The stag-headed man stands and staggers in our direction. Raze starts to shake violently.

"I need a portal," I say. My hands shake with fear, but my voice is steady. "Same conditions as last time."

"Gossamer!" someone screams again.

Gossamer flinches at the sound, and I know that he needs this just as much as I do. This is safe—as safe as it can be. "I can't do that."

An arrow whizzes past us.

"Yes, you can! You make a portal, and I'll give you use of my magic for the duration of the spell. We've already done it once!"

Gossamer puts a hand on the back of my neck, nails just barely pricking the tender skin. "I *can't*," he repeats. "I can't make an unequal exchange, and your need for a portal now is much higher than it was before. Which means the price has gone up. Offer me something else."

An imp bites my arm, and I rip it off and throw it as far as I can. Raze gasps for breath. Blood runs down my ruined sleeve, drawing attention from the monsters gathered around Briar's corpse.

"Now!" Gossamer shouts. His voice has turned harsh in an instant, and I can't tell if the emotion in it is fear or urgency or greed. We're running out of time.

"Anything," I say, before I can stop myself.

I expect Gossamer to crow in victory, to taunt me, to say *something*. Instead, he vanishes, leaving nothing but an icy breeze at the back of my neck.

But he's not really gone. I feel him, in my head, in our

hands. They move like they did in the other faerie forest, sweeping in a gesture both familiar and strange.

Anything, I promised him. I might as well have said *Everything*. I can already feel myself slipping away. I'll never have the chance to reconcile with Isolde, to make her laugh again.

But maybe Raze will live.

Gossamer seems almost disappointed at how quickly I give up, and his hold on our limbs loosens a little.

Suddenly, I realize I'm not ready to go. I'm not ready to give up my mind or my magic. I'm not ready to stop fighting. For this one fleeting moment, we're equals.

This time, when Gossamer twines together his magic, my magic, and the magic of the forest, I pay attention. I feel the moment his power flows through our hands, weaving the portal into the air.

I drop my iron knife and catch it by the blade.

Pain shoots through my hand and up our arm as the cold metal bites through my palm.

The iron cuts deep, and Gossamer starts to lose his hold. I can feel his anger and betrayal, but that only makes it easier for the iron to banish him from my body. My grip tightens on the dagger, and with each second of pain, there's also relief. It's too late to stop his magic, though. It runs through me, pouring from my fingertips, until I'm wielding it without him.

Suddenly, even though it's impossible for a mortal to create a portal, I know how to do this.

I have never felt power like this before.

The portal starts to shimmer beneath me in the discarded leaves under my feet.

Gossamer fights back, making our shoulders twitch and

our head snap back as we battle, but he's already lost. I grip the iron tighter. Blood runs over my palm. It drips, hot and dark, into the soil.

Faerie teeth snap at us.

Raze is just awake enough to fight, trying to get a swarm of imps off while still sweating and shaking. They cling to his clothes, sinking teeth into every exposed inch of skin.

I need to see Isolde again.

My hands keep moving, spinning the enchantment.

Seelie, you fool, Gossamer screams in my head, furious and betrayed. His voice is fading. *You've doomed us both. Your mortal body can't control this much magic. You'll die. We—*

I push harder, dragging his magic from its source. Letting it run over me and within me and spark in the air. It builds up painfully, and for a breathless moment, I'm terrified that Gossamer is right: I can't control this.

I need to see Isolde again.

I've almost got it, but not quite. I can feel the magic slipping through my fingers, the exact formation of the portal eluding me. But I refuse to let go. The thought of saving my sister isn't enough. I need something else.

I reach in my mind for the firedrake egg. Its magic is still encased in the shell, still dormant, but it could be anything. At Raze's side, it could save us all. With Leira, it could doom us. But it's more than that. It's a living, breathing creature, and I am going to rescue it so it can't go through everything that happened to Raze.

Its magic is pure potential. Mine is an explosion with no direction. We need each other.

My hands fly apart with a gasp, flinging blood in an arc,

and the tension breaks. I understand it now—it's like a string, tying two places together. I've knotted the first end around myself, and the second Isolde, double-looped around the egg for enough stability to hold us. For a second, there's just me, and the portal, and the magic still flooding through me.

My head is quiet.

Raze falls through the portal, taking the imps with him. He finally wakes up enough to scream before the sound cuts off and he's gone.

Cold hands reach for me, but I'm burning, brilliant, still alight with faerie magic. I'm untouchable.

Everything seems so bright as I fall and fall and fall, gripping the dagger tighter. The portal splinters and explodes into dazzling white flame above me.

And then the light swallows me whole.

chapter thirty-eight

Fire still fills my vision as I blink spots from my eyes. I'm flat on my back, and all I can see is gold and white. The flames are all around me, but I'm not burning. People are shouting in alarm all around me, but the sound feels distant in comparison to the thing that's here with me in the fire, floating in the ripples of pure magical energy.

The thing that answered when I called, and pulled me the rest of the way home.

The egg is already cracked down the middle, but I watch as light bursts from within in zigzags that cover its surface, and its occupant comes tumbling out into the world.

The fire fades, and the baby dragon and I both collapse onto a soft, thickly carpeted floor. My vision blurs, and consciousness gets slippery. There's something heavy on my chest.

Golden eyes with huge, dark pupils. A gleaming, ash-colored snout pokes into my nose as its newly hatched owner gazes down at me in pure adoration.

And then it's pulled away. Someone pries the knife, still sticky with blood, from my hand.

Magic dazzles behind my closed eyelids and consumes my mind, my body. I can feel it, insistent under my skin. Sparking on my fingertips.

I can't move.

I hear voices that I recognize but can't place, fading in and out. I don't know how long they're gone.

Gossamer thrashes in the edges of my consciousness, but he's still weakened by the iron. He can't bother me, even in my own pathetic state. Still, I feel his anger, simmering slowly as only an immortal can.

Cool, sweet water trickles down my dry throat.

The space behind my eyes pounds, stabbing me with pain over and over.

Gentle hands stroke my sweaty hair back from my face. I must have a fever.

Everything goes dark, and then the light returns, prodding at my aching head until it fades slowly away again.

Raze, I remember suddenly. I'm not fully conscious, but I remember his body twitching in the leaves as faerie venom pulsed in his bloodstream. He needs a healer. Someone needs to make sure he can see a healer. "Raze," I mumble. At least, I think I do. I don't really have control of my face, and it comes out as a soft groan. "Raze," I try again, desperately. He could be dead, for all I know. I need him to know I'm here to save him. "Raze!"

"I'm here." Warm hands—*too* warm, everything is too warm—clamp down on my shoulders. "Shh, it's okay. I'm here."

He doesn't sound like he's dying. I crack an eye open, but everything is blurred. It's hard to tell, but I think I'm in a candle-lit room, in an enormous bed. A fire crackles in the corner, warding off the early-autumn chill. Raze sits near my knees, making the mattress dip a little, and his face is a distant smudge surrounded by coppery red, but I'm pretty sure he's looking down at me with concern.

I reach up, then pull my hand back, hissing with pain. Raze catches it gently in his, turning my palm up to inspect the wound. Someone bandaged it, but it still hurts, worse than when I first cut it.

"Where are we?" I ask. My voice sounds strange, whispery and raw. "The egg! I saw…the dragon…" I look around as quickly as I can, but the firedrake is nowhere to be found. Maybe I imagined it.

Raze pauses, and I think he leans back a little. Finally, after a silence long enough to be noticeably awkward, he says, "We're safe, okay? I'll explain later. Do you trust me?"

That should set off some kind of alarm, but I'm surprised to find that I *do* trust him. I would nod my head, but I don't think I need my aching brain sloshing around up there with that kind of movement, so I just blink and hope he understands.

He seems to realize he's still holding my hand between us and drops it as if it burned him. "How are you feeling?"

I wonder if he knows what an impossible question that is to answer.

On the one hand, the weight of Gossamer's presence is gone, and I feel like I can breathe for the first time in days. I can feel my pulse in my ears and my head and my hand, electric with the faerie power still coursing through my veins. That feeling of invincibility still hasn't worn off.

On the other hand, I'm so weak that I can't get out of bed, in so much pain that I can hardly crack my eyes open, sweaty with fever, and my palm feels like there's still a knife embedded in it.

"Like I tore a hole in the fabric of reality big enough for two people to jump through," I say, eventually. I mean for it to sound light, but that's hard with the scratchy rasp of my voice right now.

Raze chuckles anyway.

I can only remember things in quick bursts, which fade as fast as they come. I catch onto one thought before it can slip away, ignoring the nagging feeling that I'm forgetting something else. "Isolde…" I say. She was all I thought of when I created the portal's direction. She should be here. Anxiety starts to rise in my chest. "Where…?"

"She's safe," Raze soothes. "You brought us back to them. Do you want me to go get her?"

I remember our last harsh words to each other in the courtyard. I remember shoving her away roughly. I remember the look on Isolde's stolen face when I drove the knife through—

"No." I'm too tired to untangle all my feelings and smooth over hers. Too drained to face her. There will be time for all that later.

I peek up through my eyelashes. Raze has always looked best in firelight. Even now, with his washed-out complexion and the shadows under his eyes. It brings out the warmth in his cheeks and the gleam of copper in his hair. His brows draw close together as he stares deep into nothing, like he's trying to figure out what to say. Finally, it all comes out in one rushed breath. "Fate, Seelie, I'm so sorry. I was useless, and I put you in danger. I don't remember what happened, I just remember waking up and you *saving me*, and I can't believe—"

I silence him with a scowl. "You were *enchanted*. Again. You couldn't have helped it." I try to crack a smile, and it sits lopsided on my face. "Besides, I kind of like saving you."

I think he smiles back. His hands move, like he wants to do something with them but he isn't sure what. After a moment, he clears his throat. "I... I should let you rest."

His weight shifts as he starts to stand, and I catch onto another thought—one that's been bothering me in the back of my mind for a while now, but which I only now have the courage to actually ask. "Wait." I reach with my uninjured hand, tugging his sleeve.

Raze comes back, this time crouching beside the bed. He's close enough now that I can actually see his face as he waits expectantly for me to speak.

Something snaps in the fire, and I swallow hard. My throat still feels dry, my head is fuzzy, and the feeling of magic searching for a release is a little overwhelming. I close my eyes, trying to ground myself. "I'm sorry."

His head tilts, making his hair fall around his face. The ends brush my cheek. "What?"

I pause, struggling to form the thought in words. This one is just practice. Eventually, I'll have to apologize to Isolde, too, and the thought makes me want to choke. Doubt wrinkles my feverish forehead. "My fault we were in danger. My portal. You almost died."

Raze shifts subtly, looking a little nervous. Then his face relaxes, and he takes my hand, looking into my eyes like he has something very important to say that can't be conveyed any other way. "I forgive you. And I hope you'll forgive me."

The way he says it makes me feel a little dizzy, for reasons I don't understand. If we have the firedrake now, then he's another step closer to taking back his place in his family, of breaking Leira's iron hold. No wonder he's feeling generous. I've messed up at every turn, and if we still have a chance to win now, that's despite me not because of me. But he looks at me like he still thinks I'll help him.

Something between us has changed. I don't know when it happened, but we're not just business partners anymore, just temporary allies until I get my money. We're linked by everything we've been through, and I suddenly realize that even if he couldn't pay me, I'd still be on his side. That's enough pressure to make anyone feel a little nauseous. A little like their heart is trying to find a new place to roost.

Raze laughs at my stricken expression. Any chance to get under my skin is enough for him to pounce on, even now. I can't tell if he's blushing, or if his face looks this pink all the time.

I frown, struggling to follow. "Forgive you for what?"

"Because... Well, when we met, I thought you were just some magical creature, like the dragon. Just a changeling."

I wrinkle my nose, struggling to remember back to the bonfire in Gilt Row. The way I mistook his smile for charming and his attention for flattering. "A *pretty* changeling," I correct, my words blurring together.

Raze snorts, but he doesn't respond to that. "But I was wrong. I see that now. I underestimated you. I thought you were less than human, but Seelie, you're…"

My stomach twists in knots as he searches for words, and I let my eyes drift closed to focus on their sound.

"You're more human than anyone I've ever met," he finally manages, surprising me. When I dare to sneak a glance at his face, he's smiling strangely. "You're passionate and funny and brilliant and terrifying. You stopped to ask what would become of the firedrake. To think of it as more than a weapon. You feel so much more than I do, and you see so much more than I do. You're unlike anyone else, and…" This time, he doesn't finish the sentence. For once, Raze has run out of words.

Now my stomach is doing acrobatics, flipping and flying around uncomfortably. Magic tingles in my hands, and my heart races.

It isn't really about *me*, what he said. It's about the dragon, and how it's a living creature with feelings that doesn't deserve the abuse that Raze suffered. For a brief second, I wonder if the dragon is safe—but it must be. He said everything was fine. But still…

No one has ever talked like that about me before.

"I—" No words seem to fit right now. "Fate," I complain weakly. "Do you *always* have to be *such* a pain?"

Well, I never claimed to be eloquent.

Raze's laughter pierces my ears and shakes me painfully, but I don't care. I put up one weak hand to feign pushing him away, pretending to be offended. The light catches gold in his lashes when he throws his head back. I can't help but join in, laughing weakly.

I realize I'm staring as our giggling subsides and look away quickly.

"I don't *have* to be a pain," Raze says, still grinning. When he notices that I'm refusing to look at him, he grabs my un-injured hand, drawing my gaze. The smile on his face teeters wildly between intentionally obnoxious and charming. "But you make it so much fun, Iselia."

I know I'm not thinking clearly, that I'm weak and con-fused but also more sure and powerful than I've ever been. For some reason, I can't resist pulling my hand free and let-ting it slip into the space under Raze's jaw. I tilt his head to me so the firelight can accurately illuminate just how awful he looks. We've been through so much.

"You know, you don't have to be my friend," I say. Thoughtlessly, my thumb brushes his cheekbone. "You're still going to have to pay up."

"I know." His lips curl in a smile. I've never really no-ticed Raze's lips before, besides when they were smashed awkwardly against mine, so the observation seems strange. They're a nice shape. Nothing extraordinary, but just right for his face. They look soft.

I've never noticed *that* about anyone before.

Before I can pinpoint why my mind is wandering to such a bizarre place, he brings his hand up, covering mine com-pletely. His palm just barely brushes against the back of my knuckles, warm and familiar.

"I just remembered," he says. "We didn't die. I guess you win the bet."

The silly bet we made in the enchanted Seelie forest seems like so long ago, but it's just been a few days. I completely forgot about it.

"So unfortunate that we lived," I say. My heart jumps into my throat as I remember the ridiculous stakes we set. "Per our previous agreement, you owe me fifty percent."

"Thirty-five, and a promise," he negotiates easily, with a charming smile.

Yes, I remember, with a sinking feeling in the pit of my stomach. *And…that.*

I raise my eyebrows, inviting him to continue. I hope he can't feel how feverishly sweaty my hand is.

It's a long moment before he speaks, a long moment of his lips parted slightly with that grin playing in the shadows at the corner of his mouth. "Seelie," he says, his voice so low that if I was any more than three inches away from his face I wouldn't hear it. "I promise that you will never have to kiss me again." His expression hovers again, like he's about to add an *unless…*

Blood rushes in my ears.

It feels like Raze is daring me, trying to do that *thing* where you can look into someone else's eyes and know just what they're thinking. But I can't do that.

All I can do is observe that our noses are inches apart, that we're staring each other deeply, uncomfortably in the eye. In silence. With our hands overlapping in the hollow of his jaw. If it was anyone else, I might think it means something that he wants me close. That I can feel the warmth of his breath on my skin when he breaks into a wider smile.

But this is *Raze*, and normal rules of human behavior don't apply to him.

My gaze strays down from his lagoon-blue eyes to my injured hand on the sheets, and the moment cracks. I'm reminded intensely of the pounding in my head and the heated magic in my blood. It's hard to keep my eyes open.

"I really should let you rest," Raze says softly, even as I feel myself start to sink into darkness.

"Yeah," I agree, lips barely moving, suddenly annoyed with him for a reason I can't explain. "Leave me alone."

Before he leaves, before I fall back into restless, delirious sleep, I think I hear a low laugh and feel his hand brush gently over my face.

chapter thirty-nine

The next time I wake, I'm alone in the dark. All the candles have burned out, and the only light is a soft red buried in the dying embers of the fire.

I sit up so fast I feel sick, shaking at the nightmare that woke me. In the moment between blind panic and fully awake, a wave of magic overwhelms me with light and heat and a roaring in my ears. Fire erupts from my fingertips, and I just barely manage to direct it into the fireplace.

My heart beats low and heavy, and nausea rises in my stomach as I watch the yellow flames crackle and try to take hold on the burned-out wood. *I can control this.*

For one horrible moment, all I can remember is the last second of the dream. The feeling of tendons snapping under the force of the knife in my hand as I drove it through my sister's heart.

Not my sister.

I collapse back onto the pillows, breathing hard, as I come to my senses. That creature *wasn't* my sister, no matter how much she briefly resembled her. But her confusing, truthful words still echo in my mind.

Everything that everyone thought they knew about changelings is wrong.

Everything that *I* thought I knew about changelings is wrong.

There were no faerie kidnappers, no babies stolen from the cradle. Only a normal human child, and a faerie spark of life. Isolde wasn't a prize that had been snatched away from our parents.

She was given. We both were.

I was the child my mother bore, but that doesn't matter—we're both hers.

Both human. Both changelings.

I have to tell Isolde, I think numbly. *I have to tell everyone.*

Not right now, though. I can't seem to move, even though all I want is to get up. My fingers brush something crackly, and I realize I've singed the sheets. Even though I just summoned a jet of fire, the magic is still overwhelming, desperate for release.

I expect to hear Gossamer's voice in my head again, scolding me, but the faerie still hasn't reappeared. I don't dare to hope that's permanent. I'll be waiting for him, ready whenever he does turn up again.

But this time, I'll have the power.

I flex my uninjured hand, fidgeting my tingling fingers. I wonder how long I've been asleep and how long it'll be until I feel like myself again. Not that I mind this—I feel like my old self would be much more concerned about where I am and how I got here and where my sister is and what's going on. About the strange, strained feeling between Raze and me, where the firedrake ended up, and getting rid of Gossamer forever. I used to be afraid of everything, every twist in the road and unexpected turn around the corner.

But I just can't seem to feel afraid anymore. It's all going to work out. I'm safe for now, and tired, and still a little feverish, but I'll be okay.

And I'll still be okay if I let myself sink back into sleep, just a little while longer.

This time, I fade into deep, dreamless sleep before the nightmares can catch up.

"Leave her alone!"

The voice that wakes me is familiar and irritated, accompanied by doors slamming and several sets of footsteps. There's enough light outside my closed eyelids to tell it's day now, which is disorienting.

I groan without opening my eyes. I'm not ready to see Isolde yet. I'm beginning to think I might never be.

She marches in, still shouting at someone. "She needs her rest, okay? Just wait—"

"I'm up." I grimace, squeezing my eyes shut tighter and stretching slowly. The pillows under my head are damp. Why hasn't this fever broken yet?

"Seelie!"

At the open delight in Isolde's voice, I finally open my

eyes. What I see makes me jerk upright in alarm, scrambling back to the other side of this seemingly endless bed on my hands and knees.

Isolde bounces on her toes, barely holding herself back from throwing herself at me. But it's the other face I see, standing between us, that stops me cold.

Aris strides forward, only stopping when my defensive hands spark with blazing gold flames. Her mouth sets in a tight line, green eyes focused on mine.

"Get away from her," I snarl, taking in the room for the first time.

Suddenly, I think that maybe I should have been much more concerned about where I am when I woke up the first time. Because it isn't an inn, and it isn't a house, and it isn't the Destiny. I still have no idea where I am, since Raze was so distracted and secretive last night. I've never seen a room like this before: ceilings so high you could fly a kite, an island of a four-poster bed, arched windows that go from the floor all the way to the ceiling. The floor is carpeted with a rich, floral pattern, vines of gold climb the walls, and it smells like roses.

Isolde doesn't look frightened, and she doesn't take the opportunity to attack Aris. She just rolls her eyes and says, "See? I tried to warn you."

Olani appears in the doorway behind them. She hardly seems to be limping and looks healthy and strong, but that's not possible. Unless they've found another healer. Concern twists her face, and gold beads glint in her hair.

I try to scramble back, but my legs are still tangled in the sheets. I must be more delirious than I thought, because I can't think of a single rational explanation for what's going on. "Wh-where am I? What's going on?" I try to keep the shake out of my voice, to sound threatening, but every instinct is telling me to torch Aris where she stands, to set this gorgeous room on fire and let it all burn to ash around me. It's all I can do to hold back the fire as the flames grow hotter and brighter in my hands.

"Raze didn't tell you?" Olani snorts. "Typical."

"I don't have time for this," Aris snaps. "She's awake. She's needed. Let's *go*."

Isolde pushes Aris aside gently, stepping towards me. She speaks with exaggerated calmness, but I can see a flurry of emotions flickering in her eyes. They glitter, almost as if she's about to start crying, set against her mouth stretched in a trembling smile. "Seelie, everything is *okay*. We're in Wildline Manor."

My head spins. What? That can't be true. The fire blows out like a candle, leaving thin trails of smoke as I struggle onto my shaking legs. We can't be in Wildline Manor. That's where Leira Wildfall lives, Leira Wildfall who took everything from us, who almost killed Isolde. I saw the firedrake. Why didn't we get away? Why are we here? Why aren't Isolde and Aris trying to murder each other? Why didn't Raze tell me?

Burn it all, says a not-so-quiet voice inside me. I could. It would be too easy.

I turn from the thought, from the flash of hot violence running through me. I need to get away from this. I can't breathe.

What I thought were floor-to-ceiling windows behind me are actually doors, panes of glass set into intricate iron frames that open to a balcony. I trip over a low table as I stumble for them, and I hear the sound of glass breaking behind me. Water splashes to the floor as a vase of flowers smashes, leaving pale pink petals in my wake.

"Seelie, wait!" Isolde calls.

I throw the doors open, letting the breeze cool my heated skin. I'm wearing a nightgown that I know isn't mine, and the silky fabric clings to my sticky skin. I sway on my feet and hold tight to the balcony's stone railing. I lean so far that for a second, I think I might fall.

That would be bad because I'm several stories up, looking over Gilt Row.

The street looks different in the daytime. I think it's still early in the morning, because there's almost no one out walking, even though it's pleasantly cool with just a few wisps of gray cloud overhead. The pastel houses snuggle tight together in their orderly rows, and the pale pavement is perfectly smooth and free of any kind of debris. It doesn't seem real. How can I be back *here*, after everything that happened? Was it all for nothing?

Anxious, half-delirious wind rushes under my fingertips and flutters my sleeves. It whips my hair from my face, chilling my skin and rushing in my ears. I can't hold it back any longer.

My bandaged hand still stabs with pain every time I move it, but I raise it anyway, reaching down into the aching hollow of my chest to summon my magic. Blood starts soaking through the white cloth. I can't focus, but the magic is already there, running as freely as my blood, white-hot power splitting through the haze of pain.

The russet leaves of the climbing ivy tremble as the wind

picks up around me, breaking off and swirling into the empty air with a hollow, brittle rush.

"Seelie!" Isolde calls my name again, but I don't turn to her, don't lower my hands. I can't stop now. There's too much of it—too much emotion, too much magic, too much confusion.

"I know how you must be feeling right now!" my twin continues, undeterred.

No. She doesn't.

"I'm so sorry about everything that happened. I— *Please.*" I don't know what she's asking for. "I missed you so much. I thought I'd never see you again. And then you just appeared, and whatever you did, it made the egg hatch, and—"

"It was *two days!*" I shout. We both have to shout now, to be heard over the wind.

"It was two months!" Isolde's voice finally breaks, splintering my heart. I hear her start to cry. "Raze told me what happened to you, but for me—here in the Mortal Realm—it was *weeks,* Seelie. I thought you were dead. Leira wouldn't let us go, just in case you came back. And when she realized you weren't going to, she offered us work. But it wasn't an offer, Seelie. We're still prisoners. We're just not in chains anymore."

Months? That…that can't be true. I all but counted the hours in the Unseelie Realm. I got back as quickly as I could. All that time, Isolde was hurting, but she never doubted me. She never even considered that I wouldn't—or couldn't—come back for her. A tear rolls down my face, the twin to hers. "I did *everything* for you. I was going to save you. To save *us.*"

"I know." Isolde takes the last step forward, closing a hand around my wrist. "It's going to be okay."

The wind wraps around me indifferently, stings my eyes

and draws fresh tears, and the sky starts to darken with thick clouds. Maybe she's right—or maybe it doesn't matter what we do. We're still trapped, running from one prison to the next. One cold raindrop falls next to my foot, and the next lands on my nose.

Magic still burns through me, more and more and more, no matter how much I pour into the storm. There never seems to be less of it. It's overwhelming, but it's the kind of overwhelming that awakens my senses and makes every second draw out longer before me.

"Seelie, I want to know everything that happened. But I need you to come inside now, okay? The dragon won't let anyone else even approach it. They think…they think it needs you. That it wants you. I tried to tell them to let you rest, but they wouldn't listen. I don't know what they'll do to you if you don't—"

"No!"

The veil of clouds opens, and rain pours down, cold and sweet. It feels like relief, like each drop is a little bit of myself I don't have to stuff away into a too-small box. I'm tired of being needed, of being told what to do and pushed around by random whims of Fate.

Isolde looks up, like she's just noticing the rain, and then she looks at me. I shouldn't be able to do this, and she knows it. But I'm not going to let the magic snap out of me, unintentional and cruel, and hurt her. Not again.

My hands slowly drop to my sides as I let the rain soak through my nightgown and drip in my hair. My breathing is still uneven, but the magic in my blood almost feels manageable again.

Lightning flashes bright white across the sky.

I can control this.

Isolde slowly lets go of my wrist, draping her arm over my shoulders. I cringe at the touch. I still don't know what to say to her. Everything feels different now. "You don't have to fix everything, Seelie," she says. Rain sticks her hair to her face and clings to her eyelashes, but she just blinks it away. "We… we're together now. We're alive. None of the rest of it matters."

I let her hold me. Despite everything I feel, my shoulders relax slightly. A roll of thunder follows the lightning, long and low like a breath held too long.

Isolde doesn't know she's a changeling, and I don't know what she's been through in the time I was gone. So much has changed, and I don't know if we can ever go back to how it was before.

But what I do know—what she promises wordlessly in the tight grip of her bony arm around me—is that she's still my sister. My best friend. No matter what happens, what changes, we will always love each other.

And we'll always come back for each other.

My arms wrap around Isolde, pulling her closer. I know we're going to fight again, and probably soon. We're going to disagree on things—lots of things. We're going to struggle expressing how we feel and make each other furious.

But after it all, no matter what, we'll still be sisters. Changelings or not. Two halves of a whole.

I squeeze her tight another moment and then pull away, trembling. I'm still delirious and feverish and overrun by faerie magic, but as the storm rages over the city, I can't feel anything but exhilaration.

We're going to come up with a way to get out from under

Leira's thumb, but first—the firedrake. It, like the rest of us, is in the hands of the enemy. A Wildline woman who can't be trusted, under any circumstances. If I can help it and I don't, how am I any less cruel?

Water droplets puddle in my hands, where magic still sits just below the skin. It feels like power. Like freedom.

"I'll go," I say, in a low voice. "Show me the way."

Isolde pauses, staring at me. Then she nods, letting go and walking back to the door.

Rain streams down my skin, and before I follow her, I step forward. My bare feet splash in the cold puddles, and the wind is like ice on my scarred, soaked arms. I lean over the balcony again, letting the wind wash over me, feeling its magic push gently at my own.

We may be captured, but the dragon is loyal to me. My magic—the same magic that I've spent a lifetime trying to escape, that has saved me and my sister and my friends count-less times—ties us together.

We may be captive at the moment, but Leira has no idea what I can do.

"You look different," Isolde says softly, from the doorway.

I twitch my uninjured hand, and thunder crashes in re-sponse. My lips curl in a smile. "I *am* different." Then I flick the other hand out, and lightning sparks against the dark-ened sky.

★ ★ ★ ★ ★

author's note

How do you write about autism without using the word autism?

This book was inspired by the theory that changeling mythology is an early description of autistic children, and, well, it kind of went off the rails from there. I wanted to write a story about someone like me, a story where the autistic character is the center of her own narrative. In a fantasy world where there's no diagnostic term for it, I can only explain autism by showing you who Seelie is, how she thinks and feels and experiences the world. Seelie is flawed and immature, but she is also loved and accepted as she is. Too many stories about autism focus instead on the parent, the teacher, the caregiver...

This is not one of those stories.

When I was diagnosed, I wasn't given access to resources by other autistic people. I had to find those perspectives myself, and it took years of searching and learning about how my brain works for me to accept it. After all, I knew the stereotypes: autism was white and male and cold. Either rude and brilliant, or nonspeaking and objectified. People tend to focus on the social aspects of autism, but it's so much more than that. Autism affects how your brain processes all information. That includes social interactions but also language, problem-solving, input from your senses, executive functioning, and so much more.

It's not a flaw or a fault. It's just a variation of the many ways that human brains are wired. And you can't separate us from the way our brains function without stripping us of everything that makes us who we are.

Too many autistic people go undiagnosed, without supports, for too long, because we don't fit the image of What Autism Should Look Like. Because, of course, there's no such thing. Autistic people, like everyone else, exist in infinite variety, in all genders and colors and shapes and sizes. We have different needs and different expressions. I can't possibly speak for all of us—but I wrote *Unseelie* to challenge that image. If I had seen characters like Seelie, I might have been able to recognize and accept myself earlier and skip over years of identity crisis.

If you enjoy this book, I'd encourage you to seek out more information about autism from autistic advocates. And if you see yourself in these pages, I want to tell you what I wish someone had told me.

You are exactly the way you were meant to be, and you are the hero of your own story.

acknowledgments

First of all, I want to thank you, reader, for picking up this book, and making it all the way to the end. I wrote this for you, so I'm pretty psyched that you're here.

This book went on quite the journey from the moment I started brainstorming it in 2017 to now. For most of that, I didn't think it was ever going to be read by anyone, and yet I kept writing/editing/rewriting, which felt a little like squeezing my heart with a citrus juicer for years on end. The only reason it exists now at all is, in some way, because of each and every one of the people listed here.

I need to thank my editor, Stephanie Cohen, for understanding my book, seeing what it could be, and being a pleasure to work with—and my second editor, Olivia Valcarce, for jumping onboard so smoothly halfway through the process. I'm incredibly grateful to the whole team at Inkyard, including Bess Braswell, Erin Craig, Vanessa Wells, Brittany Mitchell, and Justine Sha, for making my words book-shaped, and to Mona Finden, for bringing that book to life with the most beautiful cover illustration.

I owe a million thanks to my agent, Victoria Marini, for your fierceness and enthusiasm, and never making me feel bad for emailing you in a panic at pretty much every turn. This book wouldn't be nearly as good without your spot-on insight, and I'm so glad you saw the same future for it that I did.

To Sarah Kapit, and the entire Author Mentor Match program—I've said it before, and I'll say it again: I couldn't possibly ask for a better mentor. I am forever thankful for all the time and effort you poured into helping me.

To all the teachers who encouraged me to write as an outlet, who let me ask weird questions and do outside-the-box projects and sit under my desk when I needed to hide—thank you. You provided a safe place for me in the stressful, overwhelming school environment.

Heather, Dani, and the RPS Team, you guys are the best. I couldn't ask for a better Day Job.

Squadtism and Floor Time group chats, thank you for getting me through 2020.

To those who read this book when it was mostly a formless lump of potential—Kate Weiler, Elizabeth Unseth, and Aimee Mayer—I can't thank you enough. Saint Gibson and Vika Hendersen, thank you both for being much cooler than me, and sharing your knowledge of publishing with me. Huge thanks to Margaret Owen for your kindness and advice about navigating publication, Emily Thiede for book chaos empathy, and Lillie Lainoff for being the best '22 Debut Buddy I could ask for. Hannah Geist, I'm going to group you in here as an honorary mention because you're my favorite librarian (and we both know I'll never hear the end of it if I don't).

Thank you to my whole huge extended family who supported me enthusiastically without exception, who believed in me even when I didn't. There are too many of you to list here, so just know that whether you're a Clark, Ortiz, Purcell, or Mayer, I'm counting you. Y todos los Quinitos tambien.

To my brother and bonus siblings—Zeke, Kyleigh, Tanner, and however many others there are at the moment—I wish there was a less cheesy way to say it, but thank you all for filling my life with laughter and love. To all my friends, thank you for putting up with all my angst, letting me explain to you how publishing works, and celebrating every win with me. I'm lucky to be surrounded by such creative and empathetic souls.

Lyndall Clipstone, thank you for being my first real writer friend, as well as my official Australian Friend.

Catherine Bakewell, thank you for the memes. Being friends with you has made me a better writer, and I couldn't be happier that our goofy fantasy books are primas.

Thanks to my mom and dad, who would travel to the faerie realms for any of their kids. Thank you for reading to me, encouraging my love of books, and always making me feel like my stories mattered. You've created a monster.

Samantha, for being my first reader, my first fan, my opposite-but-the-same sister: thank you. I will never forgive you for the NSFW comments you left on the first draft of this book.

And finally, to my husband Sam—look up. You're in the end zone. There is nothing I can say here that I haven't already cried into your T-shirt at some point. Without you, this book wouldn't exist, and I'd be a hot mess. I love you.